A RESCUED DESTINY
THE AGE OF BRITISH TRIUMPH
1700-1763

THE DEATH OF WOLFE ON THE PLAINS OF ABRAHAM (*From the original painting by Benjamin West in the Capitol at Ottawa, Canada*)

The Real America in Romance

A RESCUED DESTINY

THE AGE OF BRITISH TRIUMPH

1700-1763

EDITED BY

EDWIN MARKHAM

AUTHOR OF "THE MAN WITH THE HOE, AND OTHER POEMS,"
"LINCOLN, AND OTHER POEMS," "VIRGILIA, AND OTHER
POEMS," "THE POETRY OF JESUS," ETC.

VOLUME VIII

Art Edition

NEW YORK   CHICAGO

WILLIAM H. WISE & COMPANY

MCMXIV

A RESCUED DESTINY

THE AGE OF BRITISH TRIUMPH

THOUGH little more than a skirmish in outward seeming, the battle of the Plains of Abraham ranks high among the decisive battles of the world. The consequences of those few pregnant minutes in the autumn of 1759 are vast beyond contemplation. Not the fascination of the fiery young Englishman's recklessly masterful movement to the rear of the French fortress, his death in the moment of victory, nor yet the brave Frenchman's fatally valiant stand against him gives vitality to the story: it is the ever-living results of that romantic morning.

It is possible that, had Wolfe lost that fateful field, we should now be a French-speaking people, with French customs and institutions. For the battle on the Plains of Abraham was the destined climax to a protracted duel between the civilizations of England and France, between republican liberty and royal autocracy. If we owe our republican institutions to our English forefathers, we owe them also to James Wolfe and his victory at Quebec.

The conflict between England and France was unavoidable. On one hand stood a people which had been ready to leave homes of cultured ease and hew a State out of the wilderness, moved only by sheer love of civil and religious liberty; on the other hand loomed a mighty despotic genius who dreamed of empire. On one hand were budding colonies which taught and practiced that government is for the benefit of the people; on the other, a supreme tyrant, who asserted that the people were for the benefit of government, which was their King by divine right.

7

Underneath it all lay the traditional racial jealousy between France and England, intensified by the imperial policy of Louis XIV, whose bitter wars for the extension of his power filled Europe with woe for many years. Each desired the New World for its wealth. Both lusted for the furs and reputed gold of America. Each was jealous lest too great power spring from this wealth.

The first clash came while Virginia stood alone. As the seaboard was settled by the English and their pioneers struck into the interior, they met the French trading-posts creeping stealthily toward the coast. At every point of contact a new crisis arose. For the most part the French fought with the help of Indian raids and massacres; yet ever the English withstood the blows, spreading steadily westward year by year, bringing greater stress upon a situation already tense.

At last the breaking-point was reached; and Wolfe, fiery, impetuous, magnificent in his desperate strategy, risked the destiny of a nation on a single stroke — and won! From that hour the United States of America, as we know it to-day, became possible. What might our fate not have been had our destiny not then been rescued! Thereupon the consolidation of the several colonies took a long step forward: their petty jealousies were foregone, their unison a fact. Into what this grew when other, more serious dangers assailed us every American knows.

And the men of America learned another lesson. They re-discovered the ancestral trick of fighting. Shoulder to shoulder with British regulars, they grew used to the smell of powder and the sting of wounds. They made themselves certain that in bravery and prowess, in coolness and general-ship, they were the equal, or capable of becoming the equal, of the best soldiery of Europe. It was a lesson that stood them in brave stead in the years, soon to come, when former comrades became embattled enemies.

CONTENTS

CHAPTER   PAGE

Chapter		Page
I	LIFE ON THE OCEAN WAVE	19
II	MEETING BEGINS PARTING	35
III	THE MAN OF GOD	45
IV	FRANÇOIS THE VENGEANCE	58
V	THE WORLD'S LAST AMEN	68
VI	LOVE HATH A WAY	84
VII	AN OLD FRIEND IN A NEW ROLE	94
VIII	THE ANSE DU FOULON	104
IX	DEVELOPMENT AND PROGRESS	117
X	THE DEBTOR	134
XI	THE DEBTOR FORGIVEN	143
XII	THE DEBTOR RECOMPENSED	153
XIII	THE FIGHTING SHIPWRIGHT	168
XIV	THE MAN ON THE ROCK	181
XV	THE BONDWOMAN	196
XVI	THE BATTLE IN THE RAIN	209
XVII	MISCHIEF AT HOME	227
XVIII	AFFAIRS AND THE MEN	244
XIX	THE GREAT GREY MAN	259
XX	LOVE THINE ENEMY	275
XXI	WHAT IS THIS STRANGE MAN?	288
XXII	THOSE WHO SERVE THE KING	299
XXIII	ARMS AND THE MEN	311
XXIV	THE DEVICES OF DAVID	325
XXV	THE SINS OF THE SON	337
XXVI	UP FROM THE VOID	355
XXVII	OUT OF THE ENEMY'S HANDS	368
XXVIII	THE PATHS OF GLORY	380
XXIX	THE LONG TRAIL HOME	391

9

XXX	After Many Years	.	.	.	.	405
XXXI	A Day of Reunion	.	.	.	.	418
XXXII	Greatest of These is Love		.	.	428
XXXIII	The Last Shuttle	.	.	.	.	440
	Index	.	.	.	.	449

ILLUSTRATIONS

		PAGE
THE DEATH OF WOLFE ON THE PLAINS OF ABRAHAM		4
(*From the painting by Benjamin West*)	*Frontispiece*	
GENERAL WOLFE		19
QUEEN ANNE		21
(*From the painting in the National Portrait Gallery*)		
LOUIS XIV		22
QUEEN ANNE'S BED IN HAMPTON COURT		23
QUEBEC, CAPITAL OF NEW FRANCE	*Full Page*	25
STREET IN THE OLD TOWN, QUEBEC		28
RURAL SCENE IN THE PROVINCE OF QUEBEC		30
QUEBEC'S IMPOSING WATER-FRONT		31
BREAK NECK STEPS, QUEBEC		33
BED OF LOUIS XIV IN THE PALACE OF VERSAILLES		34
VILLAGE OF CAUGHNAWAGA		36
THE ANCIENT WALLS OF CAUGHNAWAGA		37
COMMON AND WELL OF OLD FORT DEERFIELD, MASSACHUSETTS	*Full Page*	39
DEERFIELD STREET, DEERFIELD, MASSACHUSETTS		41
THE DEERFIELD SETTLEMENT		42
(*From a painting*)		
OLD STONE CHAPEL AT CAUGHNAWAGA		43
LUMBER CAMP ON THE CONNECTICUT		44
CASCO BAY, MAINE	*Full Page*	47
WINTER ON THE UPPER CONNECTICUT		49
OLD BLOCK HOUSE IN MAINE		51
(*From a recent photograph*)		
ON THE CONNECTICUT RIVER		53
THE FERTILE VALLEY OF THE CONNECTICUT		54
NORTH HAVERHILL AND THE CONNECTICUT RIVER		57
HERTEL DE ROUVILLE		58
(*From the family portrait*)		
THE REVEREND JOHN WILLIAMS'S HOUSE		61
BATTERED DOOR FROM THE WILLIAMS HOUSE		64
(*In the Museum at Deerfield*)		
BURIAL PLACE OF THE DEERFIELD VICTIMS		65
THE CONNECTICUT RIVER AT WHITE RIVER JUNCTION	*Full Page*	69
GRAVES OF THE REVEREND JOHN WILLIAMS AND HIS TWO WIVES		72
ON THE PENOBSCOT RIVER		74
HOCKOMOCK ROCK ON THE COAST OF MAINE		77
THE CITADEL, QUEBEC		78
STATUE OF LOUIS XIV AT THE PALACE OF VERSAILLES		81
THE SAINT LOUIS GATE, QUEBEC		82
THE HARBOR OF QUEBEC		83

MONTMORENCI FALLS 84
LOWER TOWN, QUEBEC . . . . . . *Full Page* 87
ISLE OF ORLEANS 90
THE CHATEAU FRONTENAC AND CITADEL 92
OLD HOUSE, QUEBEC 94
THE CITY OF QUEBEC FROM PARLIAMENT BUILDINGS . . *Full Page* 97
ON DUFFERIN TERRACE, QUEBEC 100
THE PARLIAMENT BUILDINGS, QUEBEC 102
SOLDIERS' MONUMENT ON SAINT FOYE ROAD, QUEBEC 103
A FRENCH MAN-AT-ARMS 104
TO THE PLAINS OF ABRAHAM 105
A SCENE IN RURAL QUEBEC 107
NATURAL STEPS, MONTMORENCI . . . . . *Full Page* 109
THE OLD SAINT LOUIS GATE 113
POINT LEVIS, FROM QUEBEC 115
NATURAL BRIDGE, VIRGINIA 117
JOHNSON AND THE MILITIA AT CHARLESTON 119
    (*From an engraving on wood*)
ON THE WAKEFIELD FARM 120
WASHINGTON'S BIRTHPLACE, WAKEFIELD, VIRGINIA . . . 120
GREENWAY COURT, HOME OF LORD FAIRFAX . . . *Full Page* 121
WASHINGTON FAMILY TOMB AT WAKEFIELD, VIRGINIA . . . 124
INITIALS OF WASHINGTON CARVED ON NATURAL BRIDGE, VIRGINIA . 125
FREDERICKSBURG, VIRGINIA, AND MARY WASHINGTON'S HOME . 127
MARY WASHINGTON'S MONUMENT, FREDERICKSBURG, VIRGINIA . 128
WASHINGTON'S LAST VISIT WITH HIS MOTHER 131
    (*From the painting by L. E. Fournier*)
WASHINGTON'S MOTHER PERSUADING HIM NOT TO BECOME A MIDSHIP-
    MAN 133
    (*From the painting by Chappel*)
JAMES OGLETHORPE 134
THE PORT OF SAVANNAH 136
    (*From the engraving after the painting by Vernet*)
OGLETHORPE'S OLD FORT ON SAINT SIMON'S ISLAND . . *Full Page* 137
THE FLEET PRISON, LONDON 141
    (*From an old print*)
BULL STREET, SAVANNAH, GEORGIA 143
SAVANNAH, FROM TOWER OF CITY HALL . . . *Full Page* 145
ON THE SAVANNAH RIVER 149
THE PORT OF SAVANNAH 150
JOHN WESLEY 153
    (*From the engraving by J. W. Paradise*)
THE HERMITAGE PLANTATION, NEAR SAVANNAH . . . 154
JOHN WESLEY'S MONUMENT, CITY ROAD, LONDON . . . 155
SAVANNAH, GEORGIA, AND THE RIVER . . . . *Full Page* 157
LIVE OAK UNDER WHICH JOHN WESLEY PREACHED HIS FIRST SERMON
    IN AMERICA 160
MONUMENT TO TOM-O-CHI-CHI 161

BETHESDA, THE FIRST ORPHANAGE IN AMERICA, AND ITS FOUNDER, THE
REVEREND GEORGE WHITEFIELD . . . . *Full Page* 163
MONUMENT MARKING SPOT WHERE OGLETHORPE LANDED AT SAVANNAH 165
CHARLES WESLEY 166
(*From an original portrait in possession of the family*)
SIR WILLIAM PEPPERELL 168
(*From the portrait in the Essex Institute at Salem, Massachusetts*)
SIR WILLIAM PEPPERELL'S HOUSE, KITTERY, MAINE 171
(*From an engraving on wood*)
WILLIAM SHIRLEY 172
(*From the portrait by T. Hudson*)
GUN CAPTURED AT LOUISBURG, NOVA SCOTIA . . . *Full Page* 173
THE HARBOR OF LOUISBURG 176
GENERAL PEPPERELL AT THE SIEGE OF LOUISBURG 178
(*From a print*)
LOUISBURG MONUMENT 180
GOVERNOR ROBERT DINWIDDIE 181
(*After an engraving from the family portrait*)
PITTSBURG, THE GATEWAY OF THE WEST . . . . *Full Page* 183
COLONEL THOMAS LEE 186
THE KENTUCKY RIVER, NEAR FRANKFORT 189
DINWIDDIE'S MESSENGERS 191
(*From an engraving on steel*)
FORT NIAGARA 194
(*From the steel engraving by J. I. Pease*)
SITE OF WASHINGTON'S CAMP ON LE BŒUF CREEK . . . 197
THE POTOMAC RIVER AT HARPER'S FERRY . . . *Full Page* 199
WASHINGTON AND GIST CROSSING THE ALLEGHENY . . . 202
(*From an old engraving*)
KENMORE, THE HOME OF WASHINGTON'S SISTER 204
CONFLUENCE OF THE MONONGAHELA AND ALLEGHENY RIVERS: THE FORKS
OF THE OHIO 205
THE OLD SPRING AT FORT LE BŒUF 207
WASHINGTON MINIATURE AND SIGNATURE 209
(*After the portrait by Peale, engraved by Rogers*)
WASHINGTON'S BIRTHPLACE AT WAKEFIELD, VIRGINIA . . *Full Page* 211
(*From an ancient etching*)
FORT CUMBERLAND IN 1755 213
(*From an old print*)
OLD BARRACKS NEAR OGLETHORPE'S FORT, ON SAINT SIMON'S ISLAND . 214
THE GATES OF SAINT AUGUSTINE 215
ROCK FORT, WHERE WASHINGTON MET HALF-KING . . . 216
THE NIGHT COUNCIL AT FORT NECESSITY 217
(*From an old print*)
WASHINGTON'S FIRST BATTLEFIELD 218
GREAT MEADOWS AND FORT NECESSITY, THE ONLY FIELD ON WHICH WASH-
INGTON EVER SURRENDERED TO A FOE . . . *Full Page* 219
JUMONVILLE'S GRAVE 222
WASHINGTON'S ROCK, FROM WHICH HE FIRED ON THE FRENCH . . 224
ROAD NEAR JUMONVILLE'S GRAVE 226

GENERAL BRADDOCK 227
   (*From an oil sketch*)
THE SCHOOL ROOM AT MOUNT VERNON 229
WASHINGTON'S CREST AND COAT-OF-ARMS 231
THE LIBRARY IN THE MOUNT VERNON MANSION 232
WASHINGTON'S MANSION AT MOUNT VERNON, VIRGINIA . *Full Page* 235
THE ROSE GARDEN, MOUNT VERNON 238
GENERAL WASHINGTON'S BEDROOM AT MOUNT VERNON . *Full Page* 241
BENJAMIN FRANKLIN AT THE AGE OF TWENTY 244
   (*From a painting in London*)
FRANKLIN'S BIRTHPLACE, BOSTON 245
   (*From Windsor's "America"*)
PHILADELPHIA'S STATUE OF FRANKLIN . . . . *Full Page* 247
IN THE PINES OF THE LAKE CHAMPLAIN REGION 250
ON HISTORIC LAKE CHAMPLAIN 253
A GLIMPSE OF LAKE CHAMPLAIN 254
WASHINGTON'S MILL, STILL STANDING, FAYETTE COUNTY, PENNSYLVANIA . 257
SIR WILLIAM JOHNSON 259
   (*From the steel engraving by Marcy*)
JOHNSON HALL, JOHNSTOWN, NEW YORK 260
SIR JOHN SAINT-CLAIR 262
   (*From the miniature by Copley, in possession of the Pennsylvania His-*
   torical Society)
BRADDOCK'S FIELD 263
   (*From an old print*)
GENERAL BRADDOCK WOUNDED 264
   (*From the drawing by Freeland A. Carter*)
BRADDOCK'S ROAD ON THE CREST OF LAUREL HILL . . . 266
CUSTIS HOUSE, WILLIAMSBURG, VIRGINIA . . . *Full Page* 267
BRADDOCK'S RETREAT 269
   (*From an early print*)
BRADDOCK'S ROAD, EAST OF FORT NECESSITY 271
BRADDOCK'S ROAD 272
GENERAL BRADDOCK'S GRAVE 273
THE MEADOWS OF GRAND PRÉ 275
THE VILLAGE OF GRAND PRÉ 278
GENERAL VIEW OF THE FORT AND CANNON, ANNAPOLIS . *Full Page* 281
THR OLD CHURCH AT GRAND PRÉ 285
THE OLD FRENCH CAVE, ANNAPOLIS ROYAL 286
THE OLD SALLY-PORT, ANNAPOLIS ROYAL 287
ON THE MISSISSIPPI RIVER AT NATCHEZ, MISSISSIPPI . . . 288
SITE OF FORT ROSALIE, NATCHEZ, MISSISSIPPI 290
THE OLD WELL AND WILLOWS AT GRAND PRÉ . . *Full Page* 293
A HISTORIC HOUSE IN NATCHEZ, MISSISSIPPI 296
RUINS OF FORT DUQUESNE 298
GENERAL WINSLOW 299
   (*From the contemporary portrait in oil*)
THE OLD ROAD AT GRAND PRÉ 300
MINAS BASIN 302

ILLUSTRATIONS

MOUTH OF THE GASPEREAUX RIVER 303
THE OLD FRENCH WILLOWS AND ROAD, GRAND PRÉ 305
INSIDE THE OLD CHURCH AT GRAND PRÉ 309
EVANGELINE 310
    (*From the engraving*) .
THE BLOODY POND 311
SHELVING ROCK, LAKE GEORGE 313
HOUSE OF GOVERNOR WILLIAM SHIRLEY, ROXBURY, MASSACHUSETTS . 316
THE RUINS OF FORT WILLIAM HENRY . . . . *Full Page* 319
GENERAL MARQUIS DE MONTCALM 322
    (*From an engraving after the portrait*)
OLD FORT ONTARIO, OSWEGO, NEW YORK 324
LORD HOWE 325
STONE MONUMENT MARKING SPOT WHERE LORD HOWE IS BURIED . 326
SABBATH DAY POINT 328
OLD FORT CADDIS, FAYETTE COUNTY, PENNSYLVANIA: LAST OF THE FRON-
    TIER FORTS . . . . *Full Page* 331
THE COURT HOUSE, PITTSBURG 334
WASHINGTON RAISING THE BRITISH FLAG AT FORT DUQUESNE . . 336
    (*From the old print*)
MARTHA WASHINGTON 337
    (*From the painting by Woolaston, engraved by Rogers*)
THE JUMEL MANSION 339
WILLIAMS FERRY HOUSE, WHERE WASHINGTON MET MARTHA CUSTIS . 341
THE SHENANDOAH VALLEY, VIRGINIA . . . . . *Full Page* 343
WASHINGTON'S FIRST MEETING WITH MARTHA CUSTIS . . . 346
WILLIAMS FERRY, ON THE PAMUNKEY RIVER 348
MARTHA WASHINGTON'S RECEPTION . . . . *Full Page* 351
    (*From the painting*)
MARTHA WASHINGTON'S BEDROOM AT MOUNT VERNON . . . 354
THE FALL OF LOUISBURG 356
    (*From an early print*)
WILLIAM PITT, EARL OF CHATHAM . . . . *Full Page* 359
    (*From the painting in the National Portrait Gallery*)
NO. 10 SAINT JAMES SQUARE, LONDON, FORMER RESIDENCE OF THE
    ELDER PITT 362
RUINS OF FORT TICONDEROGA 365
GENERAL WOLFE 368
    (*From the scarce contemporary print by R. Houston*)
THE LOFT IN THE FARM HOUSE WHERE WOLFE LAY ILL FOR TWO WEEKS
    BEFORE THE BATTLE OF QUEBEC 371
    (*From a recent photograph*)
FARM HOUSE WHERE WOLFE LAY ILL BEFORE THE BATTLE OF QUEBEC:
    SAINT LAWRENCE RIVER AND THE ISLE OF ORLEANS IN THE BACK-
    GROUND . . . . *Full Page* 373
    (*From a recent photograph*)
SILLERY, WHERE WOLFE LANDED 378
DEATH OF MONTCALM 380
WHERE WOLFE DIED VICTORIOUS 383

THE PLAINS OF ABRAHAM, AND MONUMENT MARKING SPOT WHERE GEN-
    ERAL WOLFE DIED . . . . . . *Full Page* 387

THE URSULINE CONVENT, QUEBEC 390

MONUMENT TO WOLFE AMD MONTCALM 392

THE HOME OF MONTCALM, QUEBEC 395

DE LEVIS, FRANÇOIS GASTON, DUC 397
    (*From the engraving by J. Porreau*)

HAYES PLACE, BROMLEY, LORD CHATHAM'S COUNTRY HOUSE *Full Page* 399

BEAUPORT VILLAGE, QUEBEC 404

BIRTHPLACE OF WOLFE AT WESTERHAM, ENGLAND , . . 405

WOLFE'S HOUSE ON THE BORDER OF THE ROYAL PARK, GREENWICH 407

LAKE GEORGE: THE LOCH LOMOND OF AMERICA . . *Full Page* 411

MEMORIAL WINDOW TO WOLFE IN SAINT ALPHEGE'S CHURCH, LONDON 414

LAKE GEORGE BATTLE MONUMENT 417

A LOUISIANA BAYOU 419

BROADWAY, NEW YORK, AT AN EARLY DAY . . *Full Page* 423
    (*From an old lithograph*)

DOORWAY OF A VIRGINIA COLONIAL MANSION 426

A COLONIAL MANSION IN VIRGINIA 427

TOMB OF MARY, MOTHER OF WASHINGTON 429

CHRIST CHURCH, ALEXANDRIA, WHERE WASHINGTON WORSHIPED . 432

OLD NEW YORK, FROM BROOKLYN HEIGHTS . . . *Full Page* 435
    (*From an early print*)

OLD DETROIT 439
    (*From an old engraving on steel*)

MONUMENT TO GENERAL WOLFE IN WESTMINSTER ABBEY }
MONUMENT TO WILLIAM PITT IN WESTMINSTER ABBEY } . *Full Page* 443

THE FIREPLACE IN THE MOUNT VERNON MANSION. . . . 445

THE STABLES AND FAMILY COACH, MOUNT VERNON . . . 446

A RESCUED DESTINY

A RESCUED DESTINY

CHAPTER I

LIFE ON THE OCEAN WAVE

CLOSE–HAULED on the port tack, every stitch of her white canvas taut in the spanking breeze that whirled across the sparkling sea, a corvette of twenty guns made merry way through the tossing waters. Her long, low, dark hull, sliding through the crested waves, taunted them like some live thing to come and lay hand on her. Rushing down upon her, flaring into vivid green along their tops, they reached forth their fingers, cold and sharp, only to slip from her polished sides as she rose above them, and to lie broken and twisted and frothing in her wake.

GENERAL WOLFE

As far as the eye could reach, the whitecaps broke into bloom under the morning sun. The wind, whistling out of the North, cried to them as it passed, and they shouted back to it and to each other in free and bounteous joy. And as the corvette sped on among them, the joy of it all seemed to seize upon her too, so that her taunting and their chasing of her was but a boisterous, rough play of fellow-spirits.

It was the corvette *Impudence*, a privateer, that sailed

the seas that day. For the glory of old England and miscellaneous profit to themselves, certain men of Boston had equipped this craft as a scourge, and a good investment. It was the spring of the year 1703. Good Queen Anne had been on the throne of England for a twelvemonth, and for a twelvemonth had been waging war against the French as hereditary enemies and a people to be utterly destroyed.

Two youths — midshipmen by their dress — stood in the bows looking out upon the seas in the attitude and the silence of close companionship. The elder, a lad of seventeen, with fine auburn hair and deep brown eyes, held his head high and sniffed the perfume of the singing wind. The other, lost in thought, leaned against the bulwark, gazing into the water as it swirled away from the keen fore foot of the vessel.

The first gazed at his companion, and placed his hand across his slender shoulders, as one who would cheer him.

"Elmer," he said, in tones of gentle reproach, "I fear me you like it not."

"Nay, brother," replied the younger, "that I do not. It is now close to the end of May, and for a month we have seen nothing but these waters that are never still, and these rough fellows that vie with them in tumult."

"Never fear, lad, you will see enough ere you set foot again on the green meadows of our father's plantation in Virginia; and when you have had two years of it, such as I have had, and are on the eve of being a lieutenant, you too will love it as I do."

"I might like it better if I knew what I was fighting for, George," returned Elmer. "I do not see why we should shed our blood in this quarrel. The colonies will get nothing of it. What do we care who is on the throne of Spain?"

"Would you not fight for your Queen, then?" George demanded with some show of indignation.

"Ay, as well as you, if she were in any stress of danger," retorted the younger lad, becoming warm in the discussion. "But what interests have we in their politics that do nothing but shed blood? We can better afford to attend to our affairs of peace."

QUEEN ANNE

"If there were as much wisdom in your head as there is sound in your words, you would not be guilty of such foolish utterances, and I advise you to keep silent hereafter, lest your valor and loyalty be brought into question," remarked George, the elder. "As for our Queen, is not her Majesty in danger for her throne when Louis XIV, the French King, says that she is not the Queen of England at all, but that James Stuart, son of James II, who fled from the wrath of the English people, is their rightful King, for all that Queen Anne is of the blood royal, and herself a Stuart? And has not Louis been left-handed enough through this whole business?"

"I care not what he has done; let them punish him themselves. They need not ask us to help."

"Elmer, I am grieved for you," exclaimed the elder brother. "I believe it is your longing for home that speaks. Does it not make your blood boil to think of the trickery of the French Louis? He placed his grandson, Philip of Anjou, on the throne of Spain after he had promised our good King William that he would take none of Spain upon the death of Charles II, except that in Italy. Then he sent ambassadors to Spain secretly, so that when the Spanish monarch died, it was found that he had willed the throne to Philip. Not satisfied with

Louis XIV

that, he is now trying to place on our throne James Stuart, the son of King James, who was driven out when William of Orange came. He proclaimed the young James King, when Queen Anne was already on the throne. It is time we rose and struck him down. He wants the world for France. All Europe is leagued against him."

"Let them whip him, then," growled Elmer. "He has done nothing to us."

"Nothing, lad? Know you not that he would push us all into the sea, and that he would have our colonies for France, along with the rest of the world? Come, lad, you are no Englishman to talk thus!"

Aft, on the quarter-deck, the captain paced to and fro, casting his eye at the full white sails with glad pride, glancing up and down the decks at the black guns as she heeled over before the wind, and searching the sea with his piercing gaze,

QUEEN ANNE'S BED IN HAMPTON COURT

anxious for the prize that might be his. All about her deck was the bustle and orderly confusion of the sailors and the fighters, tending to their duties, ever ready, ever anxious for the enemy.

Suddenly, above the humming of the decks, above the droning of the breeze in the cordage, above the muttering of the waves as they fell away from her, came the cry of the lookout at the masthead: "Sail ho!"

The captain paused in his pacing and looked briskly up.

"Where away?" he cried.

"On the starboard beam, sir!" the lookout answered.

"What do you make her out?"

"A big ship on the port tack, sir!"

Bounding into the after-rigging, the captain climbed to the top with an agility that was ever the joy of his crew. Glass in hand, he swept the horizon, stopping finally to gaze fixedly at a point abreast of them. The crew crowded the rail. There, faintly shimmering in the slanting sun, was a cloud of canvas. The ship was hull down, and only her topsails and topgallant sails were visible; but from the size of them she showed to be a big vessel.

Great was the excitement along the length of the decks. The captain hurried to the quarter-deck, cold, calm, intense, eager. A few quick orders, a scurrying of feet, a pulling of ropes, a twist of the wheel, and the corvette, sheering off a trifle, struggled a moment, paused, and swung into a new stride as she took the waves on the course that would intercept the vessel, be she friend or enemy.

Interminable was the time to the eager soul of George Stevens, midshipman, on the dawn of lieutenancy, as the two drew together across the everlasting water. Interminable was the time to the soul of Elmer Stevens, junior midshipman, whose taste ran rather to bucolic things than to this fighting of rough men on the uncertain element

Quebec, Capital of New France

about them, and who had yet to taste the pleasures of the conflict.

But the time came to an end. The other ship, if she had seen them, as she must have done, paid no heed, holding her course across their bows to the last. Bright on the sky floated the colors of France from the masthead. Up came her hull out of the waves. The lines of her rigging showed to those on board the corvette. Men could be seen running about her decks, and standing to her guns. Slowly they grew larger, till their faces could be made out, —and a rough-looking lot of faces they were, too, for the most part, thought Elmer Stevens, as he waited the order to begin to serve powder to the gun where he was stationed.

There was a puff of smoke, drifting swiftly across the seas, a sharp crash, and the forward gun of the corvette had spoken. George, standing beside it, could see the water leap from the top of a wave as the ball passed through it. All along the decks of the Frenchman ran a rim of fire, and she lay buried for an instant behind a cloud of smoke.

With the crash of their broadside came the balls, singing, screaming overhead, chugging through the rigging, sputtering into the water alongside. One shot, better aimed, burst through the bulwarks amidship, sending a shower of splinters about the deck. It fell on the planking, bounded, hit the breech of a gun on the port side with a sharp clang, glanced into the port bulwark, denting it, and fell into the scupper, where it ran back and forth as the vessel tossed, a thing that a child might play with.

The *Impudence* made fitting answer. There was a muttering roar that made Elmer clap hands to his ears and shut his eyes. The little vessel shuddered under the recoil. The guns, flying back from the discharge, stood inboard with their muzzles smoking, licking their chaps.

STREET IN THE OLD TOWN, QUEBEC

Elmer opened his eyes to see a bank of white smoke scurrying to leeward. It cleared. The mizzen topmast of the enemy, poising for an instant in the air, slowly toppled forward and fell into the midst of the deck. A long section of her rail was torn away. The cries of those aboard her came over the water, angry, sullen.

Some one grasped him roughly by the shoulder, and with an oath told him to fetch powder. He heard the glad, exultant voice of his brother, shouting in triumph at his station. His heart fluttered. He heard his own voice answering it, with a strange sound. He rushed below to the magazine. The zest of it was upon him. His soul was afire for the fight, and he longed for the blood of Frenchmen!

The din became stupendous. The clamor of the men, the shouts of triumph, the shrill curses of rage, the screams of those who were hit, the fierce, harsh blasts of the guns, the crunching of wood beneath the blows of the enemy's shots, wrought into the soul of the lad, and he found himself staggering back and forth from the magazine with the charges of powder under his coat, muttering soft curses under his breath the like of which he had never thought of before, and longing to plunge his cutlass into the hairy throat of some villain of a Frenchman!

George, joyous, buoyant, the vision of a lieutenancy ever before his mind, was everywhere about the forecastle. A round shot, entering the port of the gun he served, crashed against the carriage, buckled the bearings, flew into pieces, struck down several men, and sent a jagged piece of iron tearing through the sleeve of his shirt. He laughed, and cried out a challenge. Hurrying below with the wounded, he laughed again, and came up the companionway from the brig two steps at a bound.

Another ball, striking on the gun next the one he had been serving, now disabled, had wrought terrible havoc among the gunners. Leaping to the spot, George grasped the arms of a sailor who was aiming the piece, shouted orders to the gun crew, trained the cannon, and fired it. Blackened, grimy, sweaty, powder-burned, hoarse with shouting, he fought as one possessed, for the glory of the King and the profit of citizens of Boston.

The enemy was crippled. Although a bigger ship, she was not a vessel of war, and did not carry as many guns as the little corvette. Those she had were not so well served, or so skillfully aimed as the pieces of the privateer; and with each exchange her plight was worse. Her mainmast went by the top. Three of her guns were silenced. Her decks ran blood. Pools of it gathered in her scuppers, to spurt overside as she rolled, staining the white-topped waves. Still she fought, blindly, frantically. And still the little corvette fought with an enthusiasm, a spirit, an intelligence on the part of her crew, prophetic of the spirit that was to make history in the country that sprang from such sires as struggled on her decks that day.

Close and closer came the vessels. No time now to manœuver and work ship! All hands had other deeds to do!

"Stand by to board!"

The captain sang out the order.

"Stand by to board!"

The cry went up and down the deck, smothered at last in the cries of battle that followed it. The Frenchman, desperate, double-shotted his guns. The powder from the blast that followed came aboard the *Impudence*, spattering hot on the faces of the crew, and burning tiny black holes in the sails. George wiped the glowing cinders from his face, feeling the sting of them. He felt another and a sharper sting in his left arm. He brushed his hand over his sleeve to rid himself of it.

RURAL SCENE IN THE PROVINCE OF QUEBEC

QUEBEC'S IMPOSING WATER-FRONT

His eyes were fixed on the enemy. He was absorbed in calculating how soon they could board, for the two ships had drawn close together now.

His right hand, brushing along the sleeve of his shirt, came away wet and warm. He glanced it at. It was red, over the black of the fight. He looked at his sleeve. It was torn, and a red blot was spreading over it with a slow, steady, pulsing increase. As he looked, not yet thinking of it, a red drop fell from his sleeve to the deck, where it was lost in the stain there. Another drop. A little stream, spurting for a moment, and ceasing. He felt it soggy and wet beneath his arm. He tore the sleeve more. A great gash ran all across the fair white skin, opening up the muscles. As he saw it, the sight of it, and the burning, stinging pain that came with the sight, made him reel, faint and sick.

"Boarders, away!"

Some one shouted it. A hundred voices took up the cry.

"Boarders, away! Boarders, away!"

There was a grinding, and lurching together, as the two vessels struck and fell alongside of each other. Forgetting his pain, George reached down and grasped a cutlass from the scabbard of a sailor who lay groaning beside the gun, leapt forward over the gunwale, and clambered upon the deck of the enemy.

The fight had already gone far along the deck. George was behind the line that bore the brunt of it. He saw Elmer, thrust away from his place there by a sailor, struggling to get back where he might strike his cutlass into the breast of a Frenchman; with a cry, he dashed among them and pressed to the forefront.

It did not continue for great length of time. No one could have withstood that onslaught of the victorious. The enemy gave way. The attacking party followed them, in little knots, until they cried for quarter. Elmer, the tension over, sank to the deck and wept like the child that he was, gazing wistfully upon the cutlass he held in his tiny hand, which dripped blood where he had plunged it into the foe. George, seeing him, passed over to him, faint and weary from his own wound.

Out across the clamor of the men, who shouted, some for quarter and some with the joy of the victory, there came a scream of terror that sent the blood shivering up and down the veins of both lads. Many cries they had heard that day which in a day of ordinary events would have frozen them with horror, and not one had they heeded. But this cry reached into their very souls and wrung them. For it was the cry of a woman in the last fear.

Instantly alive, George leapt for the cabin, whence the sound had come. Others crowded there. He pushed through them, after the manner of youth. There was tumult within. The cry reached his ears again, above hoarse laughter and brutal jeers. Stung by it, he surged forward into the midst of the cabin.

There, on the floor, clinging to the body of a grey-

BREAK NECK STEPS, QUEBEC

bearded man whose eyes were glassy in death, was a girl of tender years. Her face was drawn and haggard with grief and anguish; but above the anguish and the grief was utter terror. For rough hands were upon her, seeking to drag her from the man, and hoarse shouts and laughter were hurled at her by men from the privateer. For the life of her she struggled, twining her arms into the limp arms that once would have struck so strongly in her behalf, livid with fear and gasping for breath to cry out again.

Leaping over the prostrate form, George struck out with his

weapon in blind wrath. "Unhand her!" he cried. One felt the bite of it, and reeled back. Another crumpled and fell across the feet of the dead man on the floor. George felt the tiny hands of the maiden about his knees, and felt that her face was turned to him. He struck again, and again. One crept behind him. He could not turn, she held so closely to him. He thrust the cutlass backward, without seeing where he aimed. It passed harmless through the air.

A terrific blow upon his head; a shower of sparkling lights before his eyes! A deep, sweet, placid calm came over him, and he sank to the floor.

BED OF LOUIS XIV IN THE PALACE OF VERSAILLES

CHAPTER II

MEETING BEGINS PARTING

THROUGH the darkness that had come so swiftly upon George there broke the faint glow of lights striking on his closed lids. Up out of the dead numbness that had possessed him came feeling, the sense of dull pain, and the experience of the swinging of the vessel, pleasurable save when it lurched too quickly. Into the utter silence struck the low muttering drone of voices, speaking in undertones, the resonant reverberations of the voice of the captain, which could not sound without the twang of command; the harsh, shaggy voice of the mate, the smooth, soothing tones of the ship's surgeon, and others that he did not recognize.

He opened his eyes. The light of the lamp in the cabin shone on his pupils. Elmer, with a long, sad face, sat beside him, contemplating him in complete dejection. A group was gathered about in the small space. Elmer, seeing him raise his lids, cried slightly in surprise, and then broke out into weeping. The captain, seeing it, looked at the prostrate form.

"So ho, Leftenant Stevens, you're with us once again, are ye?" said he, quietly. "I'm glad for that, for we should miss you sore, my lad! It's a brave lad, doctor."

George struggled to answer, but gave up for the pain in the effort. The surgeon felt his pulse, and nodded his head in satisfaction. There was a murmur of voices, and one of them said:

"She can see him, then?"

The doctor nodded again.

"There's a miss aboard who's very keen to see ye,

35

Leftenant Stevens," said the captain, with a wink and a chuckle.

There was a stir among them. Presently they stood aside. A girl, the sadness and pallor of whose face added to her soft, dark beauty, crept timidly toward him and placed her hand gently on his breast. He recognized her

VILLAGE OF CAUGHNAWAGA

as the maiden whom he had saved from the sailors in the cabin of the Frenchman.

"Is monsieur well?" she stammered. Her syllables fell in tinkling spangles of broken English.

For answer he closed his lids, and smiled, opening them abruptly again to gaze upon her. She was passing fair.

"I thank you! I cannot thank you. What shall I say? I — you —" She leaned over him and kissed his free hand. One of his arms was bound to his side. He moved his lips, yearning to reply. She placed her fingers on them, soft as the petals of a rose, smiled through her sadness, and was gone. With a sigh, George passed into slumber.

Throughout the night he fought again the good fight, crying out now and then, and awakening. Always he found the wistful eyes of Elmer gazing upon him, and the hand of the surgeon's assistant ready to soothe him, and fell again

into repose. He awoke, at last, after a long sleep, to know
the light of day flooding into the cabin, to hear the scurry
of the sailors' feet on deck as they worked ship, and to feel
the swing of the craft as she slipped rapidly over the waves.

His head, bandaged heavily, was dull and painful. His
left arm throbbed and ached. But for the most part he
was comfortable. And he was happy, for the girl who had
come the night before, came early to see him; when they
brought him gruel, she fed it to him, lisping sweetly to him
in her pretty English the while.

They found her nursing excellent for him. Before many
days he was given over into her charge, and she was constantly with him during the days. When he was strong
enough, they brought him on the quarter-deck,— for, though

THE ANCIENT WALLS OF CAUGHNAWAGA

he was but a midshipman still, his father, Robert Stevens, was a man of moment in the colonies, and he himself was already as good as lieutenant.

In the happy hours that came to him in her company, she told him her story. Her name was Marie Heuillet. Family she had none, save only a cousin in Quebec. Her father had been all that was left to her; but he had been slain, and buried in the tumbling waters of the sea. She wept in telling the tale, and he wept with her.

She was coming with her father to Quebec, she said, where he had offices to do for his government in France. Now she did not know what might befall her, having fallen into the hands of the enemy. George, comforting her, told her that he would shield her; that he had kinsfolk in Boston who would shelter her, and that in the end he would see that she came safely to Quebec.

So the days passed as they drew toward Boston. And ever there grew between them a warmth that sprang from the fateful day which had brought them together, and waxed with the tender hours of his convalescence. In the end, they spoke but little, sitting on the quarter-deck, or below in the cabin when the weather was bad. What little they spoke was in whispers, so that none might hear. Gently he led her from her sorrow, and gently she led him from his pain and weakness. So bright and pleasant were the hours, that it was with a heavy heart that they saw at last the lights of Boston breaking out of the evening sky.

Alexander Stevens, a distant cousin, was rejoiced to see the brothers. When George told him of Marie, he sent his wife post-haste to greet her. She came aboard the corvette as it lay in the stream, with many cordial words of sympathy and reassurance. Marie, weeping on her bosom, thanked her simply and went with her.

George added himself to their company. Elmer stayed

COMMON AND WELL OF OLD FORT AT DEERFIELD, MASSACHUSETTS

aboard the corvette, which was being patched up and prepared for another cruise, only awaiting the arrival of the
prize. At last she crept limping into the harbor, and came
to anchor. Great was the rejoicing of captain and crew,
and of the citizens of Boston who had interest in her, among
them Alexander Ste-
vens; for she was
richly laden.

The day of the
sale of the cargo ar-
rived, amid much ex-
citement. The profit
was large. Alexander
Stevens, with kindled
eyes, rubbed his hands
together and was ex-
ceedingly gay t h a t
night at supper.

"And so you too
found profit in the
adventure, D o c t o r

DEERFIELD STREET, DEERFIELD, MASSACHUSETTS

Williams?" quoth he, addressing himself to the Reverend
John Williams, pastor of a little church of Deerfield, Massachusetts, a distant relative, who was visiting them for a space,
and had been at the sale. "It is well for you that bells are not
much in demand. You got it at a fair bargain, my friend!"

"Ay, that I did," the minister made answer. "And
it will be a proud day in Deerfield when it rings out the call
to worship!"

George, ever gazing upon Marie, saw her cross herself
swiftly, with a look of alarm in her dark eyes, and mutter
something in French. He asked her, when he could, what
it was about the bell that had disturbed her.

"*Mon Dieu!*" she said, under her breath. "Was it

THE DEERFIELD SETTLEMENT

the sacred bell, blessed by the Holy Father at Rome for the chapel of Saint Louis at Caughnawaga? *Ah, c'est tres mal!* Evil fortune will come of it, for that bell to fall into the hands of heretics!"

He pressed her further, and she told him that on the ship was a holy bell sent from France to the chapel in the wilderness with the blessings of the Pope, and was much perturbed concerning what had befallen it. He chid her gently for her fears, and told her that he, too, was a heretic, if she chose to call him such. Whereat she sighed, and looked sadly upon him, and they spoke no more of it.

Time passed swiftly, as it will when lovers are together. Her thoughts turned toward Quebec. She desired to go to her own people. They urged her to remain with them. George made many bold plans for a youth of seventeen, with brave promises and assurances. She rested closer to him when he spoke as he did, but shook her head.

"Ah, *mon cher*, there will be a time for that, when the war is done," she whispered, with tears in her eyes. "But now I must go to mine own people."

She would not be dissuaded, so they cast about them for a way to send her to the enemy's city. In course of time there came an exchange of prisoners. A party was starting for Quebec in a week. Among them were women, the wives of officers. It was fitting that she should go with them, and it was so arranged.

OLD STONE CHAPEL AT CAUGHNAWAGA

Heavy were the hours that came then to the two lovers. Still weak and sick from the wound on his head and the gash in his arm, George bore it ill. The last night that they were to be together was at hand. With a heavy heart, they wandered forth into the moonlight for the farewell parting. For a long time neither could speak.

"Ah, Marie, Marie," said George, at last, "I cannot bring myself to think of the time when you will be gone. Almost I believe that it would be better for me to go with you, since you will not stay with us. It is not yet too late! Stay with us, and I will take you to my father. I shall go no more to sea, and we shall be very happy."

"With all that I am I love you," she said, "and the day will come when there shall be no more parting for us.

But now I must go to mine own people in mine own country. I am only a woman, and know not why it is, but I feel that it is better that I go."

"And have you no fear?" he asked, overcome with emotion. He was pitifully weak and sick.

"Ah, beloved, none! If you cannot find me, I shall seek you into the last corner of the world, so that we shall be together always at the last."

He was silent for a space. Presently he said:

"I grieve that you spoke so of that bell. I cannot forget it. It haunts me with a nameless foreboding."

She crossed herself quickly, alarmed in her turn.

"That cannot bring harm to us," she said. "Every night I pray to the saints to shield us from that. Every night I shall pray for you, and think and dream of you.

They fell then to talking of their love, until fear was gone and only sadness remained. On the morrow she left, with a heavy heart, and George turned back to the house of his cousin, now so vast and vacant that he found no joy in life.

LUMBER CAMP ON THE CONNECTICUT

CHAPTER III

THE MAN OF GOD

FOR all that the heart of George Stevens was heavy, time passed lightly over him as he stayed in Boston, until the autumn came, shutting down upon all prospect of another voyage for him that year. The *Impudence* had been in port since she brought Marie and himself ashore, but his wound had not yet healed, so that he could not go with her when she went down to the sea once more to cleanse it of the French. Now November was at hand, and the *Impudence*, making port, would not put out again until the spring.

Queen Anne's War had broken out all along the fringe of her possessions in America, in innumerable hostile raids of French and Indians, incited to massacre by the emissaries of France. Hardly a week passed that a tale did not reach Boston of horrors done at some little frontier settlement, of tomahawk and torch, of murder and pillage. The entire border-line was in a state of fear and anxiety. There was no security. None could foresee where the marauders might next swoop down in the darkness of night upon the unprotected settlements.

Governor Dudley, in June, met many Indian sachems and chiefs at Casco, seeking security for his people. With protestations and much smoking of the peace-pipe, they renewed old treaties, telling him that the French had tried to incite them again the English colonists, but that they had been true and loyal, and so would continue to be. Bomaseen, the chief sachem among the Indians, told them that the French agents had tried to incite them against the

English, but that they would not listen to the tempting offers of reward.

August 10 many bodies of Indians, acting in concert, fell simultaneously on the settlements about the Casco. They killed twenty-two at Spurwink, twenty-five at Purpooduck, five at Berwick, seven whom they took in a boat with their canoes, and many scattering settlers whom they surprised in their hay-fields. In all 150 were massacred by the same savages who had sworn allegiance in June.

The English believed that the Jesuits were responsible for the massacre. Father Rale, whom they most bitterly accused, in denial says of the Indians:

"I exhorted them to maintain the same interest in religion as if they were at home; to observe carefully the laws of war; to practice no cruelty; to kill no one except in the heat of battle; and to treat their prisoners humanely."

As a result of the treachery of the Indians, the border-land was continually in a state of dread, not knowing when or where the next blow would fall. It was the fascination of this constantly threatening danger, with its element of uncertainty and high adventure, that lured George Stevens to Deerfield, Massachusetts, early in December, in response to the invitations of the Reverend John Williams to come and see what death looked like ashore. He liked the prospect well. He sent word to the master of the *Impudence* that he would wait there until the spring. Now, in the last of February, he was as completely a member of the household of the frontier clergyman as though he had always been of it, so closely did the common hardships of the life knit the bonds of common humanity.

The weather was cold and dreary. For many days it had snowed. The sky had turned more sullen still, and sharp winds had snarled down from the North, piling the snow high about the eaves of the little log cabins of Deer-

Casco Bay, Maine

field. At last a cruel cold had come, so that the snow was frozen stiff and impassable. It was hard living those days. When they dragged in the great logs of oak and hickory, to build up their fires, the icy blasts came through the open

WINTER ON THE UPPER CONNECTICUT

door and chilled the house until the seven children shivered again, with blue lips and numb fingers.

And when the logs were piled high within the huge, wide fireplace, it was little better; for the searching wind thrust its muzzle in between the rough logs of the walls and about the hewn door-posts, and through the loopholes that were left so that they might fire upon the Indians, and gnawed at the backs of those huddled about the hearth, until they were half frozen on one side, and parched by the roaring blaze on the other.

Sitting at the end of the semicircle, next the fire, where the light was better, his work for the day all done,— for they made their guests lend a hand in those days,— George

Stevens sat reading to the family in the early evening of the last day in February. The smaller children, already tucked away in the crude, rough beds in the corner of the cabin, had been lulled to sleep by the soporific qualities of the literature upon which George was engaged. The flare of the fire made uncertain light on his book, and sent huge shadows fluttering into the far ends of the room. The members of the family circle, the rough table behind them, the spinning-wheel drawn off into a corner, all joined in sending their shadows in a mad, mocking dance over the walls and across the ceilings as the flames waved in the gusts that rushed upon them.

The door opened, and a draught that crinkled with cold blew across them all, even causing the smaller children, wrapped as they were in bedding, to shiver and draw together. The door, with its four inches of good oak, closed with a dull bang, and the Reverend John Williams stood within the light of the fire, bound to his ears in great-coat and scarf, shrunken with the cold, stamping his feet. His wife, frail and white, with a tiny infant in her arms, smiled upon him, making room for him on the bench at her side.

"Poor dear," she said, "to be out such a night. How did you find our brother Wells?"

"But poorly," replied the minister, doffing his outer garments and coming closer to the fire. "I fear that he is not long for this world."

"Does he fear death, then?" the little woman asked.

"Nay, he fears not death itself, so much as the manner in which it may come. A dread of the savages has come over him, and he cannot be comforted. It is his illness that makes him so, for a braver man, nor one more God-fearing and righteous, never lived."

"Are there Indians about, then?" asked George, eagerly.

Much had he heard of Indians, and the thought of them possessed his imagination.

"Since a month none has been known to have raised hand against an Englishman, and no news comes of any on the war-path," the minister replied. "But who can tell what evil spirit may not possess them at any moment? Since they rose against our brothers of Casco last August, after they had passed the wampum of peace and piled the rocks of fidelity, there is no refuge save in God. What God in His wisdom deemeth best, that it is which will take place."

"Ay, John," observed his wife. "But it amazes me to know how God in His wisdom permits the blasphemous French to stir up these lost souls of perdition in His name to prey upon His faithful children."

"It is not for us to inquire into the ways of the Almighty, wife," returned Mr. Williams. "We should rather raise

OLD BLOCK HOUSE IN MAINE

our voices in thanksgiving that our harvests of the last year are still sufficient in our granaries, and that we have been spared until this time.

"Our fields have flourished. There is no evil abroad in the land. Our people here and throughout the colonies are law-abiding and living in the fear of God, in goodly virtue. Think of the horror of war to those poor peasants of Europe over whose fields the hostile armies tread!

"Nay! We have only to be thankful, wife. Even our neighbors in New York are worse off than we. Thomas Litchfield, who comes at great pains to see his brother ere he dies, tells of affairs there that would make one almost to rise in wrath against the blunders of England. Their governor, Lord Cornbury, is an evil man, he says. He hath imposed much upon them, and when the legislature voted fifteen hundred pounds for forts in the Narrows, the governor, it seems, took the money from the treasury, but built no forts. So that now they have defied him, and will vote him no more money, having a treasurer whom they appoint to disburse their funds. And they petition the Queen to remove him, sending them another.

"But for that, there is no mischief abroad, and all goes well. Honor, liberty, freedom of conscience are every-where. Surely, the forays of the Indians and French are not a thing to make us forget all our benefits."

"Ay, John, it is wicked in me, I know," said Mrs. Williams, with a sigh. "But sometimes, when I am sick and weak, I am prone to wish for myself the safety and security of those of our people who do not live here on the brink of the world. It is not for myself so much, John, as for these poor innocents whom God hath sent to us. I pray that He may protect them for us."

"There is no danger, Mistress Williams, that I know," said George, seeking to reassure her. "For are we not

within the stockade, and are there not a score of soldiers
about to give the redskins as warm a welcome as they will
be like to find this side of the next world?"

"Thou art young and brave, and speak like a soldier,
George. But I am a woman, weak and helpless, and I
know the mother-
love. It is that
which makes me
afraid."

At the instant
there was the
crunching of snow
without the door,
the sound of heavy
feet, a rattling of
the latch, and the
door flew open
once more. With
a slight shriek,
which she could
not suppress, Mrs.
Williams clasped
her tiny babe to

ON THE CONNECTICUT RIVER

her breast, clutched another by the arm, and backed into
the corner farthest from the door. George felt the hair
rising on his head, and leapt for a loaded musket that
stood in the corner. Mr. Williams, rising swiftly, turned to
see who entered.

Two men, so bundled against the cold that they were
scarcely to be seen in the midst of their wrappings, came
into the firelight, closing the ponderous door behind them.
The foremost of them, throwing off a pair of mittens and
extending his hand toward the heat, advanced to the fire.
Seeing how they welcomed him and his companion, he

FERTILE VALLEY OF THE CONNECTICUT

stopped midway with a loud laugh, and snatched the muffler from his throat and chin.

"Were the redskins as feared of a soldier as ye are, 't would be merry work we should make of it," said he. "Hast any brew about? Asa and I are fair starved with the cold."

"Is it you, then!" exclaimed the minister, at sight of the rugged red face revealed beneath the muffler. "Come, wife, 't is but two of our soldiers. Never fear now for the Indians. But how comes it that you are not on guard to-night?"

"God guards us to-night, reverend sir," responded the second of the two soldiers, coming forward with his outer garments loosened. "Were any Indians to come abroad this night, I could wish them no greater evil; for it is bitter cold, and grows colder with every inch of blackness."

Mrs. Williams, with a sigh of relief, came back to her bench, trembling. George, replacing the musket, went to fetch a pot of mild beer, a common article of domestic provision in those times, and the hearth circle adjusted itself to the new arrivals.

"Then there is to be no guard to-night?" asked George, resuming his seat.

"None, by the orders of our captain," replied the first soldier. "And 't is glad enough I am. Egad, your bullet would freeze in the air to-night."

"Hast any news of the wars, reverend sir?" inquired the second soldier, as his face emerged from the mug of beer, where it had been vigorously employed for a space of time.

"Nay, none; and we are like to have none soon, too," the minister made answer.

"Belike it should be all over, and France pushed into the sea, ere we should learn of it, smothered here under this world of snow and coldness," observed the first soldier, applying himself to the beer in his turn. "Ha, a round one that!" he continued, setting down the empty pot by the side of George as a delicate intimation that he was welcome to fetch more. "And it 's well I wish, sitting snug here by the fire, that the devil would prompt some of his dear children of France to come forth on such a night as this, to prepare them for the weather in their world to come,— saving your reverence, sir!"

"'T would be worse for their craw than the meal we gave them at Berwick last August. What say you, Daniel?" said Asa, turning to his comrade.

"Pray, what was that?" demanded George, eagerly, before Daniel could reply. "Were you there?"

"Ay, that we were," answered Asa. "And when the settlers came running into our fort, with the savages at their heels, we turned loose upon them such a hell that they ran howling back to the woods, where they burnt poor Joe Ring at the stake for revenge."

George had heard the story, but never from one who had been there. He pressed them eagerly, and there followed many rough tales of the fighting of Indians; until

Mr. Williams bade them cease, lest they harrow the souls of his wife and children till they could not sleep that night. As it was growing late, they gathered in prayer, and went to their rest for the night, hurrying into bed clothed as they were because of the cold.

The flames between the logs leapt forth lazily, flapped, and crept down again into the warmth of the coals. The shadows ceased their dancing, and slept in the corners. George piled the ashes over and about the embers that were left, so that they should smoulder through the night, and there would be no need to resort to flint and tinder-box in the morning. The soldiers, rolling themselves in their outer coats and cloaks, lay down before the hearth and were soon in noisy slumber.

Little by little the red glow grew duller underneath the ashes. Little by little the smoke that poured out from the banked fire dwindled into a tiny blue ribbon that flickered and wavered from side to side within the great throat of the chimney, or streamed out into the room as the blasts rushed down into the fireplace from above. A few muffled words from the unquiet children, the hungry cry of the babe, quickly stifled, drowsy whisperings; and then silence fell upon the little band of pioneers, broken only by the breathing of the sleepers.

Struggling at last through the clouds that hung over the Connecticut Valley, the moon burst out across the night. Coldly it shone over that scene of coldness. Bleakly it looked down upon the snow-laden trees, shivering beneath the wind, casting their black shadows along the whiteness. Pale, dead, drear, it made the vast mantle of untracked snow that lay deep over the earth seem more dead and utterly desolate.

Save for the huddled huts of the settlers, standing in a clearing with a stockade about them, and a few that straggled away from the shelter toward the forest, there was in all the world no sign of life, no sign given that there was to be life on the morrow, or any other day.

And there was no sound but the rattling of the dead leaves that still clung to the oaks and the rasping together of the hard, frozen needles on the pine-trees — those, and the sibilant sighs of the sleepers in the huts.

NORTH HAVERHILL AND THE CONNECTICUT RIVER

CHAPTER IV

FRANÇOIS THE VENGEANCE

RAGGED clouds, swarming past the moon, now high in the sky, sent shadows scurrying across the frozen fields of untracked snow. They darted into the darkness beneath the trees, to hurry out beyond the other side and creep into the shadow of another tree. They stalked along

HERTEL DE ROUVILLE

the ridge, tumbling down into the valley below swiftly and silently. They gathered about the little cluster of log cabins, half buried in the snow, and mingled with the black squares that lay on the snow under their eaves.

It was midnight. There was still no sound, save only the rattling of dead leaves on the oak-trees and the rasping together of the hard, frozen needles of the pine — these, and the slight sibilant rustling of little frozen particles of snow driven over the hard crust by the north wind, which blew ever more bitterly, blast on blast.

58

But there were other shadows under the moon up on the ridge, slipping from tree to tree and dropping swiftly, silently, into the valley below,— scores of them, black and stealthy. They moved in ones and twos, and larger groups, hastening across the open reaches, and crouching low in the shadow beyond. Still there was no sound more than the winds in the treetops, and a slight rustling, as of something passing over the frozen crust of the snow.

Score on score the shadows come, gliding from tree to tree, until they merged and were lost in the shadows of a heavy clump of oaks at the base of the ridge. Two of the shadows stood apart on its top. A black patch from a flitting cloud blotted out the little stockade and the cabins within. It passed; and they lay there again under the white glow, silent, serene, placid.

Dripping from the two shadows into the vast void of silence came the sound of a low-spoken voice.

"Hark ye, François Hertel de Rouville," it said, in the French tongue. "Thou hast led us a merry dance over the frozen snows to the tune of thy bell, with none for partners but cold and hunger. And thou showest us not that thou didst speak the truth when thou saidst it was here, by my troth, I would rather be a humming-bird, to suck honey from this snow, than thou. A pinched belly goeth not with a broad heart, and I like not the mutterings of our men."

"Carest thou, then, for the mutterings of a rout and rabble of slaves and savages, my lovely Contrebras?" replied the substance of the other shadow. "But as for thee, my little grumbler, I will tell thee that our holy bell of Saint Louis hangs in yonder tower, hard within the stockade, where it calls heretics to perdition on the Lord's day."

"Ay; so say ye often enough, *monsieur le capitaine;* but know ye that the bell is truly there?" pursued the voice that had first spoken, not satisfied with the assurances of the other.

"In sooth, that I do," Hertel made answer. "For were we not told how the scoundrelly heretics stole the bell of God and brought it hither, by no less a one than the good, the true, the beautiful Marie Heuillet, our fair cousin of Quebec, who was on the ship whence it was stolen?"

"Not she of the brown eyes whom De Montreville swears to marry, yet who gives him such scant looks for his pains!" exclaimed the other.

"Ay, the same," replied Hertel. "And may God wish him well of it! For my part, I would rather fondle the sconce of some heretic of an Englishman with my good hanger here than to feel the bite of a sharp tongue. Ah, my pretty little Fanchon, my lovely little brave; love stirs the heart within me too! Look yonder at those nests of heretics, those vile holes of the enemies of God! Is it not good for the soul of one, say I, to know that ere the sun pinks through the clouds of dawn their gory locks will be dripping from the belts of my brave red brothers, and their ghosts dancing on the griddles of hell? Who hath a better love than I?"

"An thou hast not had blood enough already, my good Hertel, thou shouldst have thy fill the now," exclaimed the other. "It seems a likely land of promise."

"Blood enough, snaggle-nose? Blood enough?" cried François Hertel, extending his hands before him with a gesture of despair. "There is not blood enough for me in all the cursed veins of England! Speak not to me of blood enough to shed of those who steal our holy bells!"

The shadows vanished. There was the sound of softly spoken words from the denseness that obscured the base of the ridge, orders briefly given and received, exclamations of impatience, some hasty prayers, and the shadows passed

THE REVEREND JOHN WILLIAMS'S HOUSE

from beneath the shelter of the ridge and glided swiftly from tree to tree.

Close and closer to the settlement drew the shades, now running on, now crouching where the darkness from some tree or rock concealed them. There were no whispers now, — only the sound of something passing swiftly over the hard, frozen crust of the snow, which was like the rattling of the dead leaves on the oak-trees, or the rasping together of the stiff, stark needles of the pine, or the racing of tiny ice across the crust before the fitful blasts of the north wind.

Close and ever closer came the shadows, mysterious, stealthy. Hertel, in advance, stopped, and raised his finger toward the next following. The sign passed on. As it came to each, he stopped. There was no sound. Even the wind was silent here, though far off on the ridge came the soughing of it, as a gust gathered head. The rustling, rasping noise of it drew closer. Hertel raised his finger again; the shadows moved with the wind, as the shadows of the clouds moved. And there was no sound save one that might have been the wind in the somber, shivering wood, or the ice flakes tinkling across the crust.

Now the shadows clustered in the fringe of the wood, where it gave over to the clearing that the settlers had made. The first house was not farther than one of the Indians might have thrown his tomahawk. There was no word. Their plans were made. There was but the raising of a finger, as a blast from the North broke the stillness. The shadows swarmed from the edge of the clearing out across the open space with a noise that might have been the wind, but nothing more.

The blackness beside the houses without the stockade swallowed up some of the black and stealthy shadows. Others, gliding up the drifts of snow, where it had piled to the top of the stockade, dropped silently within the enclosure. Shadows, scurrying, found cover of shadow beneath the eaves of the cabins, within the door-posts where the round ends of the logs gave recess, and in the paths, hewn deep through the snow. And there was no sound but the wind.

Ah! If that holy bell could have spoken then! If its brazen tongue could have shouted out to the settlers, peacefully sleeping there behind those doomed walls, that the savages were whetting scalping-knives on their very sills, that François Hertel with his band of marauders was upon them, bloodthirsty and vindicative, it might have been able to forestall some of the stain of blood that came upon it. But there was no sound, save only the noise of the wind.

Another sound, more horrible than any that ear could hear — a sound that sent the heart into the throat, that drove the blood thumping through the veins, that set the hair tingling and on end! For François Hertel, the Vengeance, had raised his hand, and from three hundred and more throats burst the yell of the Indian and the war-cry of France.

There was no silence now. The crashing of war-clubs against the heavy oaken doors of the cabins, the discharge of firearms, the yells of the savages, the shrieks of women and children, the shouting of the men, joined into one horrid tumult of sound that made the heart of the bravest turn sick with dismay. Awakened from the oblivion of sleep to meet the oblivion of death, the settlers fought blindly in the dark of their cabins. Dulled by the dregs of sleep, disconcerted by the surprise and the confusion of noises, they laid their hands on what they could, and prepared to sell their scalps as dearly as might be.

A mighty shout went up about the cabin of the Reverend John Williams, the minister in whose church hung the ill-fated bell. Hertel himself was there. A treacherous Indian had told them which it was.

"Here lies our man of God!" shouted Hertel derisively. "Let him look to his God now for succor!"

Blow on blow fell on the heavy door. A musket flashed from a loophole. A dozen barked in answer, the bullets thudding against the logs harmlessly. The door quivered under the blows. It tottered. It fell. A stream of shadows flowed into the deep shadow of the cabin.

The minister had leapt from his bed. He met them bravely, pistol in hand. A savage stood before him, tomahawk poised for the blow. He pressed his pistol against the breast of the savage, and pulled the trigger. George, standing near with a sword in his hand which he had drawn from the sheath of one of the soldiers, baffled by the darkness, heard the click of the hammer descending against the flint, saw the spark, a flash in the pan; but there was no report. The pistol had missed fire.

In the instant of its failure, George, aided by the flash, acted; and the brave groveled on the floor, with hands to

BATTERED DOOR FROM THE WILLIAMS HOUSE

his head, and a stream of blood gushing through between his fingers, while his hatchet went clanging against the hearth-stone. Twice the youth swung through the darkness, and twice he felt the good feel of flesh come up to meet his blade. But they were too many, and pressed too close. He had to give way.

He saw half a dozen savage warriors leap on the minister, bearing him to the ground, and saw the figure of a French officer standing behind them. He heard an order given. The little French which he had learned from Marie was of things other than war, and helped him little now. But he at least had learned who their leader was.

A musket lay across the hearth. The dull red glow from the coals traced the barrel of it out to the eye, a crimson bar. He grasped it. He kicked the ashes from the coals, that he might have light to see. Through the ruddy gloom his eye picked out the leader. He raised musket. Aiming it carefully, he braced himself for the recoil and pressed the trigger. The heavy lock swung down. But there was no discharge. The musket had been fired through the loop-hole, and abandoned.

The two English soldiers were not brave. Daniel, throwing aside his weapons, went to the commander of the party and offered himself prisoner. Asa, the second soldier, the one who had fired through the walls, was ensconced in the chimney, whence he was making frantic efforts to reach the roof.

With frightful yells, mingled with French curses, the work went on. George, at bay in a corner next the stone chimney, fighting manfully with his borrowed sword, kept them off. He could see better now. There was some light in the room through the open door, and some from the glow of the coals.

He saw Mr. Williams, bound, lying on the floor. He saw his face, and watched a look of utter horror pass across it. He followed the glance of the brave minister. A savage held one of the smaller children by the two heels in one hand. With a shout, he swung the child over his head and dashed its skull against the door-posts, not ten feet from where George stood, hemmed in by a circle of Indians and French soldiers.

While the body of the slain infant still jerked and quiv-ered, the Indian returned with another. Ghastly was the face of the minister as George glanced upon it. Terrible was the scream of the mother, piercing the tempest of yells and screams until none other than it could be heard! In-flamed beyond all judgment, George bore in among them, seeking only to save the child. Like the tongue of a ser-pent his good blade whipped in among them. They gave way to the lad of seventeen, little by little.

But they gave way too slowly. George progressed till he stood in the midst of the hearth when the Indian with the child dangling from his hands swung it through the air against the hard stones of the fireplace, and dashed the mangled body into the face of him who fought so desperately to save it. A wild, mocking jeer went up from the circle that bore about him then. As they pressed closer,

BURIAL PLACE OF THE DEERFIELD VICTIMS

they cut him off from the corner where he had stood at bay.

He felt the kicking heels of the soldier who still tried to mount the chimney. Laying hold of them, he pulled him down.

"Vile coward," he shouted, with an oath. "Do but take a hand in the work, and we shall drive them yet!"

The soldier only cowered in the chimney-corner.

There was another scream of a woman, only less horrible. George, glancing swiftly past his assailants, saw them dragging Mrs. Williams, weak and helpless, to the door and out into the bitter cold, her babe at her breast. His swollen heart choked him. He cried out he knew not what, and fell upon the small circle about him with redoubled fury, so that it bent and broke before him.

Now his sword engaged that of the leader, skilled in the play. He was no match for the trained Frenchman. For a spell his very fury carried him toward success; but in an evil moment the point of the other's weapon slipped past his guard with a quick flash. He felt a dull, stinging blow above his wrist. His arm stiffened, aching heavily. His sword clanged to the floor.

With his other hand he grasped a chair, overturned on the floor, and would have continued the fight with that. But as he stooped, they were upon him. Stronger, heavier than he, they crushed him to the floor and bound his hands.

"*Sacrebleu!*" exclaimed the Frenchman leader, François Hertel de Rouville, as George was shaken to his feet, a bound prisoner. "Thou fightest like the devil himself. An thou wert not an Englishman and a heretic, I could love thee for that."

They led him, bound as he was, out into the cold.

CHAPTER V

THE WORLD'S LAST AMEN

FRANÇOIS the Vengeance did not tarry long: only long enough to set fire to the houses, to gather the plunder, to pluck the scalps from the brows of the dead and wounded, to distribute the living as prisoners among the members of the party; and then he started northward again, up the valley of the Connecticut, before the grey blur of dawn came into the East.

But one cabin he did not burn. Seven men and seven women, barricading themselves within, fought back the savages and French and prevented every attempt they made to set fire to the building. A party of English, overtaking the band of marauders before they had gone far, made a stubborn fight to release the prisoners, but were obliged to withdraw because of superior numbers.

Wounded, thinly clad, ill-fed, it was a cursed trip for George across the frozen snows. But he did not think of his own sufferings, so great were those of others. Mrs. Williams, weak, sick, distraught by the death of her two children slain before her eyes, trudged through the broken, knife-edged crusts till she could go no farther, and an Indian clove her skull with his tomahawk. The same fate came swiftly to all who could not keep up with the Vengeance, hurrying northward to avoid the reprisal that he feared was following.

The party reached the Saint Lawrence in two divisions. George was taken from the rest of the prisoners as soon as they reached the village of Saint Francis, and confined by himself. On a day he was taken alone to

The Connecticut River at White River Junction

Quebec by Hertel himself, and turned over as a galley-slave.

"Here, you, De Montreville!" cried François the Vengeance to the French officer who was in charge of the galley-slaves, a man of tremendous size and a wild, rough beauty. "Thou mayst teach this little cockchafer better manners, an thou wilt. It were well for him to learn to be not too brave in the fight with François Hertel de Rouville. They would have killed him had I let them; but his life is natheless forfeit, and I make this use of it."

From that moment he was a galley-slave, made to toil at menial things about the citadel and the town of Quebec; helping to build houses, to repair the wharves, to smooth the roads, and to place huge blocks of granite in the fortifications, doing all manner of heavy labor. His back bent beneath it, and his heart was near to breaking. He was fed on coarse food and quartered with villains and cut-throats, the most desperate men of the province. Only the hope of escape sustained him,— that, and the thought that perhaps Marie might still be in Quebec, and that they might be brought together again.

News of the massacre of Deerfield traveled fast. It reached Boston early in March. Alexander Stevens, by special courier, sent word to Robert Stevens, on his plantation in Virginia. Elmer, who was then preparing to leave home to meet George and go out on the spring cruise, hastened northward at once, his father with him. They went to Deerfield. They searched the ruins of the Williams house. They talked with those who had defended their house against the French and Indians. They went as far as it was safe for them to go along the route that had been taken by the marauders in retreat. They left nothing undone that might bring some news of the brother. But they found no trace. Hopeless, at last, they returned to

GRAVES OF THE REVEREND JOHN WILLIAMS AND HIS TWO WIVES

Boston, and so to the plantation in Virginia. Elmer went no more to sea. His heart for the work had been taken from him when George left the decks of the *Impudence.* Now, with no hope of his return, the younger brother was without the strength to sail against the French.

As time wore on, George took the fancy of De Montreville by his bold spirit. Too wise to be in open revolt against his imprisonment and hard usage, he nevertheless held up his head among the slaves, and looked the great man squarely between the eyes when they had occasion to discuss the work that was under way, and exhibited an independence of thought that the other admired and respected.

Gradually he was accorded certain privileges, being brought sometimes to the officers' quarters, where his intelligence and quickness of speech were always welcome.

He was given charge of gangs of workmen. Responsibility was placed upon him to a degree that was unusual. The fear that he would attempt to escape was dismissed from their thoughts. For where would an Englishman go if he should escape from Quebec, in the midst of a hostile country with no friend at hand, and a vast tract of wilderness between him and home?

Two years after the massacre at Deerfield, the surviving prisoners were exchanged. The Boston News Letter, the first paper established in America, printed in Boston in 1704, contained a list of those who were exchanged. George was not among them. When they reached Boston they had no news of him, never having seen him since the day he was separated from them and carried to Quebec. His family believed then that he was surely dead, and mourned him as such. Nor was Eunice Williams, daughter of the Reverend John Williams, with them. Indians had taken her into their tribe, and her father looked upon her as one dead.

The city was built upon a rocky promontory that towered between the Saint Lawrence River on the south and the Saint Charles on the north. The rock was crowned with church, fort, chateau and citadel, convents and seminaries. There were houses of officials and civilians along the edge of it, overlooking the vast sweep of river and forest and field, with mountains hanging dim and misty in the great distance. At the foot of the rock was Lower Town, where were the houses of the poorer people, the places of business, the docks and warehouses.

The life of the people was happy. They acknowledged no deep cares. They laughed and caroused and gambled away their substance without a thought for the morrow. Sense of personal responsibility was in large measure lacking, not because they were dishonest, but because they were careless, and the examples of integrity and honor which they beheld in those sent over to govern them were not such as would inspire a strong sense of commercial or political morals in them. The city existed largely for the fur trade, and to give France a handle on the new world. With deep water at its very door, with a country of unparalleled richness behind it, situated on a natural commercial artery which reached to the remotest parts of the fertile wealth, of stately sightliness and healthful situation, in the hands of the English it would have arisen in its early youth to a commercial importance which the following centuries would only have increased. In the hands of the French it was a rough, uncouth trading-post on a large scale, with a tinsel of elegance mimicked from France.

In the interval, affairs in the colonies were progressing without great events. The war was carried on in desultory fashion, for the most part. Parties of French and Indians descended on the outlying settlements from time to time,

ON THE PENOBSCOT RIVER

killing, plundering, and carrying off captives as they had
done at Deerfield. The English colonists retaliated in
like measures. Captain Benjamin Church, with 550 men,
ravaged all the French settlements east of the Penobscot.
Massachusetts and New Hampshire offered a reward of
£20 for every Indian captured under ten years of age,
and £40 for the scalp of every Indian over ten.

Still they continued to descend on the settlers in Maine
and New Hampshire. François Hertel, unable to be appeased in his thirst for English blood, led another expedition
against Haverhill, massacring the inhabitants on August
29, 1708. Captain Samuel Ayer, mustering a company,
went in pursuit, came up with the retreating French, offered
battle, and killed thirty of the French, including Hertel's
brother. Captain Ayer and sixteen settlers were killed,
and thirty-three wounded.

It becoming apparent that Maine was not safe, and that
Massachusetts and all the colonies were threatened, an
expedition was sent in 1708 against the French at Port
Royal, in Nova Scotia, on the Bay of Fundy. The expedition, sent by Massachusetts with such help as she
could get, consisted of a fleet bearing a thousand soldiers.
Baron Castin, who commanded the place, repulsed them.

But Massachusetts was not to be discouraged. Another expedition was got together after two years of
preparation. There were thirty-six vessels, English and
American, with four regiments of troops. The force appeared before Port Royal in 1710. Baron Castin was no
longer there. His successor, Subercase, defended the
place for eleven days, and then surrendered. The English took possession, naming the place Annapolis, to honor
their Queen. With Port Royal went all of Nova Scotia.

In 1709–10 an expedition was organized in New York
to proceed against Montreal and Quebec, in coöperation

with an English fleet that was to take Quebec. Eighteen hundred troops marched as far as South River, near Lake George, when they got word that the fleet had been ordered to Portugal, and the venture was abandoned.

At last, in 1711, vast preparations were under way for the invasion of Canada, the reduction of Quebec, and the occupation of the territory by the English. England already had her eyes on Canada. General Nicholson, with a land force, was to march against Montreal, while Sir Hovenden Walker, with fifteen men-of-war and forty transports, was to proceed up the Saint Lawrence and attack Quebec. He had with him seven regiments of veterans. The force was amply sufficient to accomplish its purpose.

The news was brought to Quebec by the Abenaki Indians. It found its way among the galley-slaves. George heard it, with great joy. There was hope! Quebec was to fall into the hands of the English, and he would be free! He did not know that Walker was a cowardly incompetent, a soft-footed parlor admiral, the creature of Newcastle; that he would loiter in Boston for six precious weeks before setting sail; that he would find it necessary to wait at the Bay of Gaspé for a space in midsummer, to devise means of preserving his fleet from the ice that might come that way in the following winter; that in the end the fleet would be broken by the wreck of eight ships in the Saint Lawrence through the stupidity and stubbornness of the admiral; and that he would send a letter to Great Britain thanking God that his 8000 men had been spared starvation at Quebec by the loss of 1000 in the marine disaster.

But even if he had known it, there would have been hope for him to cling to. For, in the fall of 1710, De Montreville had gone to Boston with an exchange of prisoners, and had taken a message from George to his family, so that they might come and ransom him.

It was now early in the summer of 1711. There was great excitement through the length and breadth of the walled city, the fortress of France in America, her stronghold on the western continent. There was much running up and down in preparation to meet the fleet that was supposed to be able to melt resistance before it. Governor Vaudreuil, worried and excited, busied himself beyond belief in devising defences.

The galley-slaves were set to work on the fortifications beside the citizens and soldiers. Huge blocks of granite were wedged into place, and the walls heightened and strengthened at weak points. There was work to do on Fort Saint Louis. George was sent there with the rest of the slaves. He had proved himself so intelligent and efficient in times past that he was given men in charge now, and had much latitude of movement. It was nearly forgotten that he was an Englishman.

It was a fair day in June. The sun shone full out of a blue sky, softened with plumy clouds of white. A breeze.

HOCKOMOCK ROCK ON THE COAST OF MAINE

THE CITADEL, QUEBEC

blowing down the river, ruffled the water slightly. Resting on his iron bar, he looked far out across the wide
sweep of the river and pictured to his mind what a sight
it would be when the fleet of Sir Hovendon Walker should
come sailing up past the Isle of Orleans. He smiled as
he bent to his task again.

There was a hushed murmur of excitement among the
men. He looked about to see what might be the occasion
of it. Governor Vaudreuil and a party of elegant persons
was coming to inspect the work done for the defence of the
city. There were ladies among them. He smiled again,
grimly, as he thought that it would be fitting for him to
be there, too, if he were not a galley-slave,— that if his
youth had not been consumed in chasing the French over
the sea, or in being locked up with French soldiers and
felons, he too might have been a fine gentleman.

He turned to his work again, not waiting to stare, as the
other slaves did. The party came on, with much magni-

ficent talk among them. The ladies admired the scenery, marveled at the work being done, and were sure that the English could never take their city away from them.

One young woman, with soft brown eyes and brown hair, more beautiful than any there, walked by the side of the governor.

"These men are slaves, you say?" she asked him, in surprised response to some remark he had made.

"Yes, mademoiselle! Galley-slaves! Convicts! Felons!"

"But what have they done?"

"Everything. Murdered! Robbed! Cheated! Everything, mademoiselle," replied Governor Vaudreuil.

"Murdered! Are there murderers here, then?" cried the young woman, in pretty distress.

He shrugged his shoulders. "Perhaps," he said. "Who can tell!"

The young woman looked at them earnestly. Pity came into her face, heightening, making more beautiful, a note of tender sadness in her expression that was a glory to the beauty of her features.

"Poor wretches!" she said, under her breath. "Might I speak with one of these, *monsieur le gouverneur?*" she added, turning to rest her hand gently on the arm of the governor.

"By all means, if mademoiselle wishes it," he replied with a bow. "I will attend you."

Her attention was caught by the slight and graceful figure of a young man who worked at the end of the line, somewhat apart from the others. Through his rough garb, through the uncouth nature of the work he did, he showed an ineffaceable trace of blood and breeding that filled her at once with a romantic interest.

"Surely," she thought, "he cannot be such a wicked man."

She passed over toward him. The governor was about to follow, when he was detained by some one who sought directions concerning the work under way. The others did not notice that she had left them.

The young man, toiling heavily with his crowbar at a huge piece of rock, paused and straightened himself to rest his back. He had not turned to stare at the fine company, as the other galley-slaves did. The young woman was upon him, and at a loss what to say to him.

On some impulse, he turned. Their eyes met. She quivered, and would have fallen had there not been so many onlookers. His face, browned, drawn, melancholy, burned with a sudden fire. He started toward her, checking himself with great effort.

"Marie!" he cried, his voice stifled with emotion.

She passed her hands across her eyes, stepped backward, gazing on him in utter bewilderment, gasping rather than speaking.

"Ah!" she moaned, in a low voice. "It cannot be. George! George! Speak again! But no; you are surely dead."

"Marie! Marie!" he cried once more, so low that none other might hear. "It is I who speak to you. Don't you know me?"

She came as close to him as she dared with the others there, weeping, convulsed with sobs.

"Ah, it is George, then," she repeated, over and over again. "But you are not a criminal?"

"Can I speak? Is it safe?" he inquired, glancing at the party, which had by this time missed her and sought to find her.

"Hurry. Yes, it is safe. I told *monsieur le gouverneur* that I would speak with a galley-slave."

Then, as though he told her some tale of adventure which all might hear, he recited with great swiftness the things that had befallen him, she listening with heaving bosom and kindled eye. When he spoke of Deerfield, she scarce suppressed the awful cry that rose to her lips. He saw her agony, and paused.

"Ah, *mon Dieu!*" she cried, under her breath. "I knew it! It is the curse of the bell! It is I who brought you here! It is I, who am so fond of all of you,

that told them where they might go to find the bell, in an evil moment, when I did not think what I said."

He tried to comfort her as best he could; but she bade him go on. The governor was already approaching, making signs for her to come.

STATUE OF LOUIS XIV AT THE PALACE OF VERSAILLES

"They brought me here," he continued, rapidly, "and placed me here as a felon."

"And you are — where?"

"In the citadel, in the west wing, beneath the roof, with the galley-slaves. And you?"

She fumbled in her reticule for a moment. Then her handkerchief fluttered to the ground. He stooped, gathered it up, felt a tiny stiff piece of card within it, slipped that into the bosom of his shirt, and passed the linen back to her.

"I live — there," she whispered, fixing her eyes on the card.

"Come, mademoiselle, the company waits," exclaimed the governor.

"Pardon, monsieur," Marie replied, with a pretty gesture. And she added, looking toward George and speaking as though she addressed an unfortunate who had only that moment enlisted her sympathy: "And be sure, my poor man, that I shall get you out of here; so have a brave heart."

George pulled off his cap as awkwardly as he might, mumbled something in reply, and turned to his work with a mist before his eyes, and the whole world swinging beneath his feet.

"Mademoiselle seems to have found our young fellow quite entrancing," observed the governor, good-naturedly, as he and Marie came again to the group.

"Ah, yes; he has a most interesting tale, monsieur," she answered him. "I am quite affected by it. He is there under a mistake and his sweetheart pines for him. I shall ask *monsieur le gouverneur* to free him!"

"Mademoiselle is romantic," returned Vaudreuil. "The man is undoubtedly an impostor, and deserves well to be there."

THE SAINT LOUIS GATE, QUEBEC

"That I will not believe," rejoined Marie, exhibiting overmuch zeal in the cause of a strange galley-slave.

They passed down the hill on the other side.

The galley-slaves still labored on the fortification of Fort Saint Louis.

THE HARBOR OF QUEBEC

CHAPTER VI

LOVE HATH A WAY

MARIE dared not think of her lover until she was safe within her boudoir at the house of her cousin. She gave out that she was over-fatigued and would not be at dinner, and ordered that they should permit her to rest undisurbed. Assured of privacy, she resigned herself to the tumultuous current of her thoughts.

Out of the swirling, twisting chaos of her emotions she could grasp but one fact: George was a prisoner at Quebec. Even that failed to appeal to her as fact at first, but rather as the vivid impression of a dream. Gradu· ally, as she became calmer, the joy which had possessed her in the beginning came to be alloyed with distress and fear for her beloved.

She searched her mind for a plan to assist him. She could not exert herself too

MONTMORENCI FALLS

84

strongly in his behalf with the governor without arousing suspicion. Especially would there be danger when De Montreville returned; for De Montreville had sworn that she should be his wife, and it would be fatal to her hopes for George if he learned that the galley-slave was her chosen lover.

All night long she pondered, seeking a way out. With the morning came little hope. She sat down to her morning repast in dejection. There was a party going to the Falls of Montmorenci. Would she go with them? No. She was indisposed, and would stay at home. But she would be left alone, then! She did not mind at all. So they went, and left her.

The sun had risen half his height, when there was a loud knock at the door. A soldier from the citadel stood there.

"Mademoiselle lost this at the fort yesterday. It was found by one of our slaves. I am to bring it back to you." The soldier spoke with a knowing look in his eye, but in a voice of the most perfunctory character. He extended to her a small packet. She glanced at him, catching the look of sympathy in his eye.

"Wait!" she said. "I am alone."

She tore the packet open. Her eyes were hot with eagerness. There was a note, in English, in George's handwriting. It was in a cipher which they had used in play when he was ill from his wounds at the house of his cousin in Boston.

"This fellow is my friend," said the note. "I have the freedom of the quarters till eight o'clock at night. He is on guard to-night, and will permit me to come to the gate. Meet me if you can. He will tell you where. I am all on fire with the hope of seeing you! All will soon be well."

That night she went to him, in the twilight. Beneath the walls of the citadel they met. She clung sobbing to his bosom. He kissed her hair, and told her to have courage, as though she were the one imprisoned. The soldier of the morning watched from a distance, respectfully, without inquisitiveness. They talked of escape.

"Wait!" said George. "We can endure it, now that we have found each other, for a little space more. Perhaps Sir Hovendon Walker may come to free me, and then you would need me again. And, too, I expect word from mine own people with the return of Monsieur de Montreville, who bears messages for me. They may come to ransom me."

At the name of De Montreville she shuddered, and drew from him slightly. He questioned her for the reason. She told him, trembling and sobbing, that he had pressed his love upon her; that he had sworn to make her his wife, and that when he had gone away he had vowed that he should do it on his return.

George was all ablaze at once, but he listened to the end.

"Marie," said he. "When it comes to such a pass, I will win you from here, though I carve my way through the flesh of the devil himself. But it is better now that I should wait."

So they parted, with a mixture of sorrow and happiness, but with hope shining through it all. She saw him infrequently. The risk was too great, and the time soon to come when they should be brought together forever. The soldier who had befriended him was sympathetic and circumspect, finding a new delight in serving them by virtue of gold from the hand of Marie, concerning which George knew nothing.

Even when they met she urged him to fly. Always he pointed out to her that this would only separate them the more, for he should have to leave Quebec if he escaped; that the best hope was to wait; that when the last extremity came he could get away as well as he could now.

Lower Town, Quebec

The days wore on. The year passed into the last of July. The rumors of the fleet came frequently, full of alarm. George's hopes were high.

Then, on a night near the last of the month, Marie came to him unexpectedly, in great agitation and distress. By great fortune, his man was at the gate, else she must have gone away without seeing him. He was strolling in the yard behind the walls of the citadel. He saw the soldier beckon him. He went, and found her trembling beside the gate.

"Marie!" he cried. "What brings you here to-night?"

"You must flee to-night!" she said, under her breath. "Come!"

She took his hand, and led him to a place where the rock broke down, and a little clump of bushes offered some concealment. The soldier was about to stop her, but she raised an imploring hand, and he suffered her to do as she wished.

It was so dark that he could scarce see her face as she raised it to him when they had come to a safe retreat. She was shaking with suppressed excitement. He felt her heart flutter as she leaned against him, clinging to him, with her soft hands stroking his weather-beaten cheeks.

"He has come!" she said, at last.

"De Montreville?"

"Yes!"

"Thank God!"

"Nay, thank not God for him! He demands my answer now! He has been to me already."

"But now I shall have word!"

"Ah, he brings but evil news," sobbed the girl.

A towering figure, huge in bulk, crept stealthily behind them, concealing itself behind the bushes not two paces away. They knew it not.

"What news? You could not have asked him for word of my people?"

"Nay, nay," she said. "But the fleet of Sir Hovendon Walker has gone upon the rocks and is wrecked in the Gulf. He will never come to release you."

George made no sign when he heard it.

"How can he know of it?" he asked, clinging to a shred of hope.

"There was a fugitive taken from the wreck, who told that the British admiral, ignoring the advice of the New England pilots, ran upon rocks with great loss."

George would not show her his dismay.

"But he may have word from my family?" he urged, seeking to cheer her.

"It will come too late," she answered. "He is importunate. I am here unprotected. My cousin favors De Montreville. He is kind to me. He loves me. He is not utterly an evil man. They cannot see why it should not be so. I cannot tell them. You must save me."

Had they been more alert, they might have heard the heavy breathing of the huge figure that crouched in the bushes, so near that they could almost have touched it. But their heed was all for one thing only.

"I will come," said George, clasping her strongly to his breast, and kissing her. "Fear not, Marie, I will come. If it is to be done no other way, I will escape from here and

ISLE OF ORLEANS

come to you. But first I will see Monsieur de Montreville, for your own sake. If I am honestly free from here, I may do much more for you than if I am a fugitive."

"But you must come!" she pleaded.

"I have told you that I would."

For a space there was silence between them, save for the beating of their hearts.

"When?" she said at last.

He looked down into her up-gazing brown eyes until his very soul floated from him.

"To-morrow night!" he made answer.

"It is a long time!"

She smiled as she had smiled when he had first known her as a child; when love had first come into her life, and she had smiled at him through the tears brimming in grief for her slain father. He kissed away the moisture from her lashes.

"You must help me!" he said.

Keenest ear could not now have heard the breathing of the figure lying crouched in the bushes, so eagerly silent was it.

"You must find clothes for me and hide them where I can get them. This garb of the galley-slave would betray me. You must place firearms there as well, and a sword. Nay, tremble not. There is little chance that I shall have use for them, yet is best that I have them. You must provide food, too, and a flask of wine."

"I will! I will! But where? And shall I meet you there?"

"Nay," he answered. "I will come to you later. And as for a place, you must think of that yourself. Somewhere away from the town, but near the citadel."

She thought for a moment.

"I will tell you where," she said presently. "At the Anse du Foulon. Look! Go along the bank of the river.

It is a mile and more. You will come to a place where the bluff recedes. There are trees about it. One great oak stands at the head of a little ravine. A path leads down. A little way from the path, half-way down, is another great oak. It is hollowed out. In that hollow you shall find what you have told me to bring, to-morrow night. I often ride that way on my horse, with only a servant. To-morrow I will go, and he shall be given that which shall stop his mouth."

"Brave child," said George.

"And then?"

"And then I will come to you early in the morning. And early in the morning we shall be married. Then let them take me if they will."

"It is dangerous, my loved one," murmured the girl, clinging still closer to him.

"I will come, my sweetheart," he answered her.

"It is a long time."

"Nay, we have waited long already. It is but a short time now."

"Until then, farewell," she said, withdrawing from his embrace with a sigh.

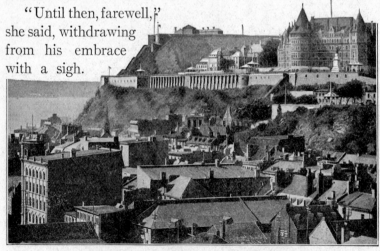

THE CHATEAU FRONTENAC AND CITADEL

"Until then, farewell!"

She left him, gliding silently from their concealment and joining the servant in waiting, who always accompanied her on these adventures. He stayed until she was gone, and turned into the gate, with many misgivings in his heart. It was a wild thing that he did!

The figure of a man of great stature rose silently from the bushes and passed in at the gate behind him, lost in deep thought.

THE SAINT JOHN'S GATE, QUEBEC

CHAPTER VII

AN OLD FRIEND IN A NEW ROLE

A MAN of great size, wearing the uniform of a captain of the French, paced up and down a large, bare room in the Citadel of Quebec. There was dust on the knee of his small-clothes. He heeded it not. There was perspiration on his forehead. He was not aware of it. He was absorbed in thought.

His great head was sunk between his shoulders. He held his hands be- hind his back, one within the other. At each turn he made, he smote the palm of one with the back of the other, and muttered a curse. There was a malignant gleam in his eye.

He contin- ued to walk up and down the room for a space. Pres- ently he paused. A grin, cunning,

OLD HOUSE, QUEBEC

malevolent, triumphant, spread across his mouth. The gleam still shone in his eyes.

"Now, let us see how it sums up," he said to himself. He raised his hands before him. The fingers of his left hand were spread abroad, with the palm toward him. His right hand was loosely clenched, save for the first finger, which was extended straight, like a pointer, and which pounded the air as he marshaled his thoughts.

"In the beginning of things, he is a knave, this Mon-

94

sieur Stevens; it is clear to the dullest — and I am by no means the dullest." He struck his extended little finger with the first finger of his right hand, knocking it over and curling it up in his left palm. He went on:

"He loves my love — which is very strange. Yet it is not strange. 'T would be stranger if he loved her not." He disposed of the finger next his smallest in the same manner.

"And my love loves him," he continued, beating the end of his middle finger with the one that he used for a marker in counting off the points he made. "That is most strange and most unfortunate — for her. She shall be cured of it.

"So they would wed, this galley-slave and my beloved; but first he needs must escape." The next finger received the attention of the pointer. "And they meet beneath the walls of the citadel, beneath my very nose, to make their plots. *Voila!* It is all very pretty! But it is well that my nose was close at hand!" He picked with his left thumb among the fingers closed into the palm of his hand, with a whimsical look on his face. "It was devilish close cramped quarters, but it is well that my nose was there. They shall not escape."

He passed to the other end of the room.

"But how to prevent it?" he said. "Most easy!"

He extended his left hand once more as he had done the first time, and counted off the points as he made them in the same way.

"Monsieur has told mademoiselle that he would fly to-morrow night if I brought him no word. I have seen monsieur's family. They send him cheering messages. They will come to get him. 'Let him have hope,' they say. But no! I have not seen them. They send no messages. They tell him to go to the devil! That they do not care for him! *Voila!* It is done! Monsieur escapes. He goes to Anse du Foulon. There are soldiers there. Who placed them there? Monsieur de Montreville, officer of the prisoners' guard, is a wary officer. Our galley-slave comes, thinking of his bride! Pouf! He goes to be a bridegroom at another festival. But could Monsieur de Montreville know who it was that was escaping?"

He shrugged his shoulders. "Impossible. *Voila! Qui donc!* The thing is done. Marie, overcome by grief, says nothing, but marries Monsieur de Montreville, whom she should marry; and all is well!"

He passed over to the bell-cord, pulled it, and sat in a chair by a plain table. An orderly entered.

"Bring before me my *monsieur chevalieur du nombre* thirty-nine," he said to him, waving his hand. His satisfaction was great. He amused himself with a little playfulness.

The soldier returned with George Stevens. The large man eyed him keenly.

"By thy looks, sirrah, thou hast had ill news!" he said.

George made no reply. De Montreville rose wrathfully and walked in a threatening manner to where he stood.

"I will brook none of thy insolence here, fellow!" he shouted in his face. "Thine arrogance carries thee far. But I have well learned what manner of knave thou art. Is it not enough for thee to flaunt me before my officers, when thou art but a paltry prisoner of war whom I would befriend? But must thou also beguile me into making a monkey of myself to suit thy bold frauds?"

George felt that De Montreville must have come upon his secret, and cast about in his mind what he should best do for advantage. Not being able to hit upon anything, he held his peace, till the crisis should be thrust upon him.

The City of Quebec from Parliament Buildings

In a moment he was glad that he had done so. For when De Montreville, who had paused to scowl at George and champ his mustachios in high rage, spoke again, George was less certain that he knew that they were rivals for the hand of Marie. But what he heard was not more welcome than such certainty would have been.

"*Sacre!* I will show you what it is to flaunt the French!" the man cried, roaring with fury. "You send me to your family in Boston! *Voila!* But you are a poor, forlorn prisoner in a French prison. Will they please to come and take you out from there? All very pretty. All very sad. They love you. They cherish you! You have a brother. He loves you. He will fly to embrace you. Certainly! Oh, a thousand thunders, how they love you, those cousins of yours."

George, utterly dumfounded, listened, marveling at what the man was saying.

"But no," continued the Frenchman, stamping up and down the room until the citadel itself must have swayed to his tread. "You are a fraud! You, a fraud, put me upon them to learn their temper. *Sacrebleu*, but I have learned it well. Wert thou not a caitiff prisoner thou shouldst learn mine by sharper tools than words."

George was still at a loss to know what the man meant.

"I meet with your brother there! He is a fine gentleman, with a gold-headed cane and small-clothes of the best. 'Your charming and gracious brother, Monsieur George Stevens, is in distress in Quebec,' I say. 'I have the honor to make it known to you, that you may fly at once to his succor.' And what does monsieur our dear brother? He draws himself up thus, with one shoulder very high, and looks over it at me as though I were a beggar asking him alms.

"'Brother!' cries he. 'Brother! Brother I have none. If that rascally fellow seeks to tell thee that I am his brother, tell him that I no longer have a brother.'

"'But?' say I, astonished.

"'But! But!' he cries, ere I have done. 'You French are nothing but "but"'—with which he claps his stick down upon the floor and rolls his eyes like the heretical English dog that he is. A plague on thy whole people! To be sent on a fool's errand by a rogue, and to be insulted by a coward under the shadow of his own flag. An I had not had better work to do, I should have wrung his little throat while it still wheezed with the insults of his tongue."

"You can never mean—" George interposed, when the other interrupted him.

"Hold thy tongue, sirrah! But if thou wilt hear more of thy loving brother, I will tell thee; for it is long since thou hast had word, by my troth. As I am holding my soul from strangling him where he fumes, he fetches me his breath and begins again upon his brother.

"'Tell your friend,'—what power of hell saved him from my hand when he called me thy friend, I know not,—'tell your friend,' he went on apace, 'that we have had quite enough of him, and would be done with him. A rascally, arrant, blackguarding knave, who stretched our temper to the break ere he was out of his

ON DUFFERIN TERRACE, QUEBEC

teens, and now whines at us when he is come up with his just deserts! And what might it be that has brought him to this?' he asks me then. 'It will make fair talk about our board. Brother! Bah!'"

George was about to speak, though he was so confused and shaken by what he had listened to that he had nought on his tongue. The other, pausing to mop his brow, looked violently at him, and bade him hold his peace.

"'A little matter of the galleys,' say I, making light of it. 'A small matter, perhaps piracy, and mayhap murder, for all I know.'

"'Let him stop where he is, then,' says thy dear brother. ''T is a good riddance of bad rubbish. Tell him that, if you wish.' With which he turns upon his high-clipped heels and leaves me so stirred with anger that the bottom of my soul was turned over."

"It is impossible," cried George, gaining his tongue. "You are not serious. If you mock me not in all you say, Monsieur de Montreville, there has been a bitter error."

"Poor fool! Poor little fool!" sneered De Montreville. "Would you say that I lie, then, in my own quarters, here alone with me? Ah, but you are too poor a foolish knave for Monsieur de Montreville to have quarrel with."

"Then there has been a mistake," insisted George, walking the room in his turn, too distressed and agitated to remain still.

"Seek not to shield thy little fraud behind such antics, youth," observed the man of France, seating himself in his chair again and pulling at his mustachios. "I know thee well. You but make yourself the more pitiful fool. I have made no mistake. I tell you truly. I have seen a little man,— *sacre!* such a tiny little man, with fragile little shoulders that came aslant to a point behind his ears, which stuck straight out from his head as though he would pass for a donkey. Eyes close together, as pale as the sick sky, hair without color, a thin head that his wisp of a neck could not hold high, a voice of string, and a tongue that tripped over it. Tell me, *monsieur le cavalier du nombre thirty-nine*, is not that thy brother, who loves thee?"

Unattractive as the picture was, George admitted that it was at the least a caricature, and was perplexed the more; for it was clear that De Montreville had seen Elmer. He could not close his mind against the conviction that the Frenchman spoke truth; that some one had prevailed over his brother; that his cupidity might have been aroused, and he sought to profit the more by George's continued absence; that some untoward circumstance had enstranged them. Surely, De Montreville, unscrupulous as he was, would not wantonly have created such a fabric of fiction without more reason than a brutal whim to chaff a helpless prisoner.

"If the man knew of Marie's love for me, he would do this thing," thought George, "but not otherwise."

He could make nothing of it except that which he recoiled from believing: that his brother had deserted him in his extremity. Yet there was one consolation for him in it all. It was clear that the man did not suspect anything between him and Marie, else he would have taken harsher measures against him than mere rough words. He had feared that in the beginning.

These things passed

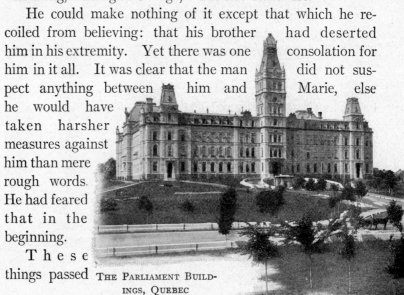

The Parliament Buildings, Quebec

rapidly through George's mind as De Montreville continued to sit silent in his chair, pulling his mustachios. He waited with trepidation to see what might come of it, determined to make a bold stand if this huge man offered any obstruction to the plan he had in mind the following night.

De Montreville, after a long space, only waved his hand, bidding them take him off to his quarters. A gleam was in his eye as the prisoner departed.

SOLDIERS' MONUMENT ON SAINT FOYE ROAD, QUEBEC

CHAPTER VIII

THE ANSE DU FOULON

SLEEP came not to refresh the troubled mind of George that night. He lay tossing on his bunk among the prisoners, burdened by the grief over his brother's defection, and worn by anxiety for the night of the morrow, until his fellows complained bitterly that he disturbed them. Then he lay still on his back, staring into the gloom, and not moving, though his bones creaked with every breath he drew.

He fought down the grief for his brother before morning. That was his own grief, which he could meet in the end in his own way. It was not pressing and immediate. Also, it might all be some hideous mistake. Neither was he anxious for himself in the matter of escape. It would be easy for him to go away from the citadel, unless De Monteville grew resentful and set stricter watch upon him. If they should take him again, it would be merely the matter of a few blows and a restriction of his liberty for a space. But what made him almost despair of his adventure was the thought of the consequences that might

A FRENCH MAN-AT-ARMS

follow to Marie. He might carry his plans so far that they would be married; but even then, would she be freed from the man she sought to escape? He could not know. His mind pictured a thousand misfortunes that might follow to her through him, and he was tormented until the sun was far into the sky, when external objects served to divert him somewhat. Yet, through it all he saw that the only chance for assisting her lay in the action he contemplated.

To the Plains of Abraham

All that day he watched with deep concern to see if there were any indications that De Montreville would hedge him about. There was none. On the contrary, he seemed to have found favor again in the eyes of the man; for, passing among the prisoners early in the afternoon, he had swung his finger at George with a whimsical leer of reproach, as though he had got over his anger, and took it all in good part now. George dissembled well the manner of one who should bend the knee, thinking the while how soon the fellow would find where the advantage lay.

Night came. Supper was finished. The galley-slaves who stood in special favor because of their good behavior or the slight nature of their crimes, patroled the yard, in twos and threes, enjoying the free air and the twilight. George was among them, joining in with them as much as ever he did. He would bide his time. There was no haste. The twilight was still bright; clouds were banking in the West; it would soon be much darker; it might rain, and a stormy night would serve his purpose much better. He strolled up and down the yard, in free conversation with his fellow-prisoners.

It grew darker. The clouds came higher in the sky
The prisoners straggled into the building one by one, idly.
George loitered by the side of the wall not far from the gate
where he knew his fellow of the guard would be on duty ere
long. Ever glancing warily about him, he seized a moment
when none was looking, to slip behind a stone buttress in
the wall. He sat there at ease on the ground as though
he were a soldier off duty. Sometimes they came into that
yard.

The prisoners were gone into their quarters. He would
not be missed at once. The soldiery were slack about many
things, in the security of their isolation. For who would care
to run away from Quebec? And where would he go if he
ran? It would be an hour before they found his empty
bunk. He would go soon; and by that time would be well
on the way to the Anse du Foulon. His friend of the ranks
was taking his station even now. In one moment he would
be away.

A door opened at a distance, sending a patch of light
across the yard. It came toward him, but the edge of it
rested at his feet. The doorway was darkened by the figure
of a man of great size. Even at the distance, George recognized him as De Montreville.

The door closed again. The night seemed darker than
before, now that the light was gone. He heard footsteps,
but could not tell which way they traveled. It was too dark
to see that distance.

They came closer. They were crunching in the gravel
near at hand. The huge figure of De Montreville took shape
in the gloom. He was not a rod away. He would pass so
close that with those long arms he would be able almost to
reach George as he sat there. He would certainly see him;
for the buttress cast no shadow of its own in the general
darkness that now prevailed.

Stevens rose hastily to his feet, standing as close to the wall as he thought he could without making his attitude appear unnatural. He drew his heels together, straightened his back, threw his shoulders into soldierly bearing, stiffened his left arm at his side, looked straight ahead of him, and raised his right hand to his forehead in military salute.

De Montreville returned it in the manner befitting an officer.

"You are abroad late, sirrah," he said.

"I am feeling ill, *monsieur le capitaine*," he replied, disguising his voice. "I came to take the air."

A SCENE IN RURAL QUEBEC

De Montreville paused and looked at him keenly.

"You have the devil's own hoarseness," he said. "See to it that you do not get too much air."

As George sat down his heart burst forth into a wild fluttering, and the perspiration stood upon his brow. He had no fear beyond an apprehension of what might befall Marie. It was that which unnerved him.

He knew by the sound of the closing gate that De Montreville had passed through it; perhaps to visit Marie, and demand her answer. The thought stung him into action. He crept close to the wall until he came to the gate, and tapped upon the wooden door that closed it in such piping times of peace. His friend of the ranks responded.

"Hello, there," he said. "You go not out here to-night."

"Pouf, Jean," responded George, lightly. "I have a tryst without to-night. You would not begrudge me a tryst, surely."

"You stand here, then, and I will go upon your errand!"

"Nay, I have an enterprise on hand to-night. Let me pass."

"What will you do, then, if I let you pass?"

"Do? I shall do what I should not do if you did not let me pass."

"Ha! You are quick. But say, then. 'T is a likely lass. Tell me what you have done when you come back this way, and I will let you through fast enough, for her account. What say you? Is it a bargain?"

"I promise you, Jean, that you shall hear of what I do until your ears burn again, and you will wish I had not done it for the very listening to it that will be your lot."

"I shall cry enough, first. Mind you, when I cry enough, it is enough!"

He let George through into the night, with a jest that seared into the soul of him, for that he could not turn and strike the man. It seemed to him that he had been talking there through ages of time. He hastened on.

It was necessary first to skirt around the foot of the walls of the citadel. He had gone out of the gate that overlooked the high bluff, the river, and the town. The Anse du Foulon was above the town, up the river, to his right. The way was steep. He had to use the greatest precautions lest he make a misstep, and be heard by the sentries on the ramparts. There was great danger of falling, too.

He picked his way carefully, slowly. There was little danger that they would look for him here, if they should miss him. When he heard the footfalls of the sentry, he hid in a clump of bushes or a cleft of rock until the soldier passed.

NATURAL STEPS, MONTMORENCI

He was near the point where the line of fortifications, passing from the citadel itself, departed also from the brink of the cliff. There lay safety for the time being; for he could walk farther from the ramparts from that point, and there was but the Cape Diamond bastion to pass then, some 200 yards above, before he would be on the Plains of Abraham, and headed for the Anse du Foulon.

There was a sharp spine running up the cliff, around which he had to pass, or go close beneath the walls. He chose the spine. It was as steep as a wall, and there were no projections on it; but it was small enough to enable him to throw his arms about it. He did so. Clinging desperately, he swung around the surface of it, suspended, without foothold.

Buttons on his coat rasped against the surface of the rock. He could not loosen his hold to release them from the contact lest he fall. He hung there breathless, uncertain what to do. To swing back to the starting-point would cause nearly as much noise as to continue, and he would then have it all to do over again. He wrenched himself farther along.

The button scraped loudly.

"Hello, there!" Some one shouted from the ramparts at the corner of the citadel.

It was the sentry. Once more George hung suspended from the rock, not daring to move. He feared that the sentry would surely hear his heart thumping against his ribs.

"Hello, there!" The man called again, louder than before. There was an answering voice from within the walls. George could not make out what was said.

"Now, then, are you never coming?" called out the sentry. "Here I have been waiting for you this half-hour, and with my eyes full of sticks for want of sleep, while you dawdle in there with your pot and your cards —"

George heard no more. It was only an impatient senti-

nel, quarreling with the one who had come to relieve him.
Laughing silently to himself in the reaction that came with
the allaying of his fear, George swung still farther across the
rock, struck his foot upon a projecting ledge, twisted, threw
himself into balance, and stood beyond the point he had
most dreaded.

It was not far now. Once past the Cape Diamond bastion, and it was a straight course with a fair wind. The
clouds had come up blacker and blacker, and the wind was
stirring into a sound that partly obliterated the noise of his
tread. He had just light enough to see the edge of the cliff.
By stooping, he could trace the outline of the line of fortification to the bastion, so that he had little difficulty in keeping
on his way.

The bastion was passed. He had seen it, the last time
he stooped, behind him to the right, fifty yards away. When
he paused, he could faintly hear the beat of the sentry's feet
on the top of the works. Before him lay the Plains of Abraham, the Anse du Foulon, Marie, and — what?

He would find out what! The feel of freedom was in
his blood. He was ready to dare now. Who was De Montreville, that he should be feared by an Englishman? He
laughed as he thought of the rage the man had been in.
He laughed, too, thinking of the story the man had told him
about his poor brother. It was some sort of sorry blunder.
He would straighten it out in a moment, as soon as he found
time.

Hurrying over the ground, thinking of the manner in
which he had deceived the great Frenchman in the citadel
by playing the soldier, he laughed so loudly that he heard
the sound of it, and was alarmed for the moment. But he
did not cease from silent mirth as he passed along. There
was much to amuse him! It was good to be free again! He
thought of the last time he was free, and laughed to recall the

way he had fought the red demons in that dusky cabin in Deerfield. Ha! But that was a long time ago. He was but a slip of a boy then. Now he was twenty-five. How many years of his life were already gone, and how little had he done. Imprisonment was a horrid curse.

Hark! Was that the alarm gun? There it came again, a sharp crash in the sky! It was the thunder of a distant storm, swiftly approaching. Just the night for a storm, thought George; and he welcomed it as appropriate to the present scheme of things. Also, it would smother the sound of his footsteps, and obliterate his tracks. A very good storm, that. And he laughed again.

He paused to look about him. He must be far enough now. He could trace the edge of the bluff indistinctly, and the rough outline of trees upon it, but could not pick out the tree that marked the place.

There was a flash of lightning. He stood close by the oak standing at the head of the gulch, as Marie had described it. There could be no mistake. Holding fast to the

THE OLD SAINT LOUIS GATE

direction in which he had seen the tree through the flash of light, he stumbled hurriedly over the ground, came to it, groped about till his feet struck a rude, narrow path, and gradually descended.

The raindrops beat through the leaves, skirmishers of the storm. His passage could not be heard above them. He did not care for that, though, for there was no one here on such a night. He waited for a second flash, to find the other tree that Marie had described to him, where the things were to be hidden.

Presently it came, splitting the heavens. His quick eyes found the huge hole, and he fumbled his way to it through underbrush and saplings. With his fingers he sought the hollow in the trunk. The bark, curving rapidly back, ended abruptly. He felt the edge of the cavity. He passed his hands down to the ground. They came to that which sent his blood spinning through his veins, he gave a little shout of joy in spite of everything.

There, in the black darkness, with the sky flashing white at intervals and the rain spouting down from the leaves of the tree, he changed his clothes, put his food carefully under his coat, slipped the wine into his pocket, and made ready to leave.

But where were the pistol and the hanger? He searched the hollow thoroughly, even waiting until another flash illuminated it, before he desisted. They were not there. Had Marie, fearful for his life, done him the mistaken kindness of withholding the weapons? Or had she been unable to get them without arousing suspicion? Never mind. He would make the best of it without. He found his way to the path, and clambered upward.

The raindrops, beating heavily, made much noise. The wind shook the wet branches of the tree, and they sobbed beneath its buffetings.

Hark! What was that? Surely, no raindrop could make such a noise! It was like the clink of metal,— bayonet against bayonet, or the cocking of a musket. A sudden terror seized him. His hair raised. He went numb.

The thing was absurd! Some sharp stick, broken by the wind, striking a dead limb on its way to the ground! The darkness is ever full of noises. He laughed at himself, and continued to climb; but the terror clung to his heart, so that

POINT LEVIS, FROM QUEBEC

he paused to rest. Another flash of lightning, prolonged, quivering, intermittent. He looked above him to trace out his way.

His heart ceased utterly to beat! The path whirled in circles about him! For standing there, not three yards away, their white coats dazzling under the dizzying light, was a body of French soldiers, bayonets fixed, muskets cocked.

His pent-up nervousness burst forth into a wild scream. He leapt down the path.

Another flash, — red, close at his back, with the sharp

thunder clinging at its heels. A long, hot pain through his body, and George Stevens fell into the mire of the path that led to safety.

A tall, huge figure of a man stood over him,— grotesquely huge and tall in that vague light, with the white flashes of the night passing overhead. The figure stooped. It felt the pulse of the body lying there so still. It stood erect again.

"Come," said the man, a bitter drawl in the tone of him. "This is a bridegroom. Bear him gently to my quarters. We shall see whether his bride shall be the sexton or the surgeon."

Soldiers, slipping in the mud, grunting, stooped and lifted the body.

The lightning flashed. A gleam of malignant triumph answered it from the eyes of the huge man.

CHAPTER IX

DEVELOPMENT AND PROGRESS

A SMALL boat, putting off from a brig that had just cast anchor in the Saint Lawrence River before the city of Quebec, drew up alongside the stone piers and made fast. It was the summer of 1715. A young man of twenty-three leapt ashore and stood looking about him with the confused air of a stranger who seeks something in a strange city. He was rather frail in build, and carried himself as though in delicate health. His eyes were pale blue. His hair was so light a brown that it was almost yellow. His head was nar-row, with ears that stood out a trifle too much. His shoulders sloped up to them at an angle. But his eyes were a-light with a something to be done, and his little body snapped with excitement and eagerness.

NATURAL BRIDGE, VIRGINIA

"Can any of you gentlemen direct me to the home of Mon-sieur de Mon-treville?" he said in English to the group that had gath-ered at the landing of the small boat. None of them understood. He repeated his question, with many inflec-tions and much emphasis, hoping to make them compre-hend. At last

one of them made out the name De Montreville, and
surmised the rest. He pointed out, with many eloquent
jerks of his thumb, a house of stone that stood on a
high hill above. The stranger thanked him and hurried
away, leaving the group to gape and wonder at him as
he went.

For surely it was a strange thing for this Englishman to
come there then, when the ink was scarce dry on the treaty
of Utrecht. It was a strange and dangerous thing, too,
for this frail Englishman to come there alone, so soon after
the passions of war had run through the country. It was
now barely July, and it was no longer ago than April that
Louis XIV, King of the French, had told the English that
he would not fight them longer. It was the more dangerous
for that they burned with anger and chagrin because the
fair provinces of Acadia and Maine, the island of Newfoundland, and the shores of Hudson's Bay had been given over
to the black heretics in the treaty that was signed at
Utrecht.

Philip V was permitted by the treaty to remain on the
Spanish throne, but it was agreed that no Bourbon should
hold the thrones of France and Spain at once, and the great-
grandson of Louis was made his successor in France. Louis
acknowledged Anne and William as sovereigns of England.
Holland was relinquished to Austria. Spain lost her
European possessions, but retained her colonies. The
balance of power in Europe was readjusted. England's
greatest gain was along lines of commercial advantages.
Antwerp was denied the use of the deep water at her doors.
The port of Dunkirk was to be filled up.

The part of the treaty which had perhaps the greatest
importance to British America was the concession made to
England in the matter of trade in negro slaves. England
agreed to furnish 4800 negroes a year to the Spanish posses-

sions for thirty years, paying a tax on them of $33.33 a
head. None but English might bring slaves to America.
Her Britannic Majesty was the exclusive slave-trader.
She took one-fifth of the stock in a projected company
to carry on the trade. Philip of Spain took another
fifth. The two sovereigns became the largest slave merchants ever known in the history of the world. The
balance of the stock was to
be divided up among British
subjects.

JOHNSON AND THE MILITIA AT
CHARLESTON

In spite of the feeling of the
French subjects against his peo-
ple, the Englishman thought little of the danger or of
the strangeness of his being among them, just as the
English always think little of danger. He bent his
way up the hill eagerly. Any other time it must have
been a weary climb for such a body, but the young man
scrambled up the steeps of the road that lead to the top
without so much as pausing for breath. He was borne

up by an elation that kept him oblivious to the defects of his physical strength.

He came at last to the house that had been pointed out to him. It was near the commandant's house, and communicated with it through a yard that had a closed passage-

ON THE WAKEFIELD FARM

way across it. Monsieur de Montreville was at h o m e. Would monsieur come in and wait? Monsieur managed to comprehend sufficient of the speech and gestures of the servant to know that he was expected to enter a large, dull room that gave upon the hall.

Presently a heavy footstep resounded through the hall, and Monsieur de Montreville entered the room. For a moment he eyed the stranger narrowly, with no expression on his face. Then a swift smile shot across his features. He advanced, holding out his hand, which the other took.

"Aha, Mister Elmer Stevens, whom I had the great honor to salute in Boston two years ago," he said in stumbling English. "It gives me a great pleasure indeed. It is well that peace has been arranged between our sovereigns, so that two such as we may be such friends as we would wish to be."

It was a French speech, and the stranger knew it, but he beamed and melted beneath its warm phrases.

"Monsieur de Montreville!" he cried. "You remember me? You know, then, why I have come all this weary way! Pardon the bluntness of an Englishman, if I come at once to

WASHINGTON'S BIRTHPLACE
WAKEFIELD, VIRGINIA

GREENWAY COURT, HOME OF LORD FAIRFAX

the point! Tell me, where is my brother George? When can I see him?"

He looked with distended eyes upon the Frenchman as he waited for the answer. De Montreville shrugged his shoulders, pulled his mustachios, turned and paced the room, and came at last before Elmer Stevens with his head bowed down upon his breast.

"It is to weep!" he said, with a sob in his voice that drowned the heart of Elmer in sadness. "How can I say it? When will you see your brother? Eyah! When you have gone where he has gone. It is two years ago since he has gone."

"You do not mean that George is — dead?" Elmer stammered, sinking into a seat.

"*Hélas!*" said the huge man, his frame shaken with emotion. "I came to him with your word, — that you would come to him soon, that he would be free, — but I came too late. He had — how shall I say it? — made an unfortunate attempt to escape from the fortress, and — ah, but I cannot say it to you, his brother! It is too bad that you came!"

Worn as he was by the fatigue and the dangers of the journey which he had made for the succor of his brother, Elmer Stevens broke under the news, delicately as it was conveyed to him by the Frenchman, and fell into a swoon. When he came to consciousness again, he was in a bed in De Montreville's best room, with a servant to wait on him. Presently De Montreville himself came, accompanied by his wife, to offer sympathy.

When Elmer saw Madame de Montreville, a flash of recollection came across his mind. Something about her face suggested another time and place, remote from the present. She looked at him with a wistful expression about the eyes. Elmer felt that she was an unhappy and disappointed woman. There was a restraint in her bearing toward her husband, which produced the impression that perhaps she did not entirely love the man, although her behavior toward him was the height of loyalty and respect. And there seemed to be a tinge of fear.

He was not certain enough of the recollection of her face which came to him to speak of it. In fact, the woman had scarcely a word with him herself, having merely accompanied her husband as a little courtesy to the stranger. He puzzled much during the night to know who she could be or whom she resembled, but was unable to recollect. At the last, his grief and disappointment and the thought of his brother banished all else from his mind, and he dismissed her face entirely.

On the morrow he left, accomodating his departure to the sailing of a vessel. It was with a heavy heart that he gazed his last upon Quebec, believing that he turned his back upon the last remembrance of his brother. He had not had even the melancholy satisfaction of seeing the grave where George lay buried, for De Montreville told him the identity of it had been lost through the carelessness of the prison grave-digger.

Elmer's sense of loss was more bitter and poignant now than it had been at any time since his brother's disappear-

WASHINGTON FAMILY TOMB AT WAKEFIELD, VIRGINIA

ance. Until now he had been able to hope. George had been his strong dependence throughout all his years. He had fallen into the habit of looking to him in all matters. Now the thought that he would never again have his inspiring love deprived him of courage. He returned to his father's plantation, near Williamsburg, Virginia, without other ambi-

tion than the even life of a planter.

The colonies prospered swiftly after the conclusion of peace. Industries of a crude description sprang up. Agriculture flourished. Settlers pushed farther and farther into the frontiers, no longer in fear of the Indians. Timber was brought down from the forests to the sea-

INITIALS OF WASHINGTON CARVED ON NATURAL
BRIDGE, VIRGINIA

shore, and shipwrights from England built vessels to carry the commerce of the colonies. Soon there was a merchant marine of swift ships that commanded the respect of merchants of other countries.

The towns of larger size throughout the colonies flourished and grew more important. Culture was introduced. Newspapers were started. Books were printed. The people read and studied and thought. The experiences of their forefathers and their own in this land where men were pitted against nature for a livelihood, and where each must fight his own fight in large measure, gave them self-reliance and firmness of character at the same time that their reading and reflection pointed out to them the good in working together. They were beginning to learn that by helping each other they could take care of themselves. The necessities of defense against the Indians from time to time taught them this. They were taking up the ideas that grew and developed into the principles of the Revolution.

Their political relations with England were not all that could be desired. The Crown had taken away the private charters of the various colonies, and they were now colonies under the Crown, with governors thrust upon them. Sometimes the governors were sincere and laborious in their efforts to improve their colonies. More often they were stubborn and dictatorial, looking rather to England for their system of governing than to the needs of the people governed.

At times the spirits of the governed became defiant. Their legislative gatherings opposed the oppressive measures of their royal governors. They breathed too much free air to be easily trodden under foot. Massachusetts maintained a stubborn quarrel with her governors over the salaries which they demanded for their appointees. The colonial assembly refused to pay for services that were not rendered by the crown officials. The governors demanded certain stipulated sums. The colonists won. In the end a compromise was effected, by which it was agreed that the assembly should vote the salaries each year.

The citizens of Carolina went a step farther. Their governor, Nathaniel Johnson, was offensive to them. Early in the century an attempt had been made to force the church of England on the colonists by severe laws. Johnson continued in the policy. "Let us have a governor of our own," said some of the citizens. "We are the ones to be governed.

We have to fight our own fights.   Why not make our own laws?"

It was the beginning of mighty things.   Johnson appointed a day for the review of the militia at Charleston.   A convention was called for the same day to elect a governor. The pioneers came trailing throught the woods, their guns on their shoulders. Johnson ordered the commander of the militia to disperse them. "I obey the convention," he replied. James Moore was chosen, and for some time there was a confu-

FREDERICKSBURG, VIRGINIA, AND MARY WASHINGTON'S HOME

sion of two governments.   Up to that time the colony had been under the rule of proprietors to whom a private charter had been granted.   In 1720, in answer to a petition of the inhabitants, the private charter was rescinded, and the colony made a crown province.   North Carolina forced its proprietors to sell to the Crown several years later.

There were turbulent times in New York over the freedom of the press. An editor named Zenger made attacks on the methods of the administration. He was arrested and placed on trial for libel. The jury promptly brought in a verdict of not guilty. The entire province rejoiced. It was a public victory. The aldermen of New York City presented the editor with a gold box when he was acquitted, as an expression of their views in the matter.

Great men were growing up in the new country. Their minds were expanding with new and big ideas. Everything about them inspired the thought of freedom. The vast territory behind them, inexhaustible in resource, suggested it. There was no old order of things with a grasp upon the minds of those born under it. Time and circumstance were ripe for great ideas, and they were bringing forth fruit. Boys were growing into manhood which was to mold doctrines that would give a new country to the world, and a new impetus to civilization.

There were sporadic troubles with the Indians during the period of peace that followed the war with France. The Tuscaroras

MARY WASHINGTON'S MONUMENT, FREDERICKSBURG, VIRGINIA

and the Yeamanses formed a conspiracy in 1715 in the Carolinas to drive the English settlers from their lands. In a bloody encounter the Tuscaroras were so nearly exterminated that they fled and joined themselves with the Iroquois nation in New York. The Indians in Maine harassed the outlying settlements. An expedition sent out in 1722, to punish them, killed Father Rale, a Jesuit who was believed to have stirred them to their attacks, and slew their chiefs, Mogg and Bomaseen. Captain Lovewell and Lieutenant Lyman went with a large force to chastise the Pigwackets. The expedition met with disaster, but the Indians were taught a lesson. They gave up their warfare, and became peaceable.

Traffic in African slaves grew apace at this time. The slaves were brought into the colonies south to work in the tobacco-fields. They were sold into service in New York and New England. The Carolinas were the center of the trade. Service was hard to obtain. Indians were also held as slaves, and servants bound themselves into servitude with the colonists for terms of years. Some of them who did this were prisoners for debt, who took that means of becoming free. Others were convicts. Some were boys who were kidnaped in Ireland and Scotland, while still others were voluntary slaves.

Elmer, settling down on his father's plantation, grew to be a leading man of Virginia. He became robust as years went on, and developed a vigor of thought and life that brought him the respect of his neighbors. Two years after he returned from Quebec in the fruitless search for his brother, he married. He had a son Robert, born in 1717, and a daughter Rebecca, born two years later.

His wife died soon after the daughter was born. Feeling the need of a companion, some one to supervise his household, he married again after several years. His second wife bore him two sons, David, born in 1728, and Noah, born in 1730. Robert at an early age went to New York, where he studied law, and practiced before the courts there, becoming in time a man of affairs. Rebecca was married to Lawrence Averill of Boston, whom she met on a visit to that place.

David was a youth lacking in imagination, whose greatest interest lay in practical matters and his own private advancement. Noah was a boy of a romantic and adventurous spirit. Often, when his father told him of his Uncle George, he would listen with wide eyes; and when he had heard the tale to the end he would say that he believed that his uncle still lived, and that he would go out into the world some day and find him. In his boyish fancy, the world lay just beyond the blue hills that lifted into the sunset a few miles from his father's plantation.

Elmer Stevens had a neighbor with whom he often went a-hunting, and who was frequently a visitor. The man was Augustine Washington. They had many long talks over their pipes by the side of the hearth on winter nights, of affairs in the colonies. Elmer was growing into a radical in the matter of colonial independence, although in his mind it never took the form of separation from the mother country.

Often there was an attentive listener at these talks,— a tall, robust lad, whose keen bright eye fixed itself on the faces of his elders with deep interest. The boy was George Washington, son of Augustine, two years younger than Noah. The two were close companions in boyhood sports. They had the same schoolmaster, named Hobby, a servant indented to Augustine Washington. In addition to being schoolmaster, he was both dominie and sexton. He was a pompous person, with imperturbable self-esteem. The school was a log cabin set on stilts. It was placed in a patch of young pines grown up on a tobacco-field exhausted by successive crops and abandoned. It was called the "old field school," from the circumstance of its location.

George, naturally equipped to lead, and trained in habits of command by his mother, whose nature was imperious as well as loving and gentle, was chief in all the games among the boys. His brother Lawrence had gone with Admiral Vernon against the Spaniards at Carthagena as captain of militia raised in Virginia. George, observing the warlike preparations for his departure upon this expedition, became imbued with military feeling, and organized a company of soldiers among his fellows, which he naturally led. Armed with cornstalks for guns, they marched and fought mimic battles under his generalship, supplying the noise so desired by boys with hollow gourds devised into drums.

In these activities Noah Stevens

Washington's Last Visit with His Mother

was lieutenant. There was only one to dispute Washington's command,— a boy named William Bustle. By force of character and arm, Washington relegated him to the ranks and kept him there, gaining an ascendancy over him which the lad never could overcome. In all the sports of boyhood Washington outdid his comrades. He could run faster and throw a stone farther than any, and the strongest fell to the ground before his grip when they played at wrestling.

The youthful Washington was a fearless horseman. He mounted and manned the most intractable steeds in his father's stables; he rode hard and fast over the dangerous countryside, following the hounds. His eye was so clear, his head so cool, and his hand so steady that one day he climbed to the top of the inner surface of the arch of the Natural Bridge, carving his name above all others, to the terror and alarm of Noah, who was with him and watched the feat.

In 1743, while George was on a visit to Noah's home, his father, Augustine, was mortally stricken. George returned in time to receive a last look of affection before death arrived. He continued to reside with his widowed mother on the plantation near Fredericksburg, as long as the advantages of the "old field school" were deemed sufficient, after which he went to live with his brother Augustine, who had inherited the old estate at Bridge's Creek, where George was born, and where the schooling was better. Here he learned mathematics and surveying thoroughly.

Later his brother Lawrence, between whom and himself there was a peculiarly strong attachment, took him to Mount Vernon, an estate on the Potomac which he had received on the death of his father. Lawrence had married Anne Fairfax, daughter of the Honorable William Fairfax, of Fairfax County, a kinsman of Lord Fairfax, whose extensive estates he managed. George, now sixteen years of age, was thrown into the company of the old noble, whose regard he won by his manly qualities, and by his fearlessness in following his hounds, a sport of which the old Briton was fond.

Lord Fairfax had obtained a royal grant to a vast tract of country extending beyond the Blue Ridge, and including much of the Shenandoah Valley. It had never been surveyed, and was overrun with squatters. Lord Fairfax, impressed with the qualities of Washington, sent him out to survey it. George accomplished the task by dint of much labor, suffering many hardships, and undergoing innumerable dangers in the wild, rough country.

But the activities of peace did not appeal so strongly to him as did a war-like career. Not forgetting the exploits of his brother Lawrence, and seeing much of naval officers who were frequently entertained at Mount Vernon, he con-

WASHINGTON'S MOTHER PERSUADING HIM NOT TO
BECOME A MIDSHIPMAN

ceived a desire to enter the navy. His ambition was approved, and the consent of his widowed mother at last obtained. Just as he was about to enter upon his career, however, she availed herself of her woman's privilege, and expressed a desire that he would abandon his plans. This he did freely. Thus was he saved to the great work that lay before him.

CHAPTER X

THE DEBTOR

IN times that have been there was a law in England which decreed that any man who did not pay his debts might be sent to prison. It was an unwise law. It no longer exists. It was intended to prevent dishonest debts and punish dishonest debtors. In a measure it accomplished this, but it fell into evil hands, and was turned into an in strument of oppression, revenge, and malice. Men were thrust into prison who intended to pay, and who could have paid if they had been permitted to remain free to make mon ey. Men who were penniless through unfor tunate ventures fell into its clutches along with the man who lived fraud ulently by his wits. They were locked up until they paid. Sometimes they were able to scrape together enough to get them out of jail. Sometimes their friends came to their assistance,— a development often relied upon by the man whom they owed. Sometimes, when they could not pay, they were forgotten of their friends and lived and died miserably within the walls of debtors' prisons.

JAMES OGLETHORPE

One unique feature of the debtors' prisons was that they were run like public houses. The inmates had to pay for their food and lodging. They were obliged to provide their own clothing. They were not furnished with anything to eat or drink. Criminals and felons fared better. Debtors were not provided with clothing. A convict's suit was more than their rags. Even the rooms in which they were kept, and for which they paid rent, were not furnished; not even with a mat of straw whereon to lie. Those who had not means of getting money were complacently left to starve, to die of the cold on the bare stones of the rooms reserved for the penniless.

This system of conducting the debtors' prisons fostered a state of affairs inconceivable at the present day. The prisons were in charge of wardens, who obtained their appointment by devices which still exist. The wardens, to spare themselves the trouble and annoyance of giving matters their personal attention, farmed out the prisons to speculators, assigning the several parts of the prisons to the highest bidders. These speculators made their profit from extortionate rentals charged for the rooms occupied by the debtors, by selling them food and drink, and by a system of fines intricate and elusive. Bullying brutality, unprincipled rascality, unlimited thievery, became custom, and grew more and more barefaced and flagrant through the years.

Each large center of population throughout England had its debtors' prison; and in smaller communities the debtors were incarcerated with common criminals. In London there were several prisons for debtors. The most famous, and the most infamous, was the Fleet prison, on the shores of the Fleet, a ditch of sewerage. It was a pile of brick, four stories in height, with two wings enclosing, with a rear wall, an exercise ground paved with brick. In one wing were the poor debtors, who could not afford to pay for their lodgings. In the other wing were the rooms rented by the warden's deputies. There were five tiers of these rooms, one beneath the ground. The vile damp from the Fleet found its way through the walls of these rooms, little better than dungeons, foul and contaminated beyond belief.

These rooms were often brought into use by the warden or his deputies for the purpose of increasing their revenue. As a means of coercion they were highly effective. Any prisoner reputed to have money, who refused to pay the fines levied by means of the adroit code of rules, was thrown into

one of these dungeons to reconsider his decision. Sometimes he was beaten; occasionally he was killed. When that happened, a jury of tradesmen, who enjoyed the patronage of the

THE PORT OF SAVANNAH   (*From a rare print*)

prison officials, would be able to discover that the dead man died of natural causes. No one paid any attention to what went on in the prisons, it not being the business of any one to pay any attention to it, and the abuses grew fat. In time they grew too fat, and aroused public interest for a space. In 1726 one warden, Brambridge, was tried for murder. He was acquitted, and corruption flourished again, until a champion arose for the defense of justice and decency in the debtors' prisons. That champion was General James Oglethorpe, cavalier, soldier, Oxford scholar, high churchman, member of Parliament, and philanthropist.

In one of these subterranean rooms of the Fleet on an afternoon early in the autumn of 1732, lay a prisoner who had angered the warden and his band. The dungeon was almost totally dark. A small opening through the bricks near the ceiling admitted a dim blur to the wall opposite.

Oglethorpe's Old Fort on Saint Simon's Island

The edges of the area of light faded into darkness. The floor was in impenetrable gloom. The window, if it could have been called a window, gave upon a small strip of ground between the walls of the prison and the Fleet. On this strip all the waste and offal of the prison was cast, to be shoveled into the vile and sluggish ditch from time to time as it accumulated. A strangling, stifling stench was in all the air that crept into the room.

The prisoner was a young man; or he had been young before they put him in here. He lay upon a heap of rotting straw, the only furniture of the room. His arms and legs were clasped in bands of iron; heavy chains connected the fetters and manacles. He lay on his side, both hands resting on the damp, putrid straw to relieve them of their weight. Beneath the iron which bound his legs — they had clamped them on as tight at they could with the strength of two men, when they brought him here — were green and agonizing sores.

Lying there, he shivered from time to time with the cold and dampness, having no covering but the thin rags remaining of the clothes worn when he came. With closed eyes he gritted his teeth and held himself from screaming as the pains of hunger twisted through his body, closing out of his mind all thought, all recollection, all fancy, lest he go mad.

Lying there, he heard a rustling in the straw,— the noise of a rat on his bed beside him. Many times had he heard the rustling; many times had he felt the rats running across his limbs and body, many times had driven them from his face, lifting his manacled arms to strike at them. He listened, wondering where the rodent would go; what it would do, speculating, clinging to thoughts of the animal frantically, to keep madness from entering his brain.

The rustling grew louder, more bold. It came closer. It ceased. He felt the light pressure of tiny feet through the thin sleeves that were left upon his arm. The rat had climbed the chain, keeping away from the hand. It had learned what the hand was.

Then a sniffling at his ear that he could feel and hear; that sent cold waves of horror up and down his aching back! Yet he could not raise his hand. A hot breath upon the lobe of his ear; a sharp pricking sensation; cold teeth and a hot tongue against his flesh! He shrieked. The rat fled, tearing his face with its claws in its haste. He shrieked again. The damp, sodden walls smothered his cries and threw them back upon him. He shrieked again, struggling to his feet, wracked, tortured with pain. Shrieking, he dragged himself to the door of the room and beat upon its oaken planks with raw and bleeding wrists. As he beat upon the door, shrieking, his chains clanked a harsh, jangling accompaniment.

Footsteps sounded through the passage. A key grated heavily in the lock. A crack of light struck across the opposite wall. The door, moving ponderously, opened. A great, hulking, burly man stood in the doorway; another behind him bore a lantern.

"Now, what the devil noise is this!" roared the first man. "No more of this, or I'll take steps that you make no more of it, mark 'ee that. You can be heard in the lodge!"

The prisoner, turning his face away that the light might not blind his eyes, crept toward the fellow.

"For the love of God, Hugo, the rats are eating me up!" he cried. "Eating me! Eating me! Do you hear? Eating me!" His voice arose again to a shriek.

"It 's vile, poor pickings they 'll find on your bones if they don't do better nor we have done." returned the man, roaring with laughter at his witticism. The one bearing the lantern joined heartily in the mirth. It was some time before the debtor could make himself heard. When he spoke again, he had recovered a degree of composure.

"You! You!" he said. "You have all I have already; if you keep me here till the flesh rots from my bones I cannot give you more. Brambridge knows that."

"Brambridge knows that you have a pleasant little wife living in luxury not two streets hence, that's what Brambridge knows," bellowed the man.

"For the love of God, Hugo," moaned the prisoner, "would the unutterable monster have me take the bread from the mouth of my wife and strip the clothing from the back of my babe? Would he have me give him the little pittance by which they live?"

"Pittance be damned!" roared the brute, "and none of your fine names." He struck the frail and starving man a blow with his heavy boot as he uttered the injunction. "As for your wife," he went on, "she is nothing to Brambridge, one way or t' other, live or die; which it is lucky for you she is n't, lemme tell you, and lucky the brat come when it did to spoil her looks. Now, let 's have no more of your howling; and I 'll come to see you from time to time to learn when you

THE FLEET PRISON, LONDON

change your mind. And none o' them fine names, mind!''

With another kick, he left the room, locking the door behind him. Their steps died along the stone corridor. Their voices, raised in rough talk and rougher laughter at the last fancy of the burly brute, passed from hearing. Silence rested in the place of abominations.

The prisoner, weakened by the panic into which the rat had thrown him and by his exertions in calling, lay on the stone floor where the boot of the man had left him. Weakened, despair crept into his brain,— despair, leading to madness. Hope was gone. There was only one way to get out of the dungeon. His wife had a few pounds to keep alive herself and infant baby. If he gave his captors this, they would let him die in the air. That he would not do. Cursing them with clenched fists, he swore he would die first among the rats, and lay along the damp flags, hoping to die soon. A blackness came into his mind. The pavement seemed to float and stir beneath him. He knew no more.

CHAPTER XI

THE DEBTOR FORGIVEN

WHEN he awoke, a breath of air was upon his brow; his lungs tingled with the exhilaration of oxygen. He had not breathed such air for two horrid months. He was too weak, too sick, to wonder at it. He only enjoyed it.

Lying where he awoke, reviving in the breath of fresh air, he was conscious by degrees that he missed some familiar sensation; that something was gone. In a moment he realized that his arms and legs no longer ached with the intolerable burden of his chains. The burning was gone from the wounds they had ground in his flesh.

Presently he became aware that there was something soft beneath him which was not rank and rancid straw. The sound of voices came to his ear. The sound of one voice above the whole world dear to him! Wondering, doubting, he opened his eyes.

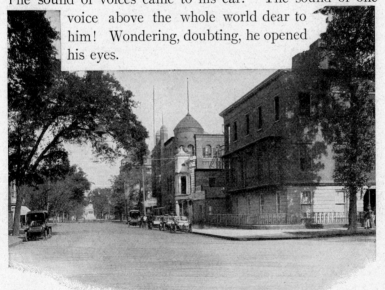

BULL STREET
SAVANNAH, GEORGIA

He was in the room of the Fleet whence he had been dragged two months before; the poor room where the indigent debtors struggled to live. About him were misery, hunger, starvation; gaunt and spectral figures; faces of gloom. But it was better than the dungeon; ten thousand times better, though the room was bare, though the air was stifling and close, though hunger stalked among them.

Trembling with doubt still, not able to believe that he was not dreaming, half dreading that he was merely a ghost lying there, he looked about for the voice which he fancied he had heard. He saw his wife, seated on a stool at the foot of the poor pallet on which he lay. In her arms was an infant to which she gave suck; the daughter he had never seen, who had been born the day before they dragged him from this room to the dungeon.

He cried out. The woman, starting, looked at him. First fear was in her eyes, then an ineffable gladness. Forgetting the babe, she glided to his side, knelt on the floor, wound one arm about his neck, holding the babe to her breast with the other. For a space they were silent, gazing upon each other; for since they had dragged him to the dungeon to extort money from him the two had never seen one another.

Gazing upon him in her gladness, a look of compassion came into the woman's face at sight of his blanched cheeks, his pallid lips, his deep sunk, staring eyes.

"Manfred!" she moaned. "My beloved!"

The tears fell fast. For a space he could not answer. The babe, missing its food, wailed, recalling the mother from her outburst of grief.

"Elizabeth! Elizabeth!" cried the man, reaching his trembling hands toward the child. "My little daughter! I have never seen her! I have never seen her face! Hold her where I may see her face!"

Savannah, from Tower of City Hall

The woman sat on the floor beside the pallet where the father might see. Her thoughts were not of the child. She continued to look fixedly upon the face of the man, with deep anxiety and solicitude. He was smiling upon the babe. The marvel of how he came there, in the air, with his chains stricken from him, with his wife and child at his side, had no place in his mind with the joy he had in seeing his daughter. It was the woman broke the spell and started thoughts flowing again.

"My Manfred! My beloved!" she said. "My poor, tortured, brave hero! Oh, why did you lie there in that loathsome place so long? Why did you not give them what they asked? Oh, think what a bitterness it is to your wife to learn now what you have been through, when she might have averted it! They told me you were ill and could not be seen by me, that it was infectious, when I came to see you. I did not know until now how it was; until a man came and told me that you were dying. Oh, why did you do it? Why did you not give them what you wanted, and let us come to live and die with you,— baby and I?"

The significance of her words came upon him gradually. He looked into her face with more and more of horror as she proceeded.

"Emma! Emma! My wife!" he murmured, when she had finished. "You do not mean that — that you gave them what they wanted? That you have nothing now? That it is all gone? That you have come here to live with me?"

His manner frightened her. "Yes, Manfred," she answered.

"Oh, beloved! Oh, the monsters! How could they take it from you like that? Now must we all die together!"

"Is not that better?" she asked, clasping his wasted shoulder in her hand.

He raised his hands above him, as he lay on the couch, in a gesture of despair. Holding them aloft, his eyes fell upon the sores that the irons had made in his wrists. "I had rather that the chains had eaten into the core of my heart with their slow, cankering rust than that you had come here, my beloved!" he replied. He turned upon her, half rising in his bed. "Do you know what it is to be here, my Emma?" he cried. "It is to die by inches; it is to live in the midst of unutterable squalor while the flesh wastes from the bones; to be cast out like a piece of carrion in the end. It is to see misery and want and despair reaping among your fellow-men through every hour of the day and night; to see the heart's blood of innocence dripping from the fingers of avarice; to see — my God! I cannot think of it! I cannot think of you, whom I took so fresh and beautiful and happy, dying here like this in the beginning of your youth and beauty! I cannot think of our little baby, our Elizabeth, shriveling up like a plant in the dark. Some day they will come and take her out of your arms. You will not know at what moment she has died, her death will be so like her life. They will take her from your arms, cold and puny. There will be none to mark where she is laid; none to lay us by her side among the worms when our time comes. It were better that I had died a thousand deaths such as I was dying; it were better that I had been eaten by the rats! Oh, God!"

He ceased. He folded his arms across his face as though he could shut out the scene which his imagination had drawn. His wasted frame shook with passionate grief and despair. His wife, overwhelmed, shrunk close beside the bed, awed.

"Manfred! Manfred!" she whispered, reaching a hand to his head. "Manfred! I did not know. Do not upbraid me. I wished to die with you, if we must die, Manfred."

In the storm of their anguish, they did not notice the man who had stood beside them almost from the beginning of the impassioned utterance of the unhappy man. He was tall, of thirty-five years or more; handsome, elegant in bearing, well dressed, alert, with a face of sympathy and generosity. He listened as the stricken man pictured the horrors of the prison with a face that reflected the anguish

ON THE SAVANNAH RIVER

of the man. As he listened, his attention, at first directed impersonally to the picture, grew fixed upon the features of the man who spoke. Throughout he watched him with close scrutiny, studying the countenance. When the woman kneeling beside the pallet uttered the name of the man, the one who stood beside them gave a cry of amazement, and bent over him.

"Merciful Heaven forbid! this cannot be Sir Manfred Hempstead," said he, under his breath.

At sound of the name, the man on the pallet started

violently and looked about with staring eyes, half fearfully, half hopefully. The woman rose to her feet with a suppressed scream, holding her child close to her. The bewildered gaze of the sick man fell upon the face of the other.

"Sir Manfred! Sir Manfred!" exclaimed the stranger, bending closer. "You remember me? James Oglethorpe, your cousin's friend! How came you here?"

The look of recognition, filled with hope that grasped at the least thing, passed, and was followed by a cold, suspicious defiance when the stranger mentioned the cousin.

"My cousin could have told you how I came here," said the prisoner.

"Come, come, my good fellow; your cousin is nothing to me, if that is what you mean," rejoined James Oglethorpe. "I am not here on his business, or to pry into yours. You must not think of it. I do not ask you to tell me how you got into prison; but I mean to tell you how you can get out, if you choose. Trowbridge!" He turned to an attendant. There were several gentlemen with him, and a number of attendants. "Here! Run and fetch steaming bowls of broth, and a cut of beef, and a pint or two of wine." He gave the attendant a sovereign as he bid him begone. "First we must eat a bite, and then we can talk. Merciful Heaven! What is this?" His eyes had fallen upon the terrible wounds made by the manacles. "Gentlemen,

THE PORT OF SAVANNAH

gentlemen!' he added, turning upon those who were with him, and who were keeping at a little distance out of delicacy, "this is done by irons, I'll take my oath. Am I not right?" He addressed his question to the prisoner, who confirmed him with a blank nod of the head.

In all this time neither the prisoner nor his wife had found command of any faculty whatsoever, except that of staring dully at the one who had come so upon them, who called him by his name, who promised freedom. The attentions of Oglethorpe passed from the prisoner to the wounds on his arms and legs. The party with him gathered about for a moment, making examinations, as though the one who bore the sores were an exhibit in a museum. It was only for a moment. Oglethorpe, with a nod and a word, requested them to await him beyond, and they passed on.

"Now, Sir Manfred, do you want to get out of here?" he inquired, when the others had left him. He was almost jocose about it, thinking in that manner to lessen the shock without resorting to circumlocution. The man could only stare back at him, with the tears starting from his eyes. Emma, his wife, sank to the floor again close by the pallet, her great eyes turned on the stranger, holding her babe closer than ever in feverish interest.

"My boy, I'll be brief," went on Oglethorpe. He addressed him as though a half-century was between them, instead of a dozen years. "This is a matter of business with me, unless of course, you care to make it closer than that." He looked beneficently into the tear-dimmed eyes fixed upon him. "I have permission from Parliament to found a colony in America. I have a tract of land from the King on the coast of the Atlantic Ocean, in a warm, tropical climate, on the southern edge of the Carolinas. I am going to settle it with insolvent debtors who will be delivered to me from the debtors' prisons of England. That, in brief, is my business here. Brief, and to the point. These gentlemen are members of a Parliamentary committee. Now, however you may have got in here, that is the way you can get out. Come! Come! Don't take it so hard! You don't have to go unless you want to, you know!"

The tears were falling so swiftly, the unspoken thanks shone so fervently through them, the crushed and bruised hearts beat so high that the philanthropist was forced to take refuge in his joke to save his dignity from tears. At that, he found it necessary for a moment to apply himself closely to an inspection of the other occupants of the room, who had been stupefied observers of all that had taken place.

In the end, the prisoner found his voice. Reaching out a hand and clasping that of Oglethorpe, he burst forth into grateful thanks, until the object of his gratitude bade him cease.

"Tush, tush, my lad; 't is business with me, you know," he expostulated, "only business. Come now. Here 's your dinner. Eat it. I 'll step back before I leave. Come, now! Come, come! Control yourself, Sir Manfred! Control yourself!"

An hour later he looked in at the door. The prisoner was sleeping peacefully. His wife was on the floor at the side of the pallet, her babe held close to her breast, her radiant face turned toward the countenance of her husband. Stepping lightly to her side, he whispered that he would be back on the morrow, and left.

As he hastened through the dark passages to overtake the investigating committee, James Oglethorpe flicked a tear from the corner of his eye. There was more of gladness than sorrow in it.

CHAPTER XII

THE DEBTOR RECOMPENSED

SIR MANFRED slept throughout the evening and the night, and far into the following morning. When he awoke at last, his wife was kneeling at his side, in some alarm at his protracted slumber. General Oglethorpe stood behind her.

"Then it is not a dream!" cried Sir Manfred, joyously. "I feared it was all a fancy, and that I should awaken to find myself in that loathsome cell, with the rats gnawing my flesh!"

Oglethorpe reassured him heartily that if it were a dream, from which he should never be aroused. He had food brought them again, and procured for them a fur- nished room on the other side of the house.

JOHN WESLEY

When they were there he sent his own surgeon to dress the wounds on the prisoner's legs and arms. He arranged to have their food sent to them regularly, at his own expense, and promised to come often to see them.

On a day when he came, he told Sir Manfred about the plans for the colonizing of America, and how it had come about.

"I had another friend in the prison six years ago," he began, "and had my attention directed to the condition of prisoners for debt in that way. I was horrified and appalled. I knew that Englishmen did not comprehend the state of

153

affairs existing in these loathsome sinks, and brought the attention of Parliament to them. A committee was appointed which investigated. I need not tell you what we found; you know more than even we were able to learn. We obtained some relief for them through laws, but could not eradicate the evil.

"In course of time the idea grew upon me to establish an asylum for worthy debtors in America, the refuge of the

THE HERMITAGE PLANTATION, NEAR SAVANNAH

abused and persecuted. Many nobles of England came to my assistance in the project. We were able to interest the Crown. The earl of Shaftesbury worked loyally. Now we have obtained a grant from the King to the territory lying between the Savannah and Altamaha Rivers, immediately south of the Carolinas. The country is exposed somewhat to the Spaniards in Florida, but we shall be able to hold our own against them. It is rich and fertile, with a delightful and healthful climate. ·

"The colony will be controlled by a council, of which Lord Shaftesbury is head. The land will be held in trust for

the poor. It will be an asylum for persecuted Protes-
tants as well as for debtors.
We shall admit Jews to the
province. None will be
debarred but Roman Catho-
lics. Those in charge will
not be permitted under the
grant to hold land or receive
any emoluments whatever.
Slavery will be prohibited.
Parliament has contributed
ten thousand pounds to the
project. Many private sub-
scriptions have raised the
sum sufficiently to insure
success. We are now making
ready to go. We are taking
great care to select for our
colonists only worthy
debtors, whom we are cer-
tain will make desirable
citizens. It is fortunate for
both of us, Sir Manfred, that
I encountered you here."

The prisoner would have
endeavored again to express
his sense of gratitude, but
his benefactor would not
listen. "Tut, tut!" he said.
"This is business, you know!"

JOHN WESLEY'S MONUMENT
CITY ROAD, LONDON

There was the same subtle invitation to confidence that
there had been the first day of their meeting. The prisoner, under some embarrassment, avoided the opportunity,

awkwardly endeavoring to make it appear that he did not apprehend. There was apparently some reason why he did not wish to tell the cause of his being there.

The wounds on the prisoner's limbs did not yield to the care of the surgeon. Their spread was arrested, but they seemed to grow deeper and more malignant. Oglethorpe assured him that a touch of sea air would cure them, and that he would be sound and whole when they arrived at their new possessions.

"You'll get your sea legs presently, you know," he laughed.

They sailed in November, 1732. There were 130 colonists in the party, every one of them a worthy debtor, eager to begin life anew with an even start. They had provisions and tools, and seeds for the planting when they should reach their haven. Oglethorpe was among them constantly, cheering and encouraging them, binding them to him in affection, establishing unity among them for the solidity of the enterprise.

The hopes of Sir Manfred for restored health did not materialize at sea. His festering sores broke out in eruptions. He could not leave his berth. His health, revived for a time by the prospect of a new beginning, fell under the disheartening effects of his affliction. His wife, whose brave heart had borne up through all his adversities, came to despair. Deprived of her courage, he sank more rapidly.

The vessel had been at sea not more than ten days when Sir Manfred sent for Oglethorpe on a morning, desiring a short confidence with him. The big-hearted leader came to him, all apprehension from the report of the messenger. His wife, sobbing piteously, left the cabin, clinging close to her child.

"Come, come, come!" he said, running to the side of his young friend. "This won't do!"

Savannah, Georgia, and the River

The other shook his head, smiling passively.

"We will not try to delude ourselves, Master Ogle-thorpe," he said. "My body has been broken in their dungeon; the fires of life have burned too low to be rekindled. I have sent for you because in the whole world there is none other in whom I can repose the secret which I must not carry with me to the grave. No, do not interrupt. I have neither strength nor courage to contend against your kind assurances. Let me go on; for the grave awaits me this side of night.

"My wife does not know,—no one knows but him,—what it is that I must tell you. My wife must never know. It would destroy her soul, for it was she who brought me to this, all unknowingly. She would reproach herself with it to her last day; though God knows she was as innocent in the chain of events that led to my ruin as the babe at her breast. Between us there has never been any other thing than love, from the first hour we met. Between her and my memory there must never be anything but love, for her sake. If she learned it while I lived, she would feel that I had something to forgive which was beyond man's forgiveness; I should never be able to make her see that I had nothing to forgive. She would feel that she had wrecked my life and made it wretched. I should never have the eloquence to make her understand that the joy I knew with her for two short years was so great that the torments of hell would not efface their memory from my mind. What power of tongue, then, could give her assurance if she should learn after I am gone? what would bring peace to her mind?

"I speak at too great length. My strength hastens from me. I must be brief. My cousin, the man you mentioned, the earl of Kildare, was the cause of my downfall. It will sound to you like romance. He loved this woman who is my wife. He would have won her. She loved me, and we were wed. I was not then of age. He cheated me of my inheritance through chancery, by way of revenge. I was complacent. His vengeance was not appeased. He sought my fur-   ther ruin. He leagued with another; one who   had my confi-   dence. He was   implac-   able. The other   — it is the old   story.

LIVE OAK UNDER WHICH JOHN WESLEY PREACHED HIS FIRST SERMON IN AMERICA

What little funds I had I invested with him. I gave bills for more. He defrauded me. The bills turned up in the hands of my cousin, the earl. He threw me into the Fleet. He came pretending friendship. He knew I would not betray him. He knew I would not tell her. And he knew her spirit. So he came as a friend, pretending that he would have obtained my freedom, but that my creditor wanted the pound of flesh and would not release me. He made a story for her that she could believe, and I, because I could not tell her, had to say it was the truth.

"You see? You see how it is? She must be guarded from this man. She must be protected. He is a beast. You know that. I see in your face you have learned that. He must not know that she came with you to America. He —" A tremor seized the man. His eyes closed. He grasped the arm of Oglethorpe. "Take me out to the deck," he gasped. "Let me die in the air!"

They did as he bade them. Life ebbed swiftly from him. He had strength only to whisper a word of parting to his wife before he died, as she knelt at his side imploring him not to leave her alone. They buried him at sea. His brave wife turned away dry-eyed to face the future, fearing, but with a sturdy heart.

Early in January, 1733, the vessel reached Charleston. There the emigrants rested, while Oglethorpe sought out a place for his colony in the new territory. Late in the month he led them to a high bluff along the Savannah River, where he founded the city which is still there, calling it Savannah, buying the ground from Tom-O-Chi-Chi, the Indian chief. Streets were laid out, and a governing body chosen, with Oglethorpe at the head. The colonists worked diligently

MONUMENT TO TOM-O-CHI-CHI

to build houses, and to make ready for the planting. Oglethorpe hired laborers from the Carolinas, including some of the planters' slaves. It was not long before the emigrants were comfortably housed, and rejoicing in social and political freedom.

Oglethorpe made treaties with the Indians before he had been there long, obtaining and retaining their friendship. In this he was nearly as wise and successful as William Penn had been in Pennsylvania. The colony prospered. Its fame as an asylum spread rapidly. It reached the Moravians and Salzburgers in Europe, who had been persecuted and tortured for their Protestantism. They came in numbers. Oglethorpe, returning to England, brought with him more debtors of the better classes, and many other Englishmen who were attracted by the religious and political liberty offered by Georgia.

Among those who returned with him in 1736 were John and Charles Wesley, founders of Methodism. Charles Wesley came as secretary to Oglethorpe; John's mission was to carry the Gospel to the Indians. He labored among them with more zeal than discretion, accomplishing little. He soon returned — to formulate his new doctrines, which had been in his mind since his years in Oxford, for which his intercourse with the Moravians in Georgia augmented his enthusiasm. He was too aggressive in his methods to make much progress with the Indians. His brother Charles remained as secretary, and continued the other's labors with similar want of success.

Five years passed from the time when Emma, with her daughter Elizabeth, set foot alone and without friends on the shores of Georgia. Oglethorpe himself had taken personal care of her, making her a member of his own household, and being sure that she wanted for nothing. She did what she could toward her own support by needlework, devoting

BETHESODEA, THE FIRST ORPHANAGE IN AMERICA, AND ITS FOUNDER, REVEREND GEORGE WHITEFIELD

her life to her daughter Elizabeth. The character of the
child was her reward. Gentle, thoughtful, loving, unsel-
fish, as she grew she gave promise of embodying all the les-
sons of adversity in herself. As she grew, she gave promise
also of attaining great beauty. On her account the mother
refused to return to England, preferring that her daughter
should grow up in the more wholesome environment of the
colony.

But the grief that was in her soul for her husband was
more potent than the joy she had in her daughter. It, together with the hardships and deprivations of pioneer life,
taxed her strength from day to day. In the spring of 1738,
five years after her arrival in Georgia, she fell ill of a fever,
which wasted her until she knew that she would never arise
from her bed. For herself she was glad enough to go, but
for her daughter she suffered great anxiety. There was no
one with whom she could leave her.

As she lay dying, she learned that Charles Wesley was
about to return to England. Wesley had befriended her
from the first. Her faith in him was complete. She sent
for him at the last, and placed her daughter in his care. She
had distant kin at home, she said, who would care for her if
he would take her to them. He promised her, and she passed
away in some peace of mind, leaving her daughter of six a
waif on the face of the
earth. In the sum-
mer Wesley left, taking
the girl with him.
The colony
throve from

MONUMENT MARKING SPOT WHERE OGLETHORPE LANDED AT SAVANNAH

the first. Slaves were not permitted in the beginning, but the practice eventually gained a foothold. George Whitefield came to take the place of Charles Wesley. He had more tact than his predecessors. He established charities in the colony and revived the religious fervor of the people. He was a vigorous orator, and a power in the community.

CHARLES WESLEY

The colony had nothing to fear from the Indians, but their Spanish neighbors on the south long threatened them. Oglethorpe, foreseeing trouble, built a fort at Augusta on the Savannah River. Twelve miles from the mouth of the Altamaha he erected Fort Darien. On Cumberland Island, at the mouth of the Saint Mary's River, he built Fort William. He carried his works into the enemy's country, erecting Fort Saint George on Amelia Island, at the mouth of the Saint John's. In 1737 he returned from England with a commission and a regiment of 600 men.

Two years later England declared war against Spain. Spain had demanded the right to search English vessels for contraband goods, and had denied the British the privilege of supplying slaves to the Spanish colonies. England would brook no interference with her commerce. Also, there was another chance for her to crowd Spain a little closer to the sea in her western possessions, and increase the British territories.

The war had little effect upon the colonies outside of Georgia, beyond keeping some of their young men in training for warfare. Oglethorpe made an attack on Spanish forts, with the original intention of investing Saint Augustine. He

took two minor posts, and returned.   The Spanish under
Don Manuel de Montiama came to attack Georgia in over-
whelming force.   They were led to believe by a ruse that the
English outnumbered them, and were frightened away by
a belief that Admiral Vernon was on the way with a large
fleet to attack Saint Augustine.

The war was brought home to Noah Stevens on his
father's plantation by Lawrence Washington, half-brother
of his youthful chum George, who was with Admiral Vernon
when that officer captured Porto Bello and Darien.   They
were fired with the spirit of adventure, and looked for the
time when they could go out to meet their country's foes.

SLAVE HUTS AT HERMITAGE

CHAPTER XIII

THE FIGHTING SHIPWRIGHT

THIRTY years and more had passed since George Stevens fell on the slippery path of the Anse de Foulon, with a shot through his shoulder. Europe was in the throes of a great war again, and again England and France were arrayed against each other. This time it was over the question of the succession to the sonless Emperor Charles VI of Austria, who had willed his throne to his daughter, Maria Theresa. In Europe the conflict was called the War of Austrian Succession, but as George II was on the throne of England, the war was called in the colonies, King George's War.

The eastern of the small Harbor, French burg, French had a great fortress on the shore of Cape Breton, in the mouth Gulf of Saint Lawrence. As a town it had been known as English but when it fell into the hands of the it was by them christened Louis- after the King. For thirty years they had been building it and had, after spending more than $10,000,000, made it one of the strongest fortifications in the world, equal almost to Gibraltar or Quebec. It was the key to the Saint Lawrence

River and protected a great bay where the French fleets could find shelter and whence they could proceed on what expeditions they chose against the commerce of their enemy.

The first blow in the war came from Louisburg. Before the English colonist knew that France had declared war, Duquesne, the French commander at Louisburg, acting under orders of his King, fell upon Canso and took the fort there. Not till the prisoners thus captured arrived in Boston, whither they were sent, did the people of Massachusetts know that war had begun. This was in June, 1744.

But the people on the frontiers knew of it, for on April 17 the Indians had fallen on Gorham, Maine, killing several; another party had attacked Boscawen, in New Hampshire, and others prowled as far as Fort Number Four, and to Charlestown, New Hampshire. The woods and fields of the settlers were no longer safe for them.

Standing in constant dread of the French fortress at Louisburg, the citizens of Massachusetts and New Hampshire determined to make an attack upon it. William Vaughn, who had an estate on the Damariscotta River and carried on a thriving trade in lumber and fish, was perhaps the first person seriously to entertain this bold project, which Parkman has called "a mad scheme." Believing that there was danger of Louisburg bringing about the destruction of the English fisheries, he thought it advisable to forestall such a calamity by taking the fortress. Governor Shirley, of Massachusetts, a man of unusual courage and resource, acting on the proposals of William Vaughn, got 3000 troops together and secured the aid of three other of the New England colonies. Connecticut and New Hampshire furnished each 500 men. Rhode Island furnished the sloop of war *Tartar* and 300 men, but they sailed too late for active service. Commodore Peter Warren was requested by

Governor Shirley to bring such ships from the West Indies as could be spared, but declined, until directed by the duke of Newcastle, to sail to Boston and give such help as he could to the cause. Before arriving at Boston, he learned that the fleet had already sailed, and Warren changed his course and joined the expedition at Canso. It was this duke of Newcastle who is remembered in American history principally for his lack of knowledge of American affairs. One day when he was told that Annapolis must be fortified, replied: "Annapolis, Annapolis! Oh, yes, Annapolis must be defended; to be sure Annapolis should be defended — where is Annapolis?"

William Pepperell, a wealthy ship-builder and justice of the peace of Kittery, Maine, was given command. Pepperell was by no means a genius, but he was a man of energy, good sense, and tact. He was a colonel of militia whose service in arms had been confined to Indian warfare; but he had never yet failed in anything he had undertaken. On taking command he was raised to the rank of lieutenant-general. Roger Wolcott of Connecticut was commissioned major-general, and appointed second in command. Pepperell had the good sense to doubt the possibility of success with a force so ridiculous; but the Reverend George Whitefield, when asked to furnish a motto for one of the flags, wrote, "Nothing is to be despaired of with Christ for the leader."

It was April 1, 1745. A beautiful young woman hung sorrowfully on the arm of her husband, resplendent in the uniform of colonel. A boy of eight clung to them, crying and distressed, he knew not for what. He knew only that his mother was crying, that his father was going away to war, and that he would have no one to ride him on his foot and take him pickaback to bed at night. The woman was Rebecca Stevens, daughter of Elmer. It was

Lawrence Averill who was in uniform, and the boy of eight was their son, named for his father.

"Come, Becky, do not be foolish, sweet," said the man, smoothing back her hair, and kissing away her tears. "Surely I will return, and I will bring with me a French duke to be your chef, and a countess to do up your beauti-ful hair."

She smiled through her tears as he kissed her

SIR WILLIAM PEPPERELL'S HOUSE, KITTERY, MAINE

again, and said she would be brave. He grasped the child and threw him above his head till the little fellow shrieked with laughter, kissed his chubby cheek, placed him in his mother's arms, and was gone. Two hours later a fleet of one hundred vessels sailed out of the harbor amid much booming of guns and shouting and waving of flags. But in one home there was no gladness.

The voyage was slow, because of the ice still afloat. The transports at last reached the bay of Canso, where they were joined by Admiral Warren with four vessels. On April 29, the fleet entered the bay of Gabarus, before Louisburg, and came to anchor outside of the range of the guns. The city and fortress stood on one point of the semicircle of land that enclosed the harbor. The granite walls of the fort were thirty feet high, with an eighty-foot ditch outside the walls. There were platforms for 180 guns. On an island in the harbor was a battery of thirty guns, and another stood on the shore of the har- bor sweeping the entrance. Behind the city lay a swamp which shielded them from land attacks.

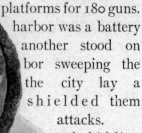

WILLIAM SHIRLEY

It was a forbidding prospect that presented itself to the ship-builder of Kittery, when he came on deck and looked out across the waters at the formidable fortress with the flag of France floating above it. But he was not used to failing. He set to work at once, landing his forces four miles below the city, behind the swamp.

Night came, and the French made merry in their impregnable fortress, laughing loudly at the little handful of raw settlers who had come to take it away from them. They quaffed their wine and grew very droll. But something wine-red spread itself through the sky. They sprang to the windows, to see the storehouse filled with pitch and tar and oakum, which stood near the land battery, blazing high into the sky. What manner of warfare was this?

"By the grace of God and the courage of thirteen men, I entered the royal battery at 9 o'clock, and am waiting for reinforcements and a flag."

GUN CAPTURED AT LOUISBURG, NOVA SCOTIA

General Pepperell received this message in the morning from Colonel Vaughn, who led an attack on the battery during the night, had fired the war-houses, and driven out the French during the confusion. By the time reinforcements arrived, the guns of the battery were trained on the walls of the fort. It was not long till other guns were trained against them. The ground of the marsh was half frozen. The provincials devised sledges, and dragged their guns into position, working at night, so that the French could not see what was going on, and throwing up their works as they went.

The guns boomed out across the marshes. Round shot struck against the granite walls, chipping out great pieces. Answering shot fell into the half-frozen mud of the swamps, throwing it over the American ranks. The fight was on.

Admiral Warren, blockading the mouth of the bay with his four vessels, desired that the battery on the island should be captured. Colonel Gorham set out with a party of troops in small boats to storm it. Colonel Averill was with him. They moved slowly across the bay, the sailors bending to the oars and the soldiers standing crowded in the floor of the boats. The sky was black and threatening. The storm broke before the expedition came to the island. Many of the vessels were swamped. A number of soldiers were drowned.

Lawrence Averill, thrown into the water, saved himself from a watery grave, and fell to assisting others out of the water into vessels that came to the rescue. The wind was bitter cold, and he was wet to the skin. Returning to camp on the marshes, he shivered and was chilled. There was a pestilence abroad, caused by the unhealthful conditions in camp. It seized him, and he wasted under it.

The bright eyes grew dim. Pain racked his bones. His breath hurt him as he drew it. He lay on a pallet of straw,

THE HARBOR OF LOUISBURG

wet with the rains of spring and with the soggy moisture from the swamps. But he kept courage and hope, speaking ever cheerfully to the men about him, urging them on to victory.

Meanwhile, an English battery placed on Lighthouse Point, across the neck of the bay from the fortress, had silenced the battery on the island, and was thumping the sea-wall of the fort with deadly monotony. From the works of the besiegers in the swamp came a ceaseless cannonade. The walls crumbled beneath it. Cracks appeared, and widened into breaches. There were assaults and sorties, bold achievements, brave deaths; but to little purpose. The lines of the English tightened; their fire continued without respite.

Lawrence Averill, lying near to death in his tent behind the works, would not let them take him aboard ship. "Leave me here," he said, "where I can hear the guns better, and see how my brave boys fight."

A French ship-of-the-line, heavily laden with material of war, appeared in the offing. There was tremendous excitement. In chasing one of the English ships of smaller caliber which she encountered in approaching the city, she was lured within reach of the whole British fleet, surrounded and captured, and all her munitions of war passed into the hands of the besiegers. The French were despondent. They had looked for succor from her. Pepperell, elated with their success and the arrival of reinforcements to the number of eight British seventy-fours, nevertheless took thought that there might be other Frenchmen on the way, and that it would be well to end matters at once. He called a council of war, and they decided to make an assault on the breached walls.

Averill was disconsolate when he learned of it, because he would not be able to go. "Take me to the door of the tent, so that I may see it," he said.

It was the morning of June 17, thirty years to a day before the fight at Bunker Hill. Averill, lying in the doorway of the tent, listened with closed eyes to the furious storm of cannonade that preceded the assault. His thoughts were of Rebecca, and of the little boy he had left in Boston such a short time ago. How full of life he was then! How sure he had been that he would come back, and how he had made merry with the fears of his wife! He opened his eyes upon the scene of war once more to forget the other scene.

The cannonade ceased. Now was the time, he thought, and he sat upright in his bed, for the first time in many a day. His was a martial spirit, and he loved the fray. But no serried ranks swept before his sight across the marshes to triumphant victory and triumphant death upon the battered walls of the fortress. Instead, a white flag hung out from the ramparts, flickering gently in the soft summer breeze that rippled over the bay.

The French had surrendered. The impossible had happened. Louisburg had fallen. A few thousand undisciplined troops, under an untutored commander who had only intelligence and determination and vigorous manhood to help him, had conquered the veterans of France, in a fortress that was the marvel of the western continent.

Rising still farther in his bed when he saw the flag, Averill joined his weak and failing voice to the hurrahs that went from the throats of the army, and sank down exhausted. He roused, presently, to find Captain Bennett, his lifelong friend, leaning over him with anxious face.

"I am starting for Boston," said Captain Bennett. "Is there any word? When shall I say you will be home?"

To the last question the sick man gave no answer, beyond closing his eyes with a look of grief on his face.

"Tell my wife — to be happy — and come to me — when she is — ready," he whispered, so faintly that the other scarce heard, though he was kneeling at his side to listen. The eyes opened, filled with light. "And tell my boy" — the voice was stronger now — "tell my boy to be a soldier, and to love his mother, just like — his — daddy."

The voice passed into silence with the last word. The

GENERAL PEPPERELL AT THE SIEGE OF LOUISBURG

light went out of the eyes.   A tremor passed over the frame.
The hand grew limp and slipped from that of his friend.

There was much in the heart of Captain Bennett as he
landed in Boston, July 2, 1745.   He was first to bring the
news of Louisburg, and had other heavy news to carry.
The bells were ringing, cannon booming, people shouting
and tapping wine-casks and lighting bonfires on the Common,
frantic with joy over the news he brought, as he passed on
his way to tell the other news.

Rebecca heard it without a tremor.   She only grasped
up her little boy to her bosom and went with him, dry-eyed,
up the stairs and into her room.

The joy of the victory reached throughout the colonies.
Guns were fired in England to celebrate it.   It was a wonderful victory!

But greater than the capture of the impregnable fortress,
of more import than the safety which it gave to New England fisherman, of higher value than the possession of the
key to the Saint Lawrence, was the lesson that it taught the
men who had gone forth alone to conquer.   They had found
themselves.   They had no need for England.   The lesson
sank home, and sent forth roots in the characters of the men
of the colonies that were to bring forth a tree and bear a
fruit the like of which the world had never known.

For three years more the war went on, waged for the most
part by the Indians.   Settlers in far-off districts were no
longer safe.   They worked the fields in parties, carrying
their guns with them.   They trained their dogs to range
through the woods, looking for Indians.   When their dogs
came bristling back to the clearing where the men were at
work, they would drop their hoes and run for their guns.

The governors of New York and Massachusetts sent the
Iroquois and Stockbridge Indians against the Canadians,
and parties of Mohawks carried the bloody trail to the walls

of the French fort at Crown Point and to the banks of the Saint Lawrence.

General Rigaud Vaudreuil, with 800 French and Indians, captured Fort Massachusetts in 1746, but failed in his attempt on Fort Number Four.

At last the war came to a close, by the treaty of Aix-la-Chapelle, in 1748. Under its terms the daring and sagacity of Pepperell and his men came to nought,

LOUISBURG MONUMENT

for all the territory taken during the war was returned and the previous boundaries restored. Pepperell, however, was created a baronet, being the first native American who attained that rank. Warren was promoted to the grade of admiral.

Louisburg Square, in Boston, commemorates the victory.

CHAPTER XIV

THE MAN ON THE ROCK

THE leaves of autumn lay in a rich carpet of color on the ground. The crisp air, stirring in among the boles of the trees, lifted the leaves and mingled them into a new pattern. The sky was grey and bleak, for the sun was gone behind the clouds, which threatened a storm.

A young man of twenty-three, with brown hair and deep brown eyes, sat on a log, a long fowling-piece across his knees. Lying in the leaves at his feet, gazing up into his face with the frank hero-worship of youth, was a lad of sixteen.

GOVERNOR ROBERT DINWIDDIE

"How do you know that your uncle George is still alive, Uncle Noah?" he asked, his eyes still wide and his face all alive with the story he had just listened to.

"Well, I don't know, Lawrence. But I am sure that he is. I know it just the way a dog or an Indian knows things that he cannot see or hear. I believe that the Frenchman did not kill him. He only hid him away for some reason. And I am going to find my uncle George, if I never do anything else to my last day. Then I am going to find that Frenchman, and the reason."

There was a light in his eyes and a far-off look that boded no good to the Frenchman when the young man found him. The two were in the forest on the plantation of Elmer Stevens, near Fredericksburg. The young man was Noah Stevens. The boy was Lawrence Averill, on a visit from Boston with his mother.

"When you go to look for him, can I go with you?" The boy looked wistfully up at his hero.

"That you may, Lawrence," replied the other, laying his hand on the boy's shoulder. "I shall probably need a little fellow like you very much. But come, we must be getting on. It grows late, and your mother will be anxious about you."

The little fellow scrambled to his feet, gathered up the game they had shot, and trudged on behind.

"I wish I did n't have to live in Boston," he said, presently. "Boston is too — well, too kind of nice for boys to live in. There are n't any Indians there, or anything."

"Never mind, Lawrence," returned Noah, "you can come down and see us once in a while. And you 're going to be a soldier, you know. Anyway, there is n't so much danger of your being scalped in Boston as there is here in Fredericksburg."

"Were you ever scalped, Uncle Noah?" asked the boy.

"Not yet, Lawrence."

"What does it seem like to be scalped?"

"I don't know. When it happens to me, I 'll try to notice what it seems like, and tell you."

"It must hurt awful," pursued the boy.

Noah merely laughed at his persistency, and the two proceeded to the manor-house of Elmer Stevens. It was a large white edifice, facing the setting sun and the rising

Pittsburg, the Gateway of the West

empire. Standing at the top of a gentle hill, a broad avenue of cottonwoods and hard maples ran to the front portico; a pillared affair of considerable state. Above the portico was a balcony, where the family were wont to sit on summer evenings to watch the sun sink behind the distant blue of the wooded mountains.

There was much commotion in the house when the two entered. They could hear the voice of Elmer Stevens raised in excitement, speaking at some length. There was the voice of Lawrence Washington, too, and at intervals a word or two in the low, even, calm tones of the young George Washington, then a youth of twenty-one.

Mr. Stevens was pacing up and down the broad parlor as the two entered the room. He had become an old man. His hair was nearly white, and grew sparsely on the top of his head. He held in his hand a long gold-headed cane, which he thumped vigorously on the floor as he passed to and fro. His head was sunken on his breast with age; his back was slightly bent; his knees gave under him in his steps; he bore the marks of his years.

"I'll tell ye, it must come to an ending," he cried, his voice shaking with agitation as he paused before the great fire rumbling in the chimney and spread out his hands to warm them. "I have not forgotten what these French did to my brother, and they need not think that I shall stay here quietly and let them overrun the entire land. No, sir! I'll take the field myself first. Confound their impudence! A plague on their arrogance! Their country indeed!"

Noah looked about the company for an explanation. He caught the blue eyes of George Washington, and passed over to where he stood, calm and quiet, at the end of the mantel-shelf. Rebecca Averill, disturbed by the tumult of voices, came into the room and passed to her father's side. She wore a dress of black; her hair was a halo of grey about her pale face; her expression held the beatitude of grief within it.

"Father dear, what is it? What disturbs you? What is the matter?" She laid her hand gently on his arm.

COLONEL THOMAS LEE

"Matter enough, daughter," exclaimed the old man. "And it's not over-pleasant for pretty ears. The cursed French are driving us into another war."

"Why, what is it now?" she said with a shudder. "We have only just had war."

"What is it now?" rejoined her father. "My child, it is everything. First they tell us that the country is theirs, from the Great Lakes to the bottom of all the rivers, because some of their wandering missionaries made a holiday through it upon a time. They warn us, the Ohio company, that the English must keep out. They build forts along our streams; they send us saucy, impudent letters that we must not trade with the Indians, and they lie about us to the red men.   And now they have fallen upon our post among the Miamis, where we had won the savages away from them, and slaughter our allies.   It makes my blood boil. If brother George had lived to see this day, he would go mad with anger.   There was a fellow of spirit!"

Rebecca, seeing him so perturbed, led him gently from the room.   Noah pressed George for further explanation.

"Captain Trent is back," Washington made answer. "Dinwiddie sent him with expostulations to the French, but he did not get half way.   He found that they had attacked Piqua, the Twightwees' town, where Gist and Croghan made the truce with the Miamis.   Then he came back. That is what disturbed your father."

"Does it mean war? asked Noah.

"In the end," replied the other, "it must come to war. There can be no other way.   They claim our country, fortify it, drive out our people, and threaten us.   There can be but one result."

"But what is going to be done about it?"

Lawrence Washington, joining them, answered the question: "George is going to Presqu' Isle, on Lake Erie, with a letter of remonstrance to the French from Governor Dinwiddie.   Then we are going to wait a little time."

"George is going?"   Noah looked at him with admiration.   Tall, handsome, there was a suggestion of reserve strength, of resource, of stored force in the young man that filled those about him with confidence in him and in themselves.   Always calm, always in perfect repose, there was a depth beneath that pale blue eye, a firmness in the lines of the sensitive lips, a vigor in the poise of the head, an intelligence in the brow that convinced those who saw him that here was a man, and held them to him.

"Yes," replied Lawrence Washington, "George is going on the mission in which Captain Trent failed."

"Good!" cried Noah. "When? Next spring?"

"Now!" returned Lawrence. "At once."

"Now!" Noah exclaimed, "in the beginning of winter? Why, it is October, and he would not reach Erie until the middle of winter."

"It is best to go at once," said George, quietly.

"Can I go with you?" It was the frank, honest outburst of loyalty to the man and the cause that spoke in Noah. George looked at him for a space in his quiet, reserved manner, nodded his head, and merely said, "I should like to have you."

The inevitable conflict was close at hand. The strife for the control of North America could not longer be avoided. France claimed the Great Lakes and the Mississippi Valley on the strength of the early explorations by La Salle, Champlain, Hennepin, Marquette, Joliet, and the others who a generation before had carried the Gospel and the flag of France throughout the middle of the continent. England claimed the continent from sea to sea, because Cabot had first sailed the length of the Atlantic coast, and the daring Drake had first landed on the Pacific coast. The claims of Spain, based on the discovery of the continent, were negligible. Spain's power was gone. It was not the intrinsic justice of the several claims that gave them strength, but rather the force of arms behind them.

France had colonized Canada and sprinkled trading-posts through the valleys of the rivers tributary to the Father of Waters. In 1718, De Bienville had established a post at New Orleans. England had settled the eastern coast and was tilling the soil far inland. The colonists did not have immediate need for more country, but England wanted more for future generations, and demanded it because France claimed it. This advance of the British frontier threatened the center of the whole French position. There

were two great natural routes between the Atlantic seacoast
and the Mississippi Valley: one a northern route from
Albany to the Niagara River, and thence westward on Lake
Erie; the other from Philadelphia to the present site of
Pittsburg, or the Gateway of the West, as it used to be called,
and thence down the Ohio River. If the English could hold
the Niagara River and the junction between the Allegheny
and the Monon-   gahela, they
could for-   ever cut
Louisi-   ana off

from   Cana-
da. The   alarming
character of   the situation
had aroused   THE KENTUCKY RIVER, NEAR FRANKFORT   the clear-
sighted Frenchman who administered the affairs of Canada.

The jealousy between the nations for the control of the
continent had been smoldering long. Twice within the
half-century it had broken into flame and been controlled
with difficulty. Much blood had been shed in Queen
Anne's and King George's Wars on that score; but the score
had been wiped out by the parent nations in their treaties
following the conflicts. They had not been ready.

But now the time was at hand. In 1749, French fur-traders began to come into the territory west of the Alleghenies, where the traders from Virginia and Pennsylvania carried on business. It was necessary to keep them out. Governor Dinwiddie of Virginia, Lawrence and Augustine Washington, Thomas Lee, president of the Virginia council, and other prominent men of the colony, among them Mr. Elmer Stevens, organized the Ohio company, receiving a grant of 500,000 acres of land on the north bank of the Ohio between the Monongahela and the Kanawha Rivers. Among other conditions of the grant, the land was to be selected immediately, and was to be settled with one hundred families within seven years.

Aware of their designs, France anticipated England. Marquis de la Galissonien, who governed Canada, responded by sending an expedition under Celoron de Bienville to inspect the country between the Niagara and Ohio Rivers and to take possession of it in the name of the French King. With a party of 250 men Bienville went up the Saint Lawrence as far as Fort Frontenac, crossed Lake Ontario in canoes, and made his way into Lake Erie. He forced a passage through the dense forest to Lake Chatauqua, and landed where Jamestown now stands. Thence the expedition proceeded once more through the woods until it reached the Allegheny River. There, on July 29, 1749, Bienville took possession of the territory in the name of Louis XV. This act of taking possession was performed by nailing to a tree a tin plate upon which was stamped the royal arms of France. At the foot of the tree a plate of lead was buried, upon which was an inscription stating that Monsieur Celoron had buried this plate "as a token of renewal of possession heretofore taken of the aforesaid river Ohio, of all streams that fall into it, and all lands on both sides to the source of the aforesaid streams, as the preceding Kings of France have enjoyed or ought to have enjoyed it, and which they have upheld by force of arms and by treaties, notably by those of Ryswick, Utrecht, and Aix-la-Chapelle." Some of these plates have since been unearthed and are now preserved in museums.

DINWIDDIE'S MESSENGERS

About the same time the Ohio company engaged the adventurous Christopher Gist to discover lands westward of the great mountains. He was summoned from his frontier home and instructed to examine the western country as far as the falls of the Ohio; to look for a large tract of good, level land; to mark the passes in the mountains; to trace the courses of the rivers; to observe the strength and numbers of the Indian nations.

In October, 1750, the bold envoy of the Ohio company and civilization set out on horseback; crossed the Blue Ridge and the Shenandoah Valley; passed through snows over "the slough and broken land" of the Alleghenies; swam his horses across the Ohio River and made his way through a rich and narrow valley to Wogstown, where he presented himself to an Indian council as an ambassador of the British Sovereign. He was received with respect, but was greeted coolly. "You are come to settle on the Indian lands," said one

of the chiefs; "you shall never go home safe." Undaunted
by this bold threat, Gist pushed on and continued his westward course almost to the falls of the Ohio River, where
Louisville now stands. Here the agent of the Ohio company turned southward and penetrated the famous blue-
grass region of Kentucky. Gist, delighted with the magnificent country he had explored, returned after an absence
of seven months to his employers by way of the Roanoke.

This was about two years in advance of the attempt
made by the French to fortify the Gateway of the West.
Considering the vital importance of this position to the English it seems strange they did not, when they had possession,
build and maintain a fortress there. But the truth is that
Pennsylvania and Virginia both claimed the spot and neither
colony was inclined to invest money in fortifying a place that
was disputed territory. Before their difficulties were settled
a new governor came to Canada, the Marquis Duquesne,
who saw at once the necessity of New France getting control of the Gateway of the West. Accordingly, in the spring
of 1753, Duquesne sent out a force of 1500 men under an
able commander named Masin. The army crossed Lake
Erie and built a strong block-house at Presqu' Isle, where the
town of Erie now stands. From that point they made a
road through the forest to French Creek, and built a second
block-house which they called Fort le Bœuf. The third
fortress was Venango, now Franklin, at the junction of
French Creek and the Allegheny. Thence they pushed on
into the Miami country, broke up an English settlement
there, conveyed the garrison back to Canada as prisoners,
and sent word to the English by means of a message to the
governor of Pennsylvania — to keep out.

The French now had a string of forts that bound to
Quebec the entire region west of the English colonies.
There were Fort Frontenac, on the northern shore of Lake

Ontario, Fort Niagara at the Niagara River, Presqu' Isle on the southern shores of Lake Erie, the two new forts, and a number of posts scattered down through the river systems. The rivers were the vital highways for the transportation of goods as well as men.

The time had assuredly come to take a stand. Governor Dinwiddie sent a messenger, Captain Trent, who became frightened and returned without delivering the message to the French. He looked about him for some one to accomplish the errand. He selected George Washington. Washington at that time was public surveyor. He had surveyed the land of Lord Fairfax in the Shenandoah Valley when he was only eighteen years old, and had already earned a reputation for courage, intelligence, and adaptability.

Washington left Fredericksburg, with a party, on the last day of October, 1753. Noah was with him. Christopher Gist, the woodsman who had explored the Ohio territory a few years before, acted as guide. They passed up the Potomac, with the wind whistling out of the North, cold and threatening; over the mountains, and down the Youghiogheny to its confluence of the Monongahela and the Allegheny, where Pittsburg stands to-day. Washington was impressed by the strategic importance of the place, and the ease with which it could be strongly fortified.

Holding a council with the Indians, whom the French were trying to enlist on their side in the controversy, Washington and his party moved northward in December. The country was a wilderness of forest, without trail or path, crossed by streams and slashed by deep ravines. The weather grew colder. There was an occasional flurry of stormy weather. Winter was upon them. But there was work to be done, and not one among them faltered. If he had, Washington, calm, determined, unafraid, would have brought him back to self-reliance again.

FORT NIAGARA

The romantic mind of Noah conceived a strange fancy as they traveled onward day by day. He thought it possible that he might meet his Uncle George among the Indian tribes. He knew that sometimes those whom the Indians captured took up their way of living. He remembered having heard that Eunice Williams, daughter of the Reverend John Williams, with whom George had been staying at Deerfield on the fatal night, had grown up among them and married an Indian, and that she would not return to her home. She had gone there on a visit once, but had hastened back to her dusky family.

One night they camped beneath a huge grey rock, against which they built their fire. It was bitter cold. Noah lay awake for a long space of time, miserable and homesick. When he finally fell asleep, his slumber was troubled much by dreams of his lost uncle. At last he dreamed with startling vividness that his uncle was there and called him. He sat upright in his blankets, trembling with excitement and the cold.

The moon had risen. The bare boughs of the trees laced across her cold white face. He could see them standing through the woods, naked and gaunt. The log that

they had placed on the fire before turning in had smoldered. Fitful flickers shot a feeble red glow across the
sleepers near him now and then, as the ghost of a wind
came rattling through the bones of the forest. He could
see the tall figure of Christopher Gist standing guard, resting on his gun, looking out into the night. That was all.

He listened. There was no sound save that of the wind,
and the rustling of the smoldering log as it settled into coals.
He lay back again to sleep. As he did so, his eyes rested
on that which sent a surge of icy fear through him, and
made him cry out sharply.

For there above him, standing on the crest of the rock,
gazing down upon him with eyes that seemed to glitter and
glow with a fire of their own beneath shaggy brows, was
the figure of a huge man. The man was dressed in a suit
of leather and a leather cap. The flood of moonlight, striking across him, streaked his locks with grey, and revealed a
face sharp-hewn and rugged, like the rock he stood on.

His first thought was that the man was his uncle. In an
instant he knew that it could not be, for his uncle would be
a man of threescore-and-four, and this man was in middle
age. When he called out, the figure vanished into the night,
without sign or sound.

CHAPTER XV

THE BONDWOMAN

ALTHOUGH they searched minutely through the woods, they found no trace of their midnight visitor, and the others held him to be a figment of Noah's brain. But he slept no more that night. Coming as the man had on the heels of his vivid dream, Noah could not rid himself of the belief that there was some subtle, mysterious relation between him and his uncle; and he pondered much over what it could be.

The party made the best of their way to Venango. On their arrival they found the English trading-house had been seized and fortified by a party of French, commanded by Joncaire. The French commander and his friends were sitting down to supper when the unbidden guests arrived upon the scene. The French and English supped together. After the wine began to flow the Frenchmen became confidential, and assured Washington that they intended driving the English out of all that country. The next day Washington and his party proceeded to Fort le Bœuf, fifty miles above, on French Creek. Legardeur de Saint Pierre, a skillful veteran, had succeeded to the command, Masin having been taken dangerously ill. Washington found him superintending the improvement of the fortifications. It was now December 11.

Saint Pierre detained the party for several days, treating them with the utmost hospitality. In the end, he told them that the letter Washington had brought, asking the French to leave British territory, must go to Montreal for an answer. As for himself, Saint Pierre politely told them that it did not become him, as a soldier, to discuss civil affairs, that he had been sent there by his superior to drive out the English, and that he was constrained to carry out his orders. They noted that he had a fleet of canoes, heavy laden, which Washington surmised were intended for use in an expedition to fortify the point he had noted at the confluence of the Allegheny and the Monongahela.

In a few days they departed, after a fruitless journey

full of hazard. But the dangers were not yet over. Washington, setting off ahead of the party with Gist, narrowly escaped with his life. Once he was thrown into a swollen river, filled with ice cakes, and barely saved himself from drowning. Another time an Indian guide proved treacherous, and fired upon him

SITE OF WASHINGTON'S CAMP ON LE BŒUF CREEK

at point-blank range. But destiny had other work for him to do, and he reached Virginia in safety early in January, 1754, with the reply of the French commander.

Traveling more leisurely and safely, Noah reached his father's home a week later. The midwinter sun had gone behind the barren hills over which he came as he crossed the portico and entered the house. His brother David was descending the stairs as he passed into the hall. Weather-worn and tired, Noah extended his hand. The other took it, limply enough, with a look not altogether as welcoming as it should have been, considering the dangers the younger brother had passed through. Noah was accustomed to surliness on the part of David, but his greeting was beyond any bounds of incivility that he had yet known.

"A pretty looking gentleman to track into his father's halls!" growled David. "Why don't you stay at home, instead of wandering about the country, driving your parents to their graves with worry."

Noah made no response to his ill-humor, but hurried into the dining-room, unkempt as he was, where the family were sitting at the table. His welcome there was more cordial. His mother clung to him, resting her head upon his shoulder and sobbing silently. His father wiped a tear from his eyes, and cleared his throat before he trusted himself to speak.

Much had he to relate to the old man concerning the impertinences of the French: how they had returned an evasive answer to the letter from Dinwiddie; how they had a chain of forts all down the Mississippi, and a strong colony at New Orleans; how they planned greater things, and were preparing new and stronger forts along the line of communication between the Saint Lawrence and the Gulf of Mexico; and with these went many tales of adventure.

So engrossed was he in the narration of these things,

The Potomac River at Harper's Ferry

that he barely had time for more than a passing glance at David, who seemed in his ill-temper still. And for a long space of time he paid no heed at all to a young woman who brought the dishes and quietly waited on his mother, supposing her to be one of the servants. At the close of the meal, the young woman leaned over Mrs. Stevens's chair, the better to hear the directions that were being given her for the night, and Noah's eyes fell fairly upon her for the first time.

Romantic as he was, the sight of her sent a little thrill of pleasure and wonder and tenderness through him. For she was wondrous beautiful! Her soft golden hair was like a cloud with the tints of a summer sunset upon it. Her face was fine and delicate, with cheeks that made him think of rosebuds. She bore herself with becoming modesty; but, though her eyes were downcast for the most part, he caught a glimpse of them, and saw that they were a blue such as he had never seen before. In the one quick glance he had of her hands, he observed that though they were roughened with work, they were exquisitely small and graceful, and that the skin of them still made a valiant fight to be soft and smooth.

So surprised was he at sight of her, so taken back by her beauty, that he stared rudely at her till his mother, noticing it, shook her head slightly, and David, upon whom he chanced to cast his eye, scowled morosely down his nose. In itself it was not a surprising thing that his mother should obtain a new servant while he was away, although servants were rare and hard to get in those days. But that such a dainty and beautiful girl should be doing menial work in a household perplexed him not a little.

"Now, Noah, don't you make tender eyes at Elizabeth," his mother abjured him, playfully, as they passed out of the dining-room. "She is a saucy minx. She is more to be feared than the Indians."

Noah could not believe that his mother spoke seriously. The marks of gentility and good breeding were unmistakable. He was at a loss what to think of the matter. He was but indifferent company that evening, and found occasion privately to inquire of his father who the girl was, before they parted for the night. He was informed that she was one who had come from England in the late autumn, bound over for five years' service. His father saw nothing extraordinary about the girl, or his question, and passed the entire matter over with a word.

All that night he pondered, sure that there must be some romantic story behind it all. He knew that nearly every boat from England brought some manner of bound servants to the colonies, who sold themselves for a space of time to do drudgery, with the final object of making a start in the new world; but he felt that Elizabeth, as his mother called her, could not be such a one. So all night long he wondered what her story might be, devising many marvelous adventures in his mind.

He arose with the resolve to have it from her. But it was not such an easy matter. When he tried to engage her in conversation, she brought

WASHINGTON AND GIST CROSSING THE ALLEGHENY

him always to a realization of his position, subtly making him feel that she was entitled to the protection of his chivalry, and that it was indelicate in him to attempt to break through the relation of master and servant. And always she did it with such decorum, such adroitness, such good taste, as almost to make him feel that he was the servant and she the mistress.

He was piqued by the consistency with which she held him aloof, at the same time acknowledging to himself the strength of her position and the weakness of his own. He knew that she had general reason to mistrust his friendliness, and resolved to disabuse her mind of such an idea, so unjust to himself. But try as he would, he found no opportunity to make matters clear to her, all his attempts only going to involve him further.

Gradually he came to realize that he regarded her with more than interest and curiosity, that she had woven herself into his fancy in quite another form of romance than that which had first appealed to him. Confronting the situation with the warmth of youth and the glamour of the unusual circumstances, he debated long, finally determining in his mind what was already determined for him,—that he was fairly in love with her, and that it was well for him to be so. For through all the time that he had seen her, he had become more and more convinced that she was worthy, and one who would do him honor if the truth were known of her.

He finally decided to speak to her fairly and freely of what was so much in his mind. The opportunity arrived in course of time. She came into the parlor one morning to set it to rights, company having been there the night before. His mother had not arisen, being fatigued, and his father and David were engaged in matters of the plantation, David having taken affairs upon his own shoulders to relieve his father's advancing years.

She barely glanced at him where he sat reading by the fire as she entered. He arose and confronted her, looking steadily into her eyes with a composure that he by no means felt.

"Elizabeth," he said, "you do me an injustice in avoiding me as you have. You receive my efforts at friendliness

KENMORE, THE HOME OF WASHINGTON'S SISTER

in a manner that wrongs me deeply. In thinking that my kindness toward you is what you suspect it of being, you not only wound my feelings, but you call in question my honor as a gentleman. You must let me speak to you now. You must let me set myself in a better light in your eyes. It is my right."

For the first time since he had returned, she was confused, casting down her eyes, and nervously dusting and re-dusting the back of a chair near which she stood.

"I am sure, Mr. Stevens," she said, "that you have always been a gentleman."

"I am not sure that you have always thought me so."

"Perhaps sometimes I have been afraid that you would forget that I am only a servant in the household, — little better than a slave."

"I forget it every time I look at you," he replied, with a fervor in his voice that his genuine nature could not possibly have assumed or concealed. "To me you are not a servant, but a good, true, brave woman, whom I respect and admire."

He would have used another word, but her agitation deterred him.

"You must not speak so," she cried. "Consider that I am helpless here. That I have only your generosity to rely upon —"

"Let me tell you how much you can rely upon that," he interrupted, speaking swiftly and earnestly. "Let me tell you how much more than that you can rely upon in me. Let me tell you, Elizabeth, that servant as you are, and humble as your place in this household, I know you only as a true, good woman, whom it would do honor to any man to love —"

"Nay, nay!" she cried, interrupting him in turn. "I cannot let you speak as you do. I believe that you are honest and that you believe for the moment what you say, but for your own sake and mine I must not listen. It would ruin both of us if I let you talk so."

THE CONFLUENCE OF THE MONONGAHELA AND ALLEGHENY RIVERS
THE FORKS OF THE OHIO

She was deeply agitated. Her face was flushed and her breath came quickly. He was stirred to the bottom of his soul by the sight, and reached forth to take her hand in his. At the moment, the door opened, and David entered the room. She fled from them both with a sound that was almost a sob. The brothers interchanged a look that forever afterward was to be a barrier between them; and Noah passed from the room without a word.

Full of concern for what might befall her as a consequence of his brother's knowledge of the conversation between them, Noah knew not what to do. He sought diligently to speak with her further, and strove to find by some glance or look in what esteem she held him, but all to no purpose. She avoided him with greater assiduity and more success than ever.

All that time his brother looked upon him with resentment and envy that shone almost like hatred in his eyes. Noah learned from what he observed in that quarter that her beauty had stricken David, too. Noah's heart sank with the knowledge, for he feared for her on his brother's account.

The winter passed swiftly into spring, without further change in the state of affairs as regarded Elizabeth. Events on the Ohio had moved swiftly into a crisis. The Ohio company, in the late winter, had sent a company under Captain Trent which had occupied the point at the confluence of the Allegheny and the Monongahela with a rude stockade. When the ice went out of the rivers, the French in their canoes descended upon the place, drove out the English, and laid the foundations of Fort Duquesne, destined to play a large and tragic part in the history of the country.

Virginia determined to expel them. There was no unity among the colonies at that time, — a circumstance on which the French largely relied for the success of their ambitious plans, for the English settlers overwhelmingly outnumbered them in the total. Virginia took steps unaided to hold the country for Great Britain. A loan of £10,000 was issued by the House of Burgesses. An army was raised. Washington received from Dinwiddie a commission as lieutenant-colonel, with orders to fortify the strategic point which he had marked out and to offer force to any who sought to interfere.

It was the last of April, 1754. Word had come to Noah to join the expedition against the French. It was with a heavy heart that he bade good bye to his family. It was with a heavy, heavy heart that he sought out Elizabeth to bid her fare-well. For he

THE OLD SPRING AT FORT LE BŒUF

was determined that he would not go and leave matters as they stood.

It was difficult to find the opportunity. He had not only her to outwit in devising a meeting, but also the jealous eye of David to avoid. He loitered for several days before the chance came. David was in Fredericksburg, whither he had been called on business affairs.

Noah found Elizabeth in the dining-room about her household work. The other members of the family were disposed about the house, conveniently out of the way.

She did not flee from him when he came to her. With downcast eyes and heaving breast, she permitted him to come and stand close beside her.

"Elizabeth," he said, "I am going to the war again."

She glanced quickly at him, to tell him that she knew he was.

"I cannot go and leave things as they are," he continued. "If I should never come back, my last hour would be bitterness itself. I have tried to tell you that I love you, but you would not let me."

She was about to stop him, but he took her hand and prevented her.

"If you will only let me tell you now that I love you, not as well as you deserve, but as truly and as fully as my heart can, — if you will let me tell you that, if you will tell me before I go that you believe me when I say it, then I can go and die peacefully, if the need may be. Elizabeth—" she struggled to free the hand that he held, but he would not let her, — "Elizabeth, I love you with all the earnest, sober devotion of my being."

"But I am only a poor slave," she sobbed, breaking from him at last.

"Never say to me again that you are a slave," he answered. "To me you are the only woman whom my heart has found among many, altogether beautiful, altogether lovely, altogether good. I only ask you to believe me. I do not ask you to tell me that you are glad, or that you are sorry. Only believe me."

Tears burst from her eyes.

"I believe you," she said, in a voice half stifled by tears. "And if I might, I would tell you — that — you are very good, and that I — I — appreciate your kindness, your generosity — that I am glad!"

She cried it out at last with a little burst of effort, and was gone from him.

He turned and left his father's house with his implements of war about him, and an abiding love in his heart.

CHAPTER XVI

THE BATTLE IN THE RAIN

WITH little thought that he was on a mission of strife and hatred, but rather with his very soul afloat in joy, Noah made all haste to join Washington at Alexandria, where he was raising a body of troops for the purpose of going into the country of the Ohio company to erect forts against the encroachments of the French.

Exasperated by the flippancy of the reply of the French commander to his letter of remonstrance, Dinwiddie had decided not to await the ponderous action of the Burgesses of the colony, but to take steps at once through the Council, under the authority of general instructions from the Government in Great Britain.

Although a young man of scarce twenty-two, George Washington had been placed in command of the troops to be raised. He was now at Alexandria, preparing for the expedition into the wilderness. Fry, who had been made colonel, died before he joined his command. The orders were to "construct a fort at the source of the Ohio; to destroy whoever opposed him in the work; to capture, kill, or repel all who interrupted the progress of the English settlements in that country." Officers and men were promised 200,000 acres on the Ohio to be divided among them.

Virginia stood alone in the struggle. Her quarrel was not

the quarrel of the other colonies. They were more concerned with matters between themselves and the home government. The need for union had not yet made itself felt; England herself was to teach them that later. For the present, Virginia stood alone, save for a small force sent from North Carolina, under a conceited officer who bore a commission from the King, and sulked because he was not allowed to take command above Washington on the strength of it, Washington's commission being merely from the provincial government.

The army was ready to move when Noah arrived. There were in all about 400 effective fighting men. They began the march in April, dragging their few small guns along the miry roads with infinite labor, and making little progress. An advance of a mile a day was sometimes all that could be accomplished. Forty men were sent ahead, under Ensign Ward, to fortify the place that Washington had picked out on his journey to Fort le Bœuf. Noah was sent with them by Washington.

Through the clinging mud in the rough road they floundered onward, with the heavy rains of spring incessantly beating down upon them. By day they had not sufficient food, and by night they had no shelter. At last they came to the appointed spot just as the sun broke through the clouds in the western sky, and sank behind a glory of crimson. They made what beds they could out of fir boughs and tree branches, and were glad enough to be at their journey's end at the last.

Noah would have been happy to roll himself up in his blanket and give himself over to thoughts of Elizabeth, as he had done each night as they came thither, but the spirits of the party were too high. Until that night it had been silent, sullen circles of men who had lain down by their fires on the wet, soggy ground, with hunger gnawing at their

Washington's Birthplace at Wakefield, Virginia

dispositions. To-night there was much mirth and rough banter.

They fell presently to telling Indian tales, and from that passed on to strange deaths and wars and high adventures. One among them, an Irishman, made very merry, and gathered about him a ring of boisterous listeners.

"Did ever you hear tell as how Oglethorpe and me played a game on the darlint that deserted on us down in Georgia now?" he cried out, in an interval. They demanded the yarn with loud clamors, and he began. "Well, then, it was this way," he said: "Me and Ogle-

FORT CUMBERLAND IN 1755

thorpe and several other inconsequential debtors thought as how it would be pleasant holiday to take a little jaunt down into Florida and drive the hoppin' Spaniards into the sea, and so we went gaily along, singin' songs and draggin' our guns behind us like the merry lads we were. Oglethorpe, with his coat all hung with braid and brocade looked very fine as he waddled along behind me, crackin' funny jokes between breaths. Oh, we were a merry lot!

"Will I ever forget the looks of him, with the tails of his pretty coat held straight over his head, a-splashin' through the swamps, him puffin' the mosquitoes off from his nose like a tea pot on the hob? 'T was a sight you should have seen. Presently we came upon a lot of them behind a

OLD BARRACKS NEAR OGLETHORPE'S FORT, ON SAINT SIMON'S ISLAND

stockade made of palm trees, pullin' their mustachios and swearin' soft and sibilant like through their little white teeth.

"'Surrender!' says we, cockin' our guns.

"'*Caramba!*' says they, or something the likes of that.

"'Divil a bit!' says we, not knowin' quite what they meant; and on we wint, yellin' like a county fair.

"Ye 'd have laughed till ye ached to see them hoppin'

out of that fort.   We could chase them no farther, for the pain in our sides.   And anon we came forninst another fort, where we had the same pleasant conversation, with similar results.   But they was too many for us, and we had to leave them in the quiet possession of their homes in Saint Augustine.

"But the matter did not end there.   We was safe at home again, explainin' things to them as paid the bills, when the whole Spanish nation, more or less, came sailin' down upon us out of the sea, which fair swarmed with craft.   We went forth to meet them like the merry lads we were; but some there were that shook so in their boots that they couldn't stay still, but had to up and run away to join the victorious hosts.

"'What shall we do?' says Oglethorpe to me, serious like.

"'Do?' says I. 'Why, lick   them, o' course. It's fine fun to see them hop.'

"'But they're too many   for   us!' says he, not scared at all, but only cautious.   He was a brave man, and a true, and I love him yet. 'An' these darlints that have run away will tell them how few we are.   I wonder what they are doin' at the club to-night?'

"At that I had a happy thought.

"'Jimmie!'

says I, takin' him by the hand, for we was close friends, me bein' heavily in debt at the time. 'Jimmie, leave it to me. Have ye got a pen about ye?'

"By good luck he had, and we sat down, him writin' what I told him to.

ROCK FORT, WHERE WASHINGTON MET HALF-KING

"'Honored Sir,' says I, addressin' the matter to the prime mover of all the desertin' darlints. 'Honored Sir: Keep up the good cause. You are doin' fine,' says I, for him to write, and he wrote. 'Don't for Heaven's sake let the hoppin' Spaniards know that we are three thousand men here, with two more thousand on the way, or they'll up and hop before we can exterminate them, bein' afraid of our numbers. Keep makin' them think that we have only a few hundred, and that it will be an easy matter to squash us. Lead 'em on, me boy, lead 'em on. And above all things, don't let them find out that Admiral Vernon is on his way to Saint Augustine with the whole blessed fleet of the English navy, or they 'll be after running back home, and we 'll miss a glorious chance to feed the fires of hell with a thousand hoppin' souls. That 's a good boy. Yours truly, Oglethorpe.'

"'But it 's not true,' says he, bein' English.

THE NIGHT COUNCIL AT FORT NECESSITY

"'Nivver you mind,' says I, takin' pity on him. 'Sign it.'"

"He did.

"'Now what 'll we do with it?' says he, not seein' clearly what I was after.

"'Sind it to our little friend, the chief deserter, by a Spanish prisoner,' says I.

"'But it 'll never get to him!' says he. 'The Spaniards 'll get it.'

"'So they will,' says I, sad like. 'Poor lad, poor lad,' says I to him further, for my heart was heavy for him, bein' English.

"'Oh!' says he, beginnin' to see.

"'Oh!' says I, by way of answer, slappin' my finger against my nose so, and winkin' somethin' prodigious.

"'Oh, yes!' says he again, doin' the same. For the matter had come to him at last.

"So we sent the letter by the prisoner, and of course it fell into the hands of the hoppin' Spaniards, as it should have done, and o' course they thought our dear lad was a spy among them, and o' course they run away. The more so, for by great good luck there were some vessels sailin' peaceful like to Savannah which they mistook to be our lovely Vernon on his way to Saint Augustine. And as they ran hoppin' to their ships, we was after them, and promptly stopped many of them from hoppin' further. An' to this day they call the place the 'Bloody Swamp.'"

WASHINGTON'S FIRST BATTLE-FIELD

"And did they hang the deserter?" inquired a soldier.

"Did they hang him?" returned the Irishman. "They hung him so high that his soul was a week in gettin' where it belonged. We found him stretched up on a tree with his tongue hangin' out and a look of hurt surprise and disappointment all on his lovely features."

So the night wore on, until one by one the men turned drowsily in their blankets, and there was silence among the sleeping soldiers, save for the crushing of the feet of the sentries among the wet grass, and the sputtering of the fires.

Great Meadows and Fort Necessity, the Only Field on which Washington ever Surrendered to a Foe

Noah awoke early and went to the river's edge to wash. As he stooped, some impulse caused him to look up. He nearly fell back against the bank as he did so, for, standing on the opposite shore of the river, which was wide at that point, was the giant figure of the man whom he had seen on the rock on that night when he was with Washington, bearing the message to the French.

For a space they gazed at each other across the water through the grey of the dawning. Noah was too overcome by a sentiment, half superstitious fear and half surprise, to make a motion or to utter a cry. In a moment the man was gone, leaving Noah trembling with excitement at the water's edge.

He spoke no word to the others of what he had seen. He tried not to think of it, for the thing was like an apparition, and filled him with an appalling sense of the weird and supernatural. In the busy labors of the day the thought wore away; for they set to with a will in the early morning to build a stockade and lay out a fort. They did not know what blood would be spilled for the possession of that point ere the problems which they sought to solve would in the end be ciphered.

Little by little the fort was assuming shape. Trees were cut down, chopped into lengths, and set upright in the ground. The earth was thrown up about their bases to give them greater rigidity. The men were rejoicing in their work, and all was going well, when the woods suddenly rang with the shouts of savages, and a fleet of Indian canoes, bearing hundreds of French and Indians, swung into view in the river. The French force under Contrecœur had come down from Venango on the same mission that had brought them thither.

There was no use in fighting. The French outnumbered them so greatly that resistance would have been more foolish than valorous. The Virginians surrendered, but were allowed to retire; the French not knowing that Washington was on the way with a larger force. They came upon Washington at Cumberland, toilfully making his way forward through the mire, dragging his cannon behind him.

Half-King, an Indian chief who had allied himself to the English, was sending runners frequently to Washington, urging him to hasten to save the Indians from the French, and informing him of the position of the enemy. He advanced to Great Meadows, thirty-seven miles from the point the French now occupied. One runner brought news that a small French detachment was in ambuscade on their route.

"Be on your guard; the French army intend to strike the English whom they shall see," was the message from the young commander's friend, Half-King. With a picked force of only forty men marching in single file along a narrow defile, Washington groped his way through the rain, in as dark a night as can be conceived, to the camp of Half-King. After a council, it was decided to strike the invaders. The Indians followed the

UMONVILLE'S GRAVE

trail of the French and found them concealed among the rocks. Washington had surprised the enemy who were lying in wait for him. The French hastened to seize their arms. "Fire!" commanded Washington, at the same time discharging the first shot. The engagement lasted a quarter of an hour. Ten of the French were killed, among them Jumonville, commander of the party; and twenty-one were made prisoners. The right wing where Washington stood received all the enemy's fire. One man was killed and three others wounded near him. "I fortunately escaped without any wound," wrote Washington to his brother; and in a postscript added, "I heard the bullets whistle, and, believe me, there is something charming in the sound."

This was the beginning of the contest known as the French and Indian War, the results of which were to prove of vast consequence to the history of America. The conflict was not to be avoided. If the French and English civilizations had not gritted together along the Allegheny over the matter of the Ohio company, there would have been friction elsewhere that would have kindled the fires. The two great forces were moving in the same direction toward control of the continent.

That they should crunch into each other was inevitable.

Although victory had rested with him in the first conflict of the war, it was impossible for Washington to press his advantage. The French, busily engaged in making the fort, which they called Fort Duquesne in honor of the governor of Canada, heavily outnumbered him. He withdrew to Great Meadows and there built him a fort which he called Fort Necessity, sending to Virginia for reinforcements.

The reinforcements did not arrive. The commander of the troops from Carolina was arrogant and sulky because he was not permitted to command the entire force, insulting Washington wantonly for that he held only a provincial

WASHINGTON'S ROCK, FROM WHICH HE FIRED ON THE FRENCH

commission. The troops were restless and hungry. Washington bore it all with quiet, placid patience, even treating the insulting scold from Carolina with distinguished magnanimity. It was well that he was being schooled in patience under the miscarriage of his plans through the faults of others. It was well for him that he was learning to bear up under adverse circumstances. It was a good thing that he was being trained to ignore the bullying arrogance of those with whom he had to do. For there was great work for him to accomplish, which required all of this drill, and much more.

Noah, constantly with him during the days when he awaited reinforcements, marveled constantly at this fortitude and serenity. Almost he thought at times that the young leader did not know the danger that he was under, so unperturbed was he.

They were working in the construction of a road, which they had pushed twenty miles toward the French fort, when a runner came to them with the news that the French, having completed the fort, were on their way to crush him.

As calmly as a laborer in the fields lays down his rake and turns to his cot at nightfall did Washington begin to withdraw his troops into Fort Necessity. The fort was built in the midst of an open meadow, taking advantage of a neighboring ravine to form part of its defense. The soldiers busied themselves during the French approach in strengthening the fort with logs, and clearing the brush away from the meadow in front.

Here, with 400 men, without bread, with nothing but fresh beef to eat, Washington awaited the arrival of a foe of 900 strong. There was no hope now of reinforcements. Walking up and down within the enclosure, his hands folded behind his back, his head high and perfect self-possession in every movement, Washington awaited the event.

A cold rain beat down upon them. The ground beneath their feet became slippery mire. There was no shelter. Cold, hungry, wet, they waited.

The sound of a shot, muffled by the rain, came over the meadow from the woods. A sentinel, slightly wounded, came running in to say that the French were upon them. Straggling through the woods, each one for himself, they saw them at a great distance making toward two hills near the fort, which were wooded and overlooked part of the stockade.

A puff of smoke, a crack of a gun, a little spurt of mud from the top of the embankment of the fort, and the fight was on. All day long, through the blur of the rain, they fought. Hidden behind the trees on the eminences within close range, or climbing into the branches, the French and Indians poured an enfilading fire into the little fort, which left but little shelter there. The swivel guns which they had with them could scarce be fired, so heavy was the shower of lead pattering about them.

Destiny guided the bullets of the enemy during that struggle. Walking stalwart among his troops, with head

erect, with even breath and low words of courage, exposed to the sight and aim of the skillful marksmen among the savages, George Washington went unhurt that day. There was work for him to do, and it was not fitting

ROAD NEAR JUMONVILLE'S GRAVE

that he should be stricken down here in a frontier fight.

At night the French called out, proposing a parley. Washington knew that to continue to fight meant annihilation. He gave word to the French that he would surrender if his troops were allowed to withdraw to civilization. The English forces delivered to the French the prisoners taken in the fight at Great Meadows, and agreed not to build a fort west of the Allegheny Mountains for a year.

So ended the first campaign of the French and Indian war. Washington began his doleful return across the mountains into Virginia on July 4. In the valley of the Mississippi no standard floated but that of France. The Gateway of the West was in the enemy's possession. In fact, the enemy seemed to be carrying everything before them.

CHAPTER XVII

MISCHIEF AT HOME

NOT at all reluctant to be honorably absolved from further participation in warfare when he had so much to lure him home, Noah made all haste to return to Fredericksburg. Washington, borne up in his defeat by a conscience that approved all he had done, returned to Williamsburg to report to the governor and council. His conduct and the behavior of his troops during the entire campaign were heartily indorsed, and he was given the thanks of the community for his efforts in defence of the country.

Having reported at Williamsburg, Washington came straight back to Mount Vernon. The death of his brother Lawrence three years before had left him the responsibilities of a large estate.

GENERAL BRADDOCK

These he had neglected for his patriotic duty, but he now found time to arrange his affairs in the intervals of drilling his old regiment into preparation for the war unquestionably begun with the first shot fired at Fort Necessity.

The regiment was stationed at Alexandria, not more than an hour's brisk ride from Mount Vernon. Coupled with the duty of whipping it into soldierly seemliness was the still more arduous one of recruiting its ranks, thinned by desertion and illness. Yet, to one as orderly and unhurried as George Washington, there was still time for the delightful life of a Virginia gentleman on his ancestral estates. His father's and brother's house was to be added to with the increasing wealth of later years, but even then it had the aspect of hospitableness, and the rather elaborate apparatus for entertainment, so necessary in that hospitable age and clime.

Its drawing-room sufficed for the gathering place of guests before they entered the spacious dining-room, where the duties of their youthful host found their highest expression. That these duties were neither few nor slight may be learned from a chronicler of the age. Says Beverley: "A stranger had no more to do but to inquire upon the road where any gentleman or good housekeeper lived, and there he might depend upon being received with hospitality." This made numerous bedrooms a nightly need, and during Washington's brief stay of five months at this time, his officers were to enjoy these as a welcome relief from the rigors of the camp.

Lawrence Washington's estate included much of the ground upon which the city of Fredericksburg is built, and once or twice Noah Stevens had the good fortune to welcome his beloved commander there. But his home-coming had not been what he had looked forward to through the weary months. Exuberant at the prospect of seeing Elizabeth so soon again, and filled with high hopes that he might this time be able to bring about complete accord with her,

with feverish eagerness spurred his staggering horse up the
avenue that led to the house.   He had ridden far and hard,
and it was now near night.

The hall was empty when he entered it.   There was
no sound of any one about, and a strange apprehension
came over his sensitive spirit.

"Mother!" he called out, softly, at the foot of the stairs.

THE SCHOOL ROOM AT MOUNT VERNON

There was no response, merely a sound as of some one moving slowly across the floor above. He looked up, and saw his father's face leaning over the balustrade. Great grief was written there on the pale features and heavy eyes. He needed not to be told what was the cause of it. With a moan he hastened up the stairs and grasped the bent and wasted figure of the old man in his strong young arms.

"Father, father! When? How?' he cried.

The old man put him from him with all his feeble strength.

"It's a pretty thing for you to come about her now with your grief, when if you had stayed at home as your brother David does, and conducted yourself as you should, she would still be alive," he said, his voice full of sorrow and anger at the same time. "It was worry for you, away at the war, and grief at the knowledge of what you had done here at home, that brought her to her grave, you unnatural son!"

Noah was too overcome with astonishment and dismay to be able to do more than stammer that there must be some heavy blunder, and to ask for explanation, when David, entering from the back part of the house, interrupted the hasty answer that was on his father's tongue.

"Noah, in God's name spare him all you can," he said. "You know well enough what it is he means. Come, father, let us go down to dinner."

He took the old man by the arm, and led him trembling and muttering to the broad staircase. As he passed Noah, he let his father go ahead, and stopped to whisper:

"Father is old and broken; pay no heed to what he says. He has a foolish notion about you and Elizabeth. See that you do nothing to provoke him further."

Glad as he was to accept the first part of the explanation offered by his brother, Noah was greatly disturbed over what had been said concerning Elizabeth. He saw in it a bold plan on the part of David to keep him from her, and bitter anger burned in him against his brother. He suspected that David might have turned his father's thoughts against him during his absence at the expense of the woman whom he wished only to cherish and protect. He was overcome by horror lest the man had also poisoned his mother's mind in the last hours of her life, and that she had gone to her grave with a black thought in which Elizabeth suffered equally with himself.

It was with a feeling of the highest agitation that he entered the dining-room half an hour later and took his seat. When the door opened presently and some one entered bearing dishes, he grew dizzy where he sat in his chair. It was the sound of the step of Elizabeth that he heard; and he knew that the eyes of his father and his brother were upon him.

He raised his own eyes and looked upon her, dissembling as well as he could the look that should have passed between a young master of a household and a servant. But for the life of him he could not keep a shadow of distress from entering into his face. For she was pitiably pathetic, as she passed to him and laid his food before him. Her agitation was as great as his own. Some heavy trouble had borne her down in the short space of time since he had gone, and a sorrow that made her face still more beautiful was written across it. In the droop of the corners

WASHINGTON'S CREST AND COAT-OF-ARMS

of the mouth, in the hollow beneath the eye, he saw traces of all that had passed; and his pity and his love rose within him until only his love and pity held him from taking her into his arms there before them.

She did not look at him, but he thought he saw a tear beneath her lids. He glanced presently at David, who

THE LIBRARY IN THE MOUNT VERNON MANSION

seemed so unconcerned and unconscious that Noah wondered if he had not really made much out of nothing, and imagined a great deal of what he had thought was tragedy. A look at his father, however, did not permit him to enter that avenue of hope. His father was gazing at him with grief in his eyes, in a manner so absorbed that he did not desist when the son returned the gaze, but continued as though he did not catch the look in the other's face of mute appeal and love hunger.

The situation did not improve with the days that came. Seek as he would, he could find no opportunity to speak with her without danger of compromising her, and she barely found chance to make a sign to him. Once she threw him a glance that was a message of understanding, and a warning. It gave him some cheer, but for the most part he was troubled and miserable. David followed him like a hound, and his father was formal and distant, even in his best moods.

His anger burned against David. He knew what Elizabeth had endured from him, by many a little indication. David had adopted a policy from the first of subtle duplicity. He would come to Noah and condone the harsh behavior toward him of their parent, explaining that it was old age, grief for his wife, worry over the wars, and other irrelevant things that had upset his calmer reason. At the same time Noah was perfectly sure that he was insinuating misconduct against him day by day, for his father grew ever more and more forbidding. Only the ties of blood withheld him from quarreling violently with David, although there was nothing but suspicion on which to base his contention. And only the consideration that his presence there was at least a safeguard for Elizabeth held him many times from going to enlist with the regular provincial troops, so grievous was the burden of his treatment at home.

It was more than a month, early in September, after his return, before he found a chance to speak with Elizabeth without risk to her. They met in a path through the woods, whither he had gone with his gun to shoot. He was greatly astonished to find her sitting by the side of the path on an overturned log as he was returning home. Hat she had none, and the slanting rays of the sun striking through the trees upon her soft hair illumined it with a warm, golden glow. She was dressed in a garment fashioned with her own hands from rough goods of a mottled greyish blue, but the delicate grace of her figure and her carriage raised it into a beauty beyond the reach of art.

She rose swiftly when she heard him coming, and he thought she would have fled if she could. He hastened to her where she stood with her head bowed low.

"Elizabeth! Elizabeth!" he cried, speaking low lest some one be near to hear them. She suffered him to take her hand for a moment. He found no words to say to her, only repeating her name again and again. At last she spoke, withdrawing her hand and standing apart.

"You have suffered heavily on my account," she said. "I was very wrong. I should not have permitted it. I knew no good could come of it."

"Elizabeth," he replied, "the time is too short and too precious for us to waste any of it in repining. We shall speak no more of suffering now. When I left here last, I told you that I loved you, and you said that you were glad to believe it. All through the weary marches, the lonely campfire, and the battle, I have permitted myself to hope that you loved me in return. I did not ask you then to answer me. I ask you now."

He paused. She trembled from head to foot, and stood for a space with her eyes cast down. When she raised them, seek to hide it as she might, they were all afloat with a light as golden as the light that played through her hair. He would have caught her in his arms, but she held him aloof with outstretched hands.

"You must not ask me that," she cried. "I told you I was glad to believe it. I should not have told you so much. Do not consider the sudden outburst of a heart that was so long pent up. Do not presume upon what was said in an ill-guarded moment to take me at a disadvantage now. Do not ask me that, I pray you. It would be better for us both if we could forget what was said at that parting."

Washington's Mansion at Mount Vernon, Virginia

He sank in dismay upon the log she had recently quitted. Her voice rang with emotion, and the golden light was upon her face as she spoke to him, but he could not understand.

"I believe I am answered," he said, staring at the path. She trembled still. "You do not love me," he went on.

She sobbed, and turned to go. He detained her. "Am I answered?" he said.

There was a deep appeal in her eyes as she turned to him again and spoke. "Would it be true love that would answer you now? Would love speak when it knew that every word meant suffering, and that the way led to nothing but trouble and disaster?"

He felt that her words were meant in part for him, and hung his head, accusing himself. "I have brought enough upon you already," she went on.

"Great God! And I on you!" he moaned. "I am but a selfish brute. I know your danger. I know my brother David's evil mind. I thought to help you, to protect you. Forgive me, Elizabeth!"

He looked up at her with an appeal in his own eyes. She pressed his hand quickly.

"No, no!" she cried, hurriedly. "You are all that is good and generous. You seek to help me. Shall I tell you how best you can do it?"

He answered her with a look.

"Wait," she said. "Wait until my years of service are ended. Leave me as you found me until then. I shall be safe while your father lives from my only danger. Then, there will be a beginning, if you choose. Then if you wish to tell me what you have told me, I will give you your answer."

"Will you promise one thing?" he said, rising.

"What shall I promise you?"

"That you will never forget what I said to you on our last parting?"

"Need I promise that?" she said, in a voice that was scarce above a whisper.

The golden light came again into the depths of her eyes as she looked at him. She permitted him to take her hand in his. She let him clasp his strong arms about her quivering body, and press her to his throbbing heart. She raised her lips that he might kiss them. For an instant she rested her head against his shoulder. Then she left him in the path and ran toward the house, with the sun striking golden through her hair, and the whole world swimming beneath her feet.

The autumn wore away into the winter. It was easier now for them to meet in the presence of Mr. Stevens and

THE ROSE GARDEN, MOUNT VERNON

David. Rarely was there word between them. When they spoke together, it was with such mutual understanding that any who listened might have heard all that passed. His father seemed to have turned to Noah again in a measure, and to have lost some of the suspicion that David had aroused in his mind. David continued to be most friendly in his protestations, and did all in his power to win his way into the confidence of his brother.

The winter was passing. Noah kept in touch with the contest that was raging fiercely on the frontier. In January, France proposed to England to leave the Ohio Valley as it was before the last war, and consider the territory neutral. England demanded as evidence of good faith on the part of France that she destroy all her forts as far as the Wabash. Both parties professed a desire to arrange all disputed points peacefully, but while negotiations were pending, a couple of regiments, each of 500 men, under Major-General Edward Braddock, arrived in the Chesapeake. When this was learned at Versailles, a force of 3000 men was started for Canada under Baron Dieskau. The health of Duquesne was failing, and with the expedition came his successor — the last of Canada's French governors, Vaudreuil, a son of the former governor of that name.

Preparations for an expedition against the French at Fort Duquesne were being made. Noah was going to join them, with George Washington and the Virginia troops. The time came when he was about to leave. He was awaiting the summons from Washington. He had been commissioned as a captain, and had a command which he must drill. He would see Elizabeth once more before he went.

The persistent guard that David had at first thrown about them was relaxed. Noah was therefore able to find his opportunity. He stood with Elizabeth in the hall, whispering softly a few words of farewell. They did not

speak of love. They had no need. The moments were few
and brief. At last he clasped her in his arms —

At the instant the door into the parlor opened, and his
father and brother stood gazing upon them. He would
have detained her where she was, and met them thus, but
she freed herself, and would have fled from them all had
not Mr. Stevens commanded her to remain.

Great was the storm of wrath that descended upon their
heads. He stamped the floor and beat upon it with his cane,
crying out all manner of reproaches and evil accusations.
David stood apart, listening passively. Aroused to anger
on his part by the words of his father, Noah made vigorous
answer, defending the girl and declaring his love for her.

"This is a pretty mess for a Stevens to bring himself into,"
cried the father, beside himself. "It would be evil enough,
without your putting a bold face on the matter. 'T were
evil enough for one of my blood thus to comport himself
with a slave, without telling me before my face that he loves
her. Away with your effrontery! Have you no pride, no
honor about you, to drag the name down in such fashion?
Do you forget that you are a Stevens? Forswear her, or on
my oath you shall fare ill at my hands. The vile baggage
shall stay here during her term, like the slave that she is;
but let me hear of your having one word with her, and out
you go forever! And if you do not tell me now that you
lied in your throat a moment since, it will fare but little
better with you now."

Incensed beyond reason by the words of his father and
the black thought he had of Elizabeth, Noah was on the
verge of laying violent hands upon his brother, whom he
conceived to be at the bottom of it, and it is not to be said
what extravagance he might not have committed, had not
his eyes chanced to rest for an instant upon Elizabeth.

There was in her face such compassion for the old man

GENERAL WASHINGTON'S BEDROOM AT MOUNT VERNON

who reviled her that he forgave too in looking upon her. Too wrought up to know the wise thing to do, he stood dumb and motionless in his father's hall, with lips parted and breath coming fast. Thoughts whirled through his brain so fast that he could not lay hold on one of them. In an instant, he decided to take Elizabeth away from there at all hazards, and was on the point of passing over to her side when she caught his eye again. She had divined his thought. With an almost imperceptible gesture, she told him to abandon the idea, and to go.

His promise held him. At the moment there was a knock at the door. A messenger was there, bearing summons for Noah to repair at once to Alexandria and join the troops. In the diversion of his entering Elizabeth left.

Noah approached his father, who still trembled with passion.

"Father," he said. "I cannot do as you ask me to do. I am going to fight the French. If I must carry your anger into battle, I — will carry it. But for the good of your soul I conjure you to believe this girl to be as good and as true as my own mother was."

He held out his hand. His father turned upon his heel and left him with a curse.

Presently he left his father's house, his accouterments of war about him, and bitter grief and misgiving in his heart.

CHAPTER XVIII

AFFAIRS AND THE MEN

ROBERT STEVENS, banker, man of affairs, member of the colonial assembly, and a person of importance in the community, entered his wife's boudoir in their home in New York City in a state of considerable excitement.

BENJAMIN FRANKLIN AT THE AGE OF 20

"Come, wife," he said, "make haste. I have great company to dine with us to-night. Come down and greet them."

"Robert!" in a tone of reproach. "Why did n't you let me know? I have n't a thing in the house to eat! Who is it, pray?"

"Well, for one there is Doctor Benjamin Franklin, the eminent statesman and philosopher, whom I met at the Albany convention in June and who proposed the scheme of union which the congress adopted. You will love him. For another there is Mr. Morris, just arrived from England to be governor of Pennsylvania to succeed Mr. Hamilton, who is sick of his bargain. For a third there is Captain Hempstead, a British officer on his way to Boston, whence he goes to join the British forces at Annapolis. And for the rest there is yourself, my dear. Come, hasten down.''

Mrs. Robert Stevens of New York was accustomed to the entertainment of her husband's fine company. His affairs brought him much with men of prominence, and his southern hospitality, transplanted to New York, had made his board and roof-tree famous. So she hastened to complete the finishing touches of her toilet, and descended to the drawing-room, whither her husband had preceded her.

A man of medium height, about fifty years old, rather stout, plainly dressed, with long, black hair, stood by the fireplace, facing the room, with his hands behind his back to warm them; it was October, and the weather had grown chilly during the day. Having seen him, for the moment she saw no one else in the room, he so held her gaze.

It was not that the face was handsome in its features. His nose was over-long for symmetry, his cheeks and chin were too full, and his mouth was large. In spite of its size, however, it was a feature that would have won her of itself; for though it was firmly drawn at the corners, it was a very Cupid bow of a mouth in its full length, sensitive, sympathetic, kindly, humorous, with the

FRANKLIN'S BIRTHPLACE, BOSTON

effect about it of always being on the point of relaxing into a smile.

But it was the eyes that held her spellbound. Never had she seen such eyes. They were large, lustrous, soft, glowing. Drooping lids made them almost languorous, but for the fire in them. They, too, looked as though they were about to smile upon her. In their depths shone the light of profound wisdom and understanding. Looking upon one, that one felt that he knew what there was to be known. Kind, gentle, sympathetic, there was that about them at the same time which would deter any one from seeking an unfair advantage. Frank, open, inviting to confidence and comfortable friendship, they at the same time were eyes that seemed always to be studying and seeking and inquiring. But above all were they truthful.

She knew at once that it was Doctor Franklin whom she looked upon. Verily her husband was right. She would love this man.

Her husband brought her forward and presented her. The smile, hovering about the lips and within the eyes, broke forth. It radiated a light and warmth of which she had almost physical sense. Every trace of formality, of outward show, of pretense, of absurd convention, melted beneath it, until she felt that she stood before him, revealed, the woman that she was — and she was glad for that, too. She loved him as every one loved him who did not hate the truth.

Some pleasant little words passed between them, and she met the others: Morris, an English gentleman with vast self-assurance and a somewhat haughty exterior, an old friend of Franklin's, for whose sake he was gracious to his hostess; Captain Hempstead, a brilliant and dashing young officer resplendent in a new uniform and a new commission, who greeted her warmly with some London phrase of the day.

PHILADELPHIA'S STATUE TO FRANKLIN

Franklin, affable, witty, genial, led the talk at table. Morris, witty also, and poignant, indulged in many merry quips at the expense of the doctor and the provinces and things in general. The captain joined in with London phrases where he could; but for the most part he found his audience with George Stevens, a lad of eighteen with military dreams, and Margaret, to whose fancy the brocade and braid of the coat spoke more eloquently than the golden words of the philosopher or the gilded phrases of the governor.

"It would appear that our friend Mr. Hamilton is leaving Pennsylvania with a bad taste in his mouth, Doctor Franklin," observed Mr. Morris, in the course of a discussion of conditions in the colony whither Morris was going to take charge of affairs.

"He has made himself somewhat uncomfortable through his contentions with the assembly," Doctor Franklin assented, with a humorous glitter in the very bottom of his eyes.

"Do you think that I must expect as uncomfortable an administration?" inquired the Englishman.

"No," replied Franklin. "You may, on the contrary, have a very comfortable one, if you will only take care not to enter into any dispute with the assembly."

"My dear friend," rejoined Morris, pleasantly, "how can you advise my avoiding disputes? You know I love disputing; it is one of my greatest pleasures. However, to show the regard I have for your counsel, I promise you I will, if possible, avoid them."

"It were well," remarked the philosopher. "You have some reason for loving a dispute, being eloquent, an acute sophister, and, therefore, generally successful in argumentative conversation. But I think the practice is not wise; for, in the course of my observation, these disputing, contradicting, confuting people are generally unfortunate in their affairs. They get victory sometimes, but they never get good will, which would be of more use to them."

Morris, in a spirit of fun, was on the point of taking up the gage of battle, when Mr. Stevens with a question intervened.

"What might be the nature of the quarrels which our friend here had best avoid?" he asked of Doctor Franklin.

"They are all at bottom owing to the proprietaries, our hereditary governors," replied the sage. "When any expense has been incurred for the defense of their province, they have, with incredible meanness, instructed their deputies to pass no act for levying the necessary taxes, unless their vast estates were in the same act expressly excused; and they have even taken bonds of these deputies to observe such instructions. The assemblies for three years held out against this injustice, though constrained to contend vigorously for their rights against the power of the governor."

"Very well, Doctor Franklin," Morris remarked. "I shall scrupulously permit the King's subjects to do as they choose, and if the King is not pleased, he must perforce find other subjects, I suppose."

The thing was said in most part as a jest, but there was a tone and tenor

IN THE PINES OF THE LAKE
CHAMPLAIN REGION

to it that aroused the young and fiery spirit of George Stevens, who had overheard it.

"Ay, sir," he burst out, "and if the King thinks that he can forever impose his arrogance upon our people, he will find us a very different kind of subject from those he has been used to!"

"Treason! Treason!" shouted Morris, making merry over it, and taking more wine on the strength of the jest.

"'Pon my honor, sir, that is a bold speech," ejaculated the captain. "I could make you smart for that."

Mr. Stevens obliterated his son with a look, and Doctor Franklin interposed with his wisdom and tact.

"Undoubtedly the son of our friend here overhears much popular talk that goes on among a certain empty class of persons in all large communities," he said blandly. "There are moments in the heat of popular discussion when things are said by thoughtless people which do not represent the results of their sober reflection and are not to be considered as the exact impression of their principles. There have been local difficulties in New York, and in all the colonies, that may have given rise to the expression of such sentiments; but the feeling has not grown up behind them."

Morris showed signs of indignation.

"Doctor Franklin," he said, "am I at liberty to infer that these subjects of the King so far forget themselves and their Sovereign as to entertain any but the most loyal thoughts of him? Do not hesitate, sir, to answer me. I am not disposed to argue the matter, for I am certain that you are not one of such a party. I ask you for the benefit I shall derive from being informed on the subject by one who is so close an observer."

"I think it will be readily agreed," began Doctor Franklin, "that there is always in every community, state, or nation some one condition of affairs, at least, which, from certain points of looking at it, might be considered capable of improvement. In only the most extravagant cases are matters past mending, and a little patience, forbearance, foresight, and concession will almost without fail extricate the most complicated problem. But there is ever in the community a class of persons who, through lack of insight, too great zeal coupled with too little sense, or a natural bodily impatience, cry out against the things they would have different, in violent fashion, letting their tongues run whither they know not, in much the same manner that our young friend here permitted his youthful enthusiasm to bring him into an indiscretion" — he bent a look on the boy which took all the sting from the reproach, but left it still effective. "They cry out, I say, in violent fashion, and either have no remedy to propose, or one that is either too wild and absurd to find favor with any but themselves, or that is a greater evil on the other side of the error than the original state of affairs may be on its own side."

"From which I am to infer," observed Morris, looking shrewdly at Doctor Franklin, "that you are too discreet to answer my direct question directly."

"From which you are to infer," rejoined Doctor Franklin, with the slightest suggestion of a compression at the ends of the lips as he spoke, and a look at the other that was all firmness, "that if the trifling difficulties which arise in the course of our state matters are met in the proper spirit of toleration by each side, I am inclined to think that complete harmony and happiness will be of permanent endurance, and the malcontents must have to seek some other game to cry after. I believe that the spirit which Master George so inadvertently expressed is for the present confined to youths and those who think little and not deeply."

"My dear sir," exclaimed Captain Hempstead, turning a stiff look upon the eminent man of affairs, "my dear

ON HISTORIC LAKE CHAMPLAIN

sir, you surely do not mean to say that the colonies would revolt, now, do you?"

"It is impossible for a man, who is without infinite wisdom, to foretell what time will bring forth," replied Doctor Franklin. "We can only observe what is in the air, and by our knowledge of the eventualities in similar cases, or our instruction in the phases of human character, arrive at some conclusions concerning what might possibly happen under given conditions. I think that it would be unwise to deny that it may become more difficult for the colonial government to be administered from the home offices with perfect mutual satisfaction, than it would be to make these adjustments now which policy might point out."

"It is a most unfortunate thing that your scheme of union which

A GLIMPSE OF LAKE CHAMPLAIN

we adopted in Albany last June was not endorsed by the various colonies," observed Mr. Stevens, noting a tendency on the part of the Englishmen present to engage in acrimonious discussion. "That would have solved the present misunderstandings and conflicts of government, and forestalled any recurrences of them, I believe. I advocated them warmly, Doctor Franklin, in our assembly last month, and they were ratified, but not as enthusiastically as we who supported them could have wished."

"Pray, sir," said Morris, "do you refer to that insolent document which was forwarded to the lords of trades and plantations from some gathering of colonists, which amounted to little less than revolt?"

Hearing his plan of union referred to in this manner, Doctor Franklin showed no sign of resentment, nor did he attempt a defense against the epithet. Mr. Stevens, however, answered the man with some heat.

"I mean, sir, that very wise and just plan for the union of the colonies under British rule which Doctor Franklin proposed to the recent colonial congress in Albany, and which the congress heartily accepted, and sent to the colonies and to the home government for ratification," he said.

"Might I trouble you to tell me, Mr. Stevens," Morris rejoined, assuming to be bored, "how it came about that such a paper was drawn up and presented? Your remarks concerning colonial congresses are somewhat obscure. I have heard of gatherings of your people to meet with Indian sachems and form alliances, but this one, judged by the results arrived at, seemed to have been for the purpose of instructing England in the matter of government."

"Your assumption that such a thing is impossible, while perfectly natural in a governor, is nevertheless unwarranted and somewhat offensive, if you will permit me to say so," returned Mr. Stevens, piqued by the off-hand manner of the other and his cool, arrogant, sarcastic attitude toward the colonies, and forgetting that he was the host. Doctor Franklin intervened to avert any wider breech between them.

"Having been the author of the document which you are discussing, and having taken a somewhat prominent part in the deliberations that preceded its adoption, I will, if Mr. Stevens will permit me, endeavor to make the matter clear to Mr. Morris."

"My dear sir, by all means do so!" exclaimed Captain Hempstead, who had remained silent for a considerable space of time, and who joined the peace party against his own countrymen for reasons best known to himself and entirely undreamed of by Margaret Stevens, whose eyes had been much on the fine uniform.

"You are aware, of course, that the congress was called under an order of the lords of trades and council, to confer with the Indians of the Six Nations at Albany, looking to bringing them to our aid in the war with the French, which threatened," began Doctor Franklin. "We accordingly met there in June and July of this year with the governors of the various provinces and representatives, who conduct the affairs for their several colonies. It was deemed necessary by them to form some manner of union among ourselves, so that we should not be so much in dependence upon England for protection of our borders against the French and Indians, but should be able to institute some mutual defense against them. The tendency toward such mutual arrangement of affairs involving us all had been growing with some headway for considerable space of time, and to some it seemed in the end it would be necessary for the colonies to unite after some fashion, so common were many of their interests becoming, and so closely had they come together in the matter of adjacent settlement.

"Among the plans submitted was the one I had drawn which was reported, and, with a few amendments and some opposition, finally adopted. By this plan the government was to be administered by a president-general, appointed and supported by the Crown, and a grand council was to be chosen by the representatives of the people, met in their respective assemblies. The appointment of civil officers, the raising of troops, the levying of taxes, the superintendence of Indian affairs, the regulation of commerce, and all the general duties of government were to be vested in this congress. The governor, however, had the veto power for the protection of the Crown.

"Its fate was singular; the assemblies did not adopt it,

as they all thought it had too much prerogative in it, objecting to the power of veto, and in England it was judged to have too much that was democratic. The different and contrary reasons for dislike to my plan makes me suspect that it was really the true medium; and I am still of opinion that it would have been happy for those on both sides of the water if it had been adopted. The colonies, so united, would have been sufficiently strong to have defended themselves, and there would then have been no need of troops from England."

What might have followed in discussion can only be surmised, for Mrs. Stevens, foreseeing dire possibilities, broke into the chain of thought by addressing herself to the young captain in a tone of voice that commanded all at the table to attend. She was a trained hostess.

"My husband tells me that you are going to Acadia to take a garrison," she said to him.

"Madame,   he tells you the truth,"   respond-

WASHINGTON'S MILL, STILL STANDING, FAYETTE COUNTY, PENNSYLVANIA

ed the young officer, glad to find himself the topic for a space. "I shall be stationed at Fort Edward, on the Bay of Fundy. The Acadians are behaving badly, madame, refusing to take the prescribed oaths; they are on the brink of treason, madame. We have serious work ahead of us, I am afraid."

"Indeed, I hope not," replied his hostess. "But did you say you were going to Fort Edward? Is n't that where Cousin Lawrence is going, George?"

"So it is!" cried the lad. "You will go together, doubtless."

"And who, pray, is Cousin Lawrence, may I ask?" quoth the officer from London.

"Lieutenant Lawrence Averill, son of my Aunt Rebecca, who lives in Boston. His father lost his life at Louisburg, ten years ago."

"I shall feel honored to be stationed with one of your family," he observed, politely, with a glance at Margaret, which lingered with her long after the company had broken up at the end of the evening; long after Captain Hempstead left New York on the following day; long after the wilderness of forest about the Bay of Fundy had swallowed him in its dark shade.

CHAPTER XIX

THE GREAT GREY MAN

WHEN Noah reached Alexandria to join his command, he found Washington on the staff of General Braddock. War had not yet been declared between England and France, wherefore the home government had deemed best only to take steps to drive out the French from the territory under contention. They spoke of it as repelling an invasion of their soil.

SIR WILLIAM JOHNSON

Braddock landed at Alexandria early in the year 1755. In April he called a convention of the governors of the colonies at Alexandria to discuss conditions and measures. Four campaigns were planned. Lawrence, the lieutenant-governor of Nova Scotia, was to complete the subjugation of that province, according to the boundaries as England considered them. Shirley, governor of Massachusetts, was to proceed against Fort Niagara, which was considered on British soil. William Johnson was to enroll a force of Mohawks, and capture the French post at Crown Point, on Lake Champlain. Braddock was to take Fort Duquesne.

Noah many times bitterly repented having left home as he had, with an uncertain fate hanging over Elizabeth, and his own case not much better. Also, there was nothing but bitter feeling in the camp between the regular and the provincial officers. An order had issued from the ministry

in England that no provincial officer should have any rank
whatever when attached to a force containing regular officers of the British army.   Washington, because of the order,
had at one time resigned and gone to his home, disbanding
his regiment; but Braddock had prevailed upon him to
return and take a position on his staff.   Noah would have
made similar excuse if Washington had not prevailed with
him to remain.

"I shall need you," he said, simply, and Noah stayed.

Many companies of recruits had volunteered from the
colonies for service.   Without exception their officers were
treated with extreme insolence, and were looked down
upon by the veteran officers of the regular army.   The
British could not believe these men capable of fighting with
judgment or bravery.   The resentment of the provincials
was bitterness itself.   There was almost open rupture, and
it was only the prospect of a common foe in the near future
that kept the peace.   It was a thing that was never for-

JOHNSON HALL, JOHNSTOWN, NEW YORK

gotten by the Americans who suffered under it, and many an English officer had occasion to regret the time when he had insulted a provincial.

Braddock himself was not behind his officers in treating the colonial troops with contempt. Even Washington, whom he called into council, he looked down upon, and would often insolently overbear. Only the American's sense of duty kept him at his post.

The convention had met, and departed. Braddock, confident, promised to send tidings of his successes, in June, by express. To Franklin he said: "After taking Fort Duquesne, I am to proceed to Niagara, and having taken that, to Frontenac. Duquesne can hardly detain me above three or four days, and then I see nothing that can obstruct my march to Niagara."

"The Indians," replied Franklin, "are dexterous in laying and executing ambuscades," and called to mind the experience on which he based his observations.

"The savages," answered Braddock, "may be formidable to your raw American militia; upon the King's regular and disciplined troops, it is impossible they should make any impression."

The little army was unable to move for want of horses and carriages. At a moment when it had seemed that the expedition must be abandoned, and when Braddock was fairly beside himself with rage, abusing the colonies and the assemblies in violent words, Franklin came to the rescue, and procured the necessary equipment from the farmers of Pennsylvania. In the latter part of April, Braddock marched to Fort Cumberland, at the mouth of Wills Creek. On the last day of May the column of British moved out from Fort Cumberland, and threaded its way into the wilderness of forest and stream that lay between them and Fort Duquesne.

Five hundred men went ahead to open the roads. Braddock, as confident of success as though he already marched through the gates of the fort, was gay enough as he rode with his staff in the middle of the line, with his selected troops of England behind him.

"These dusky red devils will find it a different matter when they come to try to make the regulars of the King run away," he cried, twitting Washington.

"You are not to be blamed, sir, for undoubtedly you did the best that you could with the poor material you had in hand; but now you shall see a fight, sir! Now you shall see men that will stand!"

"Without doubt I shall, general!" replied the staff officer without any show of resentment. "But allow me to warn you again that you will find the Indians rather different fighting."

Days passed, each one bringing insult in a new form to the provincials. Black Rifle, a noted Indian scout, offered his services to Braddock as a guide.

SIR JOHN SAINT-CLAIR

"I have experienced troops on whom I can rely for all purposes," answered the general, looking superciliously at the man clothed in buckskin. Black Rifle turned about and went into the woods, leaving Braddock in the care of his experienced troops.

George Washington, growing ill, was left behind, subsequently rejoining the command at a point on the east bank of the Monongahela, about fifteen miles from the fort. He found Braddock all impatience to push on to the fort.

"Have you reconnoitered the entire country and determined on a plan of attack?" Washington inquired.

"We are ready to attack to-morrow," replied Braddock, stiffly.

"You are quite sure there are no French and Indians about?" continued Washington. "There is grave danger

BRADDOCK'S FIELD   (*From an old print*)

of an ambuscade, general. You would do well to look closely to the matter."

"What matter a few French and Indians to the regular troops of England?" cried Braddock, giving way to anger. "I have heard enough of danger from these starveling pioneers. They are afraid of a shadow. When I find I stand in need of military knowledge, Mr. Washington, I will come to you for it."

White with wrath, Washington left the commander's tent, seeking Noah. Noah was alarmed at sight of him so pale.

"George, you should not have come," he exclaimed.
"You still are ill."

Washington's lip still quivered when he spoke. He permitted his anger to find vent before Noah.

"These stupid, arrogant officers are stumbling into a

GENERAL BRADDOCK WOUNDED

disaster which they richly deserve," he said. "Were it not for the men who must suffer for their folly, I should not regret it. They heap insults on the Virginians, and on me. They scoff at us and condemn our advice. If they so far forget that we are brothers as to treat us in this manner, God forgive us if we forget it too."

Morning came, and the camp was astir early. It was July 9. This was to be the day! It was necessary to cross the Monongahela by a ford, and to recross it at a point five miles above, in order to avoid a hill that came down to the east bank. Sir John Saint-Clair, with 150 men, went ahead to prepare the roads for the artillery and transport.

By sunrise the army was in motion. Their red coats spotless, their accoutrements clean and bright, their colors flying in the first light of the sun, their fifes and drums awakening the echoes of the primeval forests, they filed down into the water and up the other side of the stream like a great thing with life and purpose. Winding in and out beneath the great trees that rose from the smooth banks, the troops presented a sight that caused the hearts even of the Virginians to beat faster.

They reached the second ford. Gage, with his command of volunteers, was posted on the opposite side of the stream, having crossed. Sir John Saint-Clair, with his pioneers, was preparing the road. They found no enemy.

"Beware of an ambuscade," urged Washington.

"Forward!" commanded Braddock, and the files plunged into the water for the second time.

Through the ripples that turned muddy and black about them marched the red-coated regulars, the marine detachment, the blue-coated Virginians, the long train of wagons and pack-horses. They wound up the further bank, and slowly buried their head in the dense forest between them and the fort, seven miles away.

There was a path which swung away from the river and passed through heavy brush, with a hill close on one hand and a low gully on the other. Gage was still ahead, preceded by scouts and light horses. The way was cluttered with bushes and choked with the trunks of fallen trees, which the axmen under Saint-Clair were clearing up for the passage of the train.

Suddenly the horsemen in advance folded back. A Frenchman was seen running up the path. He halted, waved his cap and shouted. Instantly the woods rang with the war-whoops of the savages. In another instant the bushes to right and left and in advance blossomed into little white flowers of smoke, and stinging leaden seed came whistling down upon the soldiers. The harvest that came of them was death.

The troops under Gage formed in line, glistening red among the trees, and fired volleys into the bushes with the fatal flowers. They saw no foe, but knew they were there, for men were falling on every hand. A hill to the right was

BRADDOCK'S ROAD ON THE CREST OF LAUREL HILL

Custis House, Williamsburg, Virginia, Occupied by Governor Robert Dinwiddie

most fertile in the deadly blossoming. They sprang out white farther and farther along the flanks, and in the rear.

Braddock pushed forward, the British regulars going into action with cheers, crying "God save the King." They formed in line with Gage's troops, and poured in volleys, seeking to blight the blossoms that burst so rapidly into bloom among the trees.

From behind bushes and trees the French and Indians poured their fire into the thick ranks of the red-coated Eng-

BRADDOCK'S RETREAT

lish, massed closely together in the road, a perfect mark. The soldiers fired, they knew not at what. Their fellows fell shrieking beneath the unseen death. They wavered and huddled together, their guns resting on the ground. This was not fighting.

Braddock, furious, rode in their midst, cursing, imploring, threatening. The Virginians broke ranks and sought shelter behind trees, fighting as the Indians fought. Some of the regulars sought to do the same, but Braddock beat them back into the open with the flat of his sword. Washington, cool, calm, deliberate, forgetting the fever that had laid him low and that sapped his energy, was among them, encouraging them with word and deed. Noah, grasping a gun, knelt behind a bush and fired wherever he saw the white puffs.

A squad of Virginians rushed forward and crouched behind a log near the enemy, firing from the shelter. The regulars, seeing the smoke, aimed at it, killing many of their friends and driving the others back. Lieutenant-Colonel Burton with a hundred men led a charge against the hill. A bullet struck him down. The men returned to the ranks, running.

Frenzied by the murderous fire of an enemy they could not see, distracted by the horrible war-whoops of the savages, utterly demoralized, the men threw down their arms and waited to die as their comrades had died. Braddock, beside himself with rage and chagrin, ordered a retreat. Washington was at his side, helping him in his efforts to restore some semblance of order to the frantic troops. Noah was in the rear rank of the retreating force, firing deliberately.

It was no longer a retreat. It was a rout. The soldiers, as they came to the river, threw away their guns and plunged in, each man for himself, scrambling to the other side. Braddock had five horses disabled under him; at last a bullet crashed through his arm and into his lungs. He fell from his horse, and was assisted across by his officers.

A terrible war-whoop sounded in Noah's ears. Another and another. Before he could rise, a great weight was upon his back, and his arms were pinioned to his sides. He struggled fiercely with the Indian who held him. He rolled over upon his back. Another savage, with toma-hawk poised for the blow, stood ready to crush his skull when the opportunity came. He saw the muscles on the savage's arm tighten. He could not move. He shut his eyes and waited for the end.

The sound of a deep, sonorous voice came into his ears, saying something in French. He opened his eyes, to look up into the eyes of a great grey man, — the man whom he had seen twice before, and the sight of whom had filled him with such an unusual supernatural dread.

"Come with me," the man said in broken English. "I will keep you safe."

Noah arose and followed, glad to escape present death.

Braddock, as he lay half-dazed on his deathbed, was heard to say, "Who would ever have thought it?" and again after an interval, "We shall know better how to do it the next time," and died. His grave may still be seen near the national road, about a mile west of Fort Necessity.

Braddock has long been a well-known character to all Americans. Fiske describes him as "a British bulldog, brave, obstinate,

BRADDOCK'S ROAD, EAST OF FORT NECESSITY

and honest; but more than ordinarily dull in appreciating an enemy's methods, or in freeing himself from the precise traditions in which he had been educated." His arrogance and ill-temper are in a measure excusable if the obstacles thrown in the way of military promptness, especially by the legislature, are considered. It seemed more intent upon opposing the governor than upon attacking the enemy.

Braddock's most serious mistake — that of underrating his Indian foe — has been made by many able commanders in American warfare. The fighting qualities of the red man have often been underestimated. He has been ignorantly accused of cowardice because of his unwillingness to fight in the open; but as a matter of fact, his methods of fighting were closely adapted to the conditions of his environment. It is interesting to note that with the increase in the power and precision of death-dealing weapons, the tendency of modern warfare is to recur to Indian methods, both in looseness of order and the use of various kinds of cover.

The disaster to the British was complete. Of eighty-six officers, sixty-three were killed or disabled. Of 1373

non-commissioned officers and privates, only 459 came off unharmed. The expedition was an utter failure, and the regulars made the best of their way out of the wilderness in terror-stricken groups.

BRADDOCK'S ROAD

The same destiny that had already preserved him through so much was again about Washington. Noah expected every moment to see him fall. Two horses were shot under him, and four bullets tore through his coat, but he was unhurt. Sadly he returned to Virginia to tell the story and to read the lesson.

Noah was led by his captor to the fort. Thrice on the way the man saved him from the savages with a word or a look. Filled with wonder that grew almost into awe, he walked along by his side, unable to find words. The man's face was impenetrable. It was not harsh, it was not hard,

GENERAL BRADDOCK'S GRAVE

it was not forbidding. It was only mysterious, as was everything else about the savior of this friendless lad.

They were near the fort. The man paused and turned to him. Behind them, on the forest battle-field which was left thickly strewn with the wounded and the dead, they could hear the wild shouts of the Indians, looting the wagons, scalping the dead, holding carnival amidst the carnage. For a long space the man looked at him. Presently he spoke.

"Your name is Stevens?" he said; and his manner of saying it was as inscrutable as his face.

Utterly dumfounded, overcome with a sense of the weird about the man, astonished beyond measure at the question, Noah could only stammer that it was.

"Your uncle is George Stevens?" the man continued.

Noah merely stared wide-eyed and nodded his head.

"You know where he is?" the man asked, looking more closely at him.

"No! No!" cried Noah. "Do you? In God's name, tell me. We have sought him through the world. Is he alive?"

For answer the man merely shrugged his huge shoulders. Throughout all the journey to Quebec, whither the man took him after talk with the commander of the fort, in company with other prisoners, he spoke not one word more to Noah. The latter pressed him many times, to find who he was and what he knew, and how he knew that he was a Stevens. The man, for answer, shrugged his shoulders.

CHAPTER XX

LOVE THINE ENEMY

THE Acadian village of Grand Pré lay dozing beside the Bay of Fundy under the warm sun of early August. It was the year 1755. Simple, peaceful, docile, the inhabitants went their several ways, filled with anxiety, not knowing what to do. The English overran their country in an effort to uproot their love of centuries for France, and make them loyal British subjects overnight. They could be loyal to the English King in letter, but in spirit, never. Many had gone under the French flag. Others who remained were harassed by French emissaries, who sought to prepare the way for sedition and invasion.

Acadia was the oldest French colony in America. There the Bretons had built their dwellings, sixteen years before the Pilgrims reached the shores of New England. Their territory had been finally conceded to Great Britain at the treaty of Utrecht, after repeated conquests and restorations. Yet the name of Annapolis, a feeble English garrison, and five or six immigrant families were for many years all that

THE MEADOWS OF
GRAND PRÉ

marked the supremacy of England. The old inhabitants remained on the soil. They still loved the language and the usages of their forefathers, and their religion was graven on their souls. They promised submission to England, but such was their love for France that they would not fight against it. They were French neutrals.

For nearly forty years after the treaty of Utrecht they had been forgotten and neglected, and had prospered in their seclusion. No tax-gatherers counted their folds; no magistrate dwelt in their hamlets. The parish priest made their records and regulated their successions. Their little disputes were settled among themselves, with hardly one appeal to English authority at Annapolis. The pastures were covered with their herds and flocks; and dikes, raised by extraordinary efforts of social industry, shut out the rivers and the tide from alluvial marshes of exuberant fertility. The meadows, thus reclaimed, were covered by grass or fields of wheat. Their houses were built in clusters, neatly constructed and comfortably furnished, and around them all kinds of domestic fowls abounded. With the spinning-wheel and the loom, their women made, of flax from their own fields, of fleeces from their own flocks, coarse but sufficient clothing. The few foreign luxuries that were coveted could be obtained from Annapolis or Louisburg, in return for furs or wheat or cattle.

Happy in their neutrality, the Acadians formed, as it were, one great family. Their morals were of unaffected purity; the custom of early marriage was universal. The neighbors of the community would assist the new couple to raise their cottage on fertile land, which the wilderness freely offered. Their numbers increased, and the colony, begun as the trading-station of a company with a monopoly of the fur trade, counted, perhaps, 16,000 souls.

When the English began vigorously to colonize Nova

Scotia, as the province was now called, the native inhabitants feared the loss of possessions and independence. They were uncertain in their resolves. The haughtiness of British officers aided in fomenting disaffection. The Acadians were despised because helpless. Ignorant of the laws of their conquerors, they were not educated in the knowledge, defence, and love of English liberties; they knew no way to the throne, and under military rule, had no redress in civil tribunals. Their papers, records, titles were taken from them.

The unoffending sufferers submitted meekly to the tyranny. Under pretense of fearing that they might rise in behalf of France, or seek shelter in Canada, or convey provisions to the French garrisons on the isthmus, they were directed to surrender their boats and their firearms; and, conscious of innocence, they gave them up, leaving themselves without means of flight, and defenseless. No resistance was to be feared. The Acadians cowered before their masters, willing to take an oath of fealty to England, refusing to pledge themselves to bear arms against France. The English were masters of the sea, were undisputed lords of the country, and could exercise clemency without apprehension. Not a whisper gave a warning of their purpose.

Since June a British army had been in the province. With them was a large body of New England troops, part of a levy of 7000 that had been raised. They had captured the French forts of Beau Séjour and Gaspereaux, situated on the neck of the peninsula. A British fleet blockaded Louisburg, so that no aid could come from that stronghold, and the British were in undisputed possession of what by treaty had long been theirs, which they had been attempting to proselytize by peaceable means. Now they talked of treason among the Acadians, and threats were muttered.

Lieutenant Lawrence Averill, posted at Fort Edward, a

small fort on the Bay of Fundy, had been about much among the Acadians, seeking to reconcile them to the change in rulers. His frank, earnest boyish enthusiasm, his manifest sincerity, and his unaffected sympathy for them had won many hearts for himself, though few for his King.

One heart indeed had he won. It was with greater frequency than the political exigencies of the situation

THE VILLAGE OF GRAND PRÉ

demanded that he went to visit at the cottage of Madame de Barre, where lived Mademoiselle Madeline; for there was no man there; and what did women matter when it came to the question of the king they served?

His heart was heavy within him this afternoon as he wound his way along the path that led in among the pines and the hemlocks whither their cottage stood apart from the village, overlooking the bay. He had only just left Fort Edward, where there had been a council of officers, and he knew that on the morrow this peaceful village would be swept from the face of the earth beneath the hard hand of the English. He knew, and might not warn them of it.

The cottage of Madame de Barre was low, built of stone, and thatched. Flowers grew about the foot of the cot, and a vine climbed the arch above the gate. Before the house, beneath a slight rustic bower in the garden, Madame de Barre sat at her embroidery. At her side, on a low stool, was a beautiful young girl, with dark hair and lashes that swept her cheeks. Madame was troubled, and the girl sought to comfort her.

"Nay, Nana," she said, in tones full of caress and tenderness. "It cannot be so bad as you fear. Surely, the English cannot care for a poor old woman and her stupid little daughter. They will not molest us, Nana."

The woman only sighed, and shook her head.

"But too, Nana," she continued, with a blush over her cheeks and her head held down, "there is Lieutenant Averill. Surely he will not let evil come to us."

"He is but a lieutenant, child," answered Madame de Barre. "What could he do against the King?"

There was a crunch of feet upon the walk. Madeline, recognizing the footsteps, fled into the house, full of coquetry. In a moment Lieutenant Averill was before madame, hat in hand. She motioned him to be seated.

"Hast any news?" she asked, looking into his face, where she saw the trouble that bore him down. She spoke the English tongue, with a pretty little accent.

"News?" he cried, with a gesture of despair. "There is no news. It is all the same horrible muddle that it was from the beginning. I wish we were all well out of it."

"Is there no hope?" She looked eagerly into his face.

"I came to speak to you of hope, madame," he answered her. "You must long have been aware of the affection

which I bear Madeline. I hope you have never found
reason to doubt its sincerity."

She laid her hand on his for an instant, and dropped her
lids in pretty concurrence. For she was still beautiful, with
eyes of glorious brown and a wealth of white hair that
only added to her glory.

"I had not thought to speak to you until I could offer
myself in more worthy circumstances," the young man
continued, taking courage. "But now I feel that my love
might bring with it some benefit, and I offer it now. A thing
impends which I dare not tell you of. It is not for myself
that I would urge it upon your daughter to marry me
now, dearly as I should love to make her my wife at once.
But I feel that I can — that it would save both of you
much. Understand me, I do not seek to make this a lever-
age upon your daughter, nor would I ask her to sacrifice
herself — " He felt that he was blundering miserably
in what he was saying, and paused, looking timidly at
Madame de Barre. She was a woman of wisdom, and
she understood. He tingled with expectation of what she
would say.

"*Monsieur le lieutenant*" — she fell unconsciously into
the French, which he spoke readily enough. "Monsieur
Lawrence, my dear young friend, I know that you love
Madeline. You are honest, you are noble, you are true.
I love you, and should be glad that you love her. But it is
that which gives me grief. I grieve for you and I grieve for
her. I should have told you sooner."

"Told me? Told me what?" he cried, filled with a
thousand apprehensions.

"She is not my daughter!" The woman spoke slowly
and softly, presssing his hand the while. "Even she does
not know that, but it is your right. You love her."

He breathed with relief.

GENERAL VIEW OF THE FORT AND CANNON, ANNAPOLIS

"It is only a disappointment that she is not your daughter. And in everything but birth she is your daughter."

"Ay, and she would have been my daughter in that." The woman spoke solemnly, nodding her head with each word, and looking far out over the Bay of Fundy.

"What mean you?" he cried again, puzzled.

"Her father was — my husband." Her head sank in shame and grief. "It was your right to know. I should have told you before. Go, and forget your love, and try to learn to forgive an old woman who meant no wrong."

But Lawrence only leaned farther forward, pressing her hand in turn. "Tell me," he said.

"I took her from the woman whom my husband wronged, as she lay on her death-bed. She did not know that I was the wife. The babe was a tiny infant. I promised to cherish the child. Then she told me that my husband — since that day I have not seen him."

"Madame de Barre," he said. "Will you promise me one thing sacredly?"

"And that?"

"That you will never tell her?"

"May God keep it from her!"

"And will you promise me one thing more?"

"And that?"

"That I may take her for my wife when she lets me?"

"Is what I have told you nothing, then?"

"Nothing!"

Tears of gratitude came into the woman's eyes. She pressed her lips against the forehead of the young man, and blessed him. He could find no words.

Madeline stood beside them, pouting prettily.

"And when is it to be, may I ask?" she said archly. "After the wars are over? And may I come to it? I should be happy if I might but be flower-girl."

Madame de Barre laughed as best she could, and hurried past the girl into the house, hiding her tears.

"Sir, let me compliment you," said Madeline to him, making sure they were alone. "You have good taste."

"'T is conceit in you to say so, then," he retorted.

She looked up in pretty wonder as to what he could possibly mean, and for answer he kissed her. She cried out, softly, so that he had to kiss her again lest she give alarm.

"Monsieur forgets that I am an enemy to his King," she said, looking teasingly at him, with her arms still about his neck and her head on his shoulder.

"Madeline," he said, at last. "You must be my wife at once."

"By order of your King?" she asked, pretending rebellion.

"Nay; by order of that other king, whom we both serve."

"What king is that?"

Again he answered her, most eloquently, with a kiss.

"Must I, you say?" she resumed.

"No, I do not mean you must. I only mean that if we could marry now I could save you much, and your mother much. I cannot tell you what I mean; but something threatens which I can avert if you will marry me at once. Come, Madeline, why should we wait?"

"There is grave reason," she answered, drawing herself away from him. "I will not marry you until you have given peace to my poor country."

"But, Madeline, I cannot give you peace, of myself. Have I not sought to bring harmony here, since the first moment I arrived?"

"Nay, Lawrence, you have been ever true and noble, else how should I come to love mine enemy? But I cannot wed until there is peace."

"But, beloved, that is too unjust!"

"Unjust! Speaks an Englishman of injustice?" She laughed bitterly. "How have my poor country-people fared at the hands of the English?"

"Thou art a traitor, and I should have thee hanged for it," he cried, making light of it, for he feared the tendency of her spirits.

"You are a traitor to love a traitor, then."

THE OLD CHURCH AT GRAND PRÉ

"Come, sweetheart, let us be more serious," he exclaimed, drawing her to a seat beside him. "My time is short. I have already overstayed. Consider again. I cannot tell you why I ask you in such haste, but believe me, darling, there is strong reason why you should wed me at once."

"It is well that I know that you are not a villain, you argue so like one."

"You must be serious, beloved."

"I have told you that I would wed you when there is peace in my country."

"But I cannot bring peace, I have told you."

"Would you give up your commission in the English army on the plea of love?" she asked. "And if you did, would your soul ever cease from troubling you?"

"You must not ask me that."

"You must not ask me to wed you, then. Lawrence, you know how I love you. You know that I live only in these few brief minutes that you can steal away for me.

THE OLD FRENCH CAVE, ANNAPOLIS ROYAL

You know how happy I shall be when the time comes. But is not my King before these things. Is not thy King before them, too?"

"Is not *our* King above them all?" he asked, passionately.

She shook her head.

He knew her spirit, and that it was past hope to sway her. And his heart was heavy within him, because of that which impended.

"I will come again to-morrow for another answer, if you choose that there shall be another."

"There will be no other. It would but make us both sadder. Come not on such an errand. Come only as the subject of our King, whom we both serve!"

She crept close to him as he rose to go, and nestled once more against him.

"Long live our King!" said she.

"Long live our King!" he answered.

Passing through the rustic gate, he took up his weary way to the fort, leaving her with her head in her hands, shaken with weeping.

THE OLD SALLY-PORT, ANNAPOLIS ROYAL

CHAPTER XXI

WHAT IS THIS STRANGE MAN ?

THE young moon, fast sinking to her rest, sent splinter ing rays of silver over the eaves and about the garden of the little cot of Madame de Barre. The breeze droned through the boughs of the pine trees that clustered close beyond the stone wall. Between their boles, far away, and below, the Bay of Fundy lay sheen in the long-lingering twilight. Now and then the sound of the surf, as some larger wave came to the shore, would waft up through the woods and fall into hushful echoes about the cottage.

Madame de Barre sat beside a small table, knitting by the light of a candle. At her feet, gazing into her eyes at intervals, sat Madeline, busy with her needlework. There was constraint between them, for the first time that they could remember. The elderly woman wondered in her heart what might have passed between the two, but

On The Mississippi River at Natchez, Mississippi

dared not ask. The girl, conscious that she was keeping something from the woman, was ill at ease. Never before had there been aught which she had not shared with her.

The older woman noticed something amiss, but with the patience born of years refrained from speech — a policy that soon proved its wisdom with Madeline.

"Mother," she said at last, "who stands first before the world after God and the King?"

"Why, child, how strangely you talk. Your parents." Her voice caught, so that the girl looked up.

"Parents next? Are you sure? You hesitated."

"Nay; I but dropped a stitch in my knitting and sought to catch it up again."

"Well, then, after the parents come —?"

"Those whom we love with a pure heart."

"Would God and the King have me wed with an enemy of God" — she crossed herself and mumbled a swift prayer — "and of the King?"

"Nay, child."

"Would my parent?" very slowly, looking up into the face of Madame de Barre.

Madame's chin quivered. She shook her head.

Madeline sighed deeply, and burst into a tiny laugh of nervousness.

"Then I have done well, though my heart is dead within me."

Madeline told that which had passed between her and her lover that afternoon. The elderly woman placed a blessing upon her head, telling her she had done well, and they were once more at ease.

But they were not happy. Dread oppressed them both. They were filled with new anxiety because of what the young man had said during the afternoon. They knew that it was not an idle whim, or a thing devised by which he sought

to achieve an end.   He was honorable, if he was an Englishman.   So it filled them with a nameless foreboding the
more disquieting because they were alone and unprotected.

"Would that Pierre were here!" sighed the woman.

"Ah, blessed Pierre," sighed the girl.   "We need have
no fear if we had but his strength and courage with us."

There was a   long pause. Madeline, com-   pleting the
f r a m e   that she

SITE OF FORT ROSALIE, NATCHEZ, MISSISSIPPI

worked upon, passed silently to the spinning-wheel; and
soon the homely burring sound of it filled the house with
companionship.   Their hearts rose on the flood of busy
sound, and they ceased being so heavily sad.

"Mother, you have never told me why it is that Pierre
is away so much," said the girl presently, with a playful

note of abuse and complaint in her voice. "He is not a *coureur du bois*. He never brings me pretty furs. He is not a soldier, for he has not a white coat. What is this strange man, my brother?"

"He is one who has a mission to accomplish in this world, which you shall learn of in good time, my child," the woman made answer, gently chiding by her tone.

The girl shrugged her shoulders, and laughed as a spoiled child will when caught in petty mischief. They spoke long of Pierre then, of Madeline's lover, of the times that were and the times that they feared were to be; until the candle guttered and they were warned by it.

"Come, child, we must to bed," cried the woman then.

Madeline, rising from the wheel, went to the door and threw it open, to have a last view of the night, as lovers will.

"Make haste, Madeline, or there will not be enough candle to light you to bed," said Madame de Barre, putting away the tools of her knitting.

"Ah," sighed the young girl, "I wish I never had to go to bed, or to eat, or to sew or spin, but could stand here and dream until my lover came."

"Child, child, you will catch your death!"

There was the sound, very soft, of a footstep in the path without. Madeline started in terror.

"Lawrence!" she cried, under her breath.

A low, strong, melodious voice made answer from the darkness behind the rustic gate. "It is I," said the voice.

"Pierre! Pierre! Nana! Nana! Pierre is here!"

The two women rushed out into the darkness and gathered about a man who approached, so huge of figure, so vast in size, that he had to bend low to receive the kisses which the two pressed upon his cheeks.

"Whence come you, Pierre?" cried Madame de Barre, clinging to his arm with all her feeble strength as they made cumbrous progress to the house, for they held to him so that his way was impeded.

"I knew not the English were here. I am in danger. One sought to stop me. I know not that I killed him. I threw him far from me, and his bent musket after him."

"Was it an officer, with light brown hair?" cried Madeline, filled with a sudden apprehension.

"Nay, he was a private, with a gun, which I twisted in my hands and threw after him, lest he fire it."

They passed into the house. Madame de Barre made haste to light another candle. Its soft yellow light fell upon the huge figure, the grizzled hair, and the strong, rough face of the man of the rock, of the stream, and of the fight — the man the sight of whom had three times filled Noah with such strange sensations.

But his face was not now inscrutable. In it shone love, and tenderness, and the joy of homecoming. Over it all was infinite sorrow, infinite sadness and yearning.

"Art hungry? Hast had aught to eat?" inquired the woman, bustling about him, as he took seat by the plain deal table in the center of the room. Madeline stood beside him, looking upon him with awe and admiration.

"Since morning, nothing," he answered. "The homes of our people are gone. The country is wasted. What is it, mother? What happens? What do the English do?"

They told him the whole story as he ate and drank. His wrath rose within him at the tale and did not subside when they showed him that he could do nothing for the people.

At last he was finished.

"Come, Madeline, there is that which I must talk over with Pierre," said madame, then. "'T is time for thy bed as well."

The girl departed, taking a candle-end and climbing the steep ladder to the loft where she slept.

The Old Well and Willows at Grand Pré

"Hast any word of him?" whispered Madame de Barre, leaning close to the ear of Pierre.

"I have been from the frozen salt waters of the North to the warm currents where the sea swings up from the South, and have no word of him," replied the man. "I have turned the nose of my canoe into the last waters of the chain of inland seas, and I have lain beneath the walls of Louisburg, and have found no trace of him. I have stopped at each post on the line of forts that run to New Orleans. He was not to be found, nor in New Orleans itself. There I met a man who had been with De Bienville on his expedition, had seen him make the treaty of peace with the great chief of the Natchez, had helped him build Fort Rosalie in 1716, and had been in New Orleans when the town was settled two years later. The man I sought was unknown to him; he had never been with De Bienville. Sometimes I think that they are in league against me, that they knew of him and hide him from me, that the monster out of very spite prevents us from finding him."

"How of Quebec? Might he be in Quebec?"

"I do not know. I dare not go there. If I did we should lose all. The monster would lay hand on me if I thrust my head into his lair."

At the mention of him whom they called the monster, the woman shuddered and closed her eyes in horror.

"God save me, but I hate him!" she muttered, crossing herself.

"Know you that he is alive, then?" she began again, abruptly. "Tell me? Does he live? Or did the monster slay him, as he said he did?"

"I know not," replied the man. "Yet I feel that he lives, as you do; and that we shall yet find him."

They fell into silence, the woman weeping on the arm of the man. Once she moaned.

"*Mon Dieu*, may we never atone?" she cried.

"I have seen one of them," he said.

"Ha! How? Who was it? Tell me!" she cried, starting up and gazing into his eyes with eagerness.

"'T was not his son, that I know, though it looked like him. I knew him from that locket you showed me with his likeness painted in it. Twice had I seen him when he was with a party of English in the woods, but I could not speak with him. At last I saved him when the Indians would have slain him at Fort Duquesne. He is now a captive at Quebec. I conducted him thither, with many others, and would not let him be hurt."

"Could you not have saved him that?"

"Nay; if I had freed him, they would have slain him. I could do **no** better. He is now in the monster's hands."

"Alas! Knew **he** aught of him?"

"Nay, he did **not**. They have sought him far, as we have, and found him not."

"God help us!" cried the woman. "Think you the monster knows who is the boy he has made a prisoner there?"

A HISTORIC HOUSE IN NATCHEZ, MISSISSIPPI

"I fear it. He must know from his looks that he is of the same blood!"

"Cannot you save him still?"

"I shall ever try."

"Is she happy?" he asked softly, glancing to the loft.

"Ay," replied the woman.

"She called me Lawrence when I came. Is there — another?"

"Ay; one who loves her dearly. He is English; though not himself an Englishman. He comes from Boston. He will be our shield in any trouble that comes to us."

"Then you will not be without protection," observed the man, with a breath of relief. "She loves him?" he went on.

The woman turned a look of deep compassion upon him.

"She loves him," she said simply.

"Is he worthy of it?" he asked at last.

"Altogether worthy," she made answer.

"It is better so," he said.

"Poor Pierre!"

It was wonderful to see that great head sink upon the breast of the little woman, there to take courage.

"Poor Pierre!" she repeated. "Shall I never bring anything but sorrow to those I love?" she went on, half to herself, still stroking the grey hair and the rugged cheeks of the man. "How was I to know that you would love her? I would have spared you knowledge of the sin of your father, for the sake of your soul, and I brought this grief upon you."

He comforted her in turn; and they fell into silence. The candle fluttered in the breeze; the trees without awoke to a louder humming.

"'T is the night wind," said Pierre. "It grows late. I must be away. Can I see her before I go?"

"You surely will not go to-night?"

"Ay, mother. I would only fall into English hands;

and you have a better friend than I among them. I must go about my other task."

She took the candle and crept softly up the ladder and into the loft. Presently she beckoned him, and he followed. They passed into a low, small room. Madeline lay sleeping. The huge man knelt beside her, his frame shaking, his head in his hands. He arose, gazed once more upon her beautiful face, bent and kissed it softly on the brow, and turned away.

Softly they descended the ladder again, without a word. For a moment he lingered, supporting his mother in his strong arms. Then he was gone into the night.

The woman sank down upon a chair, her head bent forward on her breast and her hands folded. In the morning Madeline found her so, asleep, with the tears springing still through her closed lids and passing gently down her furrowed cheeks, which still held the vestiges of a former beauty.

RUINS OF FORT DUQUESNE

CHAPTER XXII

THOSE WHO SERVE THE KING

THE sun rose red on the peaceful village of Grand Pré on the next morning, and the Basin of Minas glowed red beneath it. It was the morning of August 5. The red sun, striking down through the trees of the forest, found Pierre far on his way. Up through the dark paths, past the English forts stealthily, through the desolated country-side swiftly, he had made his way in the gloom, faltering not, for his feet were trained to search out hidden tracks and his eyes were as the eyes of an owl.

Madeline, finding him gone, gave way at first to displeasure, but her thoughts dwelt elsewhere as the day wore on. The afternoon came, and they sat again in the arbor in the garden before the cottage. Madeline had brought the spinning-wheel out with her, and it was humming its song of home

GENERAL WINSLOW

and the fireside. Madame de Barre sat silently knitting. Neither spoke, for their thoughts were of many things.

Some one was at the gate. They looked, to see the widow Montenay, in great distress, fumbling with the latch. Madeline hastened to open it for her.

"Sit you here like this when the world is being pulled to pieces?" she cried, beside herself with grief and terror, pushing past the girl and confronting Madame de Barre. "Ah, but ye have no men to mourn. Oh! My Jean! My Victor!"

The woods that crept close to the wall of the garden echoed back her lamentations. She wrung her hands, crying out loudly—the cry of a woman bereft.

THE OLD ROAD AT GRAND PRÉ

"Speak, woman!" cried Madame de Barre, alarmed, her heart sinking within her. "What of thy two sons?"

"Know ye not, then, that the English have driven all the men into the church, where they are like cattle, and keep them prisoners?" The woman paused in her wailing, looking from one to the other, dumbly. They stared at her back again.

"Speak!" cried Madame de Barre once more.

"They called all the men to the church this afternoon at

three o'clock," said the frantic woman, speaking in a voice little less than a scream. "The place was full of British soldiers. They had long since taken our arms from us. They read a paper that said that all Acadians were traitors. They told us that our lands were to be taken by their King, and that we should be sent to the ends of the earth. They let only twenty of our men come forth to tell us of it."

She fell again to wailing, loudly calling the names of her sons.

Madame de Barre and Madeline looked upon each other, hopelessly, helplessly. It was the thing that Averill had meant when he spoke of something dire the day before. The blow had fallen. The English, in possession of the provinces, feared lest the inhabitants should revolt, being many. They wished to be rid of them. Governor Lawrence and Admiral Boscawen, who was present with the British fleet, conferred with the chief justice of the province, and devised a way.

They framed an oath for the Acadians to take, of such a nature that they, being Catholics, must refuse. Their priests told them to swear allegiance to the King of England, but not to take the oath. The British construed it as disloyalty. The chief justice upheld the view of it, and ruled that their lands were forfeit. The men of the province were gathered together, in such manner as was possible, and were told that because they had refused the oath they were prisoners and would be expelled from the land.

Many of them sought then to take the oath. It was refused, because they had once declined. August Winslow, nephew of the governor of Massachusetts, in charge of the forces, was obliged to hold them prisoners and to arrange to deport them. It was the news of the gathering at the church at Grand Pré and the reading of the document mak-

MINAS BASIN

ing them prisoners and traitors that the widow Montenay reported to Madame de Barre and Madeline.

Not knowing what to do, the two women with the widow hastened to the village. Everywhere was grief and despair. Women and children gathered before the church, where their men were held by the soldiers. Terrible was the sound of lamentation that arose from the gathering, answered by the cries of the men from within. Tears streaming down their cheeks, Madame de Barre and Madeline pressed among them, giving such scant comfort as their burdened hearts and fearful could devise.

Lieutenant Averill, in full uniform, with his arms at his side, stood guard with his command before the door of the church. Madeline rushed to him.

"What is this that ye do, coward?" she cried, all undone by rage and grief.

"I serve my King, Madeline," he replied. His face was deadly pale, and he dared not look at her.

"Call me not Madeline," she cried, bitterly. "Thou art a tyrant, a brute, a beast, a villain!"

A soldier presented his bayonet at her breast and commanded her to be silent, with rough words. Lieutenant Averill struck his weapon away with his sword.

"Touch her not!" he cried, furiously. "Touch her not, on your life!"

She would have broken forth again upon him in her wrath, had not Madame de Barre come at the moment and dragged her away. Averill gave the woman a beseeching look. She returned it with a gaze full of compassion, tears in her eyes.

The sun sank on the scene of misery, and the moon, coming forth, hid her cold face from the view behind the clouds. Women, wailing, returned to their empty homes, to weep through the night. Madeline and Madame de Barre went back to their cot with the last rays of the sun, mournful and heavy. Madeline's anger against her lover had given way to a hopeless despair. Her sobs clung in her throat, and racked her slender body.

There was no light in the house, when the twilight had faded. They had no heart for light. Only the moon threw a white light like a shroud about the eaves, and a fold of it lay across the threshold. They sat beside the door in the evening air, absorbed in melancholy reflections. The heart of Madeline lay dead within her, and Madame de Barre grieved for the grief of youth.

They knew not how long they had sat thus, when they heard the striking of a heel on the stone flags of the walk, and a figure of a man loomed through the shadow cast by

MOUTH OF THE GASPEREAUX RIVER

the moon behind the pines. The figure approached slowly. They felt no fear now. For what more was there that might befall them?

The man spoke.

"Madeline!" Broken by grief though it was, they recognized the voice of Lawrence Averill.

Her only answer was a convulsive sob, as she rose hurriedly and went into the house. He could hear her sobbing within as he came close to Madame de Barre.

"I feared you were gone," he said, with a voice of one whose heart lay dead within him. "Can I see her?"

Without a word the woman arose and went into the house. He waited for a space, not knowing whether to go or stay. Presently the woman returned, leading Madeline by the hand.

"Madeline!" he said. "You have done me bitter wrong. I could not let the night close over us thus."

She only sobbed.

"My loved one," he cried, his tones wringing with woe. "Can't you see that you wronged me? Can't you see that I could do nothing this afternoon? Can't you see my duty as I saw it, and pity rather than accuse me?"

She stood in the flood of moonlight, her cheeks resting on her hand and tears glimmering on the pale face.

"Madeline! Madeline! Sweetheart! Won't you speak to me?" he pleaded

She shook her head.

"I cannot, oh, I cannot!" she moaned. "I loved you so!"

"Do not say you loved me, dear heart! Do not say it that way!"

There was no word from her.

"Madeline!" His voice was husky and shaking. "I have come to save you, Madeline. You and your mother.

The question I asked you yesterday,— I have come for my answer. Come with me, and I can save you from your sorrow."

At each word her grief gave way to anger, and when he was done she spoke.

"You come to me now with your offer?" she cried. "Shame upon you! Can you so soon forget that you have betrayed my countrymen, laid waste their homes, torn open their hearts, slain that which God himself cannot bring to life again? Dare you ask me now to be your wife, you who have been a tyrant, a cruel, brutal, relentless despot? Would you have me throw my soul down before your wicked feet, to save my poor life now? Do you think that I would be so base as to go with you, with safety as the price of my beauty, when my countrymen are dying in your hands? It was bad enough as it was. I despise you for coming to press your suit in such an hour!"

Averill staggered, heartbroken under the weight of her wrath.

"I did but serve my King," he murmured.

"And I do but

THE OLD FRENCH WILLOWS AND ROAD GRAND PRÉ

serve mine," she responded, haughtily. "Thy King is not my King."

"But our King, Madeline? Is our King nothing?"

"Was he aught to you to-day when you stood there at the church with my countrymen under your hand?"

"This must not be. I love you, Madeline. Come. It is bitterness, it is fate that there should be strife between us. But we need not be enemies. Love is above all else."

"It is bitterness, it is fate; but we are enemies. You had the choice, and chose it. Have you my answer now? Begone!"

"You have lost your reason, Madeline. Be calm. Stop and consider. All may yet be well between us if you will but listen. I love you. I would save you. I would cherish and protect you. Think what may befall you. Think of your mother. Madeline!" His voice had sunk to a low, harsh whisper. His dry tongue clove to his teeth.

"Do you still seek such a time to press your suit? Thou art a dastard. Thou art loathsome."

"You love me, and will rue those words!"

"Oh, sir, desist. You kill me! Go! Go!"

"Have you — ? Is — ?"

"Go! Go! In God's name, go!"

She thrust out both her hands. He looked into the eyes that gleamed in the white light of the moon; what he saw there struck his soul dead within him. He turned and staggered toward the gate, shrunken, gasping, blinded, with the world reeling about him, leaving her with her head against the door-post, dry-eyed, racked with sobs.

Through many days he saw no more of her, and had no word. Other women came frequently, bringing food to the men in the church. Neither Madeline nor her mother came at all. He feared that she might be ill, until one day he had a glimpse of her walking through the street of the village at a distance. Once he sent a message to her. It was returned, torn to fragments.

France remembered the Acadians in the hour of their affliction, and asked that they might have time to remove from the peninsula with their effects, leaving their lands to the English; but the answer of the British minister claimed them as useful subjects, and refused the request. The blow was sudden; they had left their homes but for the morning, and they never were to return. Their cattle were to stay in the stalls, their fires were to die on their hearths. For the first day, they had no food for themselves or their children. To prevent their possible return in any event, their villages, from Annapolis to the isthmus, were laid in waste. A beautiful and fertile tract was reduced to a solitude. There was none left around the ashes of the cottages of the Acadians but the faithful watch-dog, vainly seeking the hand that fed him.

Preparations were made as rapidly as possible to convey the exiles to the colonies. Transports lay in the harbor, awaiting provisions. The Acadians were to be distributed through the colonies, from Massachusetts to Georgia. Lieutenant Averill, with nothing but love in his heart toward Madeline, arranged that they should be sent on the transport to Boston, and wrote a letter to his mother, telling her all and asking her to take care of the women for his sake and theirs.

At last he determined that he would make one more effort to see her. With his heart fluttering, he went one afternoon out along the path that led to their house. He heard no sound from within as he approached. Fear seized him, thinking they might have gone to Canada, as many of them did who were not held prisoner. Hastening on, he came to the gate, and saw Madame de Barre standing in the doorway of the cot. Madeline was nowhere to be seen. He was about to open the gate and enter, when the woman, seeing him, made a sign to him, shaking her head sadly. He beckoned to her to come. She would not, and he turned back again, without hope, with only a desire to die.

The days passed heavily. In all the woe that was on those shores, there was none more grievous than his. The time approached when the ships were to sail. It was necessary that the women should be carried on board, even if force were required. He conferred with Captain Hempstead, who was his friend, telling him as much of the story as he needed, and as little as he could. For a reason which that officer did not divulge, he readily fell into sympathy, and proposed that he himself should go, with six soldiers, and bring them aboard the ship, together with such things as they could take with them.

It was arranged. On the day before the embarkation, the captain, full of zeal, went to the cottage. Averill, overwhelmed with his own thoughts, stood near the landing-place awaiting them. For a long time he stood there, gazing at the ships, full of the bustle of preparation. He must remain in Acadia, having other work to do. There were more than 3000 to be carried away.

Presently they came, Madeline between two soldiers. Her face was white, and drawn into hard lines of defiance and resistance. He scarce knew her. Madame de Barre was behind, supported by Captain Hempstead. The soldiers followed, bearing bundles.

Looking straight before her, walking with a firm tread, Madeline approached and passed within reach of his arm. He gazed upon her with all the longing of his great love, but her eyes turned not to right or left as she marched by. Madame de Barre glanced sadly at him, and would have fallen, but that Captain Hempstead held her. So they passed into the boat that was to take them to the ship, and were rowed out. He watched on shore until the faint blue of her dress was lost in the haze of the distance, and he could see her no more.

Many were the heartbreaks and the partings. Ties of a lifetime were torn away, leaving wounds that bled until death healed them; families were shattered, leaving weary heads to sink to their last rest without the hand of love to smooth the painful pillow or stroke the fevered cheek.

INSIDE THE OLD CHURCH AT GRAND PRÉ

Lovers were separated, never to be reunited, as the ships sailed down the basin and out upon the Bay of Fundy, and so to sea, bearing the exiles away.

But none was sadder than Lieutenant Lawrence Averill as he turned to his work when the last sail vanished, a grey blur on the horizon. He could not go, for there was work that he must do for his King.

Nor was he alone in deploring the task. Many in England raised voice against the work that was done. Edmund Burke said of it: "We did, in my opinion, most inhumanly, and upon pretenses that, in the eye of an honest man, are not worth a farthing, root out this poor, innocent, deserving people, whom our utter inability to govern, or to reconcile, gave us no sort of right to extirpate." The annals of the human race do not keep the record of sorrows more wantonly inflicted, more bitter, or more lasting, than those which fell upon the French inhabitants of Acadia. The hand of the English official seemed under a spell with regard to them, and was never uplifted but to curse them. Longfellow has immortalized the sufferings of these simple,

EVANGELINE

God-fearing people in his touching poem of "Evangeline." Some may doubt the reality of the existence of such a person, yet the story it tells is far more true than most histories: the hardships of the Acadians were greater, not less, than he has painted them, and more than one family was ruthlessly torn asunder in the sad business of their exile, more lovers than one separated forever.

CHAPTER XXIII

ARMS AND THE MEN

MRS. ROBERT STEVENS was hostess again. It was the autumn of 1758, three years after she had entertained Doctor Benjamin Franklin and Governor Morris at her board. The man whom her husband had prophesied she would love was once more her guest. So was another who was with them on the previous occasion, concerning whom no one had then made any prophecies in the matter of love,

THE BLOODY POND

but who was nevertheless going the very shortest road to such a state of affairs in the direction of Margaret Stevens, the daughter of his hostess. Captain Hempstead had just come back from his post in Acadia, with many tales to tell.

"'Pon my word, I was about to forget," he cried, as they sat at dinner. "But your cousin, Lieutenant Averill, a most prepossessing youth and a brave soldier, too, came back with me, the most disgracefully disconsolate dog you ever saw.

It would seem that he fell in love with a pretty Acadian girl, deucedly pretty, too, she seemed, when no one else was about for comparison," here he looked significantly upon Margaret. "When the time came to send them on their way, she was unmercifully rough with him, so the poor dog turned them over to me to put them on a boat and ship them down to Boston, for his mother to look after. And the droll part of it is, that though I put them on the right boat, they did not disembark when it got there, and the Red Corporal himself only knows where they may have got to. He was beastly cut up about it, poor dog."

"O captain, how can you speak so lightly of the misfortunes of lovers," cried Margaret, horrified. He smiled agreeably upon her, and plunged again into talk, being pleased with himself and the company.

"It 's too confounded bad that you can't make a soldier out of your people over here, now is n't it?" he exclaimed. "Look at Averill, now. As clever a lad as you would wish to see, and the makings of a good officer, but he crumpled all to pieces when trouble showed its head. Too deuced bad! 'T would be so convenient if you could take care of yourselves over here, so that we would not have to bother."

Robert Stevens, remembering that he was the host, held his peace. Doctor Franklin drew the sensitive ends of his mouth into a little more compression than was habitual, and partook of a large piece of bread and butter. But George was down upon the British captain in an instant. He had just returned from the wars himself beyond Lake George, where he had narrowly escaped death, and had seen it in many forms.

"What!" he cried, sitting bolt upright in his chair with an abruptness which nearly upset the table. "Not able to take care of ourselves? Why, we can take care of ourselves and you too! An American soldier is worth ten regulars!"

"O, tush, lad, you are too hot-headed," replied the captain. "I am of the service, and know somewhat whereof I talk."

"And have n't I just come from the field of battle myself?" cried the impetuous George. "Have n't I seen your generals skulking to the rear and leaving our men to fight a wood full of French and Indians? Have n't I seen our soldiers standing all day and firing at a foe they could scarcely see, while the forest rang with the wild yells of the savages? Have you ever heard a war-whoop, sir?"

"Unless I am listening to one now, I cannot say that I have had the honor," returned the young captain, nonchalantly. "But do you make it a boast not to be afraid of a noise?"

"I am not afraid of any noise that an English officer makes," retorted the boy, forgetting himself in his indignation.

Captain Hempstead laughed indulgently.

"But your men are such a ragged

SHELVING ROCK, LAKE GEORGE

lot," he went on. "Why, I am told that they went to war with hatchets in their belts, in place of bayonets."

"Yes, and they made good use of them," George returned.

"But your drill!" exclaimed the captain. "You have no discipline, no knowledge of the arts of war."

"But we know how to fight, though; and do it, too," cried George, trembling with resentment. "Better than we know how to talk, perhaps. And if the time ever comes, we will show your British regulars!"

Doctor Franklin interposed in the interests of peace.

"I think that we ought not to be too harsh with Captain Hempstead," he observed, blandly. "Erroneous as his views may be, I can readily understand how he comes by them. Used as he is to the routine of war, with all its manuals and manœuvers, he has difficulty in comprehending that men can fight well with no better equipment than the manhood that is in them. If he will permit me, I think that I can satisfy him that his ill opinion of our soldiers is unwarranted, and unfounded in fact."

"By all means, doctor," replied the Britisher, gracefully. "I should be glad to be shown that I am wrong, for I must confess to a high regard for some Americans whom I have met." He looked upon Margaret again, who blushed and lowered her gaze.

"A review of the lamentable disasters of the past two years will suffice, I think, to establish a comparison between the English and the provincials which will redound to the credit of our countrymen, without, perhaps, detracting greatly from the merits of the British. I think that any one familiar with the events of Braddock's campaign will acknowledge that that officer, in some respects, erred, and that he was saved from even greater disaster by the raw troops of Virginia, and that our George Washington proved himself a hero of dimensions, with splendid judgment and courage.

"But to revert to events that took place in the same year. Shirley, of Massachusetts, who succeeded to the command of the forces here on the death of the unfortunate Braddock, made but an evil issue of the expedition against Fort Niagara. Getting as far as Oswego, with two thousand men, he returned without any attempt to accomplish the object of his errand, merely fortifying the place more strongly; whereas he could undoubtedly, with a little energy and initiative, have taken Fort Niagara, thereby cutting in two the French line of communications. Shirley's greatest ability, I apprehend, lay in the persuasive eloquence and genial tact with which he obtained the assistance of the several legislatures in his work.

"Sir William Johnson fared better in his move against Crown Point, on Lake George; but while he has all the credit for it, and was made a baronet for his achievements, General Phineas Lyman of Connecticut, second in command, was responsible for what victory attended. Johnson built Fort Edward, where the Hudson River bends to the westward, and then went into camp with his three thousand four hundred men at the foot of Lake George, preparing a fleet to transport his troops to Crown Point.

"Dieskau, the brave and energetic commander of the French, originally intending to move against Fort Edward, learned of the presence of Johnson and diverted his advance against that force, as being less strongly intrenched, attacked him in his camp. Johnson was wounded and retired to his tent. It was Lyman, an untrained fighter, who, with provincial troops, withstood the assault. In the battle Dieskau was wounded and captured and his troops demoralized. The Chevalier de Saint Pierre, whose interview with Washington at Fort le Bœuf was the first scene in the drama, was among those killed. Instead of pressing his advantage and moving to the attack on Crown Point, he merely erected a fort, which he called Fort William Henry, at the head of the lake, and retired to Albany.

"In comparison with these, let me point out to you how George Washington, that remarkable young man of Virginia, at the head of volunteers, repulsed an invasion of the

House of Governor William Shirley, Roxbury, Massachusetts

French in the Shenandoah Valley in the same year, and how Colonel Armstrong and Captain Hugh Mercer annihilated the Delaware Indians in Pennsylvania last year. It is a different mode of warfare, sir, than what you are accustomed to, and perhaps our men are better suited to it than your trained regulars, commanded by officers who govern their movements largely by rule and rote."

"Doctor Franklin has omitted to tell you how he, as colonel of Pennsylvania volunteers, carried the war to eminent success in Pennsylvania, and built many notable defences, in the same year that Washington defeated the enemy in Virginia," observed Mr. Stevens.

"That was indeed but a matter of little consequence," said Doctor Franklin, modestly. "We have now to examine the events that have taken place since the declaration of war, in July, 1756, and the advent of Lord Loudoun, including the lamentable misfortune of the loss of Fort William Henry,—an event which, I think, could have been avoided by the proper exercise of bravery and decision on the part of at least one British general."

"Indeed, it could, sir," cried George, all alert. "I was there, as you know, and if the cowardly Webb had come to our relief with his four thousand troops, we should have been saved."

Precisely as I have been informed by many," resumed Doctor Franklin. "I should sincerely hope, sir, for the sake of your contentions, General Webb is not to be considered as a representative officer. It was he who turned back from the relief of Fort Oswego, in the summer of 1756, our only post on the Great Lakes, and permitted it to fall into the hands of the French, led by the redoubtable and able general, Montcalm, who, if I mistake not, will make much mischief for our forces ere he is finished with the business.

"It is lamentable indeed, in my opinion, that he is opposed by such a man as Loudoun, who is reported on all hands to be an incompetent if not a cowardly man, and whom I have found most dilatory and lacking in the transaction of all affairs of peace. He is like Saint George on the tavern sign-boards, always on horseback, but never getting ahead. Since he came here, chief in command, in July, 1756, he has done little but embitter our citizens by billeting his soldiers upon them, and discourage our soldiers by his inaction. Among other things, he has interfered with an expedition which Shirley would have sent to the relief of Oswego, to move from thence against Fort Frontenac."

"He is a vainglorious little popinjay," exclaimed George Stevens.

"It does not beseem me to enter into this discussion of my superior officers, gentlemen, or I might have somewhat to say concerning this Lord Loudoun," observed Captain Hempstead, with a grin of deep meaning upon the company.

"It would, I think, be difficult to defend him," resumed Doctor Franklin. "It would need nothing but his expedition against Louisburg to mark him. That fortress, greatly strengthened since its return to the French by the treaty of Utrecht in 1748, at the close of King George's War, is of great importance, and the capture of it would be of inestimable service.

"Having loitered for nearly a year in idleness at Albany, where he did nothing but survey the town and dig a ditch, he sailed in June of this year to Halifax, with six thousand troops, a sufficient force to have taken every stronghold in Canada had he acted. He was joined at Halifax by Admiral Holbourn with five thousand troops, and sixteen men-of-war. And what did he do, pray? He leveled a mustering-round, where his troops were drilled in manœuvers with which they were thoroughly familiar; and planted a bed of onions, lest his soldiers get the scurvy! Hearing at last that the French had one vessel more than he had, he returned to New York, and, learning of the capture of Fort Oswego by Montcalm, has been ever since hot to fortify Long Island against an invasion by the French; when, by using due diligence, he might have been in the heart of their country for a twelvemonth. I apprehend that had Mr. Washington been at the head of affairs, young and in-

The Ruins of Fort William Henry

experienced as he is, he would have brought things to a very different issue."

"And of all villainous cowards that was ever the boast of the British army," quoth George Stevens, taking somewhat exuberant advantage of the face that Doctor Franklin had put upon the discussion, "General Webb, who left us to die at Fort William Henry, is the most atrocious and damnable."

Brushing away his mother's expostulation over his choice of words, the young man continued in much the same strain, Captain Hempstead looking on and listening with a complacency born of an exceedingly amiable condition of his mind, he having obtained many encouraging glances from Margaret during the preceding discourse.

"Here we were, five hundred strong in Fort William Henry, under Colonel Monro, a provincial, with nine hundred men in the outworks, and Webb at Fort Edward, fourteen miles away, with four thousand men, and Montcalm pressing us all along the line. Why, the man trembled like a frightened colt when he heard the guns, and was for running to Albany post-haste. We sent for help. He sent word back that he was in danger of being attacked, and could give us none! That is your officer of the line! He even told Monro to surrender! Do you suppose he would do it? No, sir! He was only a provincial, who did n't know anything about British fighting, and he did n't know how to give up.

"We held out four days. With Webb's troops we could have driven them at any time. Then we surrendered. Montcalm was glad to make terms with us, giving us safe conduct back to Fort Edward. And it was not his fault that we did not get it. The Indians with him were crazy with four days' fighting, and then they got hold of some rum. That set them wild. They fell on us at Bloody Pond, and killed eighty of us. Montcalm and all the French officers tried their best to prevent it. They pretty nearly killed me, too.

"A couple of Indians had me, and they were fighting to see which should get my scalp. All of a sudden a great big man, the biggest I ever saw, about six feet and a half high, came up behind them, took one in each hand by the

GENERAL MARQUIS DE MONTCALM

waist, squeezed the breath out of them, threw them over his head in different directions, and then went on, helping somebody else. I never saw anything like it. He was the strongest man I ever saw. He picked up those wild savages like flies and threw them over his head. And all the time he was doing it his face never moved a muscle. He might have been asleep, for any expression he had. He was not a fighter; had n't been fighting at all. One of our men had heard of him before. The Indians call him One-onto, which means 'face of the cliff.' It 's a good name too. His face looked like a rock. He is a Frenchman, and nobody knows anything about him. He goes from one end of the country to the other, alone, without saying a word to any one. I should like to find out something about him."

"I have seen the man," said Doctor Franklin. "He was at our fort in Pennsylvania. He searched about among our men, and I spoke with him. He was very courteous, speaking a broken English, and soon went away. The Indians have a superstition about him. They believe that he is a god who is seeking a star which fell from the sky; a great meteor of which they have a tradition."

The talk fell into other lines, Captain Hempstead very glad to have it diverted from the cry which he had set afoot. It taking its course among trivial matters, George was minded to inquire of his mother what had become of a servant who was a favorite with him, and who had left when he was at the war.

"Oh, George, you must not speak of such things before company," said the hostess, with a little smirk at him. "Why, his service was up, and he has left us."

"His service was up? Why, was he a bond-servant?"

"Certainly he was, George. Don't you remember?" interposed Margaret.

"Bond-servant!" cried the captain. "Egad! That sets me to thinking. I could tell you a tale of a bond-servant that would make you believe you were listening to some high romance."

There was a murmur of invitation around the board. Margaret leaned forward with parted lips in palpitating interest.

"Well, then, once upon a time,— for so the story should begin, I suppose,— there was a beautiful young girl,— another beautiful young girl, I should have said,"— with an inclination of his head toward Margaret, "and of course there was a horrible ogre, just as there always is a horrible ogre. But this ogre did not want to eat the beautiful young girl. He was a nobleman, high in the British aristocracy and close to the throne, where it is not considered polite to eat people. Nevertheless, in respect to this girl, he was the very ogre of a man, and for many years she suffered cruelly at his hands. She was the daughter of a baronet herself,— a poor devil who had got into the Fleet and been brought over to Georgia by James Oglethorpe, where he died. Her mother died too, and the beautiful girl, who was then a child, was brought back to England, where she fell into the hands of the ogre through some juggling of chancery. You see, the ogre and her father were cousins, or something like that, and had been bitter enemies, and the ogre was seeking revenge. When she ceased to be a child and became a beautiful young girl, her danger increased. At last the ogre's wife died, and the time came when she could escape him no longer. Now, what do you suppose this beautiful young girl did?"

Of course no one supposed what she did, and so he had to tell them.

"Why, she sold herself into bondage in this beautiful country of yours, and I make no doubt that at this moment she is laying the dessert upon some aristocratic table out in the backwoods."

OLD FORT ONTARIO, OSWEGO, NEW YORK

CHAPTER XXIV

THE DEVICES OF DAVID

THE days of Loudoun were at an end. The ministry of Newcastle had fallen in England. William Pitt, the great commoner, had arisen into power. He was the greatest war minister and organizer of victory that the world has ever seen. He had large ideas. He dreamed of the maritime supremacy of England and the winning of the Mississippi Valley. He was magnetic, lofty in ideals, spotless in private and public life. He had the confidence alike of the people and the government. He was equally popular in America. Strong, virile, persistent, he now stood at the head of affairs and directed the destiny of empire overseas. In the place of the grotesque Loudoun, he sent General Sir Jeffrey Amherst with James Wolfe, fiery of hair and spirit, with a body that could not contain his soul, to lead a brigade. Realizing the deficiency of Abercrombie, he would have relieved him, but for political reasons which made it inexpedient. It was one of Pitt's chief   LORD HOWE abilities that he knew men. Lord Howe, half-cousin of the King, he sent as second in command to Abercrombie, with the understanding that Howe should be the spirit of that part of the force over which Abercrombie held command.

June 3, 1758, Amherst, with 10,000 effective troops,

anchored in the Bay of Gabarus, before Louisburg. Wolfe
was with him. Wolfe stormed the French batteries, landing
in boats, and silenced the island battery. On July 28,
Louisburg surrendered. It was part of the Pitt programme.
The important part which Wolfe took in the operations led
to his being subsequently sent against Quebec, and brought
his fame in England, where he was popularly called "the
hero of Louisburg."

Abercrombie was sent with a force to take Crown Point,
with Howe second in command. Crossing Lake George,
just as the Britsh and Colonials reached Sabbath Day Point,
Howe defeated the French in a sharp skirmish. In the fight,
Howe was killed. The French, under Montcalm, had
erected a breastwork in front of their position, protected
by felled trees. The work was on the west side of Lake
George. The British engineer had never seen such a work.
He reported that it was flimsy. On the morning of July
8, the English advanced. The day was hot. With his
coat off, Montcalm, serene, unperturbed, brave, held his
troops to the defense. All day long the battle raged. The
English troops had lost their loved commander, Lord Howe,
and their hearts were not in their work. Their artillery had
not arrived. They were repulsed at last, with heavy loss.
Even then they might have returned with their artillery and
taken the position, for they
outnumbered the French three
to one. But Abercrombie
was not the man to do it.

It was in the fight before
the flimsy works of the
French that George
Stevens had his chance
to show to Captain
Hempstead what man-

STONE MONUMENT MARKING SPOT WHERE
LORD HOWE IS BURIED

ner of fighter he was — and dear was the price he paid for the proof. They were in the same command, George as a non-commissioned officer with provincial troops, and Captain Hempstead at the head of a company of regulars All day long beneath the blighting heat of the sun and the withering storm of bullets, they fought side by side, and valor knew not which was foremost.

Coming late in the afternoon where George's company fought next his own, the captain sought him out, as he stood in the ranks, smoke-blackened, his face spattered with burnt powder, his hand hot and grimy, the perspiration melting through the grit on his cheeks, his eyes red and aflame with the lust of the fight. He had plucked a musket from the hands of a dead comrade. A ball had passed through his hat, knocking it off, and cutting the scalp. He fought with a handkerchief tied about his brows to keep the blood from his eyes.

Captain Hempstead looked at him for a space without a word. George, all unconscious, fought on, loading and firing with skillful swiftness, without thought of danger, aiming ever carefully and deliberately.

"Brave work, lad!" cried the captain, at last. "You are right. You fight like a soldier.

"God, how he fights!" muttered the young man, trained to war, beneath his breath.

As he looked, the boy staggered and reeled, pitching his gun into the air at the instant when he fired it, and throwing his arms aloft.

"He is hit!" cried Captain Hempstead, leaping forward. Reeling about, his knees quaking, George was sinking to the ground when the arm of his friend went about his body, supporting it.

"Are you hit hard, lad?" demanded Hempstead, eagerly.

The boy answered him with a look that he never forgot.

There was no fright in it. There was bewilderment, there was longing, there was wistfulness, and a mute appeal to him for help. Above all there was fortitude and courage. The captain bore him behind the line, gasping, and clutching at a red spot that spread rapidly across the front of his shirt.

"Come, lad, you are safe here," said Captain Hempstead. "I'll stay with you till it's over with."

"Nay, go back. You are needed," murmured the boy.

"Nay, I'll stay here. Come, you will soon feel better."

The boy made no reply. He lay still on the trampled grass with lids closed, drawing his breath heavily, his friend bending over him, trying to staunch the flow of blood from the wound in his breast.

George opened his eyes and looked about him, dazed, unable to recall where he was. His dull gaze fell upon Captain Hempstead. A light came into his eyes, and he smiled faintly. "I am going," he said.

"Nonsense! You'll be fighting again in an hour." How the man wished that he told the truth.

"Tell mother — how — I — fought."

The other could not speak.

The boy closed his eyes. When he opened them he looked at the captain as from a great distance. His lips moved. The Englishman bent to catch the words.

SABBATH DAY POINT

"Tell — sis — that — I — died " — a long pause — "your friend."

Hempstead's chin quivered. A mist came before his eyes. "Ay, that I will, lad!" he said, grasping his hand.

A convulsive twitch of the body; a spasmodic clutching of the hand; a look of ineffable peace stealing into the eyes and over the face; and the light went out forever.

Abercrombie, instead of pressing forward against Montcalm, retired to Fort George, at the head of the lake, and sent Colonel Bradstreet with 3000 men against Fort Frontenac, at the outlet of Lake Ontario, on the French line of communication with their outlying posts and Fort Duquesne. The place fell in two days. The blow staggered the French. Canada was in desperate straits. Their crops had failed, and the French were disheartened. Montcalm, seeing the inevitable end, knowing that the very numbers of the English must in the end prevail, begged France to make peace, without avail.

John Forbes, at the head of 9000 men, moved against Fort Duquesne, as part of the Pitt programme to conquer all of Canada and drive the French from North America. Major Grant, ambitiously anticipating the main army, fell into an ambuscade while he was trying to lead the French and Indians into a similar trap. He had just reached the hill on which the court-house now stands, when he and his Highlanders were surrounded by the Indians and nearly exterminated.

November 24, Washington, at the head of the Virginia troops, led the advance. The British had learned, at much cost, the value of the provincials. When Washington was within ten miles of the fort, the French, numbering only 500, fled, burning the fortress. On the following day the English took possession, naming the place Fort Pitt, in honor of the prime minister. In 1816 when the city was incorporated, the name was changed to Pittsburg. Thus were the French being cut down to the strip that ran along the Saint Lawrence, with their stronghold at Quebec. The news of British successes was received with enthusiasm by the Americans, from Maine to Georgia. Everywhere there was rejoicing and felicitations. Everywhere, excepting in Williamsburg, Virginia, at the home of Elmer Stevens.

Broken in health and warped in mind by age, embittered by the loss of his wife, his quarrel with Noah, and his son's disappearance, he had sought a victim for his wrath and had fallen into a prejudice against the British that made him resentful of their victories. Beginning with some political differences he had had with English governors, growing stronger because of an inclination on the part of the Crown to discourage the Ohio company, his feelings had developed into a hatred of England and all things English that could see no good in them, and which was not to be explained otherwise than as a caprice of old age.

David, since the disappearance of Noah, had devoted himself to two purposes in life. One was to obtain the estate of his father, and the other was to wed Elizabeth by fair means or foul. A coward at heart, he sought to do these things by indirection. Elizabeth had repelled every advance with the utmost spirit. He had to exercise extreme caution in that quarter, for it was necessary that his father should know nothing of it. He dared not press her too far; for, believing every one to be no better than himself, he feared that she would tell his father and upset his calculations. He felt that he could do nothing while the elder Stevens remained on the plantation.

His other ambition was more easy of accomplishment. His father had come to rely entirely upon him in all matters of business, and it was only necessary to cut off the remaining heirs. He had easily manufactured a tale which

OLD FORT CADDIS, FAYETTE COUNTY, PENNSYLVANIA: LAST OF THE FRONTIER FORTS

convinced his father that his brother was dead, by bribing one who had been with Braddock to tell Mr. Stevens that he himself had seen Noah slain and scalped. He had made good use of his father's hatred of the English to dispose of . Robert, the eldest brother, who was in New York and came to Virginia only infrequently. He had skillfully brought his father to believe that Robert, a man of affairs, was in warm sympathy with the English, and secretly acted as their agent in such matters as he could. Rebecca, the sister in Boston, received her part of the estate as a dowry when she was married to Averill.

But the time approached when it would be necessary for him to bring his plans to fruition, for it was now the last of the year 1758, and early in the following year the term for which Elizabeth had engaged herself to his father would expire. She would then be free, and his opportunity gone. He was at a loss what to do, being too cowardly to make an open move, when word came that Robert and his wife and daughter would visit them for Christmas.

The news was highly disconcerting to him. He could only prepare for the event by strengthening his father's prejudice against his eldest son, which he did adroitly during the time that intervened before the visit. Robert, arriving in the state befitting a man of affairs of the commonwealth of New York, in a private coach drawn by six horses and attended by footmen, unconsciously contributed to his own downfall by offending the democratic tastes of the elderly gentleman at first view.

"Look at him, father!" exclaimed David, as the two watched the equipage draw up before the portico on a day in December. "You would think the King himself had come to see us."

"Scant welcome would he get if he did," cried the older man, in a high treble, his cane shaking under his vexation.

Trained in all of the arts of being a good hostess, Mrs. Stevens offended, too, with her many little compliments to her father-in-law and her effusive agreeableness. It was simply her manner, for she was a wholly sound and honest woman.

"Bah!" said he to himself, squirming under her conventional flattery. "She is insincere! She is spurious!"

His bias was drawn even against his granddaughter, in whose early education deferential respect for her elders had never been sufficiently insisted upon.

It was an uncomfortable gathering that drew about the board that night at dinner. Bowed in deep grief as all of the family were

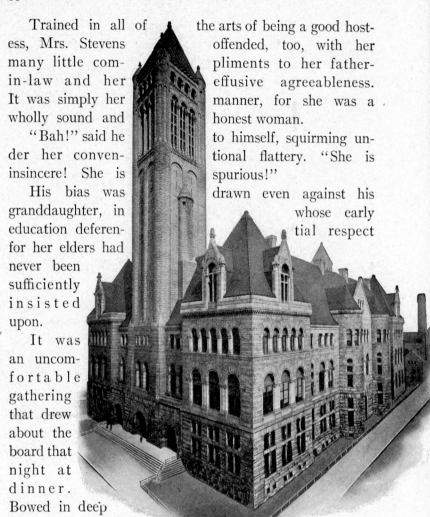

THE COURT HOUSE, PITTSBURG

over the loss of their son, the lack of cordiality in their welcome, which they could not but feel, bore heavily on the spirits of the guests. Robert, discerning the pointed disfavor with which his father regarded him, was utterly broken, and had no conversation. Her own little arts, finding no

reception, fell from Mrs. Stevens. She had so long relied
upon them that she found nothing else to take their place.
Margaret had other matters on her mind, and sat with eyes
fixed upon her plate, lost in a melancholy which, from its
very nature, could not be shared or lightened by any one
present. Her thoughts were ever of the glittering captain,
now in winter quarters at Albany.

David, playing the part he had outlined for himself, was
all graciousness. He chatted of matters at random, as nim-
bly as he could, but dully enough at best. For villains, in
their villainy, have little wit and less humor to make them
shine. He took good care to draw from his half-brother
many encomiums on the conduct of the war under Pitt,
and led him into an elaborate eulogy of that statesman, bringing out in the course of it that he had met the famous man at
one time, when on a trip to London. He contrived to make
it appear that Robert was in the habit of entertaining British
officers, a circumstance which David had learned in a visit
to New York in the previous year. He twitted Margaret
upon her captain, who was now come to be a recognized
institution in the family. During all this their aged host
looked down his nose and said never a word, to the great
discomfiture of his visiting kinsfolk.

Glancing about the room in a high state of nervousness,
Mrs. Stevens's gaze chanced to light upon the face of Elizabeth, as she passed behind their chairs in the service
of the meal. She gave a little start, and fell to staring.
When the girl had gone she turned to her husband.

"Robert," she said, "I want you to look at that girl
when she comes in here again, and tell me where I have seen
her before. I am sure that I have seen that face."

"It is hardly likely, sister," observed David, eying her
narrowly. "She came here directly from England five years
ago, and has been in our service ever since."

"Indeed!" returned Mrs. Stevens. "I must be mistaken then. But isn't she a pretty girl?"

"She has a kind of beauty," David amended, carelessly.

"She is an evil-minded baggage," exclaimed the elder Stevens, who was not in the humor to permit anything agreeable to pass without a challenge. "She is of no good, and I shall be glad when her time is up."

WASHINGTON RAISING THE BRITISH FLAG AT FORT DUQUESNE

"Indeed?" said Mrs. Stevens, again. "I am sure, I am surprised to hear it."

"Noah would have taken issue with you there, father," David slyly suggested.

Mrs. Stevens thought it discreet to slur over the remark, her training as hostess asserting itself unconsciously, and hurried on.

"I am sure I should consider it a nice face," she said. "She looks so dreadfully sad, though, I am sure she has had a life of trouble. She has such a worried look, so utterly forlorn!"

"Perhaps she is in love," murmured Margaret, innocently.

"Perhaps she is, my dear," returned Mrs. Stevens. "Anyway, I am sure she has some story, and I mean to find out what it is. Her face appeals to me."

David looked swiftly at her out of the corner of his eye, and talked of other things.

CHAPTER XXV

THE SINS OF THE SON

CHRISTMAS Day dawned bleak enough on that household in Virginia. On such a festival, when all should be happiness and joy and freedom from care, distress and misery are magnified and weigh the more heavily by contrast. It was so with the party in Elmer Stevens's house. The visitors, reminded more keenly on that day of their loss — for a twelvemonth before their son had been among them full of vigor and gayety — were sadder than they had been since the first keenness wore away from their grief. For the week they had been visiting their treatment had been of such a nature as to make all of them ill at ease and unhappy.

Elmer Stevens, stricken in conscience, was thereby aroused to more bitter hostility toward his first-born, and flayed about him with a lashing tongue at the breakfast table. The lack of joy pervaded the entire establishment, so that the servants went about with long faces taking no pleasure in the gifts which David had provided for them. The spirit of Christmas was dead.

Hastening through the meal, the gathering rapidly broke up, each going his several way. Mrs. Stevens withdrew to her room, having no other refuge in a strange house. She was gazing out of the window over the light snow that had

MARTHA WASHINGTON

fallen through the night, and at the barren trees and the sullen clouds, when she heard some one stirring in the room. She looked about. It was Elizabeth. She had had little opportunity to speak with her during their stay, and had become more and more interested in her as she watched from day to day the sad face, so full of courage and patience, so empty of hope.

"Merry Christmas, Elizabeth!" she cried.

The girl started with surprise.

"Pardon me," she said. "I did not know you were here. I was about to do my work."

She passed toward the door to leave the room.

"Do not go, Elizabeth," said Mrs. Stevens. "I shall not be in your way, shall I?"

"No, madame; if you wish it, I will go on."

A few moments passed in silence, the girl tending to her duties, Mrs. Stevens standing by the fireplace looking into the flames.

"Are you sad, too, to-day, Elizabeth?" she asked, without at all the tone of a hostess, or of a mistress. "Every one is so sad to-day."

"No, madame, I am very happy."

"I am afraid you are telling me a story, Elizabeth. I do not think you are at all happy."

"Pray, if you please, why does madame say that?"

"Because you do not look happy. You look very sad. You always look sad, Elizabeth."

Mrs. Stevens turned from the fire and gazed at her with sympathetic eyes. Elizabeth could not meet the gaze.

"It is very wrong in me, I am sure," she said. "I am sure I shall try not to look sad any more."

"You do try, Elizabeth, you do try. You always try. That is the pity of it. You cannot help looking sad. You have some great trouble, Elizabeth."

The tenderness had gone into the voice of Mrs. Stevens. Elizabeth paused at the side of the bed, irresolute, uncertain. Mrs. Stevens passed over to her, and took her hand, gently, with womanly kindness. Elizabeth looked up. The older woman laid her hand upon the shoulder of the other.

"Is it anything that you can tell me?" she asked. "Is it anything in which I can help you?"

Tears were in the eyes of Elizabeth.

"It must be dreadfully lonely for you, dear," the woman went on. "There is no one here to whom you can go. You are not like these other servants. You are — different. Somehow you do not seem like a servant at all."

More tears were in the eyes of Elizabeth.

"You need some one very badly, Elizabeth. Is there any reason why it cannot be I?"

THE JUMEL MANSION

The hand on the shoulder crept about the neck. The eyes of Elizabeth floated in tears. She raised her head, and looked at the other woman. She tried to speak. Her lips moved, but there was no sound. They passed into a smile. Then, as though her whole soul had given away at once, her frame shook with sobs, and she placed her hands before her face, weeping, weeping, weeping. Mrs. Stevens drew the bowed head upon her breast, passed her fingers softly through the golden hair, caressing her, holding her close, as a mother would a child.

At last the girl ceased sobbing and looked up. Happiness shone like a rainbow through her tears.

"How did you know?" she said.

"Are we not both women?"

"But I am a servant."

"You are a woman first. And you should not be a servant."

Tears came again into her eyes, tears of happiness.

"Is there anything that you want to tell me, Elizabeth? Come, we will sit down."

She led her to the chimney-seat, and placed her beside her, with her arm about her waist.

"Is there anything?" she repeated.

"There is nothing that I — need to tell," she replied.

"Come, dear child. Tell me." She treated her as a child, for she had become one for the moment.

"There is nothing that I — can tell."

Mrs. Stevens tactfully refrained from her intimate questioning.

"Is there anything I can do to help you?" she asked.

"Nay, you have helped me more than I could hope, already," Elizabeth replied softly, with a deep gratitude in her voice. "I have been bitterly, bitterly lonesome, bitterly in need of what you give me. I am not happy here. I cannot tell you why. If only I could feel that you will think of me when you are gone, I should be very strong again to meet my battle."

"Are you sure that you had not better tell me?"

"No; it is nothing. Pray, do not question me. If you will only have faith in me, and believe in me, and not ask me to tell you anything, I shall have stronger faith in myself, and in God."

For answer the woman pressed the girl more closely to her.

"There is one thing that you can do for me," resumed the girl timidly after a pause.

"What is that?"

"When my time is up here, will you let me come to you and be your servant? Let me live with you and serve

WILLIAMS FERRY HOUSE, WHERE WASHINGTON MET MARTHA CUSTIS

you? I ask you nothing but that. Is it asking too much of you?"

Again the woman answered her without words.

"And believe good of me? And ask me to tell you nothing? Can you have that faith?"

Mrs. Stevens drew her to her more closely still, and kissed her on the cheek. For a long space they sat then in silence. At last Mrs. Stevens spoke.

"Can't you tell me — who it is?" she asked.

Elizabeth looked at her appealingly.

"Please," she said, "you promised me that you would ask me nothing."

They sat then in silence for a long time. As they separated, Mrs. Stevens kissed her gently on the cheek again; and Christmas lived in the house.

It lived and waxed warm when they gathered about the table, staggering beneath its load of good cheer. It beamed from the features of Mrs. Stevens. It glowed in the countenance of Robert Stevens, infected by his wife's buoyancy and welcoming a change in the atmosphere. It resounded in the empty phrases of David, who dissembled a joy of the festival out of sheer love of dissembling. It rippled forth in the merry laughter of Margaret, relieved by the removal of the tension. It melted the heart of the aged parent himself, at the last, so that for the moment he became cordial.

It was in a soft and mellow heat in the afternoon, when neighboring planters came to exchange the greetings of the season, to see Robert and his family, and to felicitate with the father on his good fortune in having the son with him. Throughout the afternoon they came and went, laughing and merry, making the old house ring with new life.

There were the Lees and the Cunninghams and the Alexanders and the Jacksons and the Chamberlaynes and the Dandridges and the Custises and many others. With the Custises was Martha Custis, widow of Daniel Parke Custis, blithe, fair, plump, with brown hair and soft hazel eyes. And with Martha Custis was George Washington, not long returned from the fall of Fort Duquesne, now a general, and already broadly renowned and honored.

Mrs. Stevens, seeing him, hurried forward to greet him effusively; for he had fallen once within the circle of her guests when on a visit to New York. He had gone thither to see General Shirley, in an effort to obtain a commission which would give him more than the rank of a provincial

The Shenandoah Valley, Virginia

in the army. He had now become a man of consequence.
She looked quickly at Martha Custis, blushing upon his
arm, with her eyes cast down, and quickly into his face with
a question on her brows. Washington had his share of love
affairs, and when she had last seen him, before the Braddock
campaign, his heart had been puckered with an unutterable
woe, all for the love of Mary Philipse, one of the fair damsels
of New York.

He read her question aright, and smiled wisely upon her.
She as wisely refrained from further sign whatsoever.

"Mrs. Stevens," he said, "I am more than pleased with
this opportunity to have you know Mrs. Martha Custis; for
within a short time she will become Martha Washington."

When he had done, she looked another question at him,
flashing her eyes for an instant upon Mrs. Custis, who stood
talking with Margaret. He understood, being perfectly at
ease with her, as a man always is with a woman when he tells
her of his love for another. He nodded his head.

"Two," he said. "A boy and a girl."

"Well, Mr. Washington," Mrs. Stevens remarked
slowly, studying Martha Custis where she stood at the other
side of the room. "I cannot say that I would have done
otherwise, if I had been you. At least, I should not have
wished to do otherwise, though I doubt whether I should
have met with such marked success."

Washington bowed low, and laughed heartily again. He
was readier to laugh this Christmas than was his wont.

"Now, then," continued Mrs. Stevens, making her voice
sound like a school-master's, "tell me how it happened,
sir."

"Well, madame, it is a difficult thing to tell how those
things do happen, except that I saw her."

"No equivocation now, sir!" she cried, with mock
severity. "Tell me this instant how it came about."

"It is strange what little things fate will do to work out her purposes."

"So I have read. Pray proceed."

"Nay, I was coming to the tale. But it fell about strangely. I was hurrying to Williamsburg from Fort Cumberland on business of the campaign, last summer. On the way I met Mr. Chamberlayne, who insisted that I should

WASHINGTON'S FIRST MEETING WITH MARTHA CUSTIS

be with them to dinner. I went, urging my haste against his hospitality without avail. Well, she was there, and —"

He paused, smiling, and shrugged his great shoulders.

"And the strangest part of it is, I suppose," observed Mrs. Stevens, "that you were no longer in a hurry."

"I did not go on until the next day."

"And then?"

"And then, before I returned to Cumberland, she had given me her love."

"And never a little quiver in your heart for the beautiful Mary Philipse?" Mrs. Stevens asked, with an amused look.

"Nonsense," returned the young man. "That was a frivolous affair, of which I have long since been ashamed."

"I often wonder at men," murmured Mrs. Stevens. "I don't see how you can do such things!" Whereupon she fell to flattering him again, this time concerning the beauties and charms of Martha Custis, until Robert Stevens, discovering Washington standing in the obscure corner, came up with many expostulations.

"My dear," he said, "really, you must not be so selfish. I am sure there are others who wish to see General Washington this afternoon as much as you do."

"That is quite impossible," she cried with an arch look at the young general.

"However that may be," rejoined the hero, delighted, "I am sure there is none whom he would rather be with."

Whereat they all laughed, being in merry mood, and passed out among the other guests.

"And I am sure," whispered Mrs. Stevens to her husband, loitering for an opportunity, "that you will find him well worth while. I do not know what a man can become that is the most prominent and important position in the land, but I do feel that he will arrive there, whatever it may be. He is so strong and wise and self-contained and brave."

"I quite agree with you," Mr. Stevens replied. "He is a man much talked of throughout the colonies, and none who have met him have failed to be impressed with his worth. If a crisis ever comes to the country, he will be one on whom we can rely. You may be sure that I shall do all that I can to become intimate with him."

For that purpose Robert Stevens and his wife delayed their departure to New York until January, so that they might attend the wedding of George Washington and Martha

Custis, as Martha urged them to do that day before she left. The marriage took place on January 6, 1759, at the White House, the home of the bride. It was celebrated with great joy and much mirth, in the good old style of Virginia.

They did not know that the woman who was that day taken to wife by the diffident young gen- eral would one day be the

WILLIAMS FERRY, ON THE PAMUNKEY RIVER

first lady in the land; that the two would go down through history revered, inseparable, and beloved; that the pictures of George and Martha Washington in time to come would hang upon the walls of a hundred thousand school-rooms, draped lovingly with flags of a nation as yet unborn. These things they did not know, but they knew that true love and great happiness were there.

Elmer Stevens, after his one day of relenting, became more autocratic and abusive toward his kinsfolk than before, incited thereto by David, who observed the softening on Christmas Day and immediately took steps to counteract it. Robert and his wife would not have stayed so long at the house for any less an event than the wedding of General Washington, and made haste to get away immediately after it.

On the day when they were to leave, Mrs. Stevens, remembering that the master of the household had expressed himself against Elizabeth, asked him if she might take her with them. He flew into a rage, and accused the woman bitterly, forbidding her to speak of it. So at last they went, glad to be away from the unwelcome atmosphere, but sad of heart because of the changes in the father. Robert had made every effort to restore the old love. He had been repulsed throughout and knew not what to think.

"Father has grown very old, my dear," he said to his wife, as they rolled away in their coach.

To which view of the matter she dutifully gave her assent.

David immediately set about to carry his plans further. He feared lest Robert, suspecting something from the treatment he had received at his father's hands, would take steps that would mean disaster to himself. And the time when Elizabeth could finally elude him was drawing rapidly near.

Taking advantage of the state of mind in which his father was, he fanned his wrath against the eldest son with many devices, subtly suggesting hidden significances in many things during their stay, to work upon his feelings.

At last, in a burst of wrath, Elmer Stevens declared that he would cut Robert off, and leave all his wealth, which had become considerable, to David. Waiting, with shrewdness, until the proper moment, David suggested to his father that since Robert had proved such an ingrate in every way, the probabilities were strong that he would make trouble in the matter of the estate, and might succeed in coming into his share of it, despite his father's determination that he should not.

As his father was casting about in his mind for a way to prevent that, David, as though he had that moment hit upon it, clapped his hands and leapt to his feet.

"I have it!" he cried. "Father, if you will but make over the property to me at once, then he can never lay hand on it. But it will be yours in effect until you die."

He went to great length to show the many advantages of such a scheme. Disturbed in his conscience for the injury he unconsciously felt he had done Robert, and driven thereby to greater wrongs against him, Mr. Stevens eagerly took up the idea, and carried it out as speedily as might be, so that before another day had passed the thing was done.

The behavior of David toward his father underwent an abrupt change. He was no longer indulgent of his crabbed whims. He was no longer obsequious and dutiful. He became arrogant, intolerant, abusive, surly. He denied the man, feeble with years, many of the little luxuries to which he was accustomed. He deprived him of the room in which he had lived for many years, obliging him to remove to a barren apartment in the back of the house.

With the change in the manner of his treatment came a change in the old man. His spirit broke. He no longer grew angry at trifles and stormed, but silently wept under the abuses, humble, apologetic; like one asking alms.

At the same time, David grew overbearing and threatening toward Elizabeth. She perceived the changed relations between her masters, and feared David for the first time. She knew not what to do. Had she not been deterred by the thought that she might be of assistance to the father in extremity, she would have fled. For Noah's sake she stayed, cruelly as Noah had been wronged.

MARTHA WASHINGTON'S RECEPTION

Encountering David one day in the parlor, where she was at her task, she thought that her time had come. Making a pretence to come close to her for a book that lay on the table, he grasped her by the wrists, and, as she struggled, kissed her. She would have screamed, but he placed a hand over her mouth. Still she struggled, and at last, a servant happening through the hall, David released her.

"I will teach you that it would have been wiser for you if you had found it in your heart to meet my love with a tenderer response, girl," he said, with a malignant look in his eye. "You will soon learn that I am used to having my way at the last. What might have been very happy between us will come about in spite of you; and it will not be long ere it will be too late for gentleness between us. If you will not be my wife one way, you shall become so in another"

He left her unstrung, filled with dread and apprehension.

From that time his persecutions of his father redoubled, until the old man was fain to sit obscurely in the chimney-corner throughout the days, daring not to utter a word. It was now only a month before Elizabeth's time of service was to expire. David, growing more vicious as the time approached, was determined to be rid of his father at once. Coward that he was, he durst not bring things to a crisis with Elizabeth while the old man was in the house. It was not that he dreaded interference, but the presence of the man he had so injured deterred him from the evil.

Considering within his mind what might be done in the matter, he decided to send his father to Robert, at New York. Gathering up a few things in a portmanteau, he took him to Williamsburg on the day that the coach for Philadelphia was to leave, and placed him in it, with money enough to take him to his journey's end.

"Is not your father an old man for such travels?" asked a neighbor, who was standing by to see the coach depart.

"Nay, he is strong," replied David, "and joy bears him up. He is going to his son Robert, in New York, on a long visit. His son Robert was lately with him, and he loves him much. Now he goes to repay the visit."

Crouched fearfully in a corner of the vehicle, his portmanteau on his knees, the man of threescore-and-ten, tottering in mind and body, crushed, thrust out from his

MARTHA WASHINGTON'S BEDROOM AT MOUNT VERNON

home by his cherished son, turned face and heart toward that other son, the recently despised tory of New York.

Waiting till the coach was lost to sight, David turned back to the home now his, with an evil joy in his heart. He asked for Elizabeth. She did not answer the call. He rushed to her room. She was not within. Raging and cursing, he dashed through the house, and through the outbuildings and the fields. Long he searched, beating and cuffing those with him. In vain; she was nowhere to be found.

CHAPTER XXVI

UP FROM THE VOID

THE year 1759 opened with the French in desperate circumstances. The tendrils of their empire overseas were being loosened from their hold upon the land, one by one. Fort Duquesne had fallen. Frontenac was in the hands of the English. Louisburg was lost to them, and the command of the mouth of the Saint Lawrence. The British flag floated over the stockade at Oswego. There remained only the root at Quebec, the stem extending to Montreal, one important branch that gave shelter and promise at Niagara and struck down the Mississippi to far-off New Orleans, and another that reached far into the enemy's territory at Ticonderoga, on Lake Champlain. The vine of which her statesman had dreamed mighty dreams, whose flower and fruit they had seen in visions, was being stricken from them by the swords of their hereditary and relentless foe.

Nothing but its utter destruction, root, branch, and flower, would satisfy the pitiless energy, the far-seeing sagacity, of William Pitt, at the head of affairs in England. General Amherst was given full control of the English forces in America. Three campaigns were planned. General Prideaux was to command an expedition to proceed against Fort Niagara, by way of Oswego, which had fallen to the English in the previous year, and thence on to Montreal, down the Saint Lawrence. Amherst himself, with 11,000 men, was to move against Ticonderoga and lop that from the enemy. James Wolfe, hero of Louisburg, the courageous, the resourceful, whose burning spirit kept his frail

355

body at the front of events, was to proceed up the Saint Lawrence and reduce Quebec.   His brilliant achievement in the siege of Louisburg won for him the opportunity.

The situation of the French was hopeless.   No valor, no skill could do more than postpone the inevitable event. A mass of English and colonial troops numbering 50,000 men was in the field, with Pitt behind them, and able, re-doubtable generals in the lead.   Throughout all of Canada there were but 82,000 souls, and the army to oppose the hordes of the English had not more than 7000 able fighters.

Montcalm, wise, brave, patient, foresaw the end; and, foreseeing it, prepared to make it as bitter for the enemy as he could.   Calling in the spare forces from the length and breadth of the province, he gathered them at Quebec for   the   defense. The juice came
to the root to nur-
ture it in its
periods of ex-
tremity. Only
a feeble resis-
t a n c e w a s
made to Gen-
eral Amherst
at Ticonder-
oga. Landing
where Aber-

THE FALL OF LOUISBURG   crombie had,

he quickly drove the French before him in a slight skirmish.   They abandoned the fort that Montcalm had held so stubbornly, overborne by numbers now. Four days later, on July 26, the French were on their way northward, leaving Ticonderoga behind them, smoldering and ruined by their own hand. They paused for a space at Crown Point, but abandoned that place even before the

English came up with them, withdrawing to the Isle aux Noix, in the River Sorel. That branch withered and fell.

Prideaux invested Niagara on July 10. A mortar burst and killed him. Sir William Johnson, for whom Lyman had obtained a baronetcy in a previous year at the head of Lake George, succeeded to the command. July 24, the French general D'Aubry, came in sight with 1400 soldiers whom he had gathered at Detroit, Venango, Erie, Lebœuf, for the relief of Niagara. In a desperate battle, the French were defeated, and on the next day Niagara surrendered.

Assailed as the vine was from without, its life was threatened from within its root at the same time. For years the province had been plundered by Bigot, sent from France, through the machinations of La Pompadour, as intendant, whose duty it was to act as the King's agent between him and the governor of the province, but whose practice it was to enrich himself and his gang of fellow-robbers at the expense of everything in the State. There was division of authority, too, between the governor, Vaudreuil, and the Marquis de Montcalm, in charge of the forces. Vaudreuil was weak, vacillating, jealous, without courage, and not wise in his judgment. Montcalm, strong, resolute, magnanimous, brave, perspicacious, was dragged down by the division of authority with the governor. Neither ranked the other in command. Vaudreuil feared Montcalm would succeed; Montcalm knew Vaudreuil would fail.

Knowing that the blow would be struck at the root within the year, Montcalm had prevailed upon Vaudreuil to call the settlers to arms. All through the spring and summer they straggled in. The militia was formed and drilled. Garrisons from outlying posts arrived and took place in the forces for the defense of the stronghold. Dejected, without hope, they were for the most part but unwilling soldiers. The refractory behavior of the governor gave them an excuse to complain against the rigor of Montcalm, so that the irregular army was bound together but ill.

But all was not dejection within the fortress. To the heart of Noah Stevens, a prisoner now for nearly four years, the rumored approach of the English brought exuberance of spirit, high hope, abundant gladness. It had been a weary, weary time. Bitterly had he reproached himself through all the days and months and years that had dragged across his soul for his desertion of Elizabeth in her time of need. He knew that the time of her service was approaching an end, and was struck numb and cold by the thought of the possible calamities to her that his fear conjured before his mind. He had had no word from any of his family since he had been captured; and knew not what might have happened to them. The bitterness between him and his father, the evil tricks of David, the helplessness of Elizabeth, all filled him with the gloomiest forebodings.

Nor was this all that had weighed upon him to make his period of imprisonment one of distress and misery. He suffered brutal injustice at the hands of the man who had command of the prison, Monsieur de Montreville. Monsieur de Montreville, a large man, advanced in years, with white hair that made his wickedness strangely unseemly, was noted among his own people for an evil mind and a vicious heart. His abuses of those under his charge had even grown at times to be the scandal of the hour, and only his close friendship with the rascally intendant, Bigot, backed by the pusillanimous support of the governor, had saved him from the wrath of Montcalm himself.

From the first, his treatment of Noah had been peculiarly atrocious. The man had taken a violent prejudice against the young American on sight. When he observed him among the other prisoners for the first time, his eyes grew large for an instant, and then narrowed down to tiny slits

WILLIAM PITT, EARL OF CHATHAM

through which Noah caught sight of a gleam as of fire. From that time every indignity was heaped upon him; he was confined in solitary quarters repeatedly for the most trivial things, or for nothing at all; he was contemned and reviled by the soldiers, who sought favor with their chief through their maltreatment of the one whom that tyrant openly disfavored; he was deprived not only of all semblance of privilege, and treated like a convict, but he was also denied the ordinary rights of a prisoner of war. The height of the injustice came when Noah was withheld by De Montreville during an exchange of prisoners, and kept in continued confinement, when, by all the rules of warfare, he should have been delivered over to his own people.

Noah was completely at a loss to account for the peculiar malignancy directed against himself, and had put it down in his mind as the whim of one half insane. By degrees he had learned to bear it, and in course of time the acute phase of hatred died down to a quiescent state from which it was aroused with greater and greater infrequency; but upon the approach of the English under General James Wolfe the man's fury against him had redoubled, so that he feared for his life. De Montreville was become a perfect fiend.

It was June 27. Great excitement ran through Quebec. The English, with twenty-two ships-of-the-line and 10,000 men, were at the Isle of Orleans, four miles below the city, where the river broadened out and the tide ran in from the distant sea. The problem confronting Wolfe was difficult. Montcalm, strongly intrenched, with an army nearly equal to his own, had disposed his forces below the city along the north bank of the river, which flows to the eastward past Quebec. On his left were the Falls of Montmorenci, a perfect defense, impassable. The river above Quebec was flanked by towering cliffs, which could not be scaled. A handful of soldiers could defend the few accessible gullies that led from the water to the Plains of Abraham, behind the city. The position of the French seemed impregnable. Properly defended, it would have been so.

Wolfe erected batteries on Point Levis, opposite the citadel, seizing the place with four battalions, under Monckton. General Monckton was in command at the Point.

Wolfe grew impatient. July 7 he attempted an assault upon the French lines opposite Montmorenci. At low tide the mouth of the river could be forded. Murray and Townshend with their brigades were to cross the stream. Monckton was to cross the river in boats and support the attack. Many of the boats ran aground. The soldiers fording the stream, restive under fire, moved

No. 10 Saint James Square, London, former Residence of the Elder Pitt

to the attack before Monckton could reach the scene. They were repulsed with heavy loss. Before the attack could be renewed, the tide ran in, and a threatening storm drove the force of Monckton back across the river. The plan was abandoned, after a loss of 500 men.

August came. Wolfe learned that Amherst had taken Crown Point and Ticonderoga. He thought that the commander-in-chief would surely push on to Montreal, and descend the river in the rear of Quebec. He waited to hear the sound of his guns on the Plains of Abraham. But Amherst loitered at Ticonderoga to construct a fleet of vessels to carry him down Lake Champlain, and to build a new fort on the site of the one destroyed by the French. It was October before he was ready to move against Montreal. It was too late in the year.

The guns of the warships and of the batteries poured red-hot shot into the city of Quebec, firing it, reducing parts of it to ruins. An attempt on the part of the French to destroy the fleet by means of fire-ships had failed, early in the operations, leaving the English in complete command by water. But there, with an impassable left and an unscalable right, the French army lay in its stronghold awaiting the winter to defeat the foe and dispel the danger. Wolfe, moving his army to Point Levis, fumed and fretted, waiting vainly for Amherst, dreading the winter.

The spirits of the French arose with the plight of the English. Vaudreuil became gay, and charitable toward Montcalm. That officer, encouraged and hopeful, never relaxed his vigilance, knowing with whom he had to deal.

As the situation continued, Noah began to lose heart. Standing alone, or in groups with the other prisoners where they were confined in the citadel, he watched the fiery shots of the English as they passed through the sky; watched the bursting flames in the Upper and Lower Towns; looked out upon the lines of the French and the inactive camp of the English and gave way to dismal thoughts. Help continued to arrive in the beleaguered city, more slowly now, from distant points on the frontier. *Coureurs du bois*, farmers, old and young, with grey beards or with cheeks yet innocent of hair, garrisons from far-away posts, Indians in war-paint, came, day by day, to add their mite to the defense. Noah's heart sank within him, for it was now nearly August, and he knew what the winter was in that clime.

One early evening he stood apart from the others, watching the fiery trail of the hot shots from the English batteries and the tongues of flame that leapt to greet them in the city, thinking sadly of Elizabeth; for her time of service was ended now, and he dared not contemplate what might have befallen her ere this.

The glare from burning buildings shone sick and lurid against the pallid sky, where traces of the day still clung. It lighted up the road and quiet river, revealing the works of the English, ever winking with scarlet eyes in the drowsy dusk. It shone dimly along the entrenchments of Montcalm, and ran red over the walls of the citadel, casting leaping shadows within. And all along the heavens ran the reverberating roar of the batteries.

A small company of troops had arrived from a little post far out on the stretches of Lake Superior. They had entered the citadel, and were being greeted by their fellow soldiers. Among them Noah saw an aged man, whose flowing white beard blurred red beneath the gleaming sky. The man was not of them. Several of them stood about him, treating him as though he were a prisoner whom they waited to deliver.

Loitering over toward the group, curious to see what manner of man this aged prisoner might be, welcoming a diversion from his dismal thoughts, Noah approached. Although his beard was long and white, and his hair fell about his shoulders, white with the dust of many years, the man was strong and stalwart still. Erect, agile, active, he stood lightly on his feet with head erect, a striking figure. His face was rugged and strong. In his brown eyes there shone a half defiance, and the light of an ever-present purpose. The whole bearing and attitude of the man were such as to arouse the interest and command the attention of all who looked upon him.

Those who had him in charge remained with him after their companions had gone to quarters, waiting for some one to come and relieve them. A door in the commander's quarters opened, and De Montreville appeared, walking slowly toward where they stood.

At sight of the huge figure of De Montreville approaching through the florid light, with the gigantic shadows of the wall dancing attendance upon his steps, the light in the old man's eyes grew into a fierce blaze and he trembled with an excitement that he did not try to suppress. De Montreville, ugly of visage, with his face hardened by evil thoughts, came to them. The soldiers departed.

The great figure paused abruptly. The light of the sky and the flames was upon his countenance. Noah, standing near, saw a sudden terror come into his eyes, when they fell upon the aged man, as though he had seen that which appalled his soul more than a ghost or the legions of his sins could have done. He dashed his hands across his face and looked again, his mouth astart with fright.

"Ha, you?" he cried hoarsely. "Whence come you?"

"Out of a hell of thy making, Monsieur de Montreville," replied the other, in a voice that shook the air, "to mock thee, and flaunt thee as the devil that thou art!"

"Thou canst not frighten me with thy loud howling, sirrah!" exclaimed De Montreville, his voice quavering. "Have a care of thy

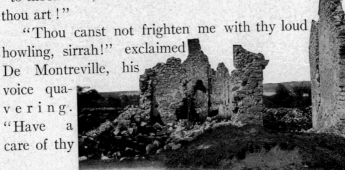

RUINS OF FORT TICONDEROGA

tongue, lest thou suffer for it. Remember that thou art my prisoner."

"Many long years have I been thy prisoner, and much have I suffered at thy hands, Monsieur de Montreville!" replied the aged man. "But thy time of reckoning is at hand; and I tell thee that thy sins will sit heavily on thy shoulders, thou perfect fiend! What hast thou done with my Marie, infamous villain, tell me that?"

The prisoner, trembling, white with fury, came close to the huge man, with hands clenched and teeth set together. De Montreville seemed to shrink in size as he drew near. He placed his hands before his face for an instant, muttering.

"Marie? What of her? What hast thou done with her?"

The old man thrust his head fiercely toward the down-turned face of the Frenchman, who brushed him aside.

"Mad dog!" cried De Montreville, in terror. "Do you come here to taunt me thus? Back! Away! Thou art a vain and frenzied fool, mouthing nothings! I 'll have thee bled for thy lunacy!"

"Lunacy, call you it?" cried the man. "How, then, of thy meeting with my brother? How, then, of the promise he gave you that he would come to my rescue, and thine infamous tale to me that he spurned me? How of thy vile lies to that pure and innocent woman, Marie Heuillet, defenseless against thy villany, whom you wed through your wicked deceptions? Am I dead, then? Was I shot and killed, trying to escape, having had no word from my brother? Base wretch! Thou 'lt find a lively ghost to track thee to hell! Stand not there thus and quake! Down on thy knees and crave a pardon of me, and of thy God!"

With a noise in his throat that was half a growl of rage and half a groan of terror, De Montreville turned on his heel and hurried into the open door of the commandant's quarters, leaving the other clutching his hands and breathing heavily.

Noah, at first a spectator held to the scene by little better than open curiosity, was by degrees quickened into a fierce and palpitating interest as the man went on upbraiding De Montreville. When he heard the name of Marie Heuillet it sprang into his memory as the name of the French girl of whom his father had told him in the story of his uncle George and the fight on the privateer *Impudence*. And the name of De Montreville itself, that had always called up in his mind some dim and intangible association which he had never before been able to fix he now recalled as that of the man who had brought word to his father many years before, and who had told his father at Quebec that the brother whom he sought was dead, shot trying to escape. The identification of the names; the circumstances revealed in the words of the aged man which he himself had heard narrated so often in another manner; his own faith that his uncle still lived, a victim of treachery, wormed swiftly within his mind into a wild fabric of thought that set him quivering.

When the old man was still pouring forth words of wrath upon the retreating figure of De Montreville, Noah leapt forward to him and grasped him by one tense arm. "You — you!" he cried, scarce knowing what he said. "You are George Stevens! God be praised! You are he!"

The aged man turned abruptly, looking upon him with eyes wide and mouth agape. "How know you who I am?" he exclaimed. "Who are you, to know me?"

"I am Noah, the son of your brother Elmer. I am your nephew, who has known these many years that you lived, and that we should find you at the last!"

Tears came into the brown eyes, quenching the fire of anger there. The man took off his hat, so that this white hair floated in the night air, and raised his face to the sky.

"God be praised!" he murmured. "My time has come!"

With a sob his heart had held pent up for twoscore years shaking his stalwart frame, he threw his arms about the young man, and clung to him, mute with joy.

CHAPTER XXVII

OUT OF MINE ENEMY'S HANDS

ACROSS the smooth and placid waters of the Saint Lawrence River the guns of the English battery boomed heavily at intervals, setting the heavens to rumbling and streaking the sky with lines of red fire, which burst into flames where they came to earth — angels of deliverance for the sore oppressed within the citadel. The knot that had gathered about George and Noah hung there dumbly till the two, conscious at last that they were the center of intrusive curiosity, withdrew beneath the shadow of a bastion, arm in arm, hearts alight with happiness, the end of long suffering.

"Are you not afraid of this man, uncle?" asked Noah, as soon as they had gained privacy. "He

GENERAL WOLFE

368

is utterly depraved. Do you not fear what he will do to you?"

"Nay, nephew — ah, how sweet the word! Nay, I fear him not. He is a coward. His conscience appals him, and he fears me; for he has these long years visited upon me an affliction that has made a criminal of him. He dreads the wrong he has done me, and at such a time as this has not the power to make himself safe from my vengeance. I have but to cry out upon him, and make known the infamy he has worked secretly upon me for many long years, and he would fall. His tenure here is slender. He dare not molest me, even if his conscience did not overwhelm him at last in his guilt."

"Come, tell me what has befallen you?" the nephew asked, eagerly, reassured by his uncle's speech. "Why did you not return to us."

"For forty long years this infamous man has held me unlawfully a prisoner among the French," George Stevens made answer. "Since the night that he waylaid me in my escape, having knowledge of it through treachery, I have been little better than the dead man he reported me to be, carried from post to post in many wildernesses, hidden from the sight of man, obliterated, through his devices."

"The unutterable knave!" cried Noah. "God send the time when I can lay these fingers about his hairy throat; and huge as it is, and slender though these may be from wasting here in prison, there is that within me which will give me strength to leave him limp and quivering at my feet. Curses fall upon his wicked head!"

"Nay, nurse not thy wrath, nephew. Vengeance is of the Lord."

"What villainous purpose had he, then, in so disposing of you?"

"My sweetheart had caught his fancy," went on the aged man, as they seated themselves in an angle of the wall.

"Marie Heuillet, whom I saved from more than death on the Frenchman which we took."

"Yes, yes; I know that tale, uncle," Noah interrupted, impatiently. "Forgive me sir, but I know of that. What of her and this man?"

"I will hasten to that," continued his uncle. "We loved. They brought me here to Quebec, from Deerfield. Hertel de Rouville, whom they call François le Vengeur, gave me over to this other devil, bearing malice against me for that I had fought so wildly on that wild night at Deerfield. They would not let me go back with the exchanged prisoners when the time came; for the malice of the Vengeur was still alive.

"Here, after seven long years, Marie found me, one day as I worked on the walls of the citadel. Ah, would to God I could go to her now and raise her drooping head to smile upon the light of Heaven!" The aged man choked with emotion, and was forced to pause ere he could proceed.

"She knew me, and our love lived, warmer than ever. We hoped soon for my release. Ah, we were happy then! Sir Hovendon Walker was on the way hither with a fleet, and De Montreville had borne a message from me to Boston, so that I expected deliverance from there. He was not then the villain that he became. She used to come at night to see me. Look! See yonder gate, beside the angle of the bastion there! There it was that we met, just without that gate. There was one among the soldiers whom I bribed, and he permitted me to see her."

His voice grew tremulous, and he was forced to wait once more.

"On a night, she came with news that Walker was wrecked," he resumed. "So we planned for my escape, waiting only till De Montreville brought word from my family; for we considered that perhaps it might not have

to be as we had planned. De Montreville had returned.
That night, as we talked, he heard us. And that night,
knowing what the effect of the news would be, he told me
that Elmer had repudiated me, and would not help me,
although Elmer had sent word that he was coming."

THE LOFT IN THE FARM HOUSE WHERE WOLFE LAY ILL FOR TWO WEEKS
BEFORE THE BATTLE OF QUEBEC

"How learned you that?" Noah inquired.

"Wait. I come to that. Hearing it, I thought some
evil chance had led to some error that prevented his succor,
and so I tried to get away to Marie. He knew my plans,
and intercepted me with soldiers at the Anse du Foulon.
They fired upon me, and I fell, desperately wounded. He
gave out that I was killed; but I recovered. Too great a
coward to kill me then, or perhaps moved by some com-
punctions, he smuggled me to a far post, saying that I was
a political prisoner.

"Telling Marie that I was dead, he at last prevailed over her to wed him; for, whatever his sins have made him since, he was not wholly bad then, and it was only the violence of his love for her that led him into his first great crime. But his sins multiplied, as you shall see.

"I was far away. Perhaps he thought to let me go to mine own people in time; but fear prevented him, and he kept me in the wilderness. For a long time I was moved from post to post at infrequent intervals. After many years, they came to move me more often; until it grew to be so that I was often not more than a week in one place. I thought then that some one, believing I lived, sought me, and hope came to me, for the first time in twenty-five years.

"Then passed a period of many years when ever-present hope, ever vanishing like a mirage before my sight, tore my soul into fragments. At last, two years ago, I was at a post by the foot of Lake Michigan, with only a few soldiers to guard me. One day there appeared in their midst a huge specimen of a man, with a face like the face of a cliff and a hand of iron, at sight of whom the Indians, of whom there were many about, fell down in terror, proclaiming him a god."

Noah uttered an exclamation of astonishment.

"A great man, with grizzled hair, and a face that never moved, and eyes that went through you like the flint of an arrowhead?" he demanded, hastily. "A man larger than any man I ever saw, save only De Montreville here?"

"The same!" cried George Stevens, surprised in turn. "The Indians called him Oneonto. Why, know ye aught of him?"

"It is he who brought me here!" cried Noah. "He saved me from the Indians at the battle of the Monongahela, where Braddock lost his life, and brought me here in safety.

Farm House where Wolfe Lay Ill before the Battle of Quebec. Saint Lawrence River and the Isle of Orleans in the Background

He knew who I was, and asked me if I knew aught of you. Who is this weird man? It is no marvel that the Indians dread him as an all-wise god."

"He saw you, then, and knew you?" exclaimed George, his surprise increasing. "That is how he knew, then, the things that he told me of Elmer. When he came among them, dropping down from the sky, it almost seemed, the soldiers, learning terror from the Indians, stood about gaping at him while he told me, speaking English the while, these things which I have related concerning the villanies of De Montreville, and that my people still sought me, believing me alive."

"And what of Marie?"

"Alas, that I know not, save that for some years De Montreville treated her cruelly until at last she fled from him, and that she still lives. Oneonto told me that, as well."

"Know ye not who the man is?"

"Nay; I have no thought about who he may be. He would give me no word of that; his face was like a stone cliff when I asked him."

"How came he to know these things that he told you?"

"I cannot say. I have marveled much. It is a blank mystery to me always."

"Think you Marie sent him to search for you?"

"I cannot believe it; and still, I have thought so."

"Did he seek to rescue you?"

"He only said that I should be free at last; and then he left me, vanishing as swiftly as he came. I am utterly at a loss to understand it."

"The man has ever filled me with a superstitious dread. But God be praised that we have come together at last!" added Noah, his joy transcending his wonder over the strange part which Oneonto had played in the lives of both of them. "We have now only to wait until this place falls into the hands of the English, when we may go home to our people. And what a joy shall I bring to them, too?"

So they sat far into the night, beneath the sky, laced over with ribbons of red fire, Noah telling the man who had been an exile for forty years of the events that had befallen his family, and the things that had taken place in the great world within the period.

But their hope of release did not grow with the days that came. Wolfe, lying across the river behind his batteries, seemed to have arrived at the last of his resources. Although he kept up a constant show of activity, transporting troops about as though intending an attack at various successive points, there had been no significant movement since the battle at the mouth of the Montmorenci.

The English officer himself, whose ardent spirit gave him no peace, was in the last extremity of hope. Burning with a bodily fever and a still fiercer fire of the mind, he saw before him the coveted citadel, inaccessible to troops and impregnable, towering on the heights above the city, with a broad river between him and it. The town was partially in ruins, and his guns knocked heavily on the door, but to no purpose.

However, it was not within the possibilities of his nature to give up. Looking out across the wide river, he saw through his glasses that at one point along the opposite cliff behind the city a path led up through a ravine filled with a dense growth of trees, and emerged at last on the Plains of Abraham. It was the Anse du Foulon. At the head of the ravine was a cluster of tents. French soldiers guarded it. But they were not many; and it was the only chance for a foothold on the other side of the river. He resolved upon the attempt.

It was September 12. The main fleet, under Admiral Saunders, appeared below the city. Montcalm, watching their activities, held himself in readiness to defend the trenches, believing that the British contemplated another assault upon his lines. Night came and found Montcalm resting upon his arms, patiently awaiting the event of an attack, secure in the consciousness that the cliffs to the west of the city along the river were well guarded at every penetrable point.

Night came, and found Wolfe with 3600 men aboard Admiral Holmes's squadron at Cape Rouge, ten miles above Quebec, ready to float down and make the perilous landing at the Anse du Foulon. It was 2 o'clock, and the tide beginning to ebb. There was a call for volunteers to go in the boat that was to land the first party at the foot of the path. In a moment the boat was full.

Foremost among them was Captain Hempstead, who, under Colonel Howe, was to assist in leading the men up the cliff. Scrambling into the boat as it lay alongside the men of war, he struck his foot against one of the men crouched in the bottom of the boat. The man, looking up, brought his face within the light of a lantern that just then swung over the rail of the ship.

"Egad!" cried Captain Hempstead, "If it is n't my little lover, the Acadian peasant, Monsieur Lawrence Averill, lieutenant of his Majesty's regiment, the Forty-Seventh Infantry. What seek you here on a night like this, lad?"

"I seek to serve my King; but if I find death it will matter little." replied Averill, gloomily. "What seek you?"

"Glory and a major's pay, lad," returned Hempstead. "'T is a merry chance we shall have for it, too, this clambering up high rocks like monkeys from Brazil. For my part, I could wish that I were not so cursedly brave as to try it."

They passed slowly down the stream. A sentinel challenged the boat at the head of the flotilla. Those in her knew from deserters who had come into camp that day that provision boats were expected down that night. Captain Hempstead answered the challenge, being able to speak the French tongue, telling the sentinel that it was the provision boats, and to have a care about letting the English hear. They passed on down the stream.

Close underneath the banks, running swiftly now on the tide, they looked up and saw a cleft in the skyline where the

SILLERY, WHERE WOLFE LANDED

lip of the cliff ran into the night. It was the place. The boat swung in, Lieutenant Averill leapt to the beach, followed closely by Captain Hempstead.

Wolfe, still in a fever, but borne up for the adventure by his spirit and determination, was in another boat. He recited Grey's "Elegy in a Country Churchyard" as they passed toward the shore.

"'The paths of glory lead but to the grave,'" he quoted. "I would rather have written those lines than take Quebec to-morrow," he said.

Vergor, in command of the Canadian guard at the head of the Anse du Foulon, was a coward, whom Montcalm had sought to deprive of rank, but who continued to hold it through the power of Bigot, a friend, and the influence of the governor, who upheld him for no other reason than that Montcalm was opposed to him.

Step by step, up through the path of the Anse du Foulon, past the spot where George Stevens had fallen before the bullet of De Montreville's soldiers nearly fifty years before, the daring body of men made their way into everlasting fame, to the destruction of French power in America and the succor of the man whose life had come upon so great a crisis in the place which they scaled.

The Canadian sentry at the top of the gully, hearing nothing, gave a shout of terror when he saw the head of Lieutenant Averill appear above the edge of the cliff, where the Anse du Foulon gave out upon it.   He fired his gun, and ran.   The other Canadians of the guard, awakening to find the British upon them, followed as fast as they might.   Lawrence, bounding after them, fired upon one who fled from his bed, dressed as he was, and brought down Vergor with a shot in the heel.

The Plains of Abraham were gained.   Wolfe had a foothold on the bank of the river, behind the city which he longed so eagerly to capture ere he died — for he felt that death was upon him, and had prophesied that he would fall in the fight.   All through the early hours of the morning the troops from the fleet came ashore, and wound up the defile, an interminable serpent, debouching upon the plain at last. Twelve hundred men came also from the other bank of the river, brought over by boats from the fleet.

When the grey of morning spread across the eastern sky, the British army was drawn up in red line of battle at the back door of the city — the fingers of William Pitt were grasped about the root of France's empire overseas, ready to drag it forth from the ground.

CHAPTER XXVIII

THE PATHS OF GLORY

THE Plains of Abraham were a grass-covered table-land, for the most part level, forming the roof of the plateau on the eastern end of which was the city of Quebec. At the right extended the inaccessible declivities of the Saint Lawrence River. Along the left of the plains ran a similar bluff, less steep and less high, which overlooked the meadows through which the Saint Charles River flowed, parallel with the Saint Lawrence.

DEATH OF MONTCALM

Reconnoitering the plains, Wolfe selected the spot where he would fight. Here the plateau was not a mile wide, and the ground in front fell away gently. Scattered about on the plain were patches of corn and clumps of bushes, but for the most part the field was clear of anything that might conceal an enemy or hide his advance.

Narrow as the heights were at the selected point, the lines of the English were not long enough to cross entirely from one declivity to the other, so that it was necessary to draw up two battalions, under Brigadier-General Townshend, at right angles to the end of the line, covering the left flanks along the Saint Charles River. Wolfe, with Monckton and Murray, commanded the front, where the pressure would come. In all, the force of the English was not more than 3500 men.

The situation of Wolfe was critical.   Defeat on the field
of battle where he had drawn up his troops meant the annihilation of the force, the failure of the operations against
Quebec, a temporary miscarriage of the Pitt programme,
and his own ruin as an officer.   In front of him was the
redoubtable, the brave and able Montcalm, with a force equal
in numbers to his own, many of its members fighting for
their homes, their country, their religion.   Behind him was
Bougainville, with 2000 soldiers.   If they should both fall
upon him at once, the danger would be great that he would be
crushed between the upper and the nether millstone.

Knowing all of these things much better than any one
else in the army, or among posterity, he walked the Plains
of Abraham behind the scarlet ranks of his soldiers, as serene,
as placid, as calm as though he threaded his way through
fashion's throng at Hyde Park.   He knew, and he had
weighed it well.   It was the one chance to grip up the root,
and he had taken it, being answerable to Pitt for the life of
the programme, and to God for the lives of his men.

Great was the consternation in Quebec when the inhabitants looked out and saw the red line drawn across the green
plains a mile away.   Excited cries ran from group to group
as the citizens came running from their houses in nightcaps
and slippers to gaze through the mirky atmosphere at the
terrifying spectacle. Dismay, despair, seized them.   The
army was lying along the trenches below the town, beyond
the Saint Charles River.   There were no defenders, and
the enemy was at the door.   But great was the joy in the
hearts of George and Noah Stevens when they heard that
the British were without.

Montcalm had passed an anxious night.   The guns of
the English ships, rumbling throughout the hours of darkness, had made him apprehensive of another attack along
his front.   He was all alertness, fearful lest some one should

fail him. And some one had. Vergor, the renegade, twice reprimanded for cowardice, had turned his back when he might have repulsed the entire British army. One craven soul lost her empire overseas to France.

In the dusk of the morning, he heard the firing of cannon above the town. It was the battery at Samos, firing on the British ships. Mounting a horse, he rode to the head-quarters of Vaudreuil, nearer to the city than his own. As he approached, accompanied by Johnstone, the country behind the town opened on their right, until they saw the British drawn up in line of battle along the crest of the heights.

Dispatching Johnstone to bring up the left from the trenches along the Saint Lawrence, where he had been awaiting the English all night, he himself hurried to Vaudreuil with the center. The right wing was already in motion. He had a few words with Vaudreuil, and pressed on across the bridge leading to Quebec, silently, with a look fixed on his face.

The army followed as swiftly as it could be brought up, pouring through the city and out through the gates of Saint Louis and Saint John a stream of white coats bearing upon its crest the sparkling bayonets of the soldiers of France. Montcalm, passing through the gates, was dumfounded. He had expected a detachment; he found an army.

He waited for Vaudreuil and the left, which he had ordered up. Neither appeared. The governor, for reasons which can only be surmised, not only remained where he was in the camp behind the trenches with 2000 or 3000 men, but he also stopped the advance of the left wing as it was marching past his position. Waiting in vain for Vaudreuil to come, and concluding at last that he had failed him in the crisis, Montcalm called a council of war.

All were for fighting at once. Bougainville's forces,

scattered along the
brought together and
rear for a number
it was feared by the
would fortify them-
Vaudreuil, with his
was not to be de-
they must, sooner or
held such a position
from all supplies by

Silently, grimly,
awaited the moment
All along that line
flapping of stand-
was no sound save
the squealing of the
landers. Three field-
commander of the
Montcalm, barked
air, and 1500 Cana-
upon them from
bushes and corn
were thrown out

river above, could not be
thrown against the English
of hours. In the interval,
French that the British
selves and be reinforced.
force of Canadians, they felt
pended upon. And fight
later, for the English now
that they cut Quebec off
land and water.

the red ranks of Wolfe
that they knew would come.
there was no stir, save the
ards in the breeze. There
the low hum of voices and
bagpipes of the High-
pieces which Ramsay,
garrison, had furnished to
at them through the dull
dians and Indians fired
behind clumps of
patches. Skirmishers
to check them. Along

WHERE WOLFE DIED VICTORIOUS

the British left, the Canadians climbed over the declivity, clinging among the bushes and firing from the lip of it upon Townshend's men.

It was 10 o'clock. Ramsay, within the garrison, would furnish no men at all, and only the three field-pieces from twenty-five that he had in readiness. Vaudreuil had clearly shown his intention of letting Montcalm take the responsibility of preserving her empire to France. Bougainville, it was thought, could not be brought up in time. The men were eager for the fight. In an hour they might sulk. The French drew up in line of battle, opposite the English.

George and Noah Stevens, in the excitement of the moment, made shift to clamber to the top of the ramparts, whence they could see the field, the red ranks of the English in the distance, the puffs of smoke springing incessantly from the cornfields and the bushes before their ranks, and the French line of battle, ready for the assault, gleaming white across the plain; their white coats shining in the sun as they slowly began to bear forward.

About the gates, along the walls, at whatever point glimpses could be had of what was taking place on the fateful field, the citizens of Quebec gathered in terror-stricken groups, whispering to each other, wringing their hands, moaning silently, in dire distress. It was not the dream of empire from which they dreaded to be awakened. It was home and religion, which were, they feared, being torn from them by the firm grip of Pitt, now strong about the roots of the French vine.

The wave rolled forward. They advanced with the war-cries of France in their throats, firing as they went. Only the answering call of the British came back to them, and the shrilling of the Scottish pipes. On moved the crested wave, rising, breaking all along its crest into a spindrift of smoke; the sting of it sharp all along the banks of red.

Close and closer they came, firing as they went. Creeping forward, catching now upon some obstructing clump of bushes for a moment, to rush forward past it in the next moment with added swiftness, bending among the undulations of the ground, ever forward swept the white-crested wave toward the scarlet banks before it, bursting ever into a stinging spindrift of smoke.

Silently, grimly, with set teeth and tense eyes, the English watched them come, closer and closer. Wolfe, passing along the right wing, gave courage to his men with low and even words, watching the crest of the advancing wave till the time should come. He was fighting for an empire that day; he needs must be cool with stakes so great.

It was scarcely past 10 o'clock. It had been but a few minutes since that white-crested wave rolled forward. It had seemed an age. They were within forty paces, closing upon that silent bank of red.

"*Mon Dieu!* Will they never fire, those cursed English!" cried a Frenchman, a huge white-haired man in the uniform of a captain, marching boldly at the head of his company. It was De Montreville, gone forth to fight.

Then, all along the British ranks burst forth a blast of flame and a mighty roar. Another volley followed the echoes of the first, as synchronous as the discharge of a cannon, and many times louder, a clattering fire springing up behind the crashing volleys.

Noah and George, standing upon the walls of the citadel, screamed with excitement as the sound of the blast swept past them, and strained their eyes to penetrate the smoke.

The smoke, clearing away, left a sight of horror. The wave had broken, and writhed in twisting torture along the face of the plain. Cursing, shrieking, gesticulating, the French battle-line was in a tumult of disorder and dismay.

"Charge! Charge! Charge!" The cry went along the

line of red. Down upon the broken wave swept the British lines, with bayonets fixed and broadswords catching the sun on their polished blades, sending it sparkling across the sky.

The white wave swept backward, a swirling, seething undertow. It caught the Marquis de Montcalm in its torrents, and bore him along. A shot passed through his body. He was supported on his horse by two men. They came in through the Saint Louis gate, their general withering in his saddle.

"*Mon Dieu! Mon Dieu! Le Marquis est tué!*" cried the people, assembled there, in the terror of despair.

"It is nothing; do not be troubled for me," replied the marquis, with a smile upon his lips.

Wolfe, leading the right wing, with a handkerchief bound about his wrist, where a bullet had torn through, was hit again. A third shot lodged in his breast. He sank to the ground. Soldiers gathered about him, awestruck.

"They run! They run!" cried one of them.

"Who run?" demanded Wolfe, rousing himself.

"The enemy, sir. Egad, they give way everywhere."

"Now God be praised, I will die in peace!"

In a moment his soul had gone. He died, knowing that the destiny of empire had been saved; that the institutions, the ideas, the light of republican England were forever afterward insured to the American continent, through him.

The rout was complete. In fifteen minutes that had happened which was to tear the root of France from the soil of America forever. Pitt's programme was working out to the end.

The English troops, victorious, could not press their victory to an immediate issue. The fugitives fled within the protection of the walls of the city, and could not be followed far; or went down across the Saint Charles meadow, a position too exposed on the flank for any pursuit. Bou-

The Plains of Abraham, and Monument marking Spot where General Wolfe Died

gainville might at any moment be down upon their rear; sleep dragged at their wits; they had been awake all night.

Within the city, all was horror and despair. The broken wave, swirling, muddied and stained with red, sucked through the town, leaving turmoil behind. With the fleeing ranks, the inhabitants bade hope farewell, and sat beside their houses to moan and pray. Frantic women rushed upon the panic-stricken soldiers, imploring them with arms about their necks to return and save the city. The soldiers only cast them off roughly, and redoubled their speed, to make up the time lost through such interference.

Montcalm was brought to the house of the surgeon Arnoux, whose younger brother, also a surgeon, examined his wound, pronouncing it mortal.

"I am glad of it," said Montcalm. "How long have I to live?"

"Twelve hours, more or less."

"So much the better. Then I shall not live to see the surrender of Quebec."

He sent advice to Vaudreuil, on request, but refused to give orders to Ramsay, commander of the garrison, who sent for them.

"I have much business on hand which must be attended to," he said, "of greater moment than your ruined garrison and this wretched country. My time is very short; therefore pray leave me."

At 4 o'clock in the morning, he died. They laid him to rest in an excavation made beneath the floor of the chapel in the Ursuline convent by an English shell, in a plain box of boards put together by an old servant of the convent.

Beside themselves with joy and exultation, George and Noah Stevens descended from the ramparts, when the retreating tide swept out of their sight behind a projecting bastion.

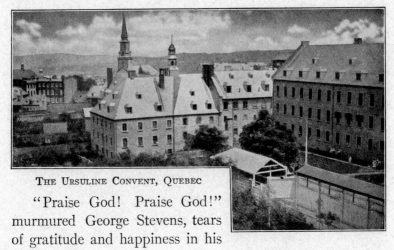

THE URSULINE CONVENT, QUEBEC

"Praise God! Praise God!" murmured George Stevens, tears of gratitude and happiness in his eyes. "After fifty years! After fifty years!"

The panic-stricken soldiers within the citadel paid no heed at the moment to their prisoners. Fugitives, streaming in, added to the tumult, and George and Noah might easily have escaped, had there been need to. Now, however, it would be only a question of hours until they should be freed by their own people.

They paused to watch the frightened stragglers come creeping in close to the walls, to fall shaking and panting on the ground under their protection.

They saw one, a man of tremendous size, making haste through the throng; but not in terror.

Seeing him, they turned and looked upon each other, dumb with astonishment.

It was Oneonto, bearing in his arms as though there were no weight in that which he carried, the huge form of De Montreville, his face writhing in pain, and unutterable fright in his eyes. He feared to go to his death.

Oneonto placed his burden close within the wall and stood erect beside it. His countenance was like the great rock, without emotion. without expression.

CHAPTER XXIX

THE LONG TRAIL HOME

SEEING De Montreville lying there, stricken mortally, gasping and staring before him in terror into the face of death, George Stevens hurried across the intervening space, with Noah following close behind.

In the face of Oneonto there was no sign. The fallen man, writhing under a sudden twinge that ran through the wound in his breast, saw them coming. Forgetting his pain, he half rose on his elbow, a greater terror still in his eyes, and cried out to George in a voice that was half a scream.

"Come not near me now to mock me in death!" he cried. "In God's name, forbear!"

"Forbear?" cried Noah, furiously, before his uncle could speak. "Did you forbear when this man lay wounded in the Anse du Foulon with a bullet of thy sending? Did you forbear through fifty years of miserable, intolerable exile from home and friends and love and hope?"

De Montreville turned a look of abject appeal upon the face of Oneonto.

"For the love of God, Pierre! let them not come near," he shrieked, holding forth one hand in the direction of the huge man standing at his side. But in the face of Oneonto there was no sign, and he moved not so much as a finger.

The wounded man fixed his eyes imploringly upon George, desperate for human charity. "Is it not enough for you that death is upon me, but that you must unhallow my last moments with thy bitter mockery?" he moaned.

George was about to reply, when Noah burst forth again in vindictive wrath.

"Nay, 't is not enough!" he cried. "Unless you had a thousand deaths to die, and I might send you to a thousand separate hells it would not be enough, thou fiend!"

MONUMENT TO WOLFE AND MONTCALM

"Thou art but a child, lad," made answer De Montreville, speaking more calmly. "Thou speakest as one who hath already escaped purgatory. Thou art young. When I was of thy years I had not sinned against man or God. Would to God I could be but given the trial again! But now the devil drags me down by the heels into the bottomless pit, and the man whom I have most grievously sinned against, comes to gloat upon it!"

"Nay, nay," said George Stevens, kneeling beside the stricken man and taking his hand, "I come not now to upbraid. I come not even to forgive. Thou art about to be in the hands of thy Maker. Before so solemn an event we should stand reverently, with bowed heads rather than in bitterness and anger. This, my brother's son, is young and hot against you. Heed him not."

Cringing at first under the touch of the grey-bearded man whose life he had so utterly wrecked, not knowing what he had to fear from him, De Montreville gazed upon him with wonder as he proceeded. Expecting malignant anger, bitter reproaches, he heard words of human sympathy, in a voice that sought to comfort. His terror of the aged man passed away from him, and with it his present terror of death.

He could not speak at first. The old man, from whose life fifty years had been torn out by him who now lay dying, knelt beside him pressing his hand gently, slow tears trickling down his beard, and the soft light of pity in his eyes. Noah, taken aback, stood staring. Oneonto made no sign.

"You forgive, then?" gasped the dying man.

"Nay, who am I that I should forgive?" replied the other, speaking softly. "Thy spirit is humbled; thou art no longer the harsh and wicked man who did me injury. Thy sins have been broken from thee. Thy naked soul stands before its God. Who am I that I should presume at such a time forgiveness?"

De Montreville uttered a cry of glad astonishment.

"Ah, monsieur," he said. "Thy kindness cuts me to the bone. Thou showest to me mine own enormity. *Mon Dieu!* but how shall I free my soul of its burden by craving your forgiveness, when you already forgive? Ah, I have done you so much evil. But how knew you what I had done unto you? How knew you of Marie?"

He asked the questions swiftly, with a sudden change in tone and mood, and anxious inquiry on his face.

George Stevens glanced up at Oneonto, who was gazing down upon the two impassively, and back at De Montreville, making no reply. De Montreville, following the quick glance, read the meaning of it. For a moment grief came into his countenance, but he swept it away with a sigh.

"Ah! 'T is well," he murmured, under his breath, speaking to himself. "An one will but be evil enough, he shall turn the whole world against himself."

Noah, impressed by the solemnity of the scene and made ashamed by the magnanimity of his uncle toward the man who lay dying, had removed his hat and stood back with bowed head. Oneonto, impenetrable, waited at one side, gazing down upon the group, devoid of visible emotion.

"Marie has suffered too," resumed the dying man, in a moment, catching his fluttering breath with an effort. "Know you aught of Marie?"

"Nay," her aged lover made answer; "only that she lived a short time since."

"Is she dead, then?"

"That I know not."

"Pray God she lives, and that you may go to her," exclaimed the Frenchman. "*Mon Dieu!* but I loved her once, cursed be the hour; for it brought misery to her and to thee, and destruction upon my very soul."

"Nay, say not that," said George Stevens, sternly. "Attribute it not to her that thou turnedst villain. 'T was the evil that slept in thy own heart, De Montreville."

"Ay, thou art right; though thou mistake my meaning," returned De Montreville, breathing more easily for a spell. "But, yes, I loved her! At the first she would have none of me, her heart being so full of you. And then, being all alone in the world with none to care for her, she came to me at the last, bringing what love she could find for a great, rough man. Ah! but I was tender with her at the first!"

"And in good time God saw fit that we should have a son. De Montreville with a son! *Hélas,* but I was happy then! And even she herself learned to smile with the little fellow rolling in her lap, making rogue's eyes at his father."

The white-haired man, kneeling beside the one who spoke, hung upon his words avidly, gazing deep into his soul as he went on. When the dying man spoke of his son, the other saw his eyes lift to the face of the huge man standing at his side with utter wistfulness within them. Turning, he saw Oneonto gazing down upon the scene with no trace of interest or understanding upon his stone-like face.

"Then it was that the devil clutched me firmly by the heels," the man groaned, speaking lower and more slowly with each breath. "Since then he has dragged me farther and farther down into the pit. I was very merry over our young son. Her heart was dead within her. It beat only for you. She loved the boy; but not as though he were our boy, but only hers. Joy she had none. God save my soul from death for it, but I blamed her! I quarreled with her. She only looked at me, saying nothing. Then it was that I went forth seeking elsewhere — for that —"

He ceased speaking, and closed his glazing eyes to shut out the memory. There was silence in the group, broken

THE HOME OF MONTCALM, QUEBEC

only by straggling shots from the field without, until he again began. He spoke now of other matters.

"I feared to let you go to your own people," he said. "Thou hadst such spirit! I kept thee far away for mine own peace; but it destroyed my peace utterly; for in the long nights the devil at my elbow would taunt me with it, driving me to new follies. As time grew over your disappearance, the greater was the difficulty of bringing you out of it. The devil had me!"

He shut his eyes with weakness, opening them with a start after a long silence.

"Ha!" he said. "I must hasten. Life slips fast. The devil tugs at my heels even now, to come with him to the pit.

Marie departed from me. I told her then that you lived, having pity on her; and she sent through me such a look that the devil will find the scar of it first on my soul. Years rolled around. I learned that there was one who sought you, I knew not whom. It was then that they bore you from place to place; for I could not tell what this man might want with you. At last, they told me what the man who sought you was like, and I knew who it was. My cup ran over. *Mon Dieu*, but I was grieved!"

Again he looked into the immobile face of the one towering above him. "At last they brought this lad here. The sight of him was like the sight of you, and was a cursed thing for my eyes. Well? What is there more? You came and frighted my soul. For the first time in ten thousand years, it seems I prayed God that night after I had seen you. It was too late! Now let the devil come for his own."

He paused. His tale was done. Breathing with great effort, he rolled his head to one side and closed his eyes, waiting. Suddenly, he opened them again with the expression of one whose mind has come upon that which it had for the moment lost. He looked at Oneonto once more, with a vast yearning in his gaze.

"Pierre! Pierre!" he whispered — for his breath had run too low for speech. "What of Marie? Does — she — live?"

"I know not."

"Pierre! . . . Pierre! . . . Find her! . . . Seek her out! . . . Monsieur — will go — to her — and tell her — that I died . . . penitent?" His eyes turned for the moment to George Stevens as he asked the question.

"Yes," murmured the grey-haired man, softly.

The eyes were back again upon Oneonto, who met their dying gaze, so full of agony, of pleading, of yearning, with the stare of a rock beneath the moon.

"Pierre — " More and more faintly came the voice, as the heaving of the breast passed into longer intervals and deeper inhalations. "Pierre —" Faint though it was, the word fell upon the ear as horrible as a scream, a sound that appalled them as they heard it.

"Pierre — Have you . . . no . . . word, . . . no . . . look for your — "

The voice failed. The last heaving of the chest passed out through the throat, a dry rattle. The head rolled back so that the eyes stared up into the faces of those gathered about, seeing nothing. Keenest eyes might have seen nothing in the face of Oneonto.

Gazing long upon the features of the dead man, which had fallen into an expression of peace and tranquillity, whence the look of evil had entirely departed, George

DE LEVIS

Stevens turned at last abruptly upon Oneonto and fixed him with his strong brown eyes.

"Thou, Oneonto, art Pierre, the son of Marie and this man," he said, as one who knew he spoke the truth.

Oneonto made no reply.

"Why did you seek me?"

"It was her will that I should."

"Why did she wish to find me?"

"To free you, and make amends for this man's sins."

"Why did you not take me with you when you found me?"

"I should have failed in the attempt. We should both have been killed. They had such instructions from the monster."

"Whom do you mean by 'monster'?"

Oneonto glanced at the body between them.

"If you have no greater regard for thine own father than to call him by such a name, sir, at least respect the dead!" exclaimed Noah, his eyes flashing reproach.

Oneonto made no manner of response. George Stevens resumed his questioning.

"You would have come back for me?"

"If we had failed in freeing you at Quebec, I should have brought her to you."

"Marie?"

Oneonto inclined his head in reply.

"But you came back?"

Oneonto made no response.

"Why not?" asked George.

The other merely shrugged his shoulders.

"Did she not wish it?"

"That happened which broke our plans," he answered, at last, evasively.

"You say you know not where she is?"

"When I returned from seeing you, she had gone."

"Where had she gone?"

"I know not."

"Where had she been?"

"In Acadia, at Grand Pré. The English took her."

"Have you searched for her?"

"Everywhere."

"Fear not!" cried George, "we shall find her yet. When they have done fighting here, we shall go in search of her, you and I, Oneonto! Pierre!"

"I shall remain at your side until we do," said Pierre.

Hayes Place, Bromley, Lord Chatham's Country House

The firing had nearly ceased. Along the British left the Canadians, lying in a thicket of bushes, had been picking off Highlanders, who had gone into the charge without their muskets, waving their broadswords, as was their use. But for the most part, it was a complete rout. Many of the soldiers came in at the gates of the city, and so on through and out the other side and over the bridge of boats that led across the Saint Charles River to their works beyond, not stopping until safe in the hornwork that defended the other side of the river. The remainder of the troops passed beneath the walls of the town, skirting it, descended into the Saint Charles meadows, and found their way across the bridge.

The English did not follow. Townshend, who had succeeded to the command upon the death of Wolfe and the wounding of Monckton, feared the approach of Bougainville from the rear, and stopped to fortify himself on the heights of Abraham.

Vaudreuil, the jealous governor, was some miles from Quebec at the time of the fight, moving with his forces toward the Plains of Abraham and complaining that Montcalm had not waited for him to come up — this in spite of the circumstance that he was three miles nearer Quebec in the beginning of things than the commander himself. In his little soul he was making shift so that it would appear that he had come to the rescue in case there should be a final victory, and could shirk the blame in case of a defeat.

Finding things in such a state, he was in abject terror and was for a capitulation surrendering the entire colony to the British. He and Bigot, the intendant, were engaged in drawing up such papers, when they were dissuaded by other Frenchmen. Distraught with the fear of the English, the governor that night ordered a retreat, which developed in an instant into a wild panic. With cries of fright, the French soldiers made the best of their way thirty miles up the river to Jacques-Cartier; making a broad detour about the English troops, where they lay in their trenches on the Plains of Abraham.

Deserted by the army, with short rations and a militia that had lost its desire to fight without the support of the regulars, Ramsay, the commandant of the city, was in despair. He waited four days in the hopes that De Levis would come to his aid, constantly urged by citizens meanwhile to give up to the foe. At last the British landed below the city and moved across the Saint Charles meadows, threatening an assault, and he surrendered.

Had he held out, his hope of De Levis would have been realized, and the work of Wolfe might still have been brought to nought. For the Frenchman, called from Montreal by the terrified governor, met and rallied the demoralized troops at Jacques-Cartier. He showed Vaudreuil that the French force would outnumber the English two to one, that they could at least so harass them as to give relief to Quebec, and prevailed upon that valiant gentleman to permit him to take the army back to the fight. He sent such word to Ramsay, but it came too late.

George Stevens and his nephew stood in the parade-ground of the citadel on the day of the surrender. They were as good as free, for the guard paid no further heed to them. Oneonto had gone to search through the city once more for Marie.

Drums beat without. The tread of soldiers made the ground rock beneath their feet. The gate swung open, and the British troops filed in. At the sight of the one who led the first company, Noah uttered an exclamation of surprise.

"Look!" he cried, pulling the sleeve of his uncle's coat. "See the one that leads them?"

"Ay! What of him?"

"That is Lawrence Averill, son of Rebecca, the daughter of your brother Elmer."

Averill, seeing Noah at the moment, came to them with a glad cry. There was much hasty inquiry and answer concerning the things that had passed in the world since the two had seen it; and when the ceremony of taking possession of the citadel was done, they went with Lawrence to his quarters, carrying with them Oneonto, who had returned.

It was a weary winter that followed in Quebec. The soldiers were not prepared for the cold, which came upon them in all the severity of the Canadian season. Rations were not scarce, but scurvy broke out and many died. The soldiers had to drag wood from the forest four miles away for their fires. The citizens were not hostile; the better class were hospitable to the English officers; yet it was a dreary winter on that bleak rock beneath the brilliant, blinding sky with the dazzling snow as far as the eye could reach.

George Stevens and Noah, burning with impatience to be on their way to the colonies, fretted and fumed through the long months, urging Oneonto to undertake to guide them to the Hudson River and so down to New York, long before the weather made it safe. He would not, and they chafed impatiently. They found little diversion in the company of Lawrence and Captain Hempstead, who was quartered with him.

April had come, and nearly gone. In a week Oneonto told them that he would take them on their journey. Then came the wild news that De Levis, the French commander, was coming to take Quebec. One of his soldiers had been rescued by English sailors in the night from a cake of ice, on which he had clambered, when the boat in which he was landing was upset. It was he who told that the French were coming.

The youthful and impetuous Murray, left in command by Townshend, longed for the glories of the name of Wolfe, and went forth to give them fight. He lost in a battle on the Plains of Abraham and withdrew within the battered walls of the town to await developments. De Levis, throwing up intrenchments, pressed the siege, hoping for the arrival of vessels from France with siege-guns and munitions. The English expected a fleet; and the reaches of the river below the city were watched with eager interest by both sides. The English fleet came first, and De Levis withdrew, first losing what vessels he had with him above the city through an attack by the British fleet. Great was the rejoicing in the beleaguered city. With the withdrawal of the French, their labors were ended.

Noah and his uncle prepared now to set out. Captain Hempstead, having urgent business in New York, obtained leave to go with them; and Lawrence, taking the infection at the last moment, was permitted by his superiors to join the caravan.

"By all means, young man, go home for a spell; and try to come back with a smile on your face," observed the officer who handed him his furlough.

In the middle part of May they set out on their long journey.

BEAUPORT VILLAGE, QUEBEC

CHAPTER XXX

AFTER MANY YEARS

A WOMAN lay asleep on her pallet in a little room that gave upon a small patch of struggling grass. Many years had worn their way across her cheeks. Her thin hair was as white as the pillow whereon her head was laid. The tiny crumpled hand that rested on the light coverlet might once have been soft and delicate and fair; the cheeks might have had the bloom of youth, the flush of love and pride; for there was that about them still which hinted of a beauty that was past and a loveliness not yet wholly gone.

The room in which she lay was bare, with scarce enough of furniture for the positive needs of the day and night. Two chairs, one of them wide-armed, the other straight, stiff, black; a small table of unpolished wood that shone white with soap and brush; a hearth patched with brick, clearly by the hand of a woman; some cooking utensils; and in the corner a spinning-wheel, formed the major part of the furnishings.

BIRTHPLACE OF WOLFE AT WESTERHAM, ENGLAND

Sitting beside the pallet where the sleeping woman lay, in the stiff, black chair, was a young woman of dark and striking beauty, who glanced frequently at the one who slept, with tender solicitude in her eyes. Her fingers flew rapidly over a frame of embroidery which she was engaged upon, and the figure, exquisite in design and tracery, rose beneath her deft touch. Other work she had in her lap, and still more on the table, some completed and some yet to be commenced.

The face of the young woman, who was scarce more than a girl, was heavy with sadness. One who could have read it aright would have seen that sorrow had clung for a long time to her heart, and that there was a tinge of bitterness in it. At times, bending over her work, she would sigh and look quickly at the one who slept, in some alarm lest she might have heard.

Although the aged woman slept, it was broad day. The door was opened wide to admit the gentle air that stirred without. It was late in June. But there was no sunlight in the room, it being on the north side of the house. In the area before the door was a willow tree, struggling feebly against the encroachments of civilization for life and a breath of air,— for the house in which the women had their room was in the city of New York, and already the population was crowding close about that part.

More than one evidence had already been given of the city's growth. It contained more than 12,000 inhabitants, Philadelphia having about 1000 more. King's College, which was to grow into Columbia University, had just graduated its first class of eight students, six years after its foundation. The neighboring towns shared this prosperity. Paulus Hook, now Jersey City, had, for example, thriven so that a ferry had just been established for the accomodation of its people. It was destined to greatness, even then.

The woman lying on the pallet stirred slightly in her sleep. The other laid down her work gently, preparing to wait on her. The sleeper stirred again, and opened her eyes. They were wonderful eyes, of a soft, lustrous brown; patient, brave, kind, tender eyes, in whose depths slept the memory of a great joy, and the ghost of much misery.

"How fares your work, daughter?" asked the woman, turning on her pallet, and watching her for a space.

"So well that I believe the saints themselves direct my fingers," answered the girl blithely.

"Well they may," returned the woman, with tears in her eyes. "God himself must weep to see thy fingers stretched thus between thy poor old mother and starvation."

"Tush, Nana, it is nothing," cried the girl, pursing her lips for emphasis. "Know you not how I used to do this thing for very love of it? Now I am just that much the happier, because I can do it for my Nana."

The other made no reply, excepting the tears that came into her eyes. For a long time they sat in silence, the one

WOLFE'S HOUSE ON THE BORDER OF THE ROYAL PARK, GREENWICH

on the bed watching the fingers of the girl and looking wist
fully into her face.

"Nana, would you like to go out and sit in the chair
beneath the willow tree?" the girl asked, at last. "It is
warm; I can take my work and we can sit there and talk,
as we used to do."

"Nay, Madeline; to-morrow we will sit there. To-day
I am not strong enough. Another day. It will, perhaps,
be warmer to-morrow."

There was another silence, broken by the older woman.

"Madeline," she said, "memory fails me. What year
is this?"

"This, Nana? Why this is the year one thousand
seven hundred and sixty, to be sure."

"One thousand seven hundred and sixty," repeated the
other. "How long, then, has it been since we used to sit
in our garden before our little cottage in Grand Pré?

"Why, that was five years ago, Nana," returned the
girl, looking upon her with a radiant face, though her heart
lay dead within her.

"Only five years, Madeline? Are you sure it is only five
years, dearie?"

"Why, yes, Nana. Sum it up for yourself. That was
the year one thousand seven hundred and fifty-five, and this
is the —"

"Nay, nay, my head cannot hold the figures, child. I
know it is but five years; though is seems deadly more."

Another pause. The aged woman gazed on the girl
absently, thinking of many things. Strive as she might,
the girl could not keep back a tear when she chanced to
glance upon her and saw her lying so.

"Madeline!" The woman, gazing afar, spoke softly.
"They have no trees here in New York, have they?"

"Why, Nana, of course they have. Don't you see this willow right in the center of our own door-yard?"

"Nay; I mean like the great pines and the hemlocks that sang to us through the night, that lifted their branches up among the stars and sprinkled the moonlight like spangles of silver about our little cottage. They have none like that here, have they, Madeline?"

"Nay, not hereabouts."

"And they have no birds?"

"Don't you hear the robin in the willow tree now, Nana?"

"Ah, that little slender song! But I mean the finches, and the song sparrows that sang swinging in the treetops when the sun hung low, and the thrushes that nested in the thicket over our wall. They have none like that, have they?"

"Only caged, and in the houses, Nana."

"I should like to see the trees again, and hear some birds singing in the forest.

"When you are stronger, Nana, I shall take you to where you shall hear plenty of them. But you must not speak of these things further, Nana. They do but make you sad. Please, sweet mother, do not talk of them more."

"Nay, child, they do not make me sad. My mind has run much upon them of late; and sometimes in my dreams I see the Basin of Minas, and the Bay of Fundy, and all our good friends, and the trees, and the flowers that grew in the hay-fields, and grow quite happy, feeling that I am soon to go back among them.

"Ah, but I forget! France, my dear France, is no longer in Acadia, and my King owns no foot of land there. And my people are scattered, all up and down this broad land; some of them are even in far-off Louisiana. I shall never see my dear France again, my child; I shall never see mine own people, or see Acadia again!"

The younger woman shuddered at the hopelessness of

the thought and sought to divert the other by showing the work to her.

"See, Nana, is not that a pretty S," she cried. But her mother paid no heed.

"Five years have we been here, and five years have thy fingers kept the soul in my body," the woman resumed, ruminating. "What a brave girl! What a brave girl!" A pause. "And in all that time we have not once seen any of our people! Verily, we are blotted from the face of the earth! How many of the living have I lost! There is my lover — ah, but soon I shall find him again; for surely he must be dead, now! And Pierre, and my husband, — God forgive him! for I cannot, — and my daughter's lover, and all mine own people — Nay, Madeline, how came we here to New York, when all on our ship went off at Boston? You have never told me that. Why was it we got not off with them at Boston? Why did you never tell me?"

The girl threw herself at the feet of the woman, spreading her arms across the coverlet, her head sinking between them, and her body shaking with sobs.

"Nana! Nana! Forgive me!" she cried. "I have not dared to tell you. I have been so wickedly selfish and stubborn and bad. It has all been my fault that you have suffered so, when you might have been with our own people, comfortable and cared for. Oh, I have done so wrong!"

The woman rose partially in her bed, stroked the hair of the girl, petted her cheeks, crooned over her as though she were but a babe, and comforted her that so at last she could look up into the other's eyes and speak.

"Nana! Nana! I would not get off at Boston, for I had learned that — "she hesitated, "that he had placed us on that boat so that we might be taken to Boston, and that he had arranged to have his mother take care of us. I could not! I could not! I loved him so! They were coming

LAKE GEORGE: THE LOCH LOMOND OF AMERICA

here with the ship. I made them bring us, swearing the captain to secrecy. I never thought! Oh, I never thought, save only of myself. But I could not bear to face his mother. Don't you understand? Don't you see?"

The other woman soothed away her agitation, caressing her and reassuring her.

"Nay, Madeline, I understand better than you could tell me; and I do not chide you," she said, lying back in her bed again; for the excitement had made her weak. "Thine was ever a high spirit, and you did what it bade you do. But you did wrong, — not on my account, but on your own. Listen, daughter, to the words of one who has learned her lesson. Love is not a thing to be thrown away for any whim. Against love there is nought which should have weight. Anger, bitterness, prejudice, unjust suspicions, jealousy, pride, yea, even patriotism should be borne under by love, for the soul's happiness. Only honor stands before it; and honor stands before it only because without honor first there can be no love."

The girl, still kneeling beside the pallet, wept as she had not wept for years.

"I know it! Alas, I know it now!" she cried.

"And there is one thing I would have you promise me before I die, Madeline," continued the woman, grasping the two hands of the girl.

"Oh, Nana, do not speak of dying. You will stay with me many, many years, to comfort me."

"Nay, do not be distressed. The time must come. I would but have your promise now."

"And that, Nana?" asked the girl, drying her eyes and controlling her emotions somewhat.

"That when I am gone, you will go forth and seek this man, Lawrence Averill, and beg his forgiveness, on your knees. For your own soul's good, and for his, as well, I conjure you to do this, Madeline as you love me, dear."

"I will, I will," cried the girl, weeping afresh at the thought of Lawrence Averill. "But what if he should not love me still?"

"He will love you forever. That no woman but an old woman can know; and I know it. Such love is given to few of us, and we should not cast it away; God help those of us who do! I have learned the lesson well!"

She raised her eyes to the low ceiling of the room, but their gaze went

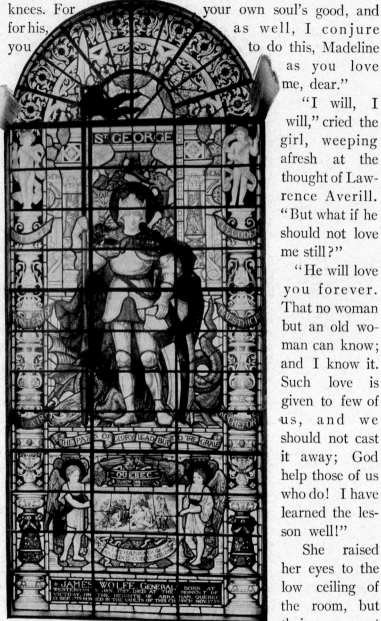

MEMORIAL WINDOW TO WOLFE IN SAINT ALPHEGE'S CHURCH, LONDON

far beyond as she lay back upon her pillow, seeking rest after the agitation of the scene. Presently they closed, and she slept again. Madeline, composing herself, went back to her work, and there was silence between them.

She had been sewing quietly for a long time, when a young woman came to the door, dressed in the garb of a servant of the rich, knocked, and entered softly. Her hair was the color of the golden leaves of autumn; her face was fine and beautiful; her hands were smooth and soft and tiny; but for her dress none would have thought her a servant. It was Elizabeth.

Madeline, glancing swiftly at her as she entered, glanced as swiftly away again to hide the traces of tears in her eyes. There was the appearance of friendship and companionship between them; for, as Elizabeth entered, she tiptoed to the pallet, and thence to Madeline.

As she bent over the back of the chair to kiss the girl, she saw the traces of tears in her eyes. She reached forward and stopped the hands that flew so busily across the cloth.

"Your eyes are tired. You must rest them," she said.

"Nay; it is not that," replied Madeline, not thinking, and releasing herself from the gentle grasp of the other's fingers.

"Let me see if it is not that, then. Come, look at me, and let me see."

Madeline would not look up. But she could not prevent a little gasp from escaping her, so affected was she by Elizabeth's sympathy.

"Come," said Elizabeth. "Come, child, you are all unstrung, sitting here forever. Jump up, now, and run about the street for a moment. I shall sit here with Madame de Barre while she sleeps. She will not mind, and I need not hurry home at once."

Madeline arose, determining her action suddenly, laid her work on the table and turned to go, without daring to utter a word; for her thoughts were heavy. Elizabeth, divining them, kissed her on the forehead as she passed, kissed her twice again to brush away the tears that started, and sent her out at last with a gentle injunction not to come back for an hour.

Sitting there by the side of the old woman, her own thoughts grew upon her, until the time slipped away without her knowledge. She was brought to present consciousness of it by the sound of Madame de Barre's voice addressing her in surprise. She faltered an explanation of her being there in place of Madeline.

"I came to get the work she is doing for my mistress, Mrs. Stevens, and —"

She got no further. At the mention of the name, Madame de Barre uttered a quick exclamation, and her whole body seemed to become electrified with excitement.

"Stevens! Stevens!" she cried. "What Stevens?"

"I am with the family of Mr. Robert Stevens," she said, looking as calmly as she might into the burning eyes before her. "He has with him his wife and a daughter, and his aged father."

"His father's name?" demanded Madame de Barre, quivering for the answer.

"His father is Mr. Elmer Stevens, of —"

"Of Virginia? *Mon Dieu!*" she cried, reading the answer in the bewildered expression of Elizabeth, who knew not what she had done. "*Mon Dieu!* It is he! Tell me, know ye aught of Elmer's brother, George? What of him? Does he live? Is he with them?"

Elizabeth, wholly at a loss to understand, shook her head. "He is not with them," she said. "Some of them think him dead; but one there was, a son of Elmer, who thought he lived, and went forth to look for him."

Madame de Barre half arose in her bed, supporting herself on one elbow. Stretching forth the other hand, tense and trembling, toward Elizabeth, she cried: "Tell them he lives! *Mon Dieu!* Tell them! Tell them to search him out in the last ends of the world, and when they have found him, let them tell him that Marie Heuillet awaits him here! For I! — I! — I am Marie Heuillet!"

The aged woman sank back on the bed, with a laugh that was all joy,

LAKE GEORGE BATTLE MONUMENT

but which sent chills creeping through Elizabeth's heart. She sprang to the side of the bed just as Madeline entered, distressed and anxious.

CHAPTER XXXI

A DAY OF REUNION

THE weather being warm, Mr. Robert Stevens, banker, member of the legislature, and man of affairs in the city of New York, sat on the porch of his house in the midst of his family, after the noon meal, until such time as it would be necessary for him to return to his counting-house. It was June; the air was still, and only a few birds twittering in the street broke the silence of the aristocratic neighborhood in which they lived.

There was Mrs. Stevens, beaming amiably upon her husband, as the wife of a banker should do to strengthen him against the struggles of the day. There was Margaret, exceedingly pretty, exceedingly spoiled, exceedingly happy in being miserably in love with Captain Hempstead. And there was an old, bent man, who sat in a large chair, his knees drawn up and his chin resting on the head of the cane thrust between his knees against the floor. His eyes were pale and watery, and were forever gazing into space. It was Elmer Stevens.

"Well, father," said Robert, raising his voice, "we have word that the French tried to take Quebec from us, and failed. It will not be long now before the whole of their possessions will be in our hands."

Elmer Stevens looked at him vaguely for a moment.

"Oh, yes, yes," he said at last, gathering his thoughts together. "Quebec. Of course. Yes, yes. So Quebec has fallen, has it?"

"No, no. I say that it is in our hands."

"Yes, yes. To be sure." His thin voice quavered.

"And I 've sent a messenger thither to look for Noah. General Washington told me, you know, that Noah was not killed at the battle of the Monongahela."

"Oh no, he was n't killed. Well, Noah was a good boy. He always was a good boy. It is strange that I thought evil of Noah. He was a good boy, and Elizabeth

A LOUISIANA BAYOU

is a good girl. I must see Noah, and tell him that I am sorry. I must ask his pardon. And I must tell Elizabeth. Where is Elizabeth?"

"Elizabeth has gone on an errand to get me some embroidery that the little Frenchwoman is doing for me, father," replied Mrs. Stevens, whose constant thought was to be tender to his old age, and who, pursuant to that object, took him into her domestic confidences to the greatest possible extent. "Those napkins, you know, father, that —"

"Mother, mother!" interrupted Margaret, in great

excitement. "Do look at that group coming down the road! Is that Captain Hempstead among them? Upon my word, I do believe it is. He ought to be ashamed of himself, if it is, coming down this street in broad daylight looking like that. I just won't speak to him. Yes, it is! It is! I never could mistake the way he pulls his mustachios. He does it so gracefully. What a disreputable-looking company. I do hope they won't stop here. And did you ever see such a huge man as that one behind? Why, one of them is cousin Lawrence, upon my word. Who is the other, I wonder; and who in the world can that perfectly fascinating old man be, with the long white hair and the beard?"

They all crowded to see the party of men that was approaching as the girl rattled on; even Elmer himself turning in his chair and straining his feeble eyes in the direction whence they were coming. The gaze of the party was as eagerly fixed upon those who stood on the porch, as they hastened along; Noah, George Stevens, and the captain ahead, and Lawrence and Oneonto as close behind at they could walk. Even Oneonto shared somewhat in the excitement.

"Noah! Noah! As I live, it's Noah!" cried Robert Stevens. "Father, father, Noah has come back! Noah is here!"

"Yes? Yes?" said the old man, rising in his chair and sitting down again. "Well, well. So it's Noah, is it? Noah always was a good boy. Yes! Yes! I shall be glad to see Noah."

Captain Hempstead, outstripping them all at the last, bounded to the top of the steps and carried Margaret forthwith to a remote corner of the porch. George Stevens, scarcely less active for all his years, was immediately behind. They stood apart, gazing blankly at him, to let him pass, waiting to greet Noah, who followed. George stood among them at last, an exile for nearly threescore years, tears streaming down his cheeks and through his beard, his hat in his hand, praising God in his heart for the moment that had come.

With a cry of joy, Noah leapt forward where his father, sitting in the chair, was staring dumbly at the white and bearded man.

"Father! Father! I am come back! Don't you know me? How come you here?"

"Oh, it's Noah! Why, Noah, I am glad to see you. Yes, yes, I am very glad to see you. How are you, Noah? How are you, boy? You were always a good boy."

Noah's heart sank to hear his father speak so feebly. George, standing beside him, looked down upon his brother with pity in his eyes. He had not known him until Noah spoke.

"See, father, whom I have with me!" cried Noah, again taking George's hand in his. Robert passed swiftly over to the chair, and laid his hand on his father's shoulder, fearing what might be the shock in store for him; for he had surmised who this white-bearded man might be.

Elmer, staring hard at George, whose features were obscured in his beard, looked blankly at Noah, and at Robert, and at the others, shaking his head.

"Come, look again, father. Don't you know who it is?" cried Noah.

There was a breathless moment, Elmer studying the face, with now and then a flash of memory passing over his own, only to flit away again; George standing before him, his heart swelling and tears streaming into his white beard.

"Why, I don't know," began Elmer, hesitatingly. "I don't know. I seem to know, though. There's something about the eyes,"— his face broke into eagerness, trepidation, hope,—"it is n't — no, no, it can't be. Is it, is it —" he dreaded to speak the word, his hope had gone so high,— "is it George?"

For answer the white-bearded man sank on his knees at the side of the chair, throwing his arms about the neck of the other, drawing him close. Those who had watched turned away, with one accord, as the two brothers, who had not seen each other for more than fifty years, who each knew nought of what had befallen the other in that time, embraced and mingled their tears of joy.

They were standing thus, overcome by the solemn joy of the reunion, when there was a light step at the door leading from the house, and Elizabeth came out on the porch, herself visibly agitated, not seeing who was there until she was well in their midst. Her eye, first falling on the two by the chair, wandered wonderingly about the group, and rested at last on Noah. For the life of her soul she could not have held the cry that burst from her lips.

Noah, hearing it, turned and beheld her, more beautiful than she had ever been, gazing upon him. He passed swiftly to her side, the others marveling. Covered with confusion, she placed one arm before her face, as though to ward off a blow, and with the other hand reaching out, sought to hold him away.

"Nay, Elizabeth," he cried. "However you came here, I know not; but I claim my privilege."

"Not here, not now," pleaded the girl. "Wait; I am a servant still."

"Your time is up. You should not be." He grasped her hand, the others too nonplussed to know whether they should interfere or find other occupation for their attention.

"I cannot stand it here and now, Noah," cried the girl, under her breath. "And I have weighty news to tell. Who is that grey-bearded man yonder? Tell me, who is he?"

Broadway, New York, at an Early Day

"That?" said Noah. "That is my uncle, whom I told you of, lost these many, many years."

The girl cried out again.

"Then I have great news for him!" she exclaimed. "I have found Marie, I have found Marie!"

She trembled under the accumulated excitements of the past hour, not knowing what to do. Noah, holding her hand, endeavored to soothe her, seeking in his mind for a way to break the word to his uncle. As they were standing thus, Captain Hempstead, who had been happily oblivious to all that went on about him, glanced over, saw Elizabeth, started, and came to them.

Placing himself before her, he swept the ground in a bow of ostentatious politeness, dragging his hat across the floor.

"My Lady Elizabeth!" he said, "I salute thee!"

Looking upon his face for the first time, Elizabeth gasped, and swooned into the arms of Noah. Robert Stevens, hastening forward with indignation flashing in his eyes, grasped the arm of the British officer.

"Out upon you, sir!" he exclaimed. "What mean you making a mock of my servant? Is it not enough that she should suffer the unseemly behavior of this rash young man without your adding insult too?"

"Insult be hanged!" cried the captain. "Do you remember the story I told you over your own table years ago of the noble lady of England who sold herself to America to escape the wicked ogre? This is she! She is no servant, but a daughter of a baronet. And who has a better right to salute her than I, who grew up with her, and who am the only blood-relative she has left in the world, now that the wicked ogre, my uncle, is dead."

"There, Robert, I always told you Elizabeth was a lady born," murmured Mrs. Stevens, breaking afresh into tears. "Oh, whatever shall we do? We are disgraced."

Robert, dumfounded, looked blankly about him. No one could find words save Noah, who called loudly for water.

Elmer, attracted by the disturbance, looked across from where he sat. "Elizabeth! Elizabeth!" he said. "What ails my Elizabeth!"

Margaret and her mother hastened to her aid, taking her from Noah's arms, who looked on helplessly as they worked

over her. At last she opened her eyes, looking about her in bewilderment and anxiety.

"There, there, Lady Elizabeth," murmured Mrs. Stevens in the most flattering tones of a hostess. "I always knew you were a lady."

"This seems a day of reunions," observed Hempstead, with an attempt at nonchalance. "Would you mind fetching me a glass of water, Lady Elizabeth? I find

DOORWAY OF A VIRGINIA COLONIAL MANSION

the excitement brings me a thirst."

Margaret laughed hysterically. The tension was broken. They lifted Elizabeth into a chair, all chattering at once, and Margaret ran to bring her brandy. She knew not what to do, sitting there bewildered. Noah, in awe at finding her a lady of the land, had no words. She looked up at him and smiled, reaching out her hand to his. He took it, timidly, uncertainly.

"Soho," said Captain Hempstead, observing it. "That

is the way the wind lies, is it? Very well, cousin. When
you seek for my consent, you shall get it readily enough."

"Whatever shall we do?" cried Mrs. Stevens, again
greatly perturbed.

"Do?" returned the incorrigible captain. "Why, the
best thing to do would be to call in a preacher."

And gathering them all together, he led them away, like
the soldier that he was, leaving Noah by Elizabeth's chair.

She looked up into his face, a radiance through all
her features. "Would you have my answer now?" she
whispered, resting her head against him.

His chin quivered. He could not speak. He leaned
over, and kissed her on the lips.

A COLONIAL MANSION IN VIRGINIA

CHAPTER XXXII

GREATEST OF THESE IS LOVE

MADAME DE BARRE lay no longer on a pallet in a corner of the room, dreaming of days that had gone. Instead, Marie Heuillet sat in the rocking-chair, with her face toward the door, a warm glow beneath the wrinkled velvet of her cheeks, her eyes alight with a vision of the days that were to come. She wore a dress of black silk, which had an underglow of brown through it from sheer age. At the neck was a piece of lace worked with her own hands half a century before.

Madeline, anxious, disturbed in spirit, hovered about her.

"Nana," she said, tenderly. "Don't you think you had better lie down again, dear? It has been so long since you sat up, I fear you will grow tired."

"Nay, Madeline, I will sit here," replied Marie, resolutely. "I will sit here to greet him when he comes. He must not think me feeble. He must not see that I am aged. I must be the same Marie when he comes; gay and light and happy. When he comes, I will arise from my chair and walk toward him. He shall not know."

"But, Nana, dear, he will not come for many days," pleaded the girl, filled with bitter grief over the infatuation of the woman. "'T was not an hour ago that Elizabeth went to them with word of you; and first they must seek him out. Perhaps they shall have to look a long way, and it will take many days."

"Nay, Madeline; he will come now. I know that he will. I know that God will not let me go without first seeing him again. God is too good."

428

"Ay, but, Nana, you will see him if it takes him many days to reach you." The heart of Madeline was wrung at sight of the woman sitting there, her face glowing with eagerness and love; and as she looked a cold fear struck her.

"Nay, sweet child, he must come soon. I have not long for this world. Else why do my thoughts run back to the woods of Acadia; to the hours I had with him, and to the earlier hours when I ran about my mother's knees in that

TOMB OF MARY, MOTHER OF WASHINGTON

garden of old France? Listen, Madeline; here was our chateau, with poplar trees leading to the door. There were many rooms; I remember them all well; and behind the house was a terrace, — nay, two terraces, one great and the second small, and at the foot of the second was a pond, with lily-pads floating upon it; and a fountain in the center; and I used to lie on the marble at the edge of the pond and peep in at the golden fishes that swam beneath the pads, frightened of them. And over there, — look, Madeline; can't you see the bower of roses over there, with the bench beneath, where my mother used to sit at her embroidery? And above the bower there drooped a yellow rose. The long branches of it, swinging in the soft breeze of summer, would pass close to her hand, and she would pluck one, and call me to her, and fix it in my hair, and kiss me, telling me how beautiful I was. Heigho! Perhaps I was! Below, in the bottom of the garden, we had wall fruit; and I had hares in a large close at one side against the wall. I played that the hares were my brothers and sisters, having none of my own; and at last one day I thought how strange it was that my brothers and sisters should be locked up, and so I let them out, and they ran away. Heigho! I see it all again. Every day I see further and further back along the path I have come; and when I get to the beginning, I shall find the end, and pass out into that whence I came, and whither we all go."

She paused, though her lips continued to move. Madeline, weeping, utterly disconsolate, stood behind the chair that her mother might not see.

A rush of hurried footsteps on the flags of the walk before the house! A creaking of the gate! A white-bearded man standing eagerly in the doorway! And Marie Heuillet arose to greet her lover, after many, many years.

Behind George Stevens, on the threshold, stood Pierre. She did not see him. His face was no longer immobile, inscrutable, passive. Across it played a thousand emotions as he saw his mother, feeble, near death, in the presence at last of that one whom she had loved all through life, and whom he himself had sought for many years. He was no longer Oneonto, "The Face of the Cliff," but Pierre, the son of Marie.

Another stood in the doorway, for a moment; but only for a moment. Lawrence Averill, borne thither by excitement alone, gazing into the room past the elbow of Pierre, cried out with surprise, and slipped quickly by the huge man, where Madeline stood dumb and motionless with stupefaction, her face set like one dead. She looked upon him vacantly and nodded her head, with a little nervous laugh. It was past belief. She feared that she had gone mad.

For one brief moment George Stevens held Marie in his embrace, supporting her. Then, finding her weak, he placed her gently in her chair, and drew up the other close beside her. There had been no word between them. There was no word that could be spoken at such a time.

For a long space their two elders gazed silently into each other's eyes, telling the story of twoscore years and ten. Even then there was no smile upon their faces. Their tale had grown past all human expression. They only sat and looked, soul upon soul.

"Marie!" he whispered at last, breathing forth the name in a sigh that was a prayer of thanksgiving.

"George!" she murmured, passing her withered hand tremulously across his brow and through his white locks.

They fell again into a long silence, ever telling the story with their eyes. Madeline, dazed and dry-eyed, was listening to the fervent words of Lawrence Averill with vague interest, not able to comprehend that they were of the moment and that he spoke to her. As he spoke, she found herself struggling against laughter. Her nerves were snapping, one by one.

"*Mon Dieu!*" she whispered to herself. "Will this never stop?"

Many times the two aged lovers essayed to speak, taking breath and moving their lips. But as often as they did, the moving lips passed into a smile, and the breath came forth again in a sigh of joy and peace and understanding.

At last Marie broke the sacred stillness.

"Have you suffered much, brave heart?" she asked.

"Nay, what I have suffered is of the past," he answered.

"Now let us think only of the happiness that is in store for us during the peace and quiet of our remaining years."

"I knew that God would bring thee to me at the end," she murmured, looking devoutly upon his glowing face. "Many years have I waited in hope and faith, and great has been the blessing that has come in my last day."

"Nay, beloved, speak not of last days," he replied.

CHRIST CHURCH, ALEXANDRIA, WHERE WASHINGTON WORSHIPED

"Thou shalt go with me hand in hand through many days. We shall be as little children together, happy and free of care."

"As God wills it, so let it be."

Lawrence Averill, seeing Madeline's face grow pale, led her forth into the air, where she rushed into the arms of Elizabeth, standing without with her lover, and wept upon her bosom, and so was comforted and brought to composure at last. Pierre stood ever in the doorway, a solemn joy over his features.

"Hast thou forgiven all?" asked Marie, after a pause.

"How could I forgive when there was nought to be forgiven? It was the hand of fate that struck between us, Marie."

"Many years have I sought thee, to repair the wrong, sending my son forth into the last corner of the world, with no creed but that thou wert to be found. Now him have I lost, too; but I have found thee!"

"Nay, he is here with us!" cried George, turning where Pierre stood in the doorway. "He found me, and brought me hither."

"He is here?" demanded Marie, half rising from her chair in her eagerness, "Where?"

He came forward in answer to a sign from George.

"Now are my blessings multiplied!" she cried. "Pierre! My Pierre!"

He knelt beside her, kissing her softly on the cheek, and she placed a withered hand on his bared head. There was long silence again. She wept now, joyously.

"Has he told you?" she asked, looking at George.

"I know all," replied her lover.

"You cannot know all. Surely, he has not told you of — that man?"

"I have heard all. From the lips of —"

"Of whom?"

"Of the man himself, as he lay dying."

"From De Montreville? Is he dead then? Tell me, how died he?"

Dread and apprehension were in her eyes. She looked in terror upon her son, half shrinking.

"Nay, mother," spoke Pierre. "He met his death in the field of battle."

The woman sighed with relief.

"I feared that I had taught the story to Pierre too well."

The huge man shook with emotion.

"God spared us that, mother," he said.

"Tell me, how died he?" she inquired of George, again.

"At peace with the world; and, I hope, with God."

"Was he humbled, then?"

"Ay, broken. With his last breath he craved forgiveness, and — I gave it him."

"'T was well."

Pierre, thinking of the last moments of his father, of the last dying, wistful plea of the stricken man, trembled with contrition, and looked imploringly at George, beseeching him with his glance. It was beyond need.

"He told you then, how he wooed me, telling me that you were dead."

George placed his hands over her lips, bidding her cease.

"Come, we shall not speak of things that are gone and past," he said. "Let us speak rather of the days of gold that are before us. Let us look upon the vision as we go walking side by side beneath the glory of the sunset sky, through the shadows of the twilight, and so into the gates of the West at last, hand in hand, where all is peace and happiness. Nay, Marie, shall we not be happy, indeed, after these years of trial?"

"Ah, beloved, I fear that the gates open to me already," murmured Marie, looking wistfully upon him. "A great light shines down the path. I am near the end."

"Nay, nay, Marie; you must not speak so. Now thou hast but begun to live."

"Ay; and perhaps it is better to go when joy is highest and hope most strong. God is good. He blesses me much. I must not complain if He takes me to Him now!"

"Marie! Marie! You shall not leave me now!"

"I am an old woman, beloved heart, worn with much waiting and many cares. It is rather for me to be thankful

OLD NEW YORK, FROM BROOKLYN HEIGHTS

that you came to me at the last, than to repine because my days cannot run on into the new happiness."

"You are not old, you are not old. Look, I am older than thou."

"Nay, let us not fill with bitterness the short space that is left for us together. Let us not grieve when we should be joyous."

He closed his lids briefly to control himself. When he opened them, Marie looked upon him with ineffable softness in her brown eyes. She reached her hand forth and rested it gently upon his. Tenderly, tenderly, he took and held it.

"George, my beloved," she said, speaking in a tone of marvelous melody. "Through all the years of my life, since thy warm young heart reached forth to protect me, friendless, pitiably alone, I have known no love but thine. It has been with me every hour of every day, and has brought me radiant dreams. Thy face has always been before me; the strength of thy spirit has made mine strong to await this day. To know at last that you live; to look upon you; to feel once more the warmth of thy love; to take strength from thy soul for the last hour; to tell thee with my passing breath of the great love I have borne for thee; and so to go into the Land Beyond, with my hand resting in thine and my soul leaning upon thine, is a happiness that makes the sorrows of the years that have gone vanish as the night mists melt before the rays of the sun."

There was no sound when she had done save the sobbing of the two men at her side. For a space she closed her eyes. Opening them at last, she looked about, searching the room. "Where is Madeline?" she said.

They called her, softly, and she came noiselessly, weeping silently, with Lawrence Averill by her side to support her in case of need.

New joy came into the eyes of Marie as they fell upon Lawrence. She looked a question at Madeline, who, for answer, fell upon her knees, reaching her arms across the aged woman's lap, with her bowed head resting between them.

Marie raised the withered hand that rested on the head of her son and held it to Lawrence, smiling a benediction upon him. Madeline lifted her face, suffused with tears.

"Mother, mother," she sobbed. "You must know — it will make you glad, I am sure. He is the grandson of his brother"; making her meaning clear by inclining her head first toward Lawrence and then to George. "They only now told me that. I thought it might make you glad to know it."

A sign of pleasure passed across the face of Marie, above the depth of joy and peace that was there.

"Verily, verily, my blessings are heaped upon me," she said. "I ever loved thee, lad, before I knew that thou hadst that precious blood within thy veins."

Lawrence bent forward and kissed her devoutly upon the forehead. Silence came once more upon them, and once again George closed his eyes to compose himself. When he opened them, Marie looked afar off.

"Madeline," she said, in a voice scarcely above a whisper. "Madeline, I told you this morning that my memory traveled the road backward over my life. I was in the garden, by the fountain, with a yellow rose in my hair, watching the fishes of gold dart among the lily-pads. Madeline, now I am in my cradle. Ah, it is many, many full years since that time! The plashing of the fountain, the hush of the breeze in the rose bower, the tender words of my lover, the whispering of the winds in the tall tree of Grand Pré, mingle sweetly in my ears with the lullaby of my mother. She calls to me now, Madeline, my sainted mother, with my father at her side. I go to her at the last, with my soul full, all the happiness of a lifetime gushing warm within it."

Silence, wonderful silence, for a pause.

"My beloved has come to me again; so the years will not be heavy now. My son, thou hast done well. Live

OLD DETROIT

in thy reward. We shall meet again. And if that man, by the grace of God, is there, him will I tell with a full heart of my great joy, and he will rejoice with me, contrite and humble. God's mercies are great!"

Further and further from them grew the gaze in her eyes. A gentle pressure on the hand of George. A quivering of the withered fingers that rested on the head of her son. A deep sigh of peace. A wonderful, wonderful silence. Her tale was done.

CHAPTER XXXIII

THE LAST SHUTTLE

BORNE up by a strength that had brought him through much tribulation, George Stevens conquered his grief and the bitterness of having lost Marie in the moment when he had found her, learning to be thankful that they had been brought together at last, and that she had gone on with her joy upon her.

In the end they buried Marie in a quiet nook of the plantation in Virginia, laying her tenderly and lovingly beneath a pine tree that overlooked the broad stretches of the Potomac, where the winds through the boughs whispered to her of peace beyond understanding, and the waters of the river rolled eternally down to the sea. On the grave they planted a yellow rose, nurturing it tenderly, till the branches of it swept the sod, filling the air with perfume and gentle memories.

Robert Stevens and Noah went to Virginia as soon as they could be spared, there to dispossess David, whom they found debauched and degraded; insolent, but making no struggle against the rights of George to the property. On the day following their first visit, when they went again to see him, he was gone, and the servants could give no word whither.

Relieved of this sorry burden, Noah Stevens took up and maintained the ancient position of his family in the Old Dominion, meeting with a glad welcome from the neighboring owners of estates, who rejoiced in the substitution of the gallant young fellow for his surly and selfish brother. The old friendship with General Washington and his gracious lady at Mount Vernon was resumed on the pleasant terms of the period, when the life led by the Virginia planters was, perhaps, the most gracious and delightful this country has ever known.

Noah went to New York in the autumn and returned with his bride, George and Elmer with them. Elizabeth, grateful for the changes fate had brought, became mistress where she had been servant, and lived rejoicing in the love of her husband and those that came to bless them with the years, ever cherishing in her heart the two old men who rambled about the lawns and sat through the long summer evenings on the portico, or joined the circle about the hearth when the cold winds of winter howled over the roof.

Elmer, taking strength from his brother, as he had ever done, came upon a happy and peaceful old age, leaning upon George to the last, glorying in his manhood, and thankful for the mercies that had come into his last days. In the end, death found George sitting beside the grave beneath the pine tree, listening to the messages it brought to him of her who had gone before. They laid him to rest at her side, secure against further parting through all eternity.

When Captain Hempstead returned to England and to private life, he took with him the petted daughter of the man of affairs of New York, who long graced his ancestral home with the arts of hostess that she had learned from her worthy mother. Madeline, forgetting at last her grief for one who had been to her a mother, whom she never knew to have been aught else, lived in Boston for many years with Lawrence Averill, the pride of Rebecca and the joy of Rebecca's son.

Oneonto, as they loved to call him still, his work done, fell quietly into the ways of peace upon the plantation on the banks of the Potomac, beloved of all, and the hero of the youth for miles around. When the grizzled locks grew thin and greyer, as he strolled through the woods with his gun he had at his heels the little toddlers of Noah and Elizabeth; and many were the tales he told them of wondrous ventures in the forests, of the Indians, of solitary nights, and the long trail that led him endlessly about the wilderness; and many were the feats of strength that he showed them in the quiet hours of his life.

The war waned from the fall of Quebec. In September, 1760, Vaudreuil surrendered Montreal to Amherst, and with it all that remained of the French claims to territory east of the Mississippi, from the Great Lakes to Lake Pontchartrain. For three years the war continued at sea, afar from the shores of America, until the French sued for peace, the English being everywhere victorious on the water. Thus faded the French dream of empire before the masterly mind of William Pitt.

In the spring of 1760, the Indians of the Cherokee nation captured Fort Loudoun in northeastern Tennessee, massacring the garrison or taking them into captivity. They were driven into the mountains by a punitive expedition, and forced to capitulate.

Other troubles arose among the Indians. The English, ignorant of the character of the savages, neglected and abused them. Their hatred of the race, instilled into them by many years of French influence, smoldered until it broke out in the Pontiac conspiracy.

Pontiac, chief of the Ottawas, the great leader of the red men, sought to reunite the tribes and drive out the invaders. Gathering the Indians of all nations from the Alleghanies to the Mississippi into the plot, he set May 7, 1763, as the day of destruction. He himself was to take Detroit, the most important of the frontier posts.

His plan was betrayed by an Indian maiden, the sweetheart of Major Gladwyn, who commanded there. When

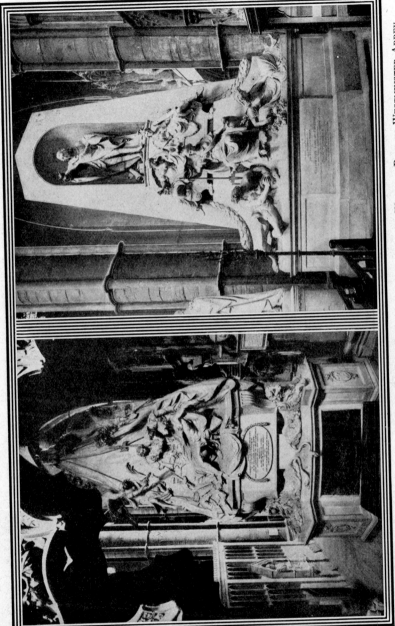

Monument to General Wolfe in Westminster Abbey   Monument to William Pitt in Westminster Abbey

the Indians came to carry out their purpose, they found the
foe ready for them, and failed. Other parties were more
successful, and by the middle of summer every outpost save
Fort Pitt, Niagara, and Detroit had fallen. Alarmed at
last by the magnitude of the undertaking, and the fear of

THE FIREPLACE IN THE MOUNT VERNON MANSION

British wrath, they sued for peace, restoring the posts and leaving the country to the English.

Thus the forms of enlightened England were introduced into the country which had been threatened by the institutions of France, which still clung to the practices of the Middle Ages. Thus the progress and civilization which had grown in the colonies was admitted to the vast territories of the Middle West, and the foundation was laid for the marvelous common- wealth which now extends from sea to sea.

THE STABLES AND FAMILY COACH, MOUNT VERNON

And the colonies, — what had they gained? They had gained freedom from the fear of the French and Indians to go their own way in the paths of peace. They had gained room to develop and room in which to grow. But more than all they had gained knowledge of war, and confidence in their own powers. They had learned that in unity lay strength; a lesson which they were to put to good purpose in the years soon to come.

So came it to pass that the destiny of these United States was rescued from the alien and unfree civilization that threatened it, while France, too long pledged to an absolute monarchy, lost by that very fact her footing upon the most magnificent domain of the modern world. England maintained her foothold in apparent security until the attempts of George III to force absolutism upon the freemen of the English-speaking race in free America led to greater liberty and even to independence. The cure for every ill attendant upon freedom is always more freedom.

THE END

INDEX

INDEX

A

ABENAKIS
Dudley renews old treaties with, 45
massacre at Spurwink, Purpooduck, and Berwick, 46
with French descend on Deerfield, 59–67
ravage New England, 74–75
harrass outlying settlements, 129
defeated and chieftains slain, 129

ABERCROMBIE, JAMES
Pitt sends Lord Howe as second in command to, 325
commanding force in America, 325
defeated by Montcalm at Lake George, 326
retires to Fort George, 329
sends Bradstreet against Fort Frontenac, 329

ABRAHAM, PLAINS OF, see **PLAINS OF ABRAHAM**

ACADIA, see also **NOVA SCOTIA,** and **GRAND PRÉ**
yielded by France to England, 118
description of, 275–277
character of inhabitants of, 275–277
Lawrence devises oath inhabitants cannot take, 301
France asks England to give inhabitants time to remove effects, 307
England refuses request, 307
England transports inhabitants, distributing them from Maine to Georgia, 307
number of inhabitants transported, 308
Burke's opinion of England's conduct toward, 309–310
Longfellow immortalizes sufferings of, 310

AFRICAN SLAVE TRADE
under treaty of Utrecht, 118–119
Queen Anne and King Philip engage in, 119
increases, 129
in southern colonies, 129
in New York and New England, 129
Carolinas center of, 129
to be forbidden in Georgia, 155

AIX-LA-CHAPELLE, TREATY OF, see **TREATY OF AIX-LA-CHAPELLE**

ALBANY, NEW YORK
on northern route from Atlantic to Mississippi Valley, 189
colonial convention meets at, 245
Franklin's scheme of union proposed at, 253–254
Loudoun loiters at, 318

ALEXANDRIA, VIRGINIA
Washington organizes expedition at, 209
Washington drills force for second expedition at, 228

ALEXANDRIA, VIRGINIA — continued
Braddock calls convention of colonial governors at, 259
campaign plans adopted at convention, 259
Christ Church in, where Washington worshiped, picture of, 432

ALLEGHENY RIVER
on southern route from Atlantic to Mississippi Valley, 189
Bienville takes possession of territory surrounding in name of Louis XV, 190–191
Masin builds fort at junction of French Creek with, 192
Washington and Gist crossing, picture of, 202

ALTAMAHA RIVER
Oglethorpe builds Fort Darien on, 166

AMELIA ISLAND, FLORIDA
at mouth of Saint John's River, 166
Oglethorpe builds Fort Saint George on, 166

AMERICAN COLONIES,
effect of treaty of Utrecht upon, 125
industries spring up in, 125
agriculture flourishes, 125
shipbuilding increases, 125
towns grow more important, 125
culture more general, 125
newspaper published, 125
books printed, 125
slavery in, 129
people read, study, and think, 125
mutual protection leads toward unity, 126
lose their charters, 126
become Crown colonies, 126
governors thrust upon them, 126
oppose oppressive measures, 126
effect of war with Spain on, 166–167
effect of capture of Louisburg upon, 179
France puts chain of forts about, 192–193
lack of unity among, 206–207
Franklin's scheme of union for, 253–254
colonies reject it, 254
size of army in field against France, 356

AMHERST, SIR JEFFERY
commands force against Louisburg, 325
anchors before Louisburg, 325–326
sends Wolfe to storm and silence batteries, 326
Louisburg surrenders to, 326
in full control of English forces in America, 355
to proceed against Ticonderoga, 356
French abandon Crown Point, 356–357
builds ships and new fort at Ticonderoga, 363
Wolfe expected at Quebec in vain, 363

ANNAPOLIS, NOVA SCOTIA
feeble English garrison, 275
general view of fort and cannon, **281**

ANNAPOLIS, NOVA SCOTIA — *continued*
the old French cave, picture of, 286
the old sally-port, picture of, 287

ANNE, QUEEN OF ENGLAND
on the throne, 20
portrait of, 21
right to the English throne denied by Louis
XIV, 21
of royal blood, and a Stuart, 21
James Stuart proclaimed king by Louis XIV
while Anne is on throne, 22
bed in Hampton Court, picture of, 23
Louis XIV acknowledges as Queen of England, 118
engages in slave trade, 118–119

ANSE DU FOULON
a gully leading from Saint Lawrence River to
Plains of Abraham, 376
Wolfe espies, 376
Howe commands leading regiment in assault
through, 377
details of assault and capture of, 376–379

ANTWERP, HOLLAND
denied deep water in harbor, 118

ARMSTRONG, JOHN
annihilates Delaware Indians, 316

ATLANTIC OCEAN
routes from Mississippi Valley to, 189

AUGUSTA, GEORGIA
Oglethorpe builds fort on Savannah River at,
166

AYER, SAMUEL
fights the French and Indians near Haverhill,
75
kills thirty of them, and is himself killed, 75

B

BEAUPORT VILLAGE, QUEBEC
picture of, 403

BEAU SÉJOUR
fort at, captured by English and colonies, 277

BERWICK, MAINE
Indian massacre at, 46

BEVERLEY
chronicler of age in Virginia, 228
quoted from regarding hospitality, 228

BIENVILLE, CELORON DE
establishes trading-post at New Orleans, 188,
295
sent by Galissonière, 190
voyages up Saint Lawrence, 190
at Fort Frontenac, 190
crosses Lake Ontario, 190
on Lake Erie, 190
reaches Lake Chatauqua, 190
lands at Jamestown, New York, 190
on Allegheny River, 190
takes possession of territory between Niagara
and Allegheny River, 190–191
builds Fort Rosalie at Natchez, 295
treats with chief of Natchez, 295

BIGOT
intendant of New France, 357
creature of La Pompadour, 357

BIGOT — *continued*
duties and pleasures of, 357
keeps Vergor in place, 378
wishes to surrender to Wolfe, 401

BLACK RIFLE
Indian chief, 262
Braddock insults, 262

BLOODY POND, NEW YORK
Indians massacre garrison of Fort William
Henry at, 321–322

BOMASEEN
chief sachem of Abenakis, 45
French seek to incite against English, 45
killed by English, 129

BOSCAWEN, EDWARD
British admiral, 301
commands fleet that transports Acadians, 301

BOSCAWEN, NEW HAMPSHIRE
Indians attack, 169

BOSTON, MASSACHUSETTS
News Letter of, first American newspaper, 73
expedition against Louisburg assembles in,
179
news of capture of Louisburg arrives in, 179
Louisburg Square in, commemorates victory,
180
Franklin's birthplace in, picture of, 245

BOSTON *News Letter*
first newspaper printed in America, 73
contains list of Deerfield prisoners exchanged
73

BOUGAINVILLE, LOUIS ANTOINE DE
commands French forces in rear of Wolfe, 381
forces scattered along Saint Lawrence River,
383
unable to come up in time for battle of Quebec,
383

BRADDOCK, EDWARD
portrait of, 227
arrives in the Chesapeake Bay with army,
239, 259
calls convention of colonial governors at
Alexandria, Virginia, 259
prevails upon Washington to accept staff
appointment, 260
treats Washington with insolence, 261
tells Franklin vainglorious plans, 261
snubs Franklin for suggesting caution, 261
Franklin obtains horses for, 261
abuses colonies and colonials, 261
at Fort Cumberland, 261
insults Black Rifle, 262
snubs Washington for suggesting caution, 262
insults Washington, 263
his field of battle, picture of, 263
wounded, picture of, 264
crosses the Monongahela, 265
his road on crest of Laurel Hill, picture of, 266
story of his defeat, 267–273
his retreat, picture of, 269
has five horses disabled under him, 270
is mortally wounded, 270
his road, east of Fort Necessity, picture of, 271
Fiske's characterization of, 272
character of, 272

BRADSTREET, JOHN
colonel under Abercrombie, 329
captures Fort Frontenac, 329

BRAMBRIDGE
warden of Fleet Prison, 136
tried for murder and acquitted, 136

BRIDGE'S CREEK, WAKEFIELD, VIRGINIA
George Washington born in, 132

BUNKER HILL
attack on Louisburg just thirty years before, 177

BURKE, EDMUND
characterization of England's treatment of the Acadians, 309–310

BURTON,
lieutenant-colonel under Braddock, 270
leads charge, 270

C

CABOT, JOHN
explorer, 188

CANADA, see also NEW FRANCE
English attack upon planned, 76–77
Vaudreuil governor of, 77
France colonizes, 188
England threatens communcation of, with Louisiana, 189
Galissonière governor of, 190
Bienville takes possession of Ohio Valley for, 190
Duquesne governor of, 192
sends out Masin to occupy Ohio Valley, 192
Vaudreuil, the younger, governor of, 239
Dieskau sails with reinforcements for, 239
crops fail in, 329
population of, 356
Ramsay surrenders Quebec, 402
De Levis beats Murray on the Plains of Abraham, 404
Vaudreuil surrenders Montreal, 442
title to, passes to Great Britain, 442

CANSO
French from Louisburg capture fort at, 169
expedition against Louisburg arrives at Bay of, 171
Warren reaches, 170, 172

CAPE ROUGE
Wolfe and Holmes at, to assault Quebec, 377

CAROLINAS, see NORTH CAROLINA and SOUTH CAROLINA

CASCO BAY, MAINE
picture of, 47

CASCO, MAINE
Dudley renews Indian treaties at, 45
Indian massacres at settlement about, 46

CASTIN, JEAN VINCENT DE L'ABADIE, BARON DE SAINT
successfully defends Annapolis against Massachusetts attack, 75

CAUGHNAWAGA, QUEBEC
picture of, 36
ancient walls of, picture of, 37

CAUGHNAWAGA, QUEBEC — continued
bell blessed for chapel of Saint Louis in, 42
old stone chapel at, picture of, 43

CELERON, see BIENVILLE, CELERON DE

CHAMPLAIN, SAMUEL DE
explorer, 188

CHARLES II OF SPAIN
under influence of Louis XIV, 22
bequeaths kingdom to Philip of Anjou, 22

CHARLES VI OF AUSTRIA
wills throne to Maria Theresa, 168
war over succession to, 168

CHARLESTON, SOUTH CAROLINA
Johnson and the militia at, picture of, 119
review of militia at, 127
people call convention to nominate governor at, 127
Moore elected governor at, 127
two governments at, 127
Oglethorpe reaches, 161

CHARLESTOWN, NEW HAMPSHIRE
Indians attack, 169

CHEROKEES
massacre garrison at Fort Loudoun, 442
are driven to mountains and captured, 442

CHURCH, BENJAMIN
attacks French settlements on Penobscot, 75

COLUMBIA UNIVERSITY
established as King's College, 406
graduates its first class, 406

CONNECTICUT, COLONY OF
sends 500 men on Louisburg expedition, 169

CONNECTICUT RIVER
lumber camp on, picture of, 44
winter on the upper, picture of, 49
scene on, picture of, 53
fertile valley of, picture of, 54
North Haverhill and, picture of, 57
Rouville leads Deerfield prisoners up valley of, 68
at White River Junction, picture of, 69

CONTINENTAL CONGRESS
held at Albany, 245
Franklin proposes scheme of colonial union at, 253–254
called under order of Lords of Trade, 256
treats with Six Nations, 256
details of plan for colonial union Franklin proposes to, 256
does not accept it, 256

CORNBURY, EDWARD HYDE, LORD
governor of New York, 52
misappropriates public money, 52
his removal petitioned for, 52

CROGHAN, GEORGE
makes treaty with Miamis at Piqua, 187

CROWN POINT, NEW YORK
Mohawks carry war to French fort at, 179–180
Johnson enrolls Mohawks against, 259
French abandon, 356–357

CUMBERLAND ISLAND, GEORGIA
at the mouth of Saint Mary's River, 166
Oglethorpe builds Fort William on, 166

D

DARIEN
  captured by Vernon, 167
D'AUBRY,
  French general, 357
  defeated by Johnson near Niagara, 357
DEBTOR'S PRISONS
  account of, 134–138
  parliamentary committee investigates, 154
DEERFIELD, MASSACHUSETTS
  common and old well in, picture of, 39
  Deerfield Street in, picture of, 41
  Deerfield settlement (*from an old drawing*),
    42
  Williams clergyman at, 46
  Williams's house in, picture of, 61
  attacked by French and Indians, 59–67
  door of Williams's house, picture of, 64
  victims of massacre in, burial place of, picture,
    66
  prisoners from, taken to Quebec, 71
  news of massacre at, reaches Boston, 71
  graves of Williams family in, picture of, 72
DELAWARES,
  annihilated in Pennsylvania, 316
DETROIT, MICHIGAN
  picture of old fort, 439
  Pontiac to take, 442
  plot betrayed, 442
  Gladwyn commandant at, 442
  held by English, 445
DIESKAU, JOHN ERDMAN, BARON
  sails for New France with reinforcements, 239
  defeated and captured by Lyman at the foot
    of Lake George, 315
DINWIDDIE, ROBERT
  portrait of, 181
  sends Trent with expostulations to French,
    187–193
  sends Washington to Presqu' Isle, 187, 193
  organizes Ohio company, 190
  his messengers, picture of, 191
  sends commission to Washington, 207
  does not await action of Burgesses, 207
  house occupied by, picture of, 267
DRAKE, SIR FRANCIS
  explorer, 188
DUDLEY, JOSEPH
  meets Indians at Casco, 45
  renews old treaties with Indians, 4·
DUNKIRK, FRANCE
  harbor to be filled up, 118
DUQUESNE DE MENNEVILLE, MARQUIS
  governor of Canada, 192
  sends Masin to take possession of Ohio Val-
    ley, 192

E

ENGLAND
  claim of, to North America, 188
  threatens communication between Louisiana
    and Canada, 189
  demands destruction of French forts in Ohio
    Valley, 239
  sends Braddock to Virginia with army, 239

ENGLAND — *continued*
  denies request of France to give Acadians
    time to move effects, 307
  transports Acadians, 307
  Burke's opinion of England's treatment of
    Acadians, 309–310
  Pitt's first campaign against the French, 325–
    326
  Pitt's second campaign against the French,
    355–356
  size of army in America, 356
  France sues, for peace, 442
  owner of North America, 442
ENGLISH HARBOR, CAPE BRETON
  name changed to Louisburg, 168
"EVANGELINE"
  Longfellow immortalizes Acadians in, 310
  ideal portrait of, 310

F

FAIRFAX, ANNE
  kinswoman of Lord Fairfax, 132
  daughter of William Fairfax, 132
  married to Lawrence Washington, 132
FAIRFAX, THOMAS, SIXTH BARON
  Greenway Court, picture of, 121
  William Fairfax manages estate of, 132
  befriends George Washingtom, 132–133
  owns land in Shenandoah Valley, 132
  sends George Washington as surveyor, 133
FAIRFAX, WILLIAM
  kinsman to Lord Fairfax, 132
  manages estate of Lord Fairfax, 132
  father to Anne, who is married to Lawrence
    Washington, 132
FISKE, JOHN
  characterization of Braddock, 271–272
FLEET PRISON, LONDON
  described, 135
  Brambridge warden of, 136
  picture of, 141
FLORIDA,
  Oglethorpe builds forts in, 166
  Oglethorpe attacks Spanish forts in, 160
  Oglethorpe abandons intention of taking Saint
    Augustine, 166
  Oglethorpe takes two minor forts in, 166
FORBES, JOHN
  moves against Fort Duquesne, 329
FORKS OF THE OHIO, *see also* PITTSBURG
  picture of, 205
FORT CADDIS, FAYETTE COUNTY,
    PENNSYLVANIA
  last of frontier forts, 331
  picture of, 331
FORT CUMBERLAND,
  picture of, 213
  Washington meets returning advance guard
    at, 222
  at mouth of Willis Creek, 261
  Braddock at, 261
FORT DARIEN, GEORGIA
  Oglethorpe builds, on Altamaha River, 166

FORT DUQUESNE, *see also* PITTSBURG
  built at forks of the Ohio, 206, 223
  Forbes moves against, 329
  Grant ambushed near, 329
  Washington leads advance against, 329
  French flee and burn, 329
  English name it Fort Pitt, 329
  name changed to Pittsburg, 329
  ruins of, picture, 298
  Washington raising flag at, picture of, 336

FORT EDWARD
  built by Johnson on the Hudson, 315
  Webb at, 321

FORT FRONTENAC
  Bienville at, 190
  on northern shore of Lake Ontario, 192–193,
    329
  Bradstreet captures, 329
  in British hands, 355

FORT GEORGE
  at head of Lake George, 329
  Abercrombie retires, 329

FORT LE BŒUF
  Masin builds, on French Creek, 172
  Masin falls ill at, 196
  Washington visits, 196
  Saint Pierre commander of, 196
  Washington hospitably treated at, 196
  site of Washington's camp near, picture of, 197
  old spring at, picture of, 207

FORT LOUDOUN
  in northwestern Tennessee, 442
  captured by Cherokees and garrison massa-
    cred, 442

FORT MASSACHUSETTS
  Vaudreuil captures, 180

FORT NECESSITY
  night council at, picture of, 217
  Great Meadows and, picture of, 217
  only field in which Washington ever surren-
    dered to a foe, 129
  Washington builds, at Great Meadows, 223
  Braddock buried near, 271

FORT NIAGARA
  part of French system of occupation, 193
  picture of, 194
  Prideaux proceeds against, 355
  invested by Prideaux, 357
  Prideaux killed, 357
  Johnson succeeds to command against, 357
  French defeated near, 357
  surrenders to Johnson, 357

FORT NUMBER FOUR, NEW HAMP-
    SHIRE
  Indians attack, 169
  Vaudreuil fails in attack on, 180

FORT ONTARIO, OSWEGO, NEW YORK
  picture of, 324

FORT OSWEGO
  Shirley strengthens, 315
  taken by Montcalm, 317
  Webb turned back from relief of, 317–318
  Loudon keeps Shirley from relief of, 317–318
  in British hands, 355

FORT PITT, *see also* PITTSBURG *and*
    FORT DUQUESNE
  Fort Duquesne taken and name changed to,
    328
  name changed to Pittsburg, 329–330
  Washington raising British flag at, picture,
    336

FORT ROSALIE, NATCHEZ, MISSISSIPPI
  site of, picture of, 290
  built by Bienville, 295

FORT SAINT GEORGE, FLORIDA
  Oglethorpe builds on Amelia Island, 166

FORT WILLIAM, GEORGIA
  Oglethorpe builds on Cumberland Island, 166

FORT WILLIAM HENRY, NEW YORK
  captured by French, 317
  Webb turns back from relief of, 317, 321
  ruins of, picture, 319
  Monro in command of, 321
  attacked by Montcalm, 321
  holds out four days and surrenders, 321
  Montcalm grants safe conduct to garrison,
    321
  drunken Indians massacre garrison, 321

FRANCE
  incites Indians against English, 45–46
  Queen Anne's War, 45–46, 59–67, 74–76
  treaty of Utrecht concludes war, 118
  King George's War, 168–180
  treaty of Aix-la-Chapelle concludes, 180
  claim of, to North America, 188
  establishes New Orleans, 188
  maintains trading-post in Mississippi Valley,
    189
  holds chain of forts about English colonies,
    192, 193
  forces Washington's retirement and surrender
    at Fort Necessity, 226–227
  holds gateway of the west, 226
  only flag in Mississippi Valley that of, 239
  proposes neutrality of Ohio Valley, 239
  sends Dieskau to Canada with reinforcements,
    239
  asks England to give time to Acadians to
    remove effects, 307
  possessions remaining, 355
  size of army in America, 356
  abandons and destroys Ticonderoga, 356
  abandons and destroys Crown Point, 356–357
  battle of Plains of Abraham ends American
    power of, 380–389
  Ramsay surrenders Quebec, 402
  Vaudreuil surrenders Montreal and all of New
    France, 442
  reasons for losing New World, 447

FRANKLIN, BENJAMIN
  portrait of, at the age of 20, 244
  birthplace of, in Boston, picture of, 245
  description of, 245
  Philadelphia's statue to, picture of, 247
  advises Morris, 250
  his scheme of union, 253–254
  details of plan of colonial union, 256
  hears Braddock's vainglorious plans, 261
  suggests caution and is snubbed by Brad-
    dock, 261

FRANKLIN, BENJAMIN — *continued*
saves Braddock's expedition by procuring horses, 261
builds defences in Pennsylvania while Washington is in Virginia, 317

FREDERICKSBURG, VIRGINIA
picture of, 127
Mary Washington's home in, picture of, 127
Mary Washington's monument in, picture of, 128
Washington starts for Presqu' Isle from, 193
built on Lawrence Washington's estate, 228

FRENCH AND INDIAN WAR
reasons for, 186–187, 188–189
beginning of, 223, 317
Braddock defeated and slain, 267–273
Shirley marches to Oswego and back again, 315
Lyman defeats and captures Dieskau at foot of Lake George, 315
Washington repulses French invasion in the Shenandoah Valley, 316
Delaware Indians annihilated, 316
Franklin builds defenses in Pennsylvania, 317
Montcalm captures Fort William Henry, 317, 321
drunken Indians massacre at Fort William Henry, 321–322
Loudoun's expedition against Louisburg fails, 318
Pitt's plans for first campaign, 325–326
Amherst and Wolfe capture Louisburg, 325, 326
Abercrombie defeated by Montcalm at Lake George, 326
Bradstreet takes Fort Frontenac, 329
Forbes moves against Fort Duquesne, 329
English take Fort Duquesne and call it Fort Pitt, 329
Pitt's plans for second campaign, 355–356
French abandon Ticonderoga, 356
French abandon Crown Point, 356
Johnson defeats D'Aubry at Niagara, 357
Fort Niagara surrenders to Johnson, 357
Montcalm rallies at Quebec, 357
Wolfe arrives before Quebec, 361
Monckton's assault on Quebec fails, 362
Amherst builds new fort at Ticonderoga, 363
Wolfe gains Plains of Abraham, 376–379
battle of Plains of Abraham, 380–389
Ramsay surrenders Quebec, 402
De Levis defeats Murray on Plains of Abraham, 404
Vaudreuil surrenders Montreal and all New France, 442
France sues for peace, 442

FRENCH CREEK
Masin builds Fort Le Bœuf on, 192
Masin builds fort Venango at junction of Allegheny and, 192

G

GAGE, THOMAS
fights at Braddock's defeat, 266–267

GALISSONIÈRE, ROLAND MICHEL BARRIN, MARQUIS DE LA
governor of Canada, 190
sends Bienville to occupy Ohio Valley, 190

GASPEREAUX
fort at, captured by English and colonists, 277

GASPEREAUX RIVER
mouth of, picture, 303

GERMANS IN AMERICA
settle in Georgia, 162

GEORGE III OF ENGLAND
seeks to force absolutism on free America, 447

GEORGIA, COLONY OF
land granted by King to Oglethorpe, 151, 154
intends settling with insolvent debtors, 151
asylum for worthy debtors, 154
Shaftesbury works for, 154
land grant for, described, 154
how to be governed, 154–155
land of, to be held in trust for the poor, 154–155
Jews to be admitted to and Catholics debarred from, 155
slavery to be prohibited in, 155
Parliament supports, 155
immigrants for, land at Charleston, South Carolina, 161
Oglethorpe founds Savannah, 161–162
compared to Pennsylvania, 162
Moravians and Salzburgers come to, 162
more Englishmen arrive in, 162
John and Charles Wesley come to, 162

GIST, CHRISTOPHER
makes treaty with Miamis at Piqua, 187
sent out by Ohio company, 191
objects of expedition, 191
crosses Blue Ridge and Shenandoah Valley 191
passes the Alleghenies, 191
swims the Ohio River, 191
reaches Wogstown, 191
in Indian council at Wogstown, 191
threatened, 192
penetrates blue grass region of Kentucky, 191
returns to Virginia by the Roanoke Valley, 191
guide to Washington, 193
left behind by Washington, 198
Washington and, crossing the Allegheny, picture, 202

GORHAM,
colonel at Lomsburg, 175
attacks Island battery, 175

GORHAM, MAINE
Indians attack, 169

GRAND PRÉ, ACADIA
description of, 275–277
meadows of, picture, 275
character of inhabitants, 275–277
village of, picture, 278
the old church, picture of, 285
old well and willows, picture of, 293
old road at, picture of, 300
inhabitants driven into the church, 300
Minas Basin, picture of, 302
mouth of Gaspereaux River, picture of, 302
old French willows and road, picture of, 305
left desolate by transportation of inhabitants, 307–309
inside the old church, picture, 309
Longfellow immortalizes, 310

GREAT MEADOWS
picture of, 219
Washington pushes forward to, 222
builds Fort Necessity at, 223
Washington surrenders at, 226

H

HALF-KING
where Washington met, picture of, 216
sends messengers to Washington, 222
Washington meets, 222

HALIFAX, NOVA SCOTIA
Loudoun sails for, 318
Holbourn arrives at, 318

HAMILTON, ANDREW
acting governor of Pennsylvania, 192
Masin sends word to, 192

HAVERHILL, MASSACHUSETTS
North Haverhill and Connecticut River,
picture of, 57
Rouville leads expedition against, 75
massacre at, 75

HENNEPIN, LOUIS
explorer, 188

HERTEL DE ROUVILLE, see ROUVILLE

HOBBY
indented servant, schoolmaster, and sexton,
130
keeps old field school, 130-131
teaches George Washington, 130

HOLBOURN
British admiral, 318
joins Loudoun at Halifax, 318

HOLMES
British admiral at Quebec, 377
takes Wolfe and his men to Cape Rouge, 377

HOWE, GEORGE AUGUSTUS, LORD
portrait of, 325
half-cousin of King George, 325
sent as second in command to Abercrombie
in America by Pitt, 325
killed at Lake George, 326
monument marking burial place of, picture,
326
defeats French in skirmish at Sabbath Day
Point, 326

HOWE, WILLIAM
British colonel under Wolfe, 377
commands advance guard in assault on Quebec, 377

I

INDIANS
Abenakis, 45, 59-67, 74-75, 129
Tuscaroras, 128-129
Yeamanses, 129
Iroquois, 179-180
Pigwackets, or Pequots, 129
held as slaves, 129
Oglethorpe treats with, 162
Stockbridge, 179
Mohawks, 179-180, 259
Twightwees, 187
Miamis, 187
Washington in council with at Pittsburg, 193

INDIANS — continued
Half-King helps Washington, 222-223
Natchez chief makes treaty with Bienville,
295
Delawares in Pennsylvania annihilated, 316
massacre at Bloody Pond, 321-322
Cherokees massacre garrison at Fort Loudoun,
442
Cherokees driven to mountains and captured,
442
Ottawas, 442
Pontiac unites the tribes and makes war, 442
Pontiac captures outposts, 445
Pontiac sues for peace, 446

INSOLVENT DEBTORS, see also DEBT-
OR'S PRISONS
condition of, in England, 134-137
Oglethorpe would settle Georgia with, 151
condition of, investigated by Parliament, 154
asylum for, in America, 154-155

IROQUOIS
Tuscaroras ally themselves with, 179
sent against Canada, 179-180

ISLE AUX NOIX
in River Sorel, 357
French occupy, 356-357

ISLE OF ORLEANS
picture of, 90

J

JACQUES-CARTIER, QUEBEC
De Levis meets and rallies demoralized soldiers at, 402

JAMES II OF ENGLAND
flees from wrath of English people, 21
driven out when William of Orange comes, 22

JAMESTOWN, NEW YORK
Bienville lands at site of, 190

JERSEY CITY, see PAULUS HOOK
ferry established to New York, 406

JOHNSON, NATHANIEL
governor of South Carolina, 126
and the militia at Charleston, picture of, 119
calls review of militia at Charleston, 127
orders militia to disperse, 127

JOHNSON, SIR WILLIAM
governor of New York, 259
portrait of, 259
to enroll a force of Mohawks against Crown
Point, 259
Johnson Hall, Johnstown, New York, picture
of, 260
moves against Crown Point, 315
builds Fort Edward, 315
goes into camp at foot of Lake George, 315
Dieskau defeated and captured by, 351-316
made a baronet, 315, 357
succeeds Prideaux in command at Niagara,
357
defeats D'Aubry, 357
Fort Niagara surrenders to, 357

JOHNSTONE,
French general under Montcalm, 382
Montcalm sends, to bring up left wing, 382

JOHNSTOWN, NEW YORK
  Johnson Hall, picture of, 260
JOLIET, LOUIS
  explorer, 188
JONCAIRE
  seizes and fortifies English trading-post at
    Venango, 196
JUMEL MANSION
  picture of, 339
JUMONVILLE
  force under, surprised by Washington, 223
  is killed, 223
  grave of, picture, 222

K

KANAWHA RIVER
  Ohio company granted land on, 190
KENMORE, VIRGINIA
  home of Washington's sister, picture of, 204
KENTUCKY
  Gist penetrates blue-grass region of, 191
KING GEORGE'S WAR
  reasons for, 168
  French attack Canso, 169
  Indian attacks in Maine and New Hampshire,
    169
  New England attacks Louisburg, 169–180
  Louisburg surrenders, 177
  Indians sent against Canada, 179–180
  Vaudreuil captures Fort Massachusetts, 180
  ended by Treaty of Aix-la-Chapelle, 180
KING'S COLLEGE
  to grow into Columbia University, 406
  established in New York City, 406
  graduates first class, 406
KITTERY, MAINE
  Home of Pepperell, 170
  Pepperell's house in, picture of, 171

L

LABRADOR
  yielded by France to England, 118
LAKE CHAMPLAIN
  pines near, picture of, 150
  on historic, picture, 253
  a glimpse of, 254
  Ticonderoga on, 355
LAKE CHATAUQUA
  Bienville reaches, 190
LAKE ERIE
  Bienville crosses, 190
LAKE GEORGE
  Shelving Rock at, picture of, 313
  Lyman defeats and captures Dieskau at foot
    of, 315
  Howe wins skirmish at Sabbath Day Point,
    326
  Montcalm defeats Abercrombie at, 326
  the Loch Lomond of America, picture of, 411
  battle monument, picture of, 417
LAKE ONTARIO
  Bienville crosses, 190

LA SALLE, ROBERT CAVELIER, SIEUR DE
  explorer, 188
LAWRENCE, CHARLES
  lieutenant-governor of Nova Scotia, 259
  to complete conquest of province, 259
  in conference with Boscawen and chief justice
    of Nova Scotia, 301
  devises oath French inhabitants cannot take,
    301
LEE, THOMAS
  portrait of, 186
  president of Virginia council, 190
  organizes Ohio company, 190
LEVIS, FRANÇOIS, DUC DE
  portrait of, 397
  Ramsay waits for, in vain, 402
  called from Montreal by Vaudreuil, 402
  rallies demoralized soldiers at Jacques-Cartier,
    402
  sends reassurance to Ramsay too late, 402
  defeats Murray on Plains of Abraham, 404
  lays siege to Quebec, 404
  withdraws on approach of English fleet, 404
LONGFELLOW, HENRY WADSWORTH
  immortalizes Acadians in "Evangeline," 310
LOUDOUN, JOHN CAMPBELL, LORD
  in command in America, 317
  character of, 317–318
  deters Shirley from relieving Oswego, 317–318
  loiters in Albany, 318
  sails to Halifax, 318
  joined by Holbourn, 318
  drills his men, 318
  plants onions, 318
  returns to New York, 318
  wishes to fortify Long Island, 318
  Pitt recalls, 235
LOUISBURG, CAPE BRETON
  formerly called English Harbor, 168
  French erect great fortress at, 168
  the American Gibraltar, 168
  key to Saint Lawrence River, 168–169
  Duquesne commander at, 169
  New England decided to attack, 169
  assembles force against, 169
  Pepperell commands expedition against, 170
  Warren arrives with aid, 169–170
  fleet sails from Boston for, 171–172
  attack begins, 172
  gun captured at, picture of, 173
  Vaughn takes battery, 175
  Gorham attacks island battery, 175
  harbor of, picture, 176
  French ships-of-the-line taken at, 176–177
  British ships-of-the-line arrive before, 177
  assault decided on, 177
  surrenders to Pepperell, 177
  lesson of capture to New England, 179
  monument, picture of, 180
  square in Boston commemorates, 180
  greatly strengthened by French, 318
  Loudoun's expedition to, 318
  Amherst anchors before, 325–326
  Wolfe storms and silences batteries, 326
  French surrender to Amherst, 326
  Wolfe called hero of, 326

LOUISBURG, CAPE BRETON — *continued*
in British hands. 355
fall of, picture, 356

LOUISIANA
New Orleans founded by Bienville, 188
England threatens communications with Canada, 189
Acadians in, 409
bayou in, picture of, 149
surrendered to English, 442

LOUIS XIV OF FRANCE
denies Queen Anne's right to English throne, 21
avers right is in James Stuart, 21
portrait of, 22
places grandson, Philip of Anjou, on Spanish throne, in violation of promises to William III, **22**
all Europe leagued against him, 22
bed in palace of Versailles, picture of, 34
equestrian statue of, at palace of Versailles, picture of, 34
yields New France to England by Treaty of Utrecht, 118

LOUIS XV OF FRANCE
Bienville takes possession of territory in name of, 190

LOVEWELL, JOHN
heads expedition against Pigwackets, 129
meets disaster, 129

LOWER TOWN, QUEBEC, *see* QUEBEC

LYMAN, PHINEAS
general of colonial troops, 315
defeats and captures Dieskau, 315

M

MAINE, *see also* ABENAKIS
old block-house in, picture of, 51
life in, not safe, 75
Hockomock Rock on the coast of, picture, 77

MARIA THERESA, QUEEN OF AUSTRIA
daughter of Charles VI, 168
receives throne from father, 168

MARQUETTE, JAMES
explorer, 188

MASIN
crosses Lake Erie, 192
builds fort at Presqu' Isle, now Erie; Fort La Bœuf, at French Creek; fort at Venango, now Franklin, 192
breaks up English settlement in Miami country, 192
sends word to governor of Pennsylvania to keep out of Ohio Valley, 192
falls ill at Fort Le Bœuf, 196

MASSACHUSETTS BAY, COLONY OF
offers reward for Indian scalps, 75
sends expedition against Port Royal, 75
Castin defeats expedition of, 75
second expedition fitted out by, 74
captures Port Royal, 75
quarrels with governors over salaries, 126
Shirley governor of, 169
decides upon attacking Louisburg, 169

MASSACHUSETTS BAY, COLONY OF — *continued*
secures coöperation of New Hampshire, Connecticut, and Rhode Island, 169
assembles 3000 troops, 160
expedition sails for Cape Breton, 169–170
rendezvous at Canso, 170

MASSACHUSETTS LEGISLATURE
refuses to pay salaries to governor's appointees, 126
governors demand stipulated sum, 126
compromise effected and salary voted every session, 126

MERCER, HUGH
annihilates Delaware Indians, 316

MIAMIS
make treaty with Gist and Croghan at Piqua, 187
Masin breaks up English settlement in country of, 192

MISSISSIPPI RIVER
at Natchez, picture of, 288

MISSISSIPPI VALLEY
France maintains trading-posts in, 188
routes between Atlantic coast and, 189

MOGG
chief of Abenakis, 129
killed by English, 129

MOHAWKS
carry war to Crown Point and banks of the Saint Lawrence, 180
Johnson enrolls, against Crown Point, 259

MONCKTON, ROBERT
British commander under Wolfe, 362
seizes Port Levis, 362
assaults French lines, 362
assault abandoned with loss, 362
commands front at battle of Quebec, 380

MONONGAHELA RIVER
on southern route from Atlantic to Mississippi River, 189
Ohio company granted land on, 190
picture of, 205
Braddock crosses, 265

MONRO
colonel of provincial troops, 321
in command at Fort William Henry, 321
attacked by Montcalm, 321
sends to Webb for help, 321
help denied him, 321
holds out four days and surrenders, 321

MONTCALM, LOUIS JOSEPH, MARQUIS DE
captures Fort Oswego, 317
attacks and captures Fort William Henry, 321
grants safe conduct to garrison, but drunken Indians massacre, 321–322
portrait of, 322
defeats Abercrombie at Lake George, 326
gathers forces at Quebec, 356
character of, 357
difficulties with Vaudreuil, 357
troubles with militia, 357
in readiness for second assault, 377
tries to deprive Vergor of rank, 378

MONTCALM, LOUIS JOSEPH, MARQUIS DE — *continued*
passes anxious night before battle of Quebec, 381
sends Johnstone to bring up left wing of army, 382
sets right wing in motion, 382
confers briefly with Vaudreuil, 382
Vaudreuil holds back left wing, 382
calls council of war, 382
decides on giving immediate battle, 382
shot through the body, 386
house in Quebec, picture of, 395
death of, picture, 380
monument to, with Wolfe, picture of, 392

MONTIAMA, MANUEL DE
comes to attack Georgia, 167
abandons attack in Georgia, 167

MONTMORENCI-FALLS,
picture of, 84
natural steps at, picture of, 109
an impassable defense for Quebec, 361
Monckton assaults French lines opposite, 362

MONTREAL, QUEBEC
New York organizes attack upon, 75–76
Nicholson to march on, 76
Vaudreuil calls De Levis from, 402
Vaudreuil surrenders, to Amherst, 442

MOORE, JAMES
elected governor of South Carolina, 127
under private charter, 127
private charter rescinded, 129
colony become Crown province, 127

MORAVIANS IN AMERICA
settle in Georgia, 162

MORRIS,
governor of Pennsylvania, 244
friend of Franklin's, 247
Franklin's judicious advice to, 250

MOUNT VERNON, VIRGINIA
property of Augustine Washington, 732
bequeathed to Lawrence Washington, 132
George Washington visits there, 132
schoolroom at, picture of, 229
library of, picture of, 232
mansion of, picture, 235
rose garden at, picture, 238
Washington's bedroom at, picture of, 354
fireplace in, picture of, 445
stables and family coach, picture of, 446

MURRAY, JAMES
British general under Wolfe, 362
assaults French lines at Quebec, 362
repulsed with loss, 362
commands in front at battle of Quebec, 380
left in command at Quebec, 404
gives battle to De Levis on Plains of Abraham, 404
is defeated and besieged, 404

N

NATCHEZ, MISSISSIPPI
Mississippi River, at, picture of, 288
site of Fort Rosalie at, picture of, 290

NATCHEZ, MISSISSIPPI — *continued*
Bienville builds Fort Rosalie at, 295
treats with chief of Natchez at, 295
historic house in, picture of, 296

NATURAL BRIDGE, VIRGINIA
picture of, 117
Washington's initials carved on, picture of, 125

NEWCASTLE, THOMAS PELHAM, DUKE OF
orders Warren to aid attack on Louisburg, 170
lack of knowledge regarding America, 170
Pitt succeeds as prime minister of England, 325

NEWFOUNDLAND
yielded by France to England, 118

NEW FRANCE
Vaudreuil last governor of, 77, 357
Bigot intendant of, 357
Vaudreuil surrenders, 442

NEW HAMPSHIRE, COLONY OF
offers reward for Indian scalps, 75
decides upon attacking Louisburg, 169
sends 500 men on Louisburg expedition, 169

NEW ORLEANS, LOUISIANA
Bienville establishes trading-post at, 188, 295

NEW YORK CITY
growth and population, 406
King's College founded in, 406
ferry to Paulus Hook established, 460
Broadway at an early day, picture of, 423
old New York, from Brooklyn Heights, picture of, 435

NEW YORK, COLONY OF
Cornbury governor of, 52
Cornbury misappropriates public money of, 52
people of, petition for Cornbury's removal, 52
organizes attack on Montreal and Quebec, 75–76
expedition of, marches to South River, 76
freedom of the press in, 127–128
Zenger's trial for libel, 128
slaves held in, 129

NIAGARA, *see* FORT NIAGARA

NIAGARA RIVER
on northern route between Atlantic and Mississippi valley, 189
English occupation of, threatens France, 189

NICHOLSON, SIR FRANCIS
to march on Montreal, 76

NORTH AMERICA
French title to, 188
English title to, 188
Spanish title to, 188
Pitt plans expulsion of French from, 325, 356, 357

NORTH CAROLINA
forces its proprietors to sell to Crown, 127
center of slave trade, 129
sends force to aid Virginia, 109

NORTH HAVERHILL, MASSACHUSETTS
picture of, 57

NOVA SCOTIA
in hands of English, 75

INDEX

O

OGLETHORPE, JAMES EDWARD
portrait of, 234
champion of justice and decency in debtor's prisons, 136
old fort on Saint Simon's Island, picture of, 137
has land grant from the King, 151
intends settling it with insolvent debtors, 151
leads colonists to Charleston and then to Savannah, 161
buys site of Savannah from Tom-O-Chi-Chi, 162
hires laborers and slaves from Carolina, 162
treats with Indians, 162
compared to Penn, 162
Charles Wesley secretary to, 162
monument marking spot of his landing at Savannah, picture of, 165
builds forts in Georgia and Florida, 166
brings commission and regiment from England, 166
attacks Spanish in Florida, 166, 213-218
uses a deserter to frighten the Spanish, 213-218

OHIO COMPANY
reasons for organization, 190
leading Virginians organize, 190
granted 500,000 acres of land, 190
sends out Gist to explore territory, 191-192
sends Trent to occupy site of Pittsburg, 206

OHIO RIVER
on southern trade route between Atlantic and Mississippi Valley, 189
confluence of, picture, 205

OSWEGO, see also FORT OSWEGO
Fort Ontario, picture of, 324

P

PARKMAN, FRANCIS
characterizes expedition against Louisburg as "a mad scheme," 169

PAULUS HOOK, NEW JERSEY
afterward called Jersey City, 406
ferry to New York established, 416

PENNSYLVANIA, COLONY OF
fur trade west of the Aleghenies threatened by French competition, 190
reason why site of Pittsburg is not fortified by, 192

PENOBSCOT RIVER
picture of, 74
Church attacks French settlers east of, 7

PEPPERELL, SIR WILLIAM
portrait of, 168
ship-builder and justice of the peace, 170
character of, 170
in command of Louisburg expedition, 170
doubts its success, 170
sails for Canso, 170
Vaughn notifies, of captured battery, 174-175
Warren assists, 169-177
French ship-of-the-line taken, 177
British reinforcements arrive, 177
calls council of war, 177
decides on assault, 177

PEPPERELL, SIR WILLIAM — continued
French surrender Louisburg to, 177
at the siege of Louisburg, picture of, 178
made a baronet, 180
first American to receive honor, 180

PEQUOTS
defeat Lovewell at Pigwacket, 129

PHILADELPHIA, PENNSYLVANIA, see also PENN, WILLIAM
on southern trade route between the Atlantic and Mississippi Valley, 189
statue to Franklin in, picture of, 267
Franklin's tomb in, picture of, 267

PHILIP V OF SPAIN
Duke of Anjou, 22
Louis XIV's grandson, 22
placed by Louis on Spanish throne in violation of promise given William III, 22
treaty of Utrecht settles on throne, 118
engages in slave trade, 118-119

PIGWACKETS, see PEQUOTS
defeat Lovewell, 129

PIQUA, OHIO
Twightwees' town, 187
attacked by French, 187
Gist and Croghan conclude peace with Miamis at, 187

PITTSBURG, PENNSYLVANIA
gateway of the west, picture of, 183
on the southern route from the Atlantic to Mississippi Valley, 189
English occupation of, a threat to France, 189
reason why site of was not fortified, 192
Washington visits and is impressed by strategic value of, 193
Washington holds council with Indians at, 193
Forks of the Ohio, picture of, 205
Trent sent to build fort at, 206
French drive English away, 206
French build Fort Duquesne at site of, 206
Forbes moves against Fort Duquesne, 329
Grant ambushed where court house now stands, 329
court house, picture of, 334
Fort Duquesne abandoned by French, 379
name changed to Fort Pitt, 329
name changed to Pittsburg, 329-330

PITT, WILLIAM
the great commoner, 325
becomes prime minister of England, 325
character of, 325
policy of, 325
recalls Loudoun and sends Amherst and Wolfe to America, 325
plans for first campaign, 325-326
plans expulsion of French from North America, 356-357
portrait of, 359
residence in London, picture of, 362
country house at Bromley, picture of, 399
realization of his dream, 442
monument to, in Westminster Abbey, 443

PLAINS OF ABRAHAM
effect of battle of, 362
situation of, 362
description of, 380

PLAINS OF ABRAHAM — *continued*
   battle on, 380-389, 401-402
   picture of, showing monument where Wolfe
      died, 387
   De Levis defeats Murray on, 404

PORT LEVIS, QUEBEC
   picture of, 115
   Monckton seizes, for Wolfe and erects batteries,
      362
   Wolfe moves army to, 363

POMPADOUR, JEANNE, MARQUISE DE
   sends Bigot to New France as intendant, 357

PONTIAC
   chief of the Ottawas, 442
   heads great Indian conspiracy, 442
   fails in his capture of Detroit, 442
   captures other frontier posts, 445
   sues for peace, 446

PORTO BELLO
   captured by Vernon, 167

PORT ROYAL, NOVA SCOTIA, *see also*
      ANNAPOLIS
   Massachusetts sends expedition against, 75
   Baron de Saint-Castin repels invaders, 75
   second Massachusetts attack upon, 75
   surrenders to English, 75
   Subercase commander of, 75
   name changed to Annapolis, 75

POTOMAC RIVER
   Washington goes up, 193
   at Harper's Ferry, picture of, 199

PRESQU' ISLE, PENNSYLVANIA, NOW
      ERIE
   Washington sent to French at, 187, 193
   Masin builds fort at, 192

PRIDEAUX, JOHN
   British general, 355
   commands expedition against Fort Niagara,
      355
   invests Niagara, 357
   is killed, 357

PURPOODUCK, MAINE
   Indian massacre at, 46

                    Q

QUEBEC, CITY OF
   picture of, 25
   street in old town, picture of, 28
   imposing water front, picture of, 31
   Break Neck steps in, picture, 33
   captives from Deerfield imprisoned in, 68-71
   description of, 73
   character of inhabitants of, 73
   reason for existence, 74
   New York organizes attack upon, 75-76
   the citadel, picture of, 78
   Saint Louis gate, picture of, 82
   the harbor of, picture, 83
   Montmorenci Falls, near, picture of, 84
   Lower Town, picture of, 87
   Isle of Orleans near, picture of, 90
   Chateau Frontenac and citadel, picture of, 92
   old house in, picture of, 94

QUEBEC, CITY OF — *continued*
   view of, from Parliament Buildings, picture,
      97
   Dufferin Terrace, picture of, 100
   Parliament Buildings in, picture of, 102
   soldiers' monument on Saint Foye Road, pic-
      ture of, 103
   to the Plains of Abraham, picture, 105
   Natural Steps at Montmorenci, picture of, 109
   old Saint Louis gate at, picture of, 113
   Point Levis near, picture of, 115
   Wolfe to proceed against, 355
   Montcalm gathers forces at, for final struggle,
      356, 361
   Wolfe arrives before, 361
   situation of, 361
   Monckton's assault upon, fails, 363
   English gunboat and batteries damage, 363
   loft in farm house where Wolfe lay ill, picture
      of, 371
   farm house where Wolfe lay ill, picture of,
      373
   Wolfe gains Plains of Abraham, 376-379
   battle on the Plains of Abraham, 380-389, 401-
      402
   Ursuline convent, picture of, 390
   monument to Wolfe and Montcalm, picture of,
      392
   Montcalm's house, picture of, 395
   condition of, after battle, 402
   De Levis defeats Murray on Plains of Abraham,
      404
   British fleet raises siege of, 404

QUEBEC, PROVINCE OF
   rural scene in, picture of, 30
   scene in rural, picture, 107

QUEEN ANNE'S WAR, *see also* TREATY
      OF UTRECHT
   breaks out, 45
   condition of, 45
   French incite Abenakis against English, 45-46
   French and Indians massacre in Maine, 46
   raid on Deerfield, 59-67
   French and Indians ravage New England
      frontier, 74-75
   Church attacks French settlements, 75
   Massachusetts and New Hampshire offer
      reward for Indian scalps, 75
   massacre at Haverhill, Massachusetts, 75
   unsuccessful attack on Port Royal, 75
   Port Royal surrenders to English, 75
   New York organizes an attack on Montreal
      and Quebec, 75-76
   general assault on Canada planned, 76

                    R

RALE
   Jesuit missionary, 46
   statement regarding Indians, 46
   killed by expedition from New England, 129

RAMSAY,
   French officer commanding garrison at Que-
      bec, 383
   sends artillery to Montcalm, 383
   waits four days for De Levis, 402
   surrenders Quebec to British, 402
   receives reassurance from De Levis too late,
      402

RHODE ISLAND, COLONY OF
furnishes sloop-of-war and 300 men to Louisburg expedition, 169

RIVER SOREL
Isle aux Noix in, 357
French occupy island, 356-357

ROUVILLE, FRANÇOIS HERTEL DE
portrait of, 58
leads attack on Deerfield, 59-67
takes Deerfield prisoners to Quebec, 68-71
leads expedition against Haverhill, 75
brother killed at Haverhill, 75

ROXBURY, MASSACHUSETTS
Shirley's house at, picture of, 316

S

SABBATH DAY POINT, NEW YORK
Howe defeats French in skirmish at, 326
picture of, 328

SAINT AUGUSTINE, FLORIDA
Oglethorpe gives up attack on, 166
gates of, picture, 215

SAINT-CASTIN, JEAN VINCENT DE L'
ABADIE, BARON DE
successfully defends Annapolis against Massachusetts attack, 75

SAINT CHARLES RIVER
Quebec built on, 73
bounds Plains of Abraham, 380

SAINT-CLAIR, SIR JOHN
portrait of, 262
commands pioneers at Braddock's defeat, 265, 266

SAINT JOHN'S RIVER
Oglethorpe builds Fort Saint George at mouth of, 106

SAINT LAWRENCE RIVER
Quebec built on, 73
Louisburg key to, 168-169
Mohawks carry war to banks of, 180
Bienville on, 190
Wolfe sails up, to take Quebec, 355
bounds Plains of Abraham, 380

SAINT MARY'S RIVER
Cumberland Island at mouth of, 166
Oglethorpe builds Fort William at mouth of, 166

SAINT PIERRE, LEGARDEUR DE
commander at Fort Le Bœuf, 196
entertains Washington, 196
has to send Washington's letter to Montreal, 196
declines to discuss civil affairs, 197
slain at Lake George, 315-316

SAINT SIMON'S ISLAND, GEORGIA
Oglethorpe's old fort on, picture of, 137
old barracks near fort on, picture of, 214

SAMOS, QUEBEC
French battery at, fires on British ships, 382

SAUNDERS, SIR C.
British admiral, 376
commanding main fleet at Quebec, 376

SAVANNAH, GEORGIA
port of, picture (from a rare print), 136
Bull Street, picture of, 143
from tower of city hall, picture of, 145
on the river, picture of, 149
Hermitage plantation near, picture of, 154
and the river, picture of, 157
site of, bought from Tom-O-Chi-Chi, 161
monument to Tom-O-Chi-Chi, picture of, 161
founding of, 161-162
first orphanage in America at, picture of, 163
monument where Oglethorpe landed in, picture of, 165
Whitefield establishes charities in, 166
Whitefield revives religious fervor of people of, 166

SAVANNAH RIVER
on the, picture of, 149
Savannah and the, picture of, 157
Oglethorpe leads settlers to high bluff on, 161
Oglethorpe builds fort at Augusta on, 166

SEVEN YEAR'S WAR, see FRENCH and
INDIAN WAR

SHAFTESBURY, ANTHONY ASHLEY
COOPER, THIRD EARL OF
works loyally for Georgia, 154
head of council for Georgia, 154

SHENANDOAH VALLEY
Washington repulses French in, 316
picture of, 343

SHIRLEY, WILLIAM
governor of Massachusetts, 169
acts on Vaughn's proposal to capture Louisburg, 169
assembles troops, 169
secures aid from Connecticut, Rhode Island, and New Hampshire, 169
asks Warren for ships, 169-170
portrait of, 172
sends Stockbridge Indians against Canada, 179
to proceed against Fort Niagara, 259
succeeds Braddock in command of American forces, 315
marches to Oswego, 315
strengthens fort at Oswego, 315
marches back again, 315
house at Roxbury, Massachusetts, picture of, 316
prevented by Loudoun from relieving Oswego, 317-318
Washington asks commission of, 342

SILLERY, QUEBEC
where Wolfe landed, 378
picture of, 378

SLAVES, see AFRICAN SLAVE TRADE

SLAVE TRADE, see AFRICAN SLAVE
TRADE

SOUTH CAROLINA
Johnson governor of, 126
attempt made to force Church of England upon, 126
revolts against Johnson, 125-126
Johnson calls review of militia of, 127
people of, call convention to elect a governor, 127
center of slave trade, 129

SOUTH RIVER, NEW YORK
expedition against Montreal reaches, 76
SPAIN
Philip of Anjou king of, 22, 118
Bourbon right of succession to throne of, limited, 118
loses European possessions, 118
England declares war on, 166
denies England right to supply slaves to colonies, 166
demands right to search English ships, 166
colonies attacked by Oglethorpe, 169
futile attack on Georgia, 167
loses her power, 188
SPURWINK, MAINE
Indian massacre at, 46
STUART, JAMES EDWARD
son of James II, 21
Louis XIV avers to be rightful King of England, 21
proclaimed King James III of England by Louis XIV, 22
SUBERCASE
in command at Port Royal, 75
surrenders to English, 75

T

TICONDEROGA, NEW YORK
on Lake Champlain, 355
Amherst to proceed against, 355
French abandon and destroy, 356
Amherst builds ships and new fort at, 363
ruins of, picture, 365
TOM-O-CHI-CHI
Indian chief, 161
sells site of Savannah to Oglethorpe, 161
monument to, at Savannah, picture of, 161
TOWNSHEND, GEORGE, MARQUIS
British general under Wolfe, 362
assaults French line at Quebec, 362
repulsed with loss, 362
covers left flank at battle of Quebec, 380
in command after death of Wolfe, 404
leaves Murray in command at Quebec, 404
TREATY OF AIX-LA-CHAPELLE
concludes King George's War, 180
restores old boundaries, 180
TREATY OF UTRECHT
yields Maine, Acadia, Newfoundland, and Labrador to English, 118
acknowledges Anne as Queen of England, 118
relinquishes Holland to Austria, 118
Spain loses colonial possessions, 118
effect of, upon colonies, 125-126
TRENT,
sent by Dinwiddie to expostulate with French, 187, 193
learns of attack on Piqua, 187
sent out by Ohio company to build fort at site of Pittsburg, 206
TUSCARORAS
ally themselves with Yeamanses, 128-129
try to drive out English settlers, 129

TUSCARORAS — *continued*
nearly exterminated, 129
join the Iroquois, 129
TIGHTWEES
attacked by French at Piqua, 187

U

UTRECHT, TREATY OF, *see* TREATY OF UTRECHT

V

VAUDREUIL, PHILLIPE DE RIGAUD, MARQUIS DE
governor of Canada, 77
capture Fort Massachusetts, 180
fails in attack on Fort Number Four, 180
VAUDREUIL, PIERRE FRANÇOIS DE RIGAUD, MARQUIS DE
son of former governor and himself governor, 239
character of, 357
jealous of Montcalm, 357
divides authority with Montcalm, 357
makes merry over Wolfe's plight, 363
keeps Vergor in place, 378
not to be depended upon, 383
in terror after battle of Quebec, 401
wishes to surrender, 401
orders a retreat, which becomes a panic, 401-402
calls De Levis from Montreal, 402
surrenders Montreal to Amherst, 442
surrenders all of New France, 442
VAUGHN, WILLIAM
originates idea of attack on Louisburg, 169
sends message to Pepperell after taking French battery, 174-175
VENANGO, NOW FRANKLIN, PENNSYLVANIA
Masin builds fort at, 192
English trading-posts seized and fortified by French, 196
Washington visits, and is entertained hospitably, 196
VERGOR,
commander of Canadian guard at head of Anse du Foulon, 378
a coward, whom Montcalm sought to deprive of rank, 378
kept in place by Bigot and Vaudreuil, 378
runs away at British assault and is wounded, 379
characterization of, 382
VERNON, EDWARD
British admiral, 131, 167
Lawrence Washington serves under, 131, 167
takes Porto Bello and Darien, 167
Spanish flee at rumored approach of, 167
VIRGINIA, COLONY OF
fur traders west of Alleghenies, 190
organizes Ohio company, 190
reasons why site of Pittsburg is not fortified by 192

VIRGINIA, COLONY OF — *continued*
Virginia determines to expel French from Fort Duquesne, 205
raises loan of £10,000, 207
organizes an army, 207
stands alone in fight for Ohio Valley, 210
force from North Carolina assists, 210
doorway of colonial mansion in, picture, 426
colonial mansion, in picture, 427

W

WAKEFIELD, VIRGINIA
scene on farm at, 120
monument on Washington's birthplace, picture of, 120
Washington family tomb at, picture of, 124
Bridge's Creek estate at, Washington born on, 132
Augustine Washington, Jr., lives at, 132
George goes to school there, 132
Washington's birthplace at, picture of, 211

WALKER, SIR HOVENDEN
to lead naval attack on Quebec, 76
loiters in Boston, 76
waits at Bay of Gaspé, 76
meets eight ships in Saint Lawrence, 76, 90
sends letter to England, 76

WAR OF THE AUSTRIAN SUCCESSION, *see* KING GEORGE'S WAR

WAR OF THE SPANISH SUCCESSION, *see* KING WILLIAM'S WAR

WARREN, PETER
British naval commander, 169
asked by Shirley for ships, 169-170
declines until ordered by Newcastle, 170
joins expedition against Louisburg at Canso, 170, 172
wishes island battery captured, 175
takes French ship-of-the-line, 176-177
at surrender of Louisburg, 177
made admiral, 180

WAR WITH SPAIN
declared, 166
reasons for, 166
effect upon American colonies, 166-167
Oglethorpe attacks Spanish forts in Florida, 166
Oglethorpe takes minor posts and withdraws, 167
Lawrence Washington in, 167
Vernon takes Porto Bello and Darien, 167

WASHINGTON, AUGUSTINE
father of George, Lawrence, and Augustine, 130-132
has servant school-teacher, 130
owns Mount Vernon, 132
organizes Ohio company, 190
dies, 132

WASHINGTON, AUGUSTINE, JR.,
brother to George, 132
George lives with, 132
inherits Bridges Creek estate, 132

WASHINGTON, GEORGE
scene on Wakefield farm, picture, 120
birthplace at Wakefield, picture of monument at, 120
his family tomb at Wakefield, picture of, 124
his initials carved on Natural Bridge, picture of, 125
his initials carved on Natural Bridge, account of, 132
son of Augustine, 130
taught by Hobby, 130
early character of, 131
brother to Lawrence, 131
athletic accomplishments of, 131-132
loses his father, 132
lives with mother, 132
lives with brother Augustine, 132
learns surveying and mathematics, 132
at Mount Vernon with brother Lawrence, 132
thrown in with Fairfax, 132
sent by Fairfax to survey lands, 133, 193
desires to enter British navy, 133
dissuaded by mother, 133
mother persuading him not to become a midshipman, picture of, 133
last visit to his mother, picture of, 131
public surveyor of Virginia, 193
goes up the Potomac, 193
over the Alleghenies, 193
down the Youghiogheny River, 193
reaches site of Pittsburg, 193
is impressed by strategic value of the Forks of the Ohio, 193
holds council with Indians, 193
meets and sups with French at Venango, 196
site of camp near Fort Le Bœuf, picture of, 198
leaves Gist, 198
narrowly escapes drowning, 198
fired upon by treacherous Indians, 198-199
and Gist crossing the Allegheny, picture of, 202
commissioned lieutenant-colonel by Dinwiddie, 207
miniature and signature of, 209
in command of army of Virginia, 209
begins his march, 210
birthplace at Wakefield, picture of, 211
Rock Fort, where he met Half-King, picture of, 216
in council at Fort Necessity, picture of, 217
first battlefield of, picture, 218
only field on which he ever surrendered to a foe, picture of, 219
begins work at the Forks of the Ohio, 221
his advance guard surrenders to French, 221-222
meets retiring force at Cumberland, 222
has messages from Half-King, 222
pushes forward to Great Meadows, 222
meets Half-King, 222-223
surprises force under Jumonville, 223
first conflict in French and Indian war, 223
builds Fort Necessity at Great Meadows, 223
sends to Virginia for reinforcements, 223
rock from which he fired on the French, picture of, 224
attacked by French at Fort Necessity, 225-226
surrenders to greatly superior force, 226

WASHINGTON, GEORGE — *continued*
crest and coat-of-arms, picture of, 321
school room at Mount Vernon, picture of, 229
library in Mount Vernon mansion, picture of, 232
mansion at Mount Vernon, picture of, 235
rose garden at Mount Vernon, picture of, 241
mill of, in Pennsylvania, picture of, 257
resents pretended superiority of British officers, 260
resigns his commission and disbands his regiment, 260
Braddock prevails upon, to accept staff appointment, 260
Braddock treats, with insolence, 261
Braddock snubs, 262
falls ill, 262
rejoins command, 262-263
defeats French in the Shenandoah Valley, 316
leads advance against Fort Duquesne, 329
raising British flag at Fort Duquesne, picture of, 336
Williams Ferry house, where he met Martha Custis, picture of, 341
seeks commission from Shirley, 342
made general after fall of Fort Duquesne, 342
first meeting with Martha Custis, picture of, 346
first meeting with Martha Custis, account of, 346
marries Martha Custis, 347-348
Christ Church, Alexandria, where he worshiped, picture of, 432
fireplace at Mount Vernon, picture of, 445
stables and family coach, picture of, 446

WASHINGTON, LAWRENCE
brother to George, 131
with Vernon at Carthagena, 131
captain of Virginia militia, 131
inherits Mount Vernon, 132
marries Anne Fairfax, 132
has George with him, 132
with Vernon at Port Bello and Darien, 167
organizes Ohio company, 190
Fredericksburg built on his estate, 228

WASHINGTON, MARTHA, FORMERLY CUSTIS
portrait of, 337
Williams Ferry house, where George met, picture of, 341
as Mrs. Custis had a son and daughter, 341
Washington's first meeting with, 346
Washington's first meeting with, picture of, 346
married to Washington, 347-348
her reception, picture of, 351
her bedroom at Mount Vernon, picture of, 354

WASHINGTON, MARY
mother of George Washington, 132
home in Fredericksburg, picture of, 127
monument in Fredericksburg, picture of, 127
dissuades George from entering British navy, 133
persuading George not to become a midshipman, picture of, 133
George's last visit to, picture of, 131
tomb of, picture, 429

WEBB,
British general, 317
fails to relieve Fort William Henry, 317, 320
fails to relieve Fort Oswego, 317
at Fort Edward, 321

WESLEY, CHARLES
comes to Georgia as secretary to Oglethorpe, 162
portrait of, 166

WESLEY, JOHN
monument to in City Road, London, picture of, 155
live oak where he preached his first sermon in America, picture of, 160
arrives in Georgia as apostle to Indians, 162
returns to England, 162

WHITEFIELD, GEORGE
portrait of, 163
first orphanage in America founded by, picture of, 163
comes to Savannah, 166
establishes charities in Savannah, 166
furnishes motto for flag in expedition against Louisburg, 170

WILLIAM III OF ENGLAND
James II flees before him, 22

WILLIAMS, EUNICE
daughter of Deerfield clergyman, 73
taken into Indian tribe, 73
given up as lost by father, 73

WILLIAMS FERRY, VIRGINIA
house where Washington met Martha Custis, 241
picture of house, 341
picture of ferry, 348

WILLIAMS, JOHN
clergyman at Deerfield, Massachusetts, 46
house, picture of, 61
battered door from house, picture of, 64
his child slain by Indians, 65
wife slain by Indians, 68
graves of family of, picture of, 72
daughter Eunice taken into Indian tribe, 73

WINSLOW, AUGUST
general commanding forces at Grand Pré, 301
portrait of, 299

WOGSTOWN
Gist meets Indian council at, 191-192

WOLCOTT, ROGER
major-general and second in command of expedition against Louisburg, 170

WOLFE, JAMES
portrait of, 19
Pitt sends to America, 325
storms French batteries at Louisburg, 326
silences the island batteries at Louisburg, 326
called "hero of Louisburg," 326
to proceed against Quebec by way of the Saint Lawrence, 355
arrives before Quebec, 357
Monckton assaults French lines and is repulsed, 362
moves army to Port Levis, 363
French fire-ships fail, 363
in command of water, 363

WOLFE, JAMES — *continued*
awaits Amherst in vain, 363
in serious straits, 363
portrait of, 368
loft in farm-house where he lay ill, picture of, 371
farm house in which he lay ill, picture of, 373
seems at last of his resources, 376
in last extremity of hope, 376
espies the Anse du Foulon, 376
determines on attempt to gain Plains of Abraham through Anse du Foulon, 376
on Holmes' squadron at Cape Rouge, 377
his part in assault on Quebec, 378-379
recites Grey's "Elegy," 378
on Plains of Abraham, 379
selects spot on which he wishes to fight, 380
line of battle and size of army, 380
Montcalm in front and Bougainville behind, 381
battle of Quebec, details of, 380-389
shot for the third time, 386
birthplace at Westerham, England, picture of, 405
dies, 386
house in Greenwich, picture of, 407
memorial window to, in Saint Alphege's Church, London, picture of, 414

WOLFE, JAMES — *continued*
monument to, in Westminster Abbey, picture of, 443
monument where he died victorious, picture of, 383
WYMAN,
in expedition against Pigwackets, 129
meets disaster, 129

Y

YEAMANSES
ally themselves with Tuscaroras, 128-129
try to drive out English settlers, 129
nearly exterminated, 129
YOUGHIOGHENY RIVER
Washington crosses, 193

Z

ZENGER, JOHN PETER
editor in New York, 128
arrested for libel, **128**
jury finds not guilty, 128
aldermen of New York city present with gold box, 128